Court of the Hawk

by

Debbie Peterson

Court of the Hawk

Cover Art by *Debbie Taylor*

The Wild Rose Press, Inc.
PO Box 708
Adams Basin, NY 14410-0708
Visit us at www.thewildrosepress.com

Publishing History
First Fantasy Rose Edition, 2015
Print ISBN 978-1-62830-801-3
Digital ISBN 978-1-62830-802-0

Published in the United States of America

He considered that for a time before he spoke. "No, I suppose it doesn't. Still, I'd like to know."

"All right, I don't have a problem giving you an answer." She cleared her throat. "The quake disturbed several portraits hanging along the hallways. I found one of them on the floor after leaving my room. So, I picked it up with every intention of replacing it, but the subject stole my attention. You see, if asked under oath in a court of law, I would swear you posed for the portrait at least two, maybe even three centuries ago."

"And you didn't stop to consider whether or not the man in the painting might be a distant ancestor to whom I bear a great resemblance?"

She extended a finger to his face, gently traced the scar that only served to enhance his looks, and shook her head. "Not when the artist painted him with this."

Praise for Debbie Peterson

"Despite being almost four hundred pages, [*SPIRIT OF THE KNIGHT*] was a one sitting book for me. I was determined to figure out the mystery of why there was a castle full of dead knights and how they got there. This was a fun, smile and 'awwwww' book, with lots of Scottish brogue, a wee bit of gore, and a very delightful couple."

~Sebella Blue, Rage, Sex, and Teddy Bears

~*~

"*SPIRIT OF THE KNIGHT* is a tender romance rife with mystery and fascinating historical references. Once again, Debbie Peterson proves she is an enchantress when weaving these elements together."

~Mae Clair, author of Eclipse Lake

~*~

"The added spells and curses from the evil hag and ancestors added to the visionary scenes making me feel as if I was literally there witnessing the whole thing and a part of the ritual itself—it actually gave me chills."

~Rhonda Tutt, Queentutt's World of Escapism

~*~

"Debbie does a wonderful job of keeping the story moving and solving all the mysteries without missing a beat."

~Paranormal Romance and Authors That Rock

~*~

"[*SPIRIT OF THE KNIGHT*] is a magnificent read! I was thoroughly entertained with the characters in this story. There was mystery, romance, ghosts, knights…everything that makes a story awesome."

~Brooke, Brooke Blogs

Dedication

In loving memory of my beloved brother and father.
Thank you for the joy, the laughter,
and all of the amazing adventures.
We've had quite a party...

Chapter One

Llys y Gwalch
Wales
Present Day

"You have returned, my Lord," said Bran.

Without relinquishing the black iron latch, Garreth turned to face his chamberlain and raised a brow. "Your powers of observation never cease to amaze me, Bran." He closed the thick wooden door and made his way to the desk tucked inside the alcove at the back of the library.

Bran merely chuckled in response.

"Did our latest epigrapher's plane land on time?" Garreth sat down and scooted his chair forward.

"That it did. Vaughn picked her up at the Liverpool International right on schedule. They should arrive almost any time now, I think."

"Good." Garreth tugged the large insignia ring off his finger and tossed it inside the topmost right hand drawer. "The minute she arrives, bring her in. I'm anxious to show her the cave."

The corners of Bran's mustached mouth twitched. "Begging pardon, my Lord, I know time, or the lack thereof, is uppermost in your mind. However, it's already past the midnight hour. The frail old girl has flown all the way from New York City. I'm certain that by now fatigue is ever her companion. Therefore, perhaps you might allow her to get a bit of sleep before you shackle her to the wall."

Garreth rubbed a weary hand across his forehead as he expelled a heavy sigh. "I suppose you're right. Come the morning, she'll need all her wits about her, won't she? Still, I'd like to get the tedious introductions over with tonight, if it's all the same to you."

"Of course, I'll bring her in the moment she arrives." Bran bobbed his head and vacated the room.

Not that he minded his chamberlain's departure. Garreth craved a few moments of solitude. Yet, even as he contemplated the epigrapher's imminent arrival, and her purpose for making the trip, his mind drifted to the cataclysm that all but destroyed his father's kingdom. Despite the vast number of years that followed, he recalled the day with absolute clarity. They had no warning. At least, *he* didn't have any warning. On that fateful day the morning began with a spectacular, though eerily brief, total eclipse of the sun. Once the midnight shadows passed, the day progressed to the noon hour with the normalcy of any other. He closed his eyes and leaned his head back against the chair as the memory engulfed him.

One instant the sun had shone bright over a cloudless sky. In the next, a thick blanket of darkness spewed over the horizon like dammed-up waters escaping their bounds. Massive lightning bolts hurled toward the earth with raging voracity, burning and destroying. Tumultuous winds shattered everything within its path. What the winds didn't obliterate, the colossal waves of the sea did. For in one fell swoop, those waves swallowed the entire realm of Llys y

Gwalch. As impossible as it seemed, those who still lived suddenly found themselves nestled inside the belly of the sea with what few structures remained of a once thriving province.

He and his men rushed to the castle from the bailey during those first moments of panic and confusion. For all the destruction, the number of survivors amazed him far more than the vast number of the dead. As he strode into the great hall, he spied the crumpled, lifeless body of his father near the doorway. Two paces to the left lay his father's advisor, bloodied from the impact of toppled stones. With weakened fingers, Glodrydd motioned him to his side. As Garreth knelt beside him the old man grabbed his wrist.

"Garreth," he wheezed as he dropped his father's ring into his hand. "The words of the omen...have come to pass...just as I feared. I tried to...to warn your father about the...approaching disaster. He wouldn't listen to the foolish beliefs of...of a feeble old man. Therefore, the king wouldn't...prepare. He would not...seek."

Garreth said nothing in response to his nonsensical ramblings. He clasped his hand and offered what comfort he could in Glodyrdd's final moments of mortality.

A moan escaped Glodrydd's lips, his body convulsed, and he grimaced in pain. Nonetheless, he continued his tale even though the struggle cost him dearly. "Be wiser, Garreth...this happened once before. The event will happen again, four hundred years to the day, and four hundred years after that in a continuing cycle...of annihilation. Each time, ingesting more land and more people...unless you...unless you..."

3

Glodrydd couldn't say any more, for death chose that moment to silence his tongue. Confusion beset him as he considered Glodrydd's final admonition. *Unless he what*? At that precise moment, he didn't know, nor did he really care. For in all likelihood, they wouldn't last down here very long anyway. How could they? The ocean waters would inevitably invade whatever impossible pocket of shelter protected them now.

Bran stooped down beside him then and placed a hand upon his shoulder. He said nothing as he took in the mayhem that surrounded them. Finally, he pinned his solemn gaze to his. "You're the king now, Garreth. The people will look to you for guidance. They'll need a sense of calm, and your strength in the days ahead."

Garreth shook his head as he wiped a hand across his mouth and chin. Visions of the dead plagued his mind. "There's no need for a king in a kingdom that no longer exists, Bran."

He had not thought it possible he would live to see the next apocalypse. But he did—

The subtle knock on the door ended his troubled thoughts. He opened his eyes, inhaled a ragged breath, and rose to his feet. How many times had he repeated this same wearisome exercise over the last three hundred plus, years? Yet, each one had concluded the same way and without any real deviation. Why should he harbor any hope this expert would be any different from the others he had employed?

"Come in," he said as he stepped away from the desk and made his way to the center of the room.

Garreth caught sight of Bran's uncontrolled smirk before he shifted his gaze to the woman who stood just a step behind him. Did the shock register on his face?

This girl looked nothing like the old, decrepit Dr. S.E. DeSpencer they envisioned, worried over, and discussed at length before retaining her services. No, the beguiling woman standing before him took away his breath. Her dark chestnut hair hung in thick layers almost to her waist. She possessed large, enchanting, golden-brown eyes, and her full luscious lips begged—

"Garreth, may I present Dr. S.E. DeSpencer, or Essie, as she prefers us to call her. Essie, I would like to introduce Lord Garreth ap Daffyd," said Bran with a low bow and an exaggerated wave of his hand. Garreth suppressed the need to roll his eyes over the ridiculous display.

****

Essie swallowed past the dryness in her throat as she gazed into the man's dark, forest green eyes. Eyes made even more striking as contrasted by his wavy black hair that fell several inches below his collar.

The tall, handsome, powerfully built, Lord Garreth ap Daffyd, dressed casually in black button down shirt and jeans, extended a hand. Despite his commanding presence that all but left her witless, she accepted the invitation without hesitation. However, he made no move to release her from his grasp as he scrutinized her face and form from head to toe. His thorough perusal left her feeling a little uncomfortable. Did she have an unsightly spot on her tailored white pantsuit? She fought off the urge to look.

His gaze remained fixed on hers. She found it obvious that he waited for some kind of response to Bran's introduction, and she sought to find one amidst the clutter of her thoughts. Did one use the term "ap" when addressing the man? Did anyone even use "ap" anymore? How archaic. Nonetheless she would use the name as presented.

She offered a friendly smile along with a slight nod. "Hello, it's nice to finally meet you in person, Lord Garreth ap Daffyd."

"I would prefer you just address me as Garreth if it's not too much trouble." His unique accent, detected in both Vaughn and Bran, captivated her. She had never heard one quite like it before.

"No, it's not too much trouble," she said as he finally relinquished her hand.

A trace of amusement filled his eyes as he flashed a charming grin. Essie noticed then, the slight scar residing next to the dimple on the left side of his face. She had the strangest desire to trace along its arc with the tip of her finger and that absurd notion left her feeling more than a little unsettled.

"I hope we didn't inconvenience you too greatly by asking you to come on such short notice?"

"Not at all. My only regret is not arriving early enough to enjoy your beautiful Welsh landscapes during the drive from the airport. The twists and turns we made from the mountain down into the valley must be breathtaking." Something flickered within his eyes as she made the comment, but she didn't have time to name it.

"Perhaps we can find an opportunity to remedy that before you leave. However, I'm sure at this particular moment the need to sleep outweighs the need to see the sites."

"Yes, I am a little tired. However, I don't mind staying up awhile longer if you'd like to show me the writing on the—"

"That can wait until the morning and you're rested from your journey," interrupted Garreth. He shifted his gaze to her companion. "Bran, would you be kind enough to call Lowri and ask her to show Dr. DeSpencer to her room?"

The man with laughing blue eyes and long, sandy-brown hair bowed slightly and then exited the impressive library. As he did so, she returned her attention to the lord of the castle.

"Please, Dr. DeSpencer just sounds so antediluvian. The pairing makes me feel like some shriveled up old prune that putters about with a cane and permanent scowl etched across her face. So, if I must use Garreth, you must reciprocate by calling me Essie." She perceived a slight grin as he dipped his head in response to the request.

"Fair enough." The opening of the door drew his gaze upward. "Ah, here's Lowri now. She'll conduct you to your room and see to any needs you might have before you retire."

Essie turned and faced the new arrival. The middle-aged woman with silver scattered throughout her light brown hair, wore a kind expression. If someone asked for a description of the hazel eyes returning her gaze, she would say they were of ancient origin and full of wisdom. Fanciful notion at best and at once she blamed her fatigue.

The woman extended a hand in welcome. "Are you ready to go Miss DeSpencer?"

"Essie, please, and yes, I am." She directed her gaze toward Garreth. "I'll see you in the morning then?"

"You can count on it."

She could feel his eyes boring into her form as she followed Lowri out of the library. The woman escorted her down the antiquated stone hallway with their arms linked together as if they were already the best of friends. Despite the friendly overture, Lowri refrained from speaking. Not that she minded the silence, for it gave her a moment to look around.

Bran had hustled her from the car to the library so fast she didn't have time to take in her surroundings until now. Except, of course, for an all too brief glimpse of the enchanting castle's exterior in which Lord Garreth ap Daffyd resided.

As they traversed the long hallway, she spied several pieces of antique furniture representing several different time periods. A host of fascinating portraits adorned the walls, which depicted a variety of men and women throughout the ages of the castle. Then, as they made a turn at the end of the hallway, several men and women stood in a line in apparent expectation of her arrival. At once, the sea of faces turned toward her.

"Essie, before you retire to bed, I'd like to introduce the members of Garreth's personal staff. Though we don't expect you to remember all of our names tonight, we want you to know you can ask assistance from any one of us for anything you might need while you're here," said Lowri.

The woman then extended her hand toward a lovely, but very pregnant redhead. "Now, this is Anne, Bran's wife. She assists with various clerical duties as needed and as able in her current expectant condition. Aeron oversees the maintenance of the castle alongside Rhys and Philip. Next we have Glenda and Bethann, in charge of housekeeping. At the end of the line, we have

Vaughn, whom you've already met, and Gerald. Both of these men take on a variety of duties as required by Lord Garreth, both in and outside the castle."

Each welcomed her warmly, and she returned each greeting in like manner. After the introductions, she and Lowri continued their journey. They made their way down two additional hallways before they climbed a flight of stairs and then stopped at the second doorway off to the right. Lowri opened the door and waited for her to enter before following her inside. The exquisite room delighted her at first glance. Her gaze wandered over the elegance of the sheer white draperies dressed with an ice-blue swag that framed a set of arched, diamond-paned glass doors. Those doors led to a gorgeous, private balcony. A richly ornate, white-and-gold iron bed, with blue coverlet and bed skirt, sat in the middle of the left hand wall. The blue floral Persian rug underneath the bed and mahogany night tables set the decor off to perfection. To complete the setting, a magnificent arrangement of ice blue roses topped the antique chest of drawers across from the bed. What's more—those flowers looked real.

"What a beautiful bedroom," she breathed out.

Lowri's smile broadened. "Yes, the blue room is a favorite of ours and is always reserved for our most special guests."

"Oh." Her hand rested against the lapel of her jacket. "Well, I feel honored that you placed me in such a category."

Lowri clasped her hands in front of her waist and tilted her head as she regarded her. "Are you hungry or thirsty, perhaps? If you like, I could bring you some sort of refreshment before you retire."

"No, I'm fine, thank you. They served dinner on the plane."

"All right then, you'll find your luggage inside the wardrobe. The door there in the corner leads to your bathroom. Should you need something in the night, you need only use the intercom system. Most every room in the castle has one now. The station to this room is just left of your light switch. You shouldn't have any trouble locating the designated place or person you seek. The buttons are all clearly marked."

Essie glanced at the device and nodded. "Don't worry. I think I can figure it out."

"Sleep well, and either I, or Anne will be around to escort you to breakfast at seven a.m. if that meets with your approval."

"Of course, thank you. I'll make sure I'm ready."

Lowri inclined her head and bid her a good night.

After a refreshing shower, Essie donned her white nightgown and wandered out to the balcony. She gazed up at the night sky for several minutes and took in the view. The thick clouds prevented her from seeing the moon or the stars. Despite the lack, she could see a smattering of twinkling lights originating from the village in the distance. She took in a deep breath of fresh air, turned around, and stepped back inside the room as exhaustion set in. After she latched the doors, she shut off the lights. She climbed into bed, nestled deep into the satin pillows, and closed her weary eyes.

But then, her eyelids fluttered a bit. Something didn't feel right. Her heart raced, muscles tensed of their own accord. She held her breath and remained absolutely still. Someone inside this room fastened his gaze to her face at this very moment. She could feel it.

Without moving her head, her eyes peeked out from beneath her lashes and drifted over every possible nook, corner, and crevice in search of the invader. The air grew ever heavier with each breath she took. Whispers bounded from out of nowhere and encircled her bed. She couldn't understand a word they said, yet they seemed repetitious in nature. Once the voice or voices ebbed, a metal click, a slow, stuttered creak, and the rustle of fabric drew her gaze to the door now inching its way shut.

Essie bolted upright, scrambled from her bed, and flew to the door that closed just as she extended her hand. She took hold of the handle, squeezed the latch, and yanked it open. Light from the gilded gas sconces lit up the empty hallway. She stood there for a moment as she considered this quandary. No one could have escaped the hall that quickly. No one—

From her peripheral vision, she caught sight of a moving shadow. Without a moment's hesitation, she followed the fleeting movement through the hallways and over to the landing. The thing disappeared even as she arrived at the steps. Despite her uncertainty, she took hold of the banister and descended the stairway in search of the specter. Nothing out of the ordinary greeted her vision at ground level. So where did the thing go? She cast her gaze over every inch of her environment.

Beams of celestial light danced through the glass doors off the right hallway and beckoned her toward them. Perhaps her shadow escaped this way. She exited the castle and made a thorough sweep of the surrounding area. Nothing stirred but the gentle sway of ancient, windswept trees. She halted her steps and rocked back on her heels. Did she dream it, then? Possible, but the experience just seemed so real—

The glimmer of light now rising over the distant hills told her the dawn approached. Muted colors haloed the few scattered clouds that strolled across the heavens. So much for the distinct impression that she had just climbed into bed and closed her eyes. She wrapped her hands around her bare arms as she ventured onto the stone pathway, followed it past the elegant, gothic-styled arch, and into the garden.

The dark green-blue stonework of this castle piqued her interest and she took a moment to rub a hand over the polished surface of a beautiful monolith cut from the same substance. She couldn't identify the rock because she had never seen anything quite like it before. She shifted her gaze to the castle then and drank in its splendor. Did it pass through generations of family members, or did Garreth buy and restore the place himself? From what she could see upon her arrival, someone had updated the singular structure with all the modern conveniences one might desire, yet retained the old world charm.

She closed her eyes and let go a sigh as the thought of Garreth instantly produced his arresting image inside her mind—an image that disturbed a swarm of butterflies resting deep inside her belly. The response surprised her. Though nothing surprised her more than Lord Garreth ap Daffyd himself. For whatever the reason, she expected someone far older, and far less intriguing. Something about him just seemed to take hold of—

"Are you all right?"

Essie muffled a gasp as she turned in the direction

of Garreth's voice. He stepped out of the shadows to her left and ambled toward her. She released the breath and nodded. "Yes, I'm fine."

"Then, you had trouble sleeping."

A breath of laughter accompanied the shake of her head. "No, not at all. From all indications, I slept very well."

He cocked his head to the side as he gazed at her. "Then may I ask what brings you outside this time of morning, barefoot and still dressed in your night clothes?"

Essie could feel the heat rise to her cheeks as she peeked down at her attire. Why not tell him the truth then? She lifted her shoulders. "Chasing a dream."

He gave her a sideways glance while he advanced a bit closer. "Chasing a dream?"

"Yes. I dreamed I woke up inside my room, perceived an unseen hobgoblin of some sort, and listened to his unintelligible whispers. I then stared in wide-eyed wonder as said hobgoblin slipped out of the open door and closed it behind him," she said using a light-hearted tone. "In all likelihood, I woke up at that precise moment. In my half-awake state I lunged for the door, and followed some kind of commonplace shadow down the stairs."

A look of curiosity entered his eyes. "You dreamed you had an otherworldly male inside your room?"

"Oh, I don't know—man, men—maybe even a woman for that matter. At that particular moment, I found it difficult to tell. I only saw a shadow."

"That whispered."

She shrugged. "All just part of the dream, I suppose."

He scratched at the corner of his mouth. "You weren't afraid of your—hobgoblin?"

"No, not really."

He considered that for a moment. "Did he lead you out here to the garden?"

"No, he didn't. Although I did wonder if he passed this way, the dwindling starlight is to blame for luring me out of your castle without my robe."

The power of his gaze unsettled her far more than she cared to admit. Why did he affect her so? She needed a distraction. After forcing herself to take a breath, she gave him a smile. "Your castle is magnificent to say the least. I've never seen one with stones quite like the ones used to construct it. Do you know where they came from?"

"In a quarry not far from here."

"I suppose that helps when repairs are needed," she said.

A slow nod agreed with the comment, but the fleeting expression which accompanied it made her feel as if she walked a path she didn't dare traverse any farther. She sought an immediate change in subject. Again.

She cleared her throat. "Well, since we're both up, why don't you give me a minute to get dressed and we'll go take a look at your wall. As you know, I'm quite anxious to see it."

He shot a downward glance as a slight grin emerged. "I'm afraid we can't do that. Lowri would be most displeased if I deprived you of the grand breakfast she has so meticulously orchestrated before I put you to work, and I'd never hear the end of it."

"Well, it's still early and it shouldn't take all that

long to take a quick peek, should it? You did say you discovered the pictograph in an underground chamber leading away from the castle, did you not?"

"Yes, I did."

"Then it can't be that far away. We could make a quick trip to your cave, decipher what I can of the message, and get back in plenty of time for breakfast."

"Your task might not be that easy," he replied. "In fact, I guarantee it won't."

"No?" She tilted her chin. Did he doubt her proficiency because of her age as so many others did? The thought rankled. Nonetheless, she gave him the benefit of the doubt. "Why do you say that? Is the main portion of the Ogham faded or missing?"

"No, the symbols are quite vivid."

"Then you doubt my ability to translate it?"

He gazed at her for several long moments and then let go of a breath. "You're not the first epigrapher to make the attempt, Miss DeSpencer. I should probably tell you that over the years, we've engaged many experts in the hope one of them could interpret the inscription. The writing on the wall left each of them baffled and me without answers."

"Do you mean to tell me that no one has ever been able to read *any* part of it?"

Garreth shook his head and shrugged. "I'm afraid none of them possessed the ability. So the question is— dare I nourish any hope you possess the skills they did not?"

Chapter Two

"She's not quite what you expected—is she?"

Garreth tore his gaze away from the doorway through which Essie—looking quite delectable in blue jeans, lavender scoop-necked top, with her hair swept up into a high ponytail—had just disappeared and focused his attention upon Bran. The man wore the infuriating grin he had retained all throughout breakfast as he made his statement. He shook his head. "You're trying to make a point of some kind?"

Bran shrugged and exchanged a mischievous glance with his wife. "Oh, I don't know. Do you think there's a point to be made here, Anne?"

Anne tossed a length of her hair over her shoulder, rested a hand on top of her belly, and rose to her feet. "Can't say for certain. But I think it obvious Garreth believes there is. Therefore, perhaps we ought to assist the man in finding one." She gave her husband a wink.

Garreth dropped his napkin on top of his plate, looked away, and released an irritated huff.

Bran chuckled in response. "If only I had the time. Unfortunately, I have other priorities this morning. So, in light of that fact I'll bid you a good day, Garreth. I'll see you later this afternoon. In the meantime, I wish you and Essie all the best in your endeavors."

That regained his attention. "You're not coming along with us?"

"No, I don't believe I will this time. I have things to do, various places to go, a lot people to see. I'm quite certain Anne has a list of chores she wants done as well, isn't that right, Anne? Seems to me you mentioned something about that last night."

"That's right, I did—and it's a very long list, I'm afraid. The bothersome thing could keep you tied up for several weeks. I'm so sorry Garreth, but as you know, we're preparing for the birth of our babe. There's still so much we need to do. Therefore, you just might have to attend Essie yourself while she's here."

The opportunity to respond to their blatant, ridiculous, scheming escaped Garreth, for at that moment their subject of conversation returned with a small bag in her hand.

She took in each of their faces before she settled her gaze upon his. "I'm sorry, did I interrupt something?"

Garreth shook his head, rose from his seat at the table, and made his way to her side. "You didn't interrupt a thing. Are you ready to go?"

"Yes, I am."

He placed a gentle hand against her back, and cocked his head to the right. "This way."

She didn't speak as they traversed the various corridors of the ground floor. But when he led her down the length of the northernmost hallway, down a flight of steps and then entered through the small door at the end of the corridor, a look of confusion beset her. She glanced about the room and then fastened her bewildered gaze to his. "Your cave entrance is connected to the castle itself?"

He nodded. "Unexpected, I know. However, a very

long time ago, the—calamitous forces of nature enshrouded our entire province, causing great destruction to the land and its structures. During that time, the—uh—lord of the castle stumbled across the passageway while assessing the damage inside this room. He constructed the doorway in the corner after he discovered the writing found within the cave because he believed it might hold some importance to later generations."

A true enough statement, he mused. This solar once belonged to Glodrydd. Therefore, when they happened upon the writing on the cave wall, he hoped the man either carved it for their benefit or discovered it himself. Either way, he felt certain it had something to do with preventing the next devastation.

"How very intriguing."

"Yes, it is." Garreth retrieved the powerful, battery-operated torch from off the small, wooden table, approached and opened the corner door. "Watch your step, now. Thick, gnarly roots are growing up from out of the ground and have a way of tripping a person. There are several areas of loose stones along the way, as well."

"I'll be very careful, I promise."

Garreth forced his rising hope into its cage as they negotiated the twists and turns of the ten minute walk. Yet, as they approached the wall the hope escaped its fragile confines, just as it always did. He held his breath and waited for her to say something. His gaze never once wandered away from her lovely face as she studied the carving, accentuated with red pigment. He didn't see so much as a shred of recognition lighting her eyes throughout the entire process. Disappointment, and a regret he couldn't identify, all but consumed him.

No matter. Although the woman's reputation and credentials far exceeded all others, he would immediately send for another epigrapher on his list. Today. The moment they returned to the castle, in fact. With a bit of luck, he could have another here by week's end. Better yet, he might find it more productive if he sent for them all at once. He paused as the idea took firm hold. Why hadn't he entertained the notion before? Perhaps many minds could succeed where one, by itself, could not.

"This is the first time I have ever examined a painted example. The style of the symbols is unique, as well. I've never seen anything quite like this particular alphabet before," she murmured, breaking into his thoughts.

He swallowed down the ridiculous knot forming in his throat, and nodded. "Well, I can't say I'm surprised to hear you say it. Nonetheless, I want to thank you for coming all the way to Wales to offer your thoughts and assistance. We will, of course, arrange to get you on the first available flight to New York."

She whirled around to face him while clutching her bag to her breast. Anger flashed in her eyes, and indignation stained her cheeks. Her penetrating gaze bore into his for several moments before she spoke. He had the distinct impression she used that time to bring her temper under tight control.

She lifted her chin a notch as she narrowed her eyes. "Are you kidding me? Is this the way you've treated all of your former epigraphists? If so, then it's no wonder you're still standing here, searching for answers."

Her outrage and comments caught him off guard and he quite literally, took a step back. His head all but met his lifted shoulder. "Well, I don't think that I have—"

"Let me tell you something, *Lord* Garreth ap Daffyd," she cut in. "All forms of writing evolve in curious and specific ways from one culture to another. They even evolve from one village to another—one family to another. Time itself will make changes to the language as well. Yet, with a bit of patience and perseverance, a person can step backward both in time and place to make sense of the dialect. Now, do you want to know what this wall says, or do you not?"

Garreth rubbed a hand back and forth against his mouth, mostly to mask the grin solicited by her fury. He raised his brows in concert and drew in a breath. "I did bring you out here with that intention in mind, so—"

"Then allow me some space, a little bit of the time you promised to give me, and let me do the job you hired me to do. If at the end of the allotted time you're not satisfied with my progress, you can send me packing and with my blessings."

He turned his head and waved a hand at the wall. "By all means, please proceed."

"Thank you." She tossed her head and yanked on the zipper of her bag so hard, he found it a wonder she didn't damage the thing. Once she extracted a camera, notebook, and pencil, she dropped the bag onto the ground. She stood back, took several photos of the etching, and then painstakingly replicated each symbol onto the pages of her book. He didn't speak during the entire process. Finally, she released a satisfied sigh, turned around, and fastened her gaze with his.

Curiosity, it seemed, had replaced her anger. Pity that, for her anger had done naught but intensify her comeliness.

"Is this the only example you have uncovered?"

"Example?" he repeated as he brought his wayward thoughts under tight control.

She shook her head and pointed a finger at the wall. "Have you ever seen this style of writing anywhere else? Rock etchings, remnants carved on ancient monuments. The trunk of a dead tree?"

The question startled him a bit. No other epigrapher had ever asked it. "Yes, I have. There are two of which I am aware. I don't know if the style is exact, of course, but I believe they're similar."

"Can you take me to see them?"

"Certainly, but I don't see what they would have to do with the message on this particular piece."

"The more examples I have, the easier it will be to decipher the dialect. We use a variety of tools to decode ancient, lost, or forgotten languages. Therefore, it helps to have more than one source for comparison."

"Exactly how do you go about accomplishing such an objective?"

She retrieved her pack and tucked away her tools. "All languages have a list of common words used repeatedly. For example, in English, we have approximately one hundred words or so that fit in this category. Words like—"the" "of" "and" "a" "to" "that" and, well—I'm sure you get the idea. Therefore, epigraphers look for common patterns to find the equivalent of these words and implement decipherment algorithms. This in turn will lead to the placement of known letters or symbols, which help decipher the other words in the text. The more examples I have, the easier, and faster, the language is to decode."

"I see." Garreth took a moment to consider her insightful explanation and for the first time in centuries, he allowed the glimmer of hope to take flight. He tucked his hands inside his pockets and gave her a sideways glance. "Tell me, Miss DeSpencer, are you capable of riding a horse?"

Her irritation returned. "The name is Essie. For heaven's sake, please use it, and yes, I am quite capable of riding a horse. Why do you ask?"

"Because the only way to see the other known etchings is by way of horseback, unless you want to start walking. Should that be the method you choose, I can't guarantee you'll see them both today."

"Riding is fine."

"Are you finished here then?"

She hesitated for a moment and glanced at the wall. "Well, I am unless you'll allow me to collect a miniscule amount of the color. I promise I won't damage the pictograph. I'll just take a tiny portion at the bottom, right down here," she said, pointing to the extended leg of the final symbol.

"Do what you think necessary, of course. But if you don't mind my asking, what are you going to do with the sample?"

As she set about the task she spared him a glance. "I'll use it to date the paint. I think it'll aid our quest if we know the approximate age of the pictograph. That is, if the creator painted the thing right after he carved the symbols into the rock. If nothing else, we'll have the date someone painted over it."

He lifted a brow. "Isn't radiocarbon dating on rock

a bit problematic?"

"Yes, and that's why, if you'll provide the transportation, I'll take this sample to a lab in London that uses a process called accelerator mass spectrometry. Unlike radiocarbon dating, this process requires very little carbon to provide a fairly accurate date."

The same fleeting expression she detected when first they met passed through his eyes yet again. She almost had the feeling he wanted to hide something from her. But the notion seemed absurd and she immediately tossed it aside.

"You needn't spend your precious time taking the sample to London yourself," he said. "If you just give me the address and some instruction, I can have Vaughn and Gerald, take it in for you. They're heading that way later today, anyway."

"That would be wonderful, thank you. I'll get it prepared for delivery now, so you can give it to them whenever you wish. Then if you're still willing to act as my guide, we can see those other carvings you mentioned."

Less than one hour later, the men set out on their errands while she and Garreth rode north on a pair of gorgeous Welsh Cobs, bay in color. They passed the time talking about a variety of things and she found him both an intelligent and amiable companion. They arrived at their first destination within the hour. After she finished her study of the first site, they rode on to the second. The journey itself consumed an additional hour.

"The pictograph is just around that bend, there," said Garreth as they dismounted.

She untied the laces from around her pack as he gathered the reins and tethered the horses. Once she had tools in hand she gave him a nod. "All right, I'm ready to go if you are."

The worn, oblong rock stood taller than the first, and unlike the first, moss crept over the face, obscuring a portion of the writing. She approached for a better look and then brushed a hand over the rough, pitted surface. "This is going to take a bit more time, I'm afraid," she murmured.

"Take as much time as you need. I'm in no hurry."

"Thank you." She retrieved her digital camera, switched it to infrared capability first, and took a series of photographs she hoped would enhance the symbols. She followed up with a series of visible light shots in every conceivable angle. Then she made use of her tools and took the photographs again. All the while Garreth remained at her side and quietly observed.

"Okay, I think I'm finished—at least for now," she said as she turned around to face him.

"Good. Are you hungry? Now before you answer that question, I'll give you fair warning—should we return without consuming the greater portion of our meal, we'll earn Lowri's disdain. She might not forgive the slight for days, and at such times she's quite difficult to live with."

Essie laughed and leaned toward him. "In that case, I'm starving."

"Excellent choice. The shade of that tree looks inviting, don't you think?"

She followed the direction of his gaze and nodded. "Yes, I would."

He gave her a wink. Her body responded to the

simple gesture by filling her with fluid warmth and that perplexed her. Countless men had winked at her without any effect whatsoever.

"Give me a minute and I'll be right back."

Essie silenced her thoughts by placing her full concentration on the lush, hilly surroundings. Varying shades of green dominated the landscape filled to capacity with a variety of grasses, shrubbery, wildflowers, and trees. But with the ever-present humidity, she expected no less, especially if they were close to the ocean.

"I hope you're hungry," he said upon his return.

She eyed the large leather bag he held aloft and shook her head. "Oh boy, I think you better invite a few friends."

Garreth merely chuckled, the low rumble of which instantly charmed her. She helped him spread the small quilt underneath the shade of the tree and divvy up the food. While they ate, she gazed up at the hazy, swirling clouds that strolled across the sky like lazy ocean waves. She had never seen anything quite like the formation before and finally said so after their conversation ebbed. Yet, the moment the comment left her mouth, she witnessed that same curious, fleeting, expression. What did it mean?

He took a healthy swig from his water bottle and shrugged. "You'll find them quite common here, I assure you. In all likelihood, it has something to with our atmosphere."

Reasonable enough reply, she supposed. Perhaps her vivid imagination worked overtime. No surprise there, and in a place such as this she expected no less. Far better for her to turn her full attention to her job than chase fanciful notions that didn't exist. A finger wiped at the corner of her mouth as she gazed at her companion and wondered—

"Garreth, can you speak Welsh?"

A touch of amusement filled his eyes as he swallowed down the last of his sandwich. "Yes, I can."

She tilted her head to the side as she gazed at him. "Fluently?"

He leaned his back against the tree, propped a booted foot on top of the other, and shrugged. "You could say that."

"But then again, what I really need is someone who has knowledge of the old Welsh, since the text could easily date back to the fifth or sixth century," she mused aloud.

He hesitated for a small moment. "I have a bit of experience with that as well."

Her mouth dropped. "Really? I mean, you do?"

"I do, but if I may ask, why do you have such a need?"

"Because at best, I only know a basic word or two of the modern tongue, and I think we might discover our ancient author carved the inscription using a form of old Welsh."

"I suppose that's a logical assumption given our present location," he said.

"Yes, it is. So, if the supposition proves accurate, and you can spare the time, I'll need your help in translating the text once we fix the symbols in their proper sequence."

"Of course I'll help you in any way I can, Essie. The work you do here is for my benefit. Therefore, I'm quite eager to help you however I can."

"I appreciate that, Garreth, thank you."

"All right. Now that we've settled that, I believe it's my turn to ask a nagging question of my own," he said.

She lifted her brows and shrugged. "Ask away."

"What do the initials S.E. in your name represent? I never did find anything on the internet providing that information."

Heat rose from her belly and splashed outward onto her cheeks. She could feel it. The humor returned to his eyes. He obviously noted the ridiculous blush as well. She cleared her throat as she sought a response.

"What makes you think they represent anything?" She feigned indifference. "There are numerous cases of parents in this world who give their children meaningless initials when they are born, simply because they like the sound of the pairing."

"Um-hmm, but I don't think that situation applies to you," he said while refusing to relinquish her gaze.

The intensity of his relentless scrutiny fueled her discomfort. She forced a breath of laughter. "Oh, come on. Use a little imagination here. If you say S.E. fast enough, you'll hear Essie."

He shook his head. "No, that might be why *you* chose the name, but that isn't the one your parents gave you."

She took in a breath and held on to it. How did he know that? "What makes you think not?"

He cocked his head to the side as he studied her face for what seemed like minutes rather than seconds. "You must abhor the name, am I right?"

Essie slowly released the breath, but said nothing in response.

Garreth mowed over the stubble on his chin with the tip of his fingers. "Let's see then, could they have named you Sigfreda?" He paused as his eyes danced with merriment. "No? How about Sigrid or Stockard, perchance?"

She picked up the remnants of their picnic, and put them back inside the bag. "Not even close."

"Not. Even. Close," he repeated. "Care to give me a hint that would point me in the right direction then?"

"Nope."

He bowed his head and chuckled. "All right, in deference to your discomfort I'll let the subject drop for now. But know this, Miss S.E. DeSpencer, before you leave here, I *will* know your name in full."

"I wouldn't count on it."

The return only served to fuel his mirth. "We'll see. If nothing else, I can be quite persistent in my chosen quests."

She retained his gaze as she rose to her feet and dusted off the back of her jeans. He followed a miniscule instant behind and then as he approached her, she shrugged. "Well, then I wish you the best of luck on your impossible quest, Lord Garreth ap Daffyd."

He chuckled anew. Yet, true to his word and much to her relief, Garreth dropped the subject as they made their way back to the castle. Instead of badgering her, he turned to the subject of her work and asked a series of questions about the history of Ogham. He seemed surprised when she said that existing inscriptions in both the ancient Irish and Pictish languages still waited deciphering.

Could they harbor any real hope then, he had asked, of decoding the message inside the cave?

Of course, she had replied, and she meant what she said. She assured him she wouldn't leave this castle until she completed her task unless he should will it otherwise. The comment surprised him, though he said nothing in return.

After she entered the great hall, she hurried up to her room, anxious to download her photographs to her laptop. Yet, the moment she opened the door, a slender, willowy, shadow, darker than the natural darkness inside her bedroom, scurried over to the balcony doors that now stood slightly ajar.

Essie rushed inside, dropped her bag on the bed, and chased after it. Before she could take hold of the handle, the doors inched their way shut. She reopened them a scant moment later, knowing full well the intruder couldn't escape the confines of the private veranda. But somehow he did just that. Just as he had once before.

She raised a hand to her mouth while her gaze swept over every inch of the marble flooring, the railing, the exterior walls, and even the grounds below. Nothing seemed out of place, nor did she see or hear anyone outside. That could only mean one of two impossible things. She either had some unearthly creature running amuck inside her bedroom—or she was in fact, losing her mind. Truly, neither option gave her any comfort.

Chapter Three

"Has our charming guest awakened yet this morning?" Bran removed his gloves as he sauntered toward him from the direction of the stables.

Garreth shifted his gaze to the castle where he had caught sight of Essie working not one hour ago. He had fought off the urge to disturb her then—a battle he lost more often than not since the evening of her arrival. Yet, allowing his attraction to his lovely epigraphist free reign would not be wise. "Yes, she has. She's in the library, studying her notebooks and a table full of photographs, just as she has every day these past two weeks, Bran."

"Is she making any progress?"

He nodded. "Some."

"Well, that's more than we could say for any of the others."

"You're right. I have to say that I'm very pleased with her dogged determination to decipher the pictograph. She's already exceeded my expectations, and for the first time in centuries, I find myself hoping we'll finally uncover this piece of our puzzle."

"I'm happy to hear that, Garreth, given our ever waning time frame. However, I must say I'm surprised you're not hovering over her."

Garreth shifted his stance and gave the man his full attention. "Now tell me, Bran, why should such a thing surprise you?"

"Because if I were single, I'd be hovering," he said with a firm nod of his head. "That is one mighty fine woman in there, both inside and out."

Garreth shot a glance at the library window yet again and chuckled. "Better not let Anne hear you say that. You might find yourself sleeping in the hallway without benefit of pillow or blanket."

"Trust me, I won't mention it again and certainly not to anyone but you. Still, if I were in your boots, I would seize every opportunity to dwell in the girl's company. In fact, I might even invent a few."

"To what end? You and I both know she'll leave once she completes her task."

"Not, I should think, if you encourage the obvious attraction the two of you feel for each other. You've gone on far too long by yourself, Garreth. Now, at long last, the perfect woman stands before you. All you need do—is take advantage of that fact."

"Don't be absurd. In the first place, neither of us feels any attraction for the other. In the second, she doesn't belong here, and you know it."

"How can you say that? We've amassed a few outsiders over the centuries," Bran said, ignoring his first point altogether. "As I recall, none of them have ever elected to leave."

"True, but none of them are like Dr. DeSpencer. I don't think a woman with a spirit like hers would be content living her life within the boundaries of our realm."

The smirk returned. "You're so sure about that are you?"

Garreth let loose a snort and shook his head. "How

are you coming along on that vast list of chores Anne assigned you?"

Bran slapped him on the back, threw back his head, and laughed. "All right, I can take a hint. I'll leave you to your own devices then. But you might want to think on what I said, and for pity's sake, don't let the grass grow under your feet while doing so. Because while you're sitting there mulling it over, someone else will surely come along and steal her away from beneath your very nose. That, my friend, would be a very regretful thing." He winked. "If I were single, you'd already have competition, our friendship notwithstanding."

Garreth followed Bran's jaunty retreat until he disappeared from view. The man should mind his own business and not encourage thoughts better left alone. Especially since, with the passing of each day, those thoughts chipped away at his resolve to keep the girl at arm's length.

His gaze drifted over the castle exterior and rested on the large library windows. He could see Essie inside, as she paced back and forth, holding two photos at shoulder height. She seemed absorbed by them. Did she stumble upon something new? Perhaps he ought to check on her and see if she found something that needed discussion.

Pathetic, Garreth, that's really, really, pathetic, he muttered inwardly. He shook his head in defeat, and hastened his pace toward the castle entrance.

****

Essie dropped her photos on the table and rubbed a hand along the sleeve of her chocolate brown sweater. She stared at Garreth's exquisite George the II barometer without really seeing the piece. Rather than focusing on her work, her mind insisted on reliving the conversation she had with Lowri the morning following her second unexplained experience with the elusive shadow. The woman had entered her bedroom with a fresh bouquet of richly scented blue roses and a friendly smile.

"Good morning, Essie," she sang out as she placed the porcelain vase on top of the bureau. "Did you sleep well?"

Essie had wavered for a moment before answering. Should she tell her about the ethereal being that visited her room, not once but twice? She opted against it. "I slept very well, thank you."

"I'm so glad to hear it. You know, there are many people who have trouble sleeping in a strange place or in a strange bed, me included." She paused for a moment and then shrugged. "But then again, each home has its own unique noises. Some of those sounds take some getting used to. Ours is no different from anyone else's, I suppose. Especially, after we installed the plumbing. We found out in a hurry those pipes could play some eerie tunes. Took us a while to get used to that."

"I bet it did. I've always thought those distinctive sounds are the reason so many people conjure sightings of ghosts or what not," she said, using a jocular tone. "And I can definitely see where something might happen like that in a castle as old as this one."

Wait a minute. Just how long did this castle exist without plumbing? The fixtures themselves seemed so much older than what Lowri indicated. Her cast iron, claw foot bathtub and sink looked of late nineteenth century design. Did they find antique fixtures and simply restore and install them for authenticity?

Lowri retrieved a fresh set of linens from the large bathroom closet, and on her way out, wagged her head back and forth in response to her remark. "I suppose so. But, I think I can say with a fair amount of certainty, we don't have any ghosts living amongst us here. They have a tendency to reside in the village—although some of them do visit us on occasion."

What?

The woman paused for a moment and turned her gaze toward her balcony doors. "We also receive visits from various members of the Tylwyth Teg from time to time. They always manage to stir a bit of excitement whenever they come around."

Confusion beset her. Essie drew her brows together and gave her head a little shake. "The Tylwyth Teg?"

Lowri fanned out the sheets and let them flutter on top of the mattress. "You know—the Fair folk," she stated matter-of-factly. "Every now and again they'll stop by and leave a gift for one reason or another. Why, some say this castle has even had a few visits from Gwynn ap Nudd, himself. Not that Garreth has ever spoken of such a visit, mind you. But then again, the man keeps a great many things to himself."

Gwynn ap Nudd? Essie clasped her hands, drew her shoulders together, and braved a reply. "I'm afraid I don't know who you're talking about."

She laughed as she smoothed and tucked the sheets. "I suppose not. The ruler of the otherworld keeps a low profile these days, and I can tell you, it's not every day he deigns to visit humankind. So, when he does—"

Oh, dear. The woman believed in fairies of all things and she didn't quite know how to respond to that.

"Essie?"

She whirled around, surprised to see Garreth standing just behind her. The beat of her heart took flight the moment he fastened his gaze to hers. "Hmm?"

His forest green eyes probed deeply into hers. "Is everything all right?"

"Yes, everything's fine. Why do you ask?"

"Well, you look troubled for one thing, and for another, you didn't hear me when I entered the room."

What to say to that? Should she pretend that nothing troubled her mind? She needed to confide in someone and Garreth did seem the likely choice. Perhaps he could offer a sane, logical explanation for her experiences since he already knew about the first. "I'm not quite sure where to start—" The knock at the door interrupted the admission.

"Come in," said Garreth, without releasing her from his gaze.

Vaughn strode inside the room and offered her the large envelope he held in his hand. For some reason, and despite his six-foot, slender frame, the middle-aged, blue-eyed blond reminded her of a storybook elf. Perhaps she could blame the slight point of his ears and features that seemed far too refined for an ordinary man.

"The results of the lab work in London," he said.

"Oh, thank you, Vaughn." She returned his smile as she accepted the package. Excitement replaced all other thought as she slid her fingers underneath the seal and extracted the report. She glued her eyes to the page and hurried through the paragraphs, seeking the age of the paint.

Once Vaughn quit the room Garreth gave her his full attention. "What does it say?"

She lifted her chin a notch as she gave him a brief glance. "They estimated the age of our pigment at about 820 A.D., plus or minus forty years."

"Well, that's interesting."

"Yes, and that date eliminates a ton of headaches and needless research. We won't have to concentrate on or consider anything beyond that time frame. I think I'll give Eli a call, and see if he can provide an opinion on some of the more common symbols I have isolated this far alongside the date the lab provided."

"Who is Eli?"

She detected a slight edge to his tone and at once, she looked up from the report but found nothing amiss in his penetrating gaze. "He's a well-known expert in the Pictish culture. His knowledge far exceeds my own in this area, so perhaps he can help us." She dipped her hand inside the pocket of her tan cargoes and withdrew her cell phone.

Garreth closed his fingers around her hand and shook his head. "I'm afraid we don't have cell phone reception here."

"Oh," she glanced down at her phone as he released his clasp.

"However, I do have an old archaic landline phone you're free to use whenever you wish."

"Well, I have to call New York, and that's—"

"Not a problem." He slipped a hand about her waist, led her over to his massive desk, and slid the phone toward her. "Go ahead and make your call. It is, after all, for my benefit, right?"

"Yes, I suppose it is. Thank you."

"I'll give you some privacy, but if you find you need me, just give me a holler. I won't be far," he said as he turned away.

She placed a light hand on top of his arm and halted his progress. "No, you don't have to go. You can stay. This will only take a minute, and I guarantee I won't say anything you can't hear."

Garreth sat down on the edge of the desk and waited while she placed her call.

"Hello?" the voice at the other end sang out.

She smiled over the mere sound of Eli's voice. "Hello, Eli, it's Essie—"

A chuckle followed a slight pause. "Well, as I live and breathe. How in the world have you been, darlin'? I can't tell you how much I've missed you."

Garreth's jaw tensed and his eyes narrowed a bit over the exchange. Perhaps he needed her to forgo the idle chitchat and get right to the point.

"I'm just fine," she said. "Look, I'm working on a project that has a great deal of importance attached to it, and I'm wondering if you'd mind evaluating some of the symbols for me. We have dated the carving to around 820 A.D., so the possibility of a Pictish connection exists. I'm hoping you can either confirm or dismiss the notion altogether."

"Are you telling me you're unfamiliar with these symbols?"

"They're different than most in a unique sort of way and kind of hard to explain without seeing the photographs yourself."

"Really? Now you have me intrigued. Just send me

the file via my personal email and I'll get back to you right away. I promise."

"Thank you, Eli, I appreciate your help."

"Anything for you, darlin', you know that."

Essie replaced the remote phone on top of the cradle as she glanced about the room. "You did say you have internet connection?"

"Yes, I do." Garreth pointed to the antique secretary that sat beneath the side window. "Again, we must use cable connection. However, it is high speed. So, either you can plug it into your own laptop or use mine if you wish."

"I'll just go ahead and use yours if you don't mind logging into your system. That way I won't have to push your things aside just to email a file that'll only take a moment to send."

Garreth gave her a nod, rose from the desk and made his way to the secretary. "This Eli—is he a good friend of yours?"

"My uncle, actually," she replied. "He's the one who fueled my interest in the field of epigraphy by dragging me off on some of his expeditions during my childhood. I suppose that's where I fell out of the habit of addressing him as "uncle," for he refused to allow it while in the field. He said it made him feel even more old and cantankerous than what his reputation alleged."

"Is that right?" Amusement filled his eyes long before the grin appeared at the corner of his mouth. "Then he'll surely know the answer to my little mystery, wouldn't you agree?"

She turned her head to the side. "What mystery? I'm not sure what you're talking about?"

"Your name. Most assuredly, an uncle, who would

condescend to take his niece on expeditions, would know her name in full. Perhaps I'll take my quest to him."

Essie laughed. "You can go ahead and try if you like. However, I should warn you, the man has made a solemn oath to carry the secret to his grave."

"Hmm. Perchance you're named for him then," he replied. "Does the mysterious 'E' stand for Eli? If so, then maybe the 'S' is a male name as well. Your father's?"

Essie approached her worktable and extracted her flash drive from her computer. She said nothing as she made her way to his side and plugged the device into an empty hub.

"How about Shamus? That name would work well with Eli. In fact, it kind of flows off the tongue, don't you think? Shamus Eli DeSpencer. Or, how about Safford or Sawyer Eli DeSpencer?"

She made every effort to concentrate on sending the file, rather than fueling his mirth.

"Stuart—Stuart Eli DeSpencer," he said, pointing a finger at her.

After the completion of her task, she removed her data stick and turned to face him. She bowed her head in playful deference. "Once again, m'lord Garreth, your guesses are ice cold." In all truth, she would prefer any one of the names he had guessed this far to that of her own.

He eyed her with a bit of suspicion. "I'm not so sure I should take you at your word. You probably wouldn't tell me even if my guess approached red hot."

She paused, feigned consideration as to his statement, and then shook her head. "Probably not."

Her amusement over his exasperation accompanied her as she climbed into bed that night. The handsome lord of this castle might succeed in gleaning most every detail of her life should he seek the knowledge, but the one thing he would never get, is her given names. She snuggled into her covers, and closed her eyes as, despite all effort to banish them, thoughts of Garreth lulled her to sleep.

****

Hours later, an odd, muffled rumble inched Essie toward awareness. Her eyes refused to open as she attempted to make sense of the unusual sound. She had nothing with which to compare it. Then, of a sudden, her bed shook back and forth, gently at first. As it abruptly increased in strength, she shot into a seated position and opened her eyes. Moonlight filtered in through the balcony doors providing a bit of light. The possibility of an earthquake stormed her mind. She glanced about the room. Her lamps and the fragile adornments on top of the various pieces of furniture bounced precariously, giving credence to the notion. A gasp escaped her lips. She grabbed hold of the lamp to her right, just as it pitched forward.

"Essie?" Her name accompanied a knock on the door. Garreth didn't wait for an answer. He burst into the room, made his way to her bed, and sat beside her. At once, he gathered her into the protective embrace of his arms and held her close. She let go of the lamp and clung to him. His arms tightened in response. She welcomed the warmth and the strength he offered.

The doors of her wardrobe flung open a scant moment later. The chandelier swung in violent circles above them. Her luggage and laptop case slammed to the ground while her clothing pitched wildly on the secured hangers. The roses tumbled to the floor, shattering the vase upon impact. Bureau drawers slid back and forth on their rollers. Each time, they threatened to break loose from their confinements.

She couldn't say how long the episode lasted. However, she did breathe a sigh of relief when the event finally subsided. Garreth leaned back, and as he brushed his fingers through her hair he connected his gaze with hers.

"Are you all right?"

She could see his concern and reassured him with a nod. "Yes, I'm fine. Thank you." Her reluctant fingers finally slid away from his chest as she looked over the disarray. She lifted a shoulder as she returned her gaze to his. "But your beautiful room didn't fare quite so well, I'm afraid."

"Nothing major—the place just needs a bit of clean-up and we can take care of that in no time at all."

"I can help. If someone will bring me a dustpan and broom, I can sweep up the glass."

"No. I won't hear to that. We have an excellent staff that manages the castle, and since these quakes are somewhat common here of late, they're quite adept at setting things to right. Therefore, I want you to stay right here in your bed until they clear away the shards. We don't need you cutting up your feet." He rose from the bed and made his way to the door. "I'll be back in just a minute."

Once he left the room, she righted the heavy bronze lamps. They didn't receive any damage during the quake that she could see. Essie inspected the bureau, the wardrobe, her luggage, and finally settled her gaze upon her laptop case. She drew her brows together as she leaned forward and focused on a piece of yellowed paper peeking out of the side pocket. A paper she didn't recognize.

In that same moment, Garreth announced his return with a couple of knocks on her door. Again, he didn't wait for an invitation to enter. He lifted the flashlight he carried at shoulder height and looked about the darkened room. "We'll have the emergency generators on in just a few minutes."

"Garreth," she said pointing to the mysterious page. "Can you hand me that document inside my case?"

He followed her gaze, extracted the sheet from the pocket, and then placed it in her hands. "What is this?"

"I don't know. I've never seen it before."

He sat down beside her. "Then how did it get inside your bag?"

"I have no idea." Her fingers glided lightly over the page. "This feels more like parchment than vellum," she murmured aloud.

"Is there a difference?"

"Well, for most it's one in the same, I suppose. But the more modern experts in the field denote the use of calfskin as vellum, while parchment refers to all other animal skins. Could you shine some light on it for me please?"

Her heart picked up its pace as she examined the document. Uncertainty bade her draw the parchment closer to the light. "I don't believe it. But where on earth did this come from?"

"You recognize it now?"

She turned her head in order to meet his gaze. "I

recognize what it is. This is a palimpsest, Garreth. This type of ancient manuscript is a page from out of a book or even served as a scroll that someone has used repeatedly—kind of like an antiquated chalkboard. That person, or any number of people for that matter, will scrape away the original text and write over the parchment again and again. But over time, the layer underneath the topmost layer will eventually show through, if even faintly. Look, can you see the telltale sign of markings here and here?"

Garreth dropped his gaze to the sheet and studied it. "Yes, I can see them now that you've pointed them out. Are you able to make sense of the message?"

"No—at least, not right now, anyway. I'm going to need better light and a source of magnification."

Just then, several members of Garreth's staff entered the room and changed out the bulbs in the lamps. She recognized only two of them by name— Glenda and Philip. They both gave her a reassuring smile.

"Don't worry, Miss DeSpencer," said Glenda after she switched on the light. "We'll have this mess cleaned up and be out of here in no time at all."

"I'll get out of your way then." Garreth took hold of her hand, gave it a gentle press, and then rose from the bed. "Try to get some sleep, Essie. We can finish our conversation a little later."

She glanced at the clock that had just passed the five a.m. hour. "I don't think I can sleep—"

"Please, at least give it a try. There's no need for you to arise so early."

She lifted her brows and shrugged. "All right, I'll try."

Essie didn't realize until he made the comment that despite the early morning hour, he had already donned a pair of jeans and a T-shirt. A combination—she couldn't help but notice—that enhanced his brawny form. Did he always arise so early or did he just have weighty concerns that troubled his sleep? Would the writing on the wall have anything to do with those concerns? If so, what made the pictograph so important? Though the questions nagged, she resisted the need to ask. After all, he didn't hire her to pry into his business.

One hour later, she gave up all efforts to close her eyes. The lure of the palimpsest prevented it. She slipped out of bed and dressed for the day in a pair of black jeans and burgundy top. After she brushed her teeth and the tangles from her hair, she scooped the parchment off the table, and exited the room.

The quake left many of the portraits askew. As she followed the hallways heading for the library, she stopped here and there to straighten them. About half way down the final hall, she spied one of the smaller portraits face down on the floor. She stooped down, took firm hold of the oval frame, and gazed up at the wall in search of the hanger. Once located, she turned the antiquated portrait around and assessed it for damage.

She gasped as she stared down at an exact replica of Lord Garreth ap Daffyd, dressed in eighteenth century attire. Did she see a direct line ancestor perhaps? If so, he bore an uncanny resemblance to the man. But then, just as she made ready to hoist the painting into position, she halted all progress. Her mouth dropped, and her heartbeat accelerated as she fixed her gaze on the slight scar next to the dimple—on the left hand side of the handsome man's face.

Chapter Four

How long she stared at the painting before replacing it, she couldn't say. Two men, separated by centuries, simply could *not* share the same, identical scar. The reverse side of the canvas showed distinct signs of antiquity, no doubt about that. Therefore, no one could possibly have painted it within the last year or two as the painting might suggest *if* Garreth posed for it. Her hands trembled as she fixed the oak frame on top of its hanger.

She glanced at the parchment she clutched in her hand. Her enthusiasm to examine it waned in the face of this new dilemma. She needed a moment to think— to sort through the countless thoughts that invaded her mind, each demanding attention. A walk and a breath of fresh air might clear away some of the clutter. At least, she hoped so. She returned to her room, abandoned the parchment to the tabletop, grabbed a light sweater, and headed outside.

Essie turned her gaze in the direction of the village. She had yet to visit the place, but right now, she wanted solitude. The green, woody hills to the west looked promising, and so she started walking. She refused to let anything enter her mind as she crossed the hilly terrain, save the beauty of the pristine landscape. But once she arrived on top of the tallest hill and gazed out over the valley, Garreth slipped into her thoughts, just as he had so many times since her arrival. She could never stop them, no matter how hard she tried, and she did try, for nothing could ever come of her growing attraction to the lord of the castle. There—she admitted it. She loved the way he looked at her and the way he said her name whenever they came in contact with each other. When he cradled during the quake, she had no desire to remove herself from his arms. She'd quite willingly go back and experience that delightful encounter again. This new quandary concerning the man and his perplexing portrait didn't change that in the least.

She eased herself down onto the ground and rested her back against the natural incline of the hill. The lush, tall grass made for a comfortable bed. She gazed up at the thick, swirling clouds that suggested it might rain. Not that it mattered. She would brave a storm if it meant putting a bit of order and reason to her chaotic thoughts. For now, she pushed the dilemma the painting posed to the back of the list.

When Garreth first contacted her in regards to the writing, she detected more than mere curiosity in the tone of his voice. She noted heavy concern, and she chalked that concern up to worry over ownership and preservation. Yet, the location and condition of the pictograph eliminated the need for both. So what worries did Garreth carry? Why the insatiable need for the inscription's translation?

Her mind wandered aimlessly over their encounter in the garden when she related her first experience with the mysterious shadow. He seemed truly interested in hearing all the details concerning her hobgoblin. Why? Did it have anything to do with his worries or did it lean more toward Lowri's comments concerning ghosts and fairies? *Oh, but how ridiculous*, she silently scoffed.

As ridiculous as a painting of Garreth, far older than what he appears? her mind taunted. She took in a deep breath and gave it a slow release as her thoughts danced around the notion of mythical creatures that weren't so mythical after all. Lowri said that from time to time, fairies entered the castle leaving gifts behind. Today, right after the quake, she discovered the parchment inside the pocket of her laptop case. Could the elusive shadow be responsible for that occurrence? If so, then it must reveal something the ethereal shadow wanted her to know. Right?

She leaned forward, wrapped her arms around her knees, and gazed up at the heavens. "What are you thinking, Essie? Phantoms and fairies belong in fairytales and well you know it," she berated aloud. "The existence of such creatures? Well, such a thing just isn't possible."

"What isn't possible?"

Essie's heart accelerated as she turned her head in the direction of Garreth's voice. He sat down beside her, placed a finger underneath her chin, and tilted it upward, forcing their gazes to meet. A shiver traveled down her spine in response.

He searched her eyes for several moments. "Please, Essie, tell me what it is that troubles you so. Perhaps I can help."

"Oh, where to even begin with that," she murmured, more to herself than to him.

"Why not begin with the thing that troubles you most."

She gazed into his eyes as she measured his level

of sincerity. He didn't shy away from the intensity of her search. "I need full and complete honesty from you, Garreth. Without it, there's no need to have this discussion, or even a need for me to stay here any longer."

"You shall have it. I give you my word, will that suffice?"

"Yes, that'll do."

He gave her an encouraging nod. "All right then— first question."

"How old are you?" She held her breath and waited. In fact, she waited so long she wondered if he'd answer the question at all.

Finally, he dropped his gaze and returned a slow nod. He made the gesture more in response to an inner resignation than directing it toward her. "First, if I might ask, what gave rise to your curiosity?"

She combed the windblown hair away from her face and shrugged. "Does it make any difference as to how you'll respond?"

He considered that for a time before he spoke. "No, I suppose it doesn't. Still, I'd like to know."

"All right, I don't have a problem giving you an answer." She cleared her throat. "The quake disturbed several portraits hanging along the hallways. I found one of them on the floor after leaving my room. So, I picked it up with every intention of replacing it, but the subject stole my attention. You see, if asked under oath in a court of law, I would swear you posed for the portrait at least two, maybe even three centuries ago."

"And you didn't stop to consider whether or not the man in the painting might be a distant ancestor to whom I bear a great resemblance?"

She extended a finger to his face, gently traced the scar that only served to enhance his looks, and shook her head. "Not when the artist painted him with this."

****

Garreth had quite forgotten about that damning portrait as did everyone else. Not that they could correct the oversight now. No wonder she fled the castle. The decision to follow her as he spied her heading for the hills seemed a good one now.

He resigned himself to answering her questions in a forthright manner, despite the possible consequences of such a course. "I can't answer your question with exactness, since I truly don't know the day of my birth. However, I can tell you I have surpassed eight hundred years of life by at least eighteen years."

Her mouth dropped as she stared at him and pondered the notion. "That's just not possible."

"No, it isn't." He shrugged. "Yet, here I am."

Her widened eyes filled with disbelief and a touch of fear. "What...what are you, Garreth? A ghost? A...a vampire? An immortal of some kind? I just can't..."

"None of the above, Essie. I'm a man who's lived an incredible number of years. Over the centuries, my body has slowly aged from a man in his nineteenth year, to that of a man in his very late twenties, perhaps early thirties by your way of reckoning. However, it's a thing for which I have no reasonable explanation. Will I die someday? I should certainly think so, for many inside this realm have already met their death. We've a lovely cemetery in the village to prove the claim if you care to take a look."

Trembling fingers covered her mouth, and then dropped into her lap as she lifted her face to the sky.

She drew in a short breath and then released it as she closed her eyes. He could see her inner turmoil. An overwhelming need to shield her—to banish the turmoil—overcame him, and with a strength that caught him off guard.

He took hold of her hand and rubbed lightly across the top of it with his thumb. She didn't shy away from his touch. "Perhaps it might help you to come to terms with all of this if I offered you a bit of history regarding this province?"

She opened her eyes then and fastened her gaze to his. "You have my attention."

"And I appreciate that." He answered the slight smile she gave him with a broader one of his own. "Somewhere in the spring after I completed my eighteenth year of life, the province of Llys y Gwalch suffered through a catastrophic event that began on an ordinary day, with an extraordinary eclipse of the sun—"

Essie didn't interrupt as he recited the details of the destruction, his experience with Glodrydd, or the brief account of their lives during the four hundred years that followed. At that point in his narrative he paused, giving her leave to ask her questions. For he could see she had them. He could also see that she doubted the truth of his tale. Then again, if their positions were reversed, he wouldn't believe a word of it either.

"I take it then, after what Glodrydd said, you experienced the event again. Yet, according to your story, your realm already existed underneath the sea in some kind of protective enclosure that not only allowed a continuation of your lives, but preserved them for an extraordinary period of time, do I have that right?"

"You do."

"Then I have to confess that I don't understand or even believe such a thing is possible—"

"Neither did I." He shrugged. "Nonetheless, time proved otherwise. All the while, I don't know if I didn't believe it would happen again, or if I just didn't think it would cause us any further harm. As we approached the deadline, and over the course of several months, a series of quakes like the one you experienced this morning, preceded the event. Then, right on schedule, and just as Glodrydd warned, the calamity began anew. Once again, death claimed many of our citizens. Walls tumbled. Homes and other structures collapsed. Then another immense land mass crashed beneath the sea and adjoined with ours. Tremendous fear and panic ran rampant in the dark hours that followed."

He paused for a moment as the recollection washed over him. "I decided then and there that I would do whatever necessary to avoid the next one. All my efforts from that day to this are prioritized with this goal in mind."

"And you think the inscription in the cave has something to do with avoiding the next cycle of destruction?"

"From the moment we discovered it, we hoped it would. As I said when you first arrived, we found the cave right after our second experience. The room to which it connects once belonged to Glodrydd. The fact remains that despite all our efforts and exploration within the entire realm of Llys y Gwalch, we've uncovered nothing else to assist the endeavor."

"Oh, I don't know, Garreth, I just find all of this so hard to accept. I've always been one to put my faith in facts and logic, not mystical places or mythical creatures that exist only in the imagination or the storybooks of children."

"That's the second time you've said that. What mythical creatures are you referring to?"

"Well, Lowri mentioned ghosts and fairies right after I saw the shadow for the second time and she said that—"

"Am I to understand you encountered your shadow again?" he interrupted. Why didn't she tell him? For some reason, the omission offended him a bit.

"Yes, I chased it out onto the balcony. The thing disappeared just as it did before when I assigned the event to a dream."

"And you confided in Lowri?"

She shook her head. "No, not confide really. We spoke in generalities. That's when she mentioned all the strange noises the freshly installed plumbing created, which didn't make any sense at all considering the age of the fixtures, but now—" She released a small laugh, waved a hand, and then dropped it into her lap. "Anyway, at the same time she said your ghosts lived in the village and that fairies visited the castle on occasion to offer their gifts. I thought the whole thing so ridiculous."

She asked for honesty. He would give it. "They've been known to do that."

Her eyes widened and her mouth dropped. "Are you seriously telling me you believe Tinker Bell flutters in and out of your castle leaving fairy dust in her wake?"

Essie's stark amazement made him laugh. "The tiny fictional character with the absurd little wings that couldn't possibly hold the weight of her body? No, not at all. But there *is* an ancient race of beings the Welsh people interacted with for centuries. We refer to them as the Tylwyth Teg, or the Fair folk, from the long lost kingdom of Llys y Helig. For as a whole, they are tall, fair-haired, and quite attractive beings. As I understand it, they were victims of the first apocalypse.

"Their entire realm disappeared beneath the water four hundred years before our own. As you can imagine, over time people distorted the facts concerning their race. They created so many tales and legends that the reality of who and what they are, is now lost to modern knowledge. They prefer to keep it that way."

She said nothing for several minutes. He didn't know where her thoughts had taken her and chose not to ask. Not right now. He simply held her hand for the simple pleasure it gave him and waited for her to speak.

Finally, a very small smile curved the corners of her lips. "I'm sorry, but I'm having a difficult time buying into all of this."

He gave her hand a gentle squeeze. "I know. I can see that."

"Especially since you just seem so normal—"

"Thank you."

The comment made her laugh. "What I mean is that you speak perfect English, albeit with a fascinating accent. You don't use archaic terms. Your castle is equipped with every modern convenience imaginable. You're quite up to date with current events, terminology, and even fashion."

Garreth looked down at his clothing and grinned. "You think so?"

"Yes, I do. So, how can you accomplish all that

living down here while isolated from the world?"

"For the first couple of centuries, we didn't do any of those things. We put all of our efforts into rebuilding and acquiring self-reliance for every needful thing. In all honesty, I didn't know we could return to the surface."

"How did you learn that you could?"

"By discovering an obscure passageway nature had tunneled through the mountain," he said. "We did have to widen it and make improvements to it over the years, but once it could handle a team of horses, wagons, and finally motor cars, we visited the surface once or twice each year. Over the ensuing centuries, we made careful study of, and welcomed, the newest technological advances. Our men of science then adapted them to our environment. This, of course, is an ongoing process in our ever changing world."

"You never wanted to leave here?"

"A few of our inhabitants have assimilated into your world over the centuries and vice versa. But most of us have never had the desire to abandon this realm. This is our home. We're content here with our way of life."

He could see the doubt and consternation still lingering within her lovely, expressive eyes. Yet, he could also see a growing need to believe him. Perhaps he could help put the matter to rest.

He pushed away from the ground, rose to his feet, and offered her his hand. She readily accepted it. "Come with me, Essie. I'd like to show you something that might make this easier for you to accept."

One hour later, he pulled his car over to the side of the gravel road just shy of the tunnel exit. They said very little to each other as they made the drive from the castle and ever upward through the winding turns of the passageway. Yet, even when they did speak, her gaze remained fixed on the rocky walls of the tunnel she couldn't have seen through the tinted windows of the car Vaughn drove.

He switched off the engine, and turned his gaze toward her. "Since the sun is still shining, I think it best if we park here, and walk out. That way we won't attract unwanted attention or curiosity should anyone be passing near the gate."

"You usually drive in and out at night?"

"Yes, unless the need outweighs the risk. Even then we'll ensure that no one is in close proximity before we take a vehicle out into the open."

She nodded and while she unbuckled her seatbelt, he made his exit. He rounded the car and opened her door. After she vacated the car, he again claimed possession of her hand. "This way."

He led her down the gravel road, over to an overhang of dense foliage, and then stepped out into the sunshine. At once, the roar of ocean waves captured her attention. Absolute shock, in seeing the seashore straight ahead instead of far down below, finally gave way to calm acceptance. He could see it.

She turned a slow circle, taking in the sight of the small stone cottage they built two centuries ago, the stable, and the handful of horses grazing in the pasture. A bemused smile touched her face. "I take it you own this property as well?"

"Yes, to ensure our continued seclusion we bought the surrounding property a few centuries ago. We then built the stone fence as well as the cottage and stable."

"Does anyone live there?"

"From time to time. Right now, it's empty. However, I do have a variety of caretakers that visit on a daily basis. They tend to the animals, make sure the place looks lived in, and see to any needed repairs." He cocked his head in the direction of the ocean. "Want to chance getting your feet wet?"

She met his comment with an impish smile. "You know, I think I do."

"Then let's go." He escorted her across his cobblestone byway, down the slope of the hill, and over to the beach. Once they arrived, she kicked off her shoes and abandoned them to the sand in favor of walking barefoot.

She gave him a sideways glance as they strolled along the shore. "I truly expected to come out of the tunnel at the top of some mountain, or at the very least, midway. But you suspected that, didn't you."

"I figured you might. So, alongside that unexpected observation, do I win the day?"

She released a sigh of resignation and nodded. "Yes, you've finally convinced me your entire province resides beneath the sea, and that means I'm going to have a million questions. So get ready for them."

"No doubt you will. But like I said, since I had them once myself, I won't mind answering them."

Essie turned her gaze toward the waves and for a few minutes, they walked along in silence. "When is the next event scheduled to take place?"

"In a little over six months."

The widening of her eyes accompanied a gasp. She halted her steps and turned to face him. "That isn't very much time to solve the riddle, Garreth."

"No, it isn't. Therefore, for the past several decades, we've prepared for the worst and hoped for the best."

She drew her brows together as she combed her wayward locks away from her face. "By doing what?"

"Fortifying our buildings to withstand the onslaught, stockpiling emergency supplies and equipment. We've also gathered food and the like for those who may ultimately join us."

"Did you receive additional people with the last calamity?"

He returned a slow nod. "A fair number from one small village managed to survive the onslaught."

She cast her gaze in a sweeping circle, taking in the countryside and the vast array of boats sailing the sea. "Look at them, Garreth. Innocent people going about their lives and none of them have any idea that within a few short months—" She gulped. "No, we have to find a way to stop this from happening again."

The comment surprised him. "After knowing all of this, you're willing to stay and continue your work?"

She fastened her gaze to his. "Down to the last possible moment if you so desire."

He paused. "The time far exceeds our agreement. What about your work in New York?"

"I don't care about that right now, Garreth. My present obligations and schedule can be rearranged if I wish. If there's something I can do to help, then I will. Unless, of course, you'd rather I leave?"

Would he rather she leave? From the moment Bran first escorted her into his library he had asked himself that question. The answer continued to plague him. Every day he waged a war with the growing need to explore the attraction escalating between them. For reasons known only to her, Essie fought against it too. If she stayed, he had no doubt they would both lose the battle. But would losing this particular battle be such a terrible thing after all?

"I would welcome any help you're willing to give. Perhaps if we work on this thing together, we can figure it out in time," he said.

"What about the Tylwyth Teg? Are they doing anything to circumvent this looming catastrophe?"

"I don't know."

"But Lowri said they have visited the castle. She said that even the ruler—what's his name?" She shook her head as she dropped her gaze while bringing the memory to mind, and then snapped her fingers. "Gwynn ap Nudd made an appearance on a couple of different occasions. Didn't you ever discuss the situation with him during one of those times?"

He shook his head. "Despite what you may have heard from Lowri, Gwynn has only appeared to me twice, Essie. The first event happened shortly after we dropped under the sea. He wanted me to know his people experienced the same devastation we had just experienced four hundred years previously and offered to assist in our recovery in every possible way. Then just before he left the castle, he turned toward me and looked me in the eye. He said we would have exactly four hundred years to discover a way to stop the recurring destruction or endure it again. I shrugged it off and told him that I, most certainly, wouldn't be here to worry about it. My callous, indifferent response offended him and he disappeared.

"I didn't see him again until after the second

devastation. He said nary a word as he stood inside my hall, surveying the damage. But the expression on his face spoke volumes. 'What think ye now, Lord Garreth,' it said, and 'will you do something about it now?' Then just as before, he disappeared."

"Yet, every now and again, someone from the Tylwyth Teg visits your world and leaves a gift behind, correct?"

"Yes, such has occurred many times over the centuries," he replied. "However, we've never discussed the apocalypse, strange though that may seem."

She considered that for a moment. "What kind of gifts do they leave?"

"Oh, I don't know. They've given us exotic seeds of all kinds, flowers, fruits, and vegetable. We now have some amazing works of art, and perhaps, even a sheet of parchment."

Essie put a hand inside her sweater pocket and nodded. "I considered that, as well. If they did provide me with the palimpsest, then they know I'm here and why. Therefore, there must be something on the parchment they want us to know."

"Then I think it's time we return to the castle and take a look at the thing, wouldn't you agree?" Yet even as he made the suggestion, she drew her brows together and fumbled around inside the pocket.

"Is something amiss?"

"I don't know." She withdrew a clenched hand, turned it palm up, and extended her fingers. "Now what in the world is this?" she whispered as she stared at the piece.

"I'm not sure. Perhaps it's an old pendant or even a

coin of some kind."

She scraped away at the top of it with her fingernail. "The piece is so dirty and worn that I can't make out a single detail. At least not here. But, how do you suppose this ended up inside my pocket."

He gave her a sideways glance. "Come now, Essie. You did say the shadow has now visited your room twice."

Chapter Five

Garreth faced the glorious colors of the setting sun without seeing them as once again thoughts of Essie took full possession of his mind. That no longer surprised him, but the why of it did. He had known and enjoyed the company of countless women over the centuries. None of them captured his attention for any length of time, nor had he intended that any of them would. He didn't want or need a commitment of any kind. Not after Nia, and especially not while the prevention of another disaster consumed his time and energy. Yet, despite the resolve he had maintained with relative ease for centuries, Essie had somehow walked into his life and turned his well-structured world upside down. If he had any intelligence about him at all, he would thank her for her time and service. He would then put her on the next plane bound for New York before that resolve vanished and he—for the first time ever—lost his heart altogether.

"Tell me Garreth, what has you so deep in thought on such a beautiful evening?"

Just the mere sound of Essie's voice caused a sudden lurch in his heart and proved his point. He turned around and took a slow step toward her as he fastened his gaze to her alluring golden-brown eyes. The ridiculous thoughts of sending her home disappeared in that same instant. Indeed, right now he wanted nothing more than to take her into his arms as he did the morning of the quake. She fit so perfectly there.

As she awaited his answer, he sought one that held a bit of truth. While so engaged, he invited her to sit down on one of the courtyard chairs with a simple sweep of his hand. She accepted the invitation without hesitation.

As he made himself comfortable in the chair opposite her he shook his head. "Nothing to worry over, I assure you. A breath of fresh air sounded good and the garden seemed a good place to get it."

Essie looked over the lush vegetation and nodded. "Yes, it is. You have the most beautiful garden I have ever seen. I find myself coming out here often and for that very reason."

"I'm glad you enjoy it." He briefly dropped his gaze to the book she held to her breast. "However, I'm afraid you won't get in much reading time, if that's what you came out here to do. As you can see, the sun is about to set."

Essie glanced first at the book, shifted her gaze to the waning sun, and then again gave him her full attention. "No, I started reading this particular volume in the series during my lunch break and found it really fascinating. So I thought I'd take it up to my room and read a little bit more before I go to bed. I hope you don't mind."

"Not at all. But what has you so fascinated if you don't mind my asking?"

She turned the title so he could see it. "This book focuses on the Irish myths."

"Is it Ireland or the myths in general that drew your

interest?"

"Both, I suppose. However, what's really interesting is the legend concerning the Tuatha Dé Danann. According to the author, they are a race of people gifted with magic and represent the main gods of the pre-Christian era in Gaelic Ireland. After a battle with the Milesians in which they were defeated, they too, *disappeared* from off the face of the earth, just like the realms of Llys y Helig and Llys y Gwalch. However, they didn't disappear underneath the sea. The Tuatha called upon a Milesian poet named Amergin to divide the land between them, since he is credited with winning the battle through a magic poem he had written. In a very shrewd move, he gave the land above the ground to the Milesians and allotted the land underground to the Tuatha. Once he announced the decision, Manannán mac Lir led the Tuatha Dé Danann underground and into the Sidhe mounds where—according to legend—they live to this very day."

Essie's excitement over the discovery solicited a grin and though he fought hard to contain it, he lost the fight. "Is that right?"

"That's what the author says, and it made me wonder if the myth has a base in fact. I mean, considering your own fate as well as the fate of the Tylwyth Teg, do you think the Tuatha might really exist?"

"There's a touch of truth found in every legend, Essie. If one searches hard and long enough, one can usually find it."

She gave him a sideways glance. "You didn't answer the question, Garreth. Is there a reason for that?"

Her suspicion made him chuckle. "Do I believe the Tuatha really exist? I don't have to believe, Essie, I know they do. However, just as with the Fair folk, who and what they really are, is far removed from the myths you read in books."

Her mouth dropped as she stared at him. "Wait a minute. Are you telling me that Manannán mac Lir is still hanging around inside the mountains? Do you how old that would make him? These myths are ancient."

"I didn't say that. Manannán died a very long time ago. However, a succession of direct line descendants has ruled their world from the day of his death and to the present."

Essie let go of a lengthy sigh as she gazed up at the darkening heavens. "I don't think I'll ever be able to wrap my head around all of this. There's just too much that goes against the grain."

He chuckled anew as he leaned forward and took hold of her hand. "Don't let it trouble you. After all, I seriously doubt your paths will ever cross." Then, in an effort to move past the subject that troubled her so much, he turned his gaze toward the castle. "How is the cleaning of your coin coming along?"

"Very well, actually, and I thank you for sending Vaughn and Gerald out for the supplies I needed."

"No problem there. How long do you think it will take us to see it in all of its glory?"

"Shouldn't be too long—a few more days, maybe. I'm just sorry I can't say the same thing for our mysterious palimpsest."

"Ah, you needn't worry over that. You have proven yourself more than capable of the task. I know that sooner or later, you'll make sense of the text."

****

Essie dabbed at the moisture gathering in the corner of her eyes as she studied the small portion of document resting beneath the microscope. Every discernible symbol on the faded palimpsest ran together and looked identical to the one beside it. Despite the confidence Garreth expressed the evening they shared in the garden—

At once the recalled memory silenced the remainder of her thought. She leaned back against her chair and closed her eyes. That night in Garreth's company, the hours fled. They talked until well past midnight without either of them realizing so much time had passed. Once he noted the time, he apologized for keeping her up so late, rose to his feet, and offered his hand. Though she had no desire for the evening to end, she placed her hand in his and with slow, unhurried steps, he escorted her to her room. All the while she reveled in the close proximity of his body and the feel of his fingers entwined within her own—

You've got to stop this Essie! You're acting like a silly schoolgirl with her first high school crush.

She needed a change in scenery if even for a moment. Perhaps if she checked the progress of the coin, the break would see her through the rest of the day. A couple of knocks interrupted her thoughts. She turned her gaze toward the door in hopeful anticipation of seeing Garreth standing there. Yet, only Lowri entered the library. She carried a tray piled high with food. Guilt washed over her.

"We missed you at lunch," Lowri said.

Essie didn't miss the disapproval in her tone. She scrunched her shoulders together in silent apology. "I know. I'm so sorry, but I just couldn't leave the parchment. You see, right now I'm at the point where I need to—"

"Oh, pshaw!" She waved a hand in disdain as she swept away the clutter, making room for the tray. "An interruption might've served you well if you'd chosen to take it. The human body needs a bit of fuel to keep going you know. Unless that document has sprouted a pair of legs, I can guarantee it'll remain safely on this table long enough for you get a bite to eat."

Essie bit down on her lip, mostly so she wouldn't laugh while Lowri assumed the role of perturbed mother and scolded her in like fashion.

"For the love of heaven, slow down a bit, child. I don't think it's wise to push yourself at such a grueling pace. Especially when you're not taking the time to eat or sleep properly. Of course, I probably shouldn't nourish the hope that you'll listen to me any better than what Garreth does," she muttered.

"Oh come on, Lowri, don't be so grumpy. You know how important this work is, and you also know that we're facing a very real time issue here."

"What good will it do any of us if you fall ill and can't complete that work?"

"Well, allow me to set your mind at ease. You have my solemn word that I won't starve myself to death while I'm here."

"The work is important. I know that better than most," Lowri said as she poured a glass of lemonade and set it before her. "But it's not going to help a whit if you drive yourself to the point of exhaustion."

"I'm not going to work myself to exhaustion, I promise."

"That's just what Garreth always says, yet he does. Why, it's no wonder he's never acquired a wife or experienced a shred of normalcy to his mundane existence," she groused.

Now that the woman drew Garreth's marital status to her attention as well as the many years he'd had ample opportunity to find a wife, she found the comment surprised her. She also discovered, for whatever the reason, it pleased her. "He's never married?"

Lowri shrugged. "Well, in all fairness, I do have to admit he almost married once—a very long time ago. But Nia died a few weeks prior to the scheduled ceremony. He didn't want anything to do with the state of matrimony after that. No amount of talking has ever changed his mind, either—not that he's lived the life of a monk, I assure you."

"Oh, I didn't know." Questions filled her mind. Did Garreth still grieve Nia's loss? Is that why he never sought a wife after her death? How did the woman die? Did she die during an apocalypse? If so, which one? Essie didn't get the opportunity to ask, for at that very moment, Garreth entered the room and fastened his gaze to hers.

"Am I interrupting a serious discussion of some kind?" His eyes darted between her and Lowri.

Lowri put a hand to her hip, raised her nose a notch, and waved a hand at the tray. "I'm trying to convince our lovely lady that she needs to eat regularly—and a bit more sleep wouldn't hurt either."

Essie picked up her sandwich, shoved a healthy bite into her mouth, and nodded. "I'm eating, see?"

Garreth worked at suppressing a grin as he

approached them. "Yes, I can see that."

"Only because I forced the issue," Lowri stated with a firm nod of her head.

"And I appreciate your concern as well as your loving dedication to all your charges. How would we ever get along without you?" Garreth gave her a little hug and kissed the top of her head.

The comment pleased her well enough it seemed, for Lowri readily returned his smile. "The heavens willing, you won't need to find out anytime soon. You'd never make it on your own, Lord Garreth, and I'm beginning to have serious concerns about Essie's ability to do the same. Now then, as your errand kept you far later than I expected, I suspect you're hungry."

"Famished."

"Good. Would you like your lunch served here so you can eat with Essie or would you prefer the comfort of the dining room?"

"Here, if you don't mind." He took hold of a chair opposite her and sat down.

"I don't mind at all. I'll be right back."

Essie lifted a hand. "Wait a minute, Lowri. You really don't have to bother with that. There's plenty of food here for the both of us," Essie said as she slid the tray between them.

Lowri shook her head and laughed. "My dear, it's quite evident you've never made careful study of Garreth's appetite."

Once she vacated the room, Garreth grabbed hold of an apple, turned to face Essie, and then locked his gaze to hers. "She's right, you know. You do need to take better care of yourself."

Essie picked up her glass and took a drink to wash

down her sandwich. "I know—it's just that the morning got away from me. Especially now that I have Eli's comments and observations in hand."

"Are they helping?" He took a bite and crunched it.

"Only as a process of elimination. Nevertheless, I've finally isolated the more common symbols on all of our samples. Now I just need to make sense of them."

"Anything I can do to help you with that?"

"Yep, if you have some time and don't mind the boredom and drudgery of it all."

"I have the time, and I don't mind the drudge. So, what would you like me to do?"

Essie turned her notebook around and slid it in front of him. "Take a look at each symbol grouping and try to come up with common words in the old Welsh language that have the same number of letters. Write a list for each. The key is to find words that use the same letter in the correct placement. For instance, it wouldn't do any good to come up with the word "can" or "the" for this particular grouping, when the three symbols don't have any letters in common. In like manner, the words "can" and "and" both use the letter "a" and "n" to create the word. Does that make sense?"

"Perfect sense. Let me see what I can come up with."

"All right then, while you're doing that, I'll focus on the mystery of our palimpsest."

Lowri entered the library a short while later, gave Garreth his tray, and left without saying a word. Perhaps the fact she'd devoured most of her sandwich and worked at her grapes had something to do with it. Or maybe Lowri simply didn't want to break their concentration—a thing Essie found increasingly difficult to maintain as the minutes ticked off the clock. Particularly since the current symbol looked no more than a smeared stain underneath the microscope.

She leaned back in her chair and hid a yawn behind her hand. What she wouldn't give to have a magic wand at her disposal right now. With a mere flick of the wrist, she could have the details magnified, perfected, and the parchment translated into any number of languages.

"Where's one of those fairy godmothers when you need one," she murmured aloud.

Garreth chuckled in response to the comment.

She looked up from her task, rested her chin on top of her hand, and met his mirthful gaze. "Surely you have one flitting about the place?"

He flashed a grin. "I think you need a break."

"No, we just had lunch."

He scooted his chair back and nodded. "That we did, over an hour ago."

She glanced at her watch. "So I don't need another quite this soon."

"You're not taking into account the long hours you've put into this project during the past few weeks." He rose from his chair, rounded the table, and made his way to her side. "As Lowri pointed out, you rise far earlier than what's necessary, and you take to your bed far later than you should. Therefore, the lord of this castle insists you take a break." He extended a hand in silent invitation.

She took hold of the offered hand, and at once he tugged her to her feet. "Where would the lord of the castle have me go?"

"Well, let's see. Either you can go up to your room and take a well-deserved rest or if you'd rather, we can go for a little walk and get the blood pumping."

She took a moment to consider her choices, for both tempted. In spite of her fatigue, the anticipation of a walk with Garreth far outweighed the need for sleep. "I think half my exhaustion arises from not getting enough exercise, so maybe—"

He gave her a wink. "A walk it is."

"Do you have a destination in mind?"

"None whatsoever. Is there a specific place you'd like to explore?"

She paused and then nodded. "Yes, I'd like to revisit the cave."

He shook his head and firmed his jaw. "Absolutely not. We're taking a break, remember?"

She hastened to explain. "I've yet to return, and I just want to see if I overlooked something the first time around."

"You didn't."

"But what if I did?"

"You didn't, you were very thorough."

"Please, Garreth, I need to know that for myself. I promise we won't stay long."

"How about we visit the cave first thing in the morning, instead. That way you'll have the benefit of a good night's sleep and can look at the wall with fresh eyes."

"I suppose you have a valid point. All right, I'll wait for the morning, if you insist—but only until the morning."

"Agreed. Now then, are you ready for that walk?" He offered her the crook of his arm.

"Yes, I think I am." As she accepted the invitation he gently gripped her fingers with his opposite hand and held onto them. The simple act thrilled her from head to toe.

They strolled out of the castle and headed for the wooded area behind it. She fell silent during their walk so she could take in her surroundings without the distraction of conversation. Tall ancient trees rose majestically toward the sky. Wild flowers grew by the wayside, providing a vast array of color. Birds warbled their sweet music from the branches high above them. Best of all? A feeling of peace and contentment permeated the area.

Essie took in a deep breath of the heady woodland fragrance and slowly released it. She shifted her gaze to her handsome, gallant escort and gave him a smile. "I don't find it any wonder you're so content to live here. This place is absolutely amazing. Everything about it makes a person feel at home," she said.

He gave her a side-ways glance. "You really feel at home here?"

A small grin accompanied her nod. "Strange, isn't it?"

"No, it doesn't sound strange at all. At least, not to me. However, I'm happy to hear *you* say it." He pulled away the sweeping branches of an ancient willow tree and ushered her inside a charming glade.

Her lips parted as she took in a sharp breath. A waterfall, sparkling like diamonds against the afternoon sun, splashed into a clear blue lake that nestled against the rolling hills. She had never seen anything quite like it.

"Oh, Garreth, what a beautiful sight," she

whispered.

His eyes swept over the dell. "I've always thought so."

For a moment, she watched the sunlight play with the rippling water and it called to mind her recent research on the legends concerning the Tylwyth Teg.

"I wonder if Gwynn ap Nudd and his people use this lake to enter your province," she mused aloud.

"What would make you say something like that?"

She shrugged. "Just something I read in one of the books I borrowed from your library, and according to what you said the other day, there's a touch of truth found in every legend, right?"

"Well, at least I believe there is most of the time. So, tell me, what did you read?"

"Tradition tells us they make their homes in lakes, streams, or in the hill hollows that surround the waters. People have reported seeing them rise up out of the water to dance in the moonlight. If we look for truth within the myth, it might stand to reason that as you use a mountain tunnel, they use an underwater pathway to make their way between realms."

"You could be right at that. Did your research yield anything else?"

"Well, the author also said the fairies were drawn to children with blonde hair. She said they would steal these children, at times substituting them for changelings, or simply leave valuable gifts in their place. As you might suspect, the gifts caught my attention since you've received your fair share of them."

Garreth chuckled in response. "Trust me when I tell you that the Fair folk don't have any need to steal children with blonde hair. They have plenty of their own."

"I should think so, given the description you gave me. But now that we're on the subject of offspring, I've a question about that as well. After so many centuries, I would think you'd be running out of space to house a growing populace, given your boundaries. Yet, from what I can see, that doesn't seem to be the case."

"No, it isn't. Death took quite a toll during the calamities I've witnessed, especially the first. That event significantly reduced our population. For those affected by age, disease, or accident, death continues to reduce it. Though I cannot explain it, our birth rate is far below that of what takes place on top of the surface. Our pregnancies take longer to achieve. The time it takes the babe to develop in the womb far exceeds a nine month period, and our children take a great deal of time to mature."

"Given your life span, that makes perfect sense. Do the women complain about the extended pregnancies?"

"To my knowledge, they don't even seem to notice." He gazed at her for several long moments. She wondered then if his thoughts had settled on Nia and the children they might've had. The notion didn't set well. After what seemed like a forever amount of time, his expression softened. The embers deep within her being burst into flame for the way he looked at her right now. At that instant she knew with absolute certainty, his thoughts didn't center on Nia at all. She—not Nia—had his full attention.

"You have no idea just how glad I am that you're here, Essie," he whispered as his fingers brushed through her hair and swept the locks behind her back.

****

A pretty blush graced her cheeks in an obvious response to both his comment and his touch. She understood his meaning. He could see it in her eyes. But then, a moment later, something made her uncertain. Doubt crept in and that doubt flustered her a bit. No matter, he would overcome that in time, for he no longer had the will or the strength to fight the enchantment that existed between them. He wouldn't even try.

She briefly dropped her gaze and studied the play of her fingers as she suddenly developed an interest in her nails. "Well—I hope I don't disappoint you in the end. There is nothing I want more right now, than to help you stop the impending destruction."

"I know that—and just so *you* know, you couldn't possibly disappoint me. Even if you have nothing more to offer in the days ahead. Because for the first time in a very long while, I'm looking forward to the future."

For one precious moment, their gazes locked as she took in a breath and held it. Again, she understood the meaning behind his words. Even so, she turned her attention in the direction of the castle. "Speaking of that future, perhaps we'd better get to work. I want to look over the list you've created, and I still need to check on the progress of my coin," she said in a breathless rush.

He bit back a grin, but he couldn't resist the need to stroke the length of her jaw with the tip of his finger. She responded with a slight shiver. "All right, let's go take a look at your coin."

Once they entered the castle, they made their way to the small washroom just off the hallway leading into the kitchen. Essie flipped on the light, approached the bowl, and retrieved the coin from the solution she made weeks ago. After a quick rinse, she picked up an old toothbrush and scrubbed both sides. She rinsed it again, and then raised it to the light.

"This looks pretty good now, but I still can't make out the writing. I think I'm going to need the microscope."

"Come on then. Let's go take a look," he said as he dropped a hand to her waist and turned her in the direction of the library. He too, wanted to take a closer look at that coin.

The moment they entered the room, Essie headed straight for the microscope. She placed the piece on top of the slot and adjusted the power of the lenses. While she studied her coin, he studied her lovely face, hoping against hope she'd see something identifiable. He didn't have long to wait.

She sucked in a breath, extended a hand, and while keeping her gaze locked on the microscope, rose from her chair. "Garreth, come take a look. The symbols on this coin are identical to those in the cave."

Her hand rested on top of his shoulder the moment he sat down. Her simple touch, given without thought, threatened his given task. In response to that threat, he gave himself an inward shake and forced his attention on the coin. Though worn with the passing of time, he could see the similarity.

"You're right," he said as he turned the piece around and studied the face engraved on the front. He recognized it. But from where? He looked up from the microscope as he struggled for memory.

"What is it, Garreth? Do you recognize something?"

He turned his gaze toward her. "I know this face, Essie. But I don't remember how or why I know it, or even from where."

"Could you have a portrait of him hanging on one of your walls? You have so many of them and from what I have seen, the men and women represent every age of this castle's history."

"Yes, they do all of that. But, I don't think that's it. At the same time, I can't rule out the possibility, either."

"Then come on. Let's at least take a look. If nothing else, we'll have taken the paintings off of our list of possibilities. Right?"

She grabbed the coin, took hold of his hand, and all but dragged him out of the door and down the hallway. Together they studied each portrait they passed to no avail. By the time they exhausted their search on the main floor, Lowri called them to dinner. Yet, he could see Essie's reluctance to give up the hunt.

Nonetheless, he cocked his head toward the dining room. "I don't think it wise to incur her displeasure a second time today, and we can easily finish our search after dinner."

She nodded. "All right."

He escorted her into the already crowded dining room, held her chair as she sat down, and then settled into the chair beside her. "Smells good, Lo."

"I'll go along with that," said Bran.

Lowri beamed her pleasure as Glenda and Bethann rounded the table with food-laden carts.

Bran picked up his glass and took a swig of the contents while the women served them dinner. He turned his gaze to Essie first, and then made Garreth the focus of his attention. "You look a bit frazzled. In fact, if you don't mind my saying so, you both do."

"That's because we've been traipsing through the hallways looking at portraits of grumpy old men and women with sour faces," he said.

"Why? Are you looking for someone in particular?" Anne directed the question to Essie.

She offered Anne the coin she clutched in her hand, which the woman readily accepted. "Garreth recognizes the face, but can't place how or why. I hoped we'd find our subject hanging on one of the walls."

Anne's shrug accompanied the slow shake of her head. "I'm sorry. I don't recall seeing this face among the castle portraits or anywhere else for that matter."

"Here, let me take a look at the thing," said Bran. He held the piece between his finger and thumb as he set his elbow on top of the table. "Garreth is right. We do know this face. But I don't think it comes from any of the portraits."

"Well, we wanted to make sure so we could eliminate them from consideration," Garreth replied.

Anne raised her fork to her lips. "Could the man be a Roman emperor, perhaps?"

Essie shook her head. "No, I don't think so. I'm fairly certain this isn't a Roman coin."

"I don't associate the face with either a coin or a portrait." Garreth struggled to bring the elusive image to the forefront of his mind.

"I don't either." Bran narrowed his eyes and drew his brows together. "It's something else—"

Anne gazed at her husband. "Could you have encountered the man on some battlefield? Perhaps he's someone of importance from a rivaling kingdom of the past."

The comment startled Essie. She turned rounded eyes toward him, melding her gaze with his. Obviously, it had never occurred to her that he participated in the battles of his time. Nonetheless, he restrained his laughter as he shook his head. "No, that isn't it either."

Vaughn strode into the dining room, with Gerald but a step behind. "What isn't what? Sorry we're late. Our errand took far longer than what we expected."

"No matter," said Garreth. "You're here now, and in answer to your question, we were just trying to identify the face on Essie's coin."

Vaughn spared Gerald a glance as he took hold of his napkin. "You have it all cleaned up then?"

"Yes, Essie just finished it today," Bran said, holding it aloft. "Care to have a look?"

"Don't mind if I do," said Vaughn.

The coin made its way down the table and into Vaughn's hands. He made careful study of the piece and then lifted his chin. He gazed first at Essie and then at him.

Vaughn offered Gerald the coin. "If I'm not mistaken, there is, or at least there used to be, a replica of this face on one of the sepulchers, inside the tomb of the kings. I believe I saw it last time we cleaned up in there. Do you remember, Gerald?"

Gerald took possession of the piece, studied it for a bit, and then nodded. "Yes, I do remember seeing the likeness of this face somewhere in there."

Garreth stared at both men as he struggled for recollection amidst the muddled fog clouding his mind. Suddenly the mist gave way to clarity. During his childhood, his father showed him the tomb and recited the tales of the various kings that rested there. "You're right, and I even know where to find it."

Essie curled her fingers on top of his own and fixed her excited gaze to his. "The sepulcher still exists?"

He grinned as he gave her hand a gentle press. "Well, at least it did the last time I looked. But it's been quite awhile since I last entered the tomb. Time and the elements might've changed or damaged things inside."

"There's only one way to find out," she said. "Is there any way we can pay a visit to this place tonight?"

Chapter Six

How could Garreth expect her to sleep now? Yet, he insisted they wait for the morning to visit the tomb. He wanted her well rested, he said. Despite the directive, her mind simply wouldn't settle down long enough for sleep to overtake her. She tossed her covers off to the side, switched on her lamp, and donned her robe. Perhaps if she read for awhile—

She took hold of the book she finished earlier and headed for the library. Light from the open doorway spilled into the hall. As she peeked inside the room, she could see Garreth sitting at the worktable. He had a pencil in hand as he labored over her notebook. The mere sight of him invoked the memory of their walk in the glade—the way he looked at her and the way he touched her that left her wanting so much more. She shook away the thought, and as she entered, he glanced up from his work and tossed his pencil aside.

"You're supposed to be sleeping," he said.

"So are you." She made her way to the shelves on the right hand side of the room, returned the book to its proper place, and looked over the nearby titles in search of another. "But it seems neither one of us is having any luck. Just goes to show that you should have let me visit the tomb tonight, don't you think?"

"What? And risk the wrath of the ghosts?" he teased. "The night belongs to them, you know."

She turned around to face him. "Do you really have ghosts?"

He nodded. "Spirits are everywhere, Essie. Just because one's mortal body dies, doesn't mean every soul chooses to leave the home he loves. Many of them elect to remain behind, and their reasons are just as diverse as they are."

A sigh escaped as she selected a book and removed it from the shelf. "Oh, why not? If I have to believe in fairies and mortals that defy death for hundreds of years, we might as well throw a few ghosts into the mix. I suppose it's good for the character. Right?"

Garreth chuckled and nodded at the book she now clutched to her breast. "You found a book of interest already?"

"Yes, according to the title, this one is on the ancient legends of Great Britain. I'm slowly plowing through your entire collection of such books."

"I'm not surprised. You seem to have an avid interest in the topic."

"You know, I find that I do. Although I have to admit in the beginning, my desire to understand the mystical things within your realm fueled that interest."

"Well then I'm happy I included those volumes in my library."

She cast her gaze around the room, taking in the vast array of books on the gorgeous oak shelves lining the walls. "You have a most impressive library, Lord Garreth. Your selection of antique books boggles the mind, and since I've made use of them, I've often wondered just how many of them are the only copies now in existence."

"That, I wouldn't know. However, you must

remember I've had a considerable number of years to amass the collection."

"That you have." Then, as she approached the table, she looked at the notebook in front of him. "So, instead of taking to your bed, you decided to work on your list of words for the symbol groupings?"

"The activity seemed a bit more productive than pacing."

"I bet." She sat in the chair beside him and read over his list of words. "Wow, you've accomplished quite a bit here," she murmured. "Maybe we can try to figure some of this out right now."

He shook his head, took hold of the notebook, flipped the cover over the pages, and pushed it aside. "Not tonight, Essie. We'll take a look at this after we return from the vault in the morning."

"I don't see where that's fair. If you're going to stay in here and work, then I don't see why I can't work with you."

He rose to his feet, offered his hand, and looked pointedly at the clock. "You're right, and therefore, we'll both take to our beds. After all, it's getting late. The morning will be here before we know it."

She tilted her head to the side and took a moment to search his eyes. He steadily met her gaze in return. "You promise you're not going to work any longer tonight?"

He raised his right arm to the square. "I give you my word. After I escort you to your room, I'll go to mine."

"And you'll sleep?"

"I'll sleep."

She let go of a sigh and placed her hand on top of

his open palm. At once, his fingers closed around hers. The contact sent a shiver through her body, just as it always did when he touched her. Even more annoying, Garreth seemed aware of that fact, though he had the good sense not to mention it aloud. Nonetheless, as had become his habit, he chose not to relinquish her hand as they made the journey from the library and to her bedroom door.

She turned to face him then, and as she dipped her head downward, she presented him with a playful curtsey. "Thank you for the escort, Lord Garreth. Barring anymore quakes or visits from otherworldly creatures, I guess I'll see you bright and early in the morning."

He aimed a thumb across the hall. "I'm just two doors down and across from you. If something happens and you need me, just call out. I promise I'll make all haste to your side."

She shot a glance at the designated room. "Well, I guess that explains how you got to me so quickly during the quake, and I don't think I ever thanked you for your concern that night. Your presence during the event gave me a sense of calm amidst the chaos. I hope you know that."

"You don't need to thank me for watching over you, Essie. Right now, I find it one of the greatest pleasures in my life."

Heat rose from her belly and flushed her cheeks as his wondrous, forest-green eyes gazed deeply into her own. Butterflies again took flight. She gulped and nodded. "Oh…well, that's a very kind thing for you to say…" she stammered.

"Kindness has nothing to do with truth, Essie.

Surely you know that."

Garreth's words echoed inside her mind as she climbed into bed. Yet, what exactly did he mean by the comment? Did watching over her give him pleasure because she chose to stay until she deciphered the pictograph? Or, dare she hope he harbored some of the same feelings for her, she now had for him? There were times when he gazed at her, touched her, or held her hand that she truly thought so, but now, after what Lowri said about Nia... She looked up at the ceiling and scoffed at the thought.

If no other woman has had the ability to capture the man's heart since the death of his Nia, what makes you think you can?

Better yet, where could such a relationship even lead given their very different backgrounds?

For the distraction it promised, she took hold of her borrowed book. She then retrieved her blue notebook in which she jotted down notes of the legends that intrigued her, grabbed her pen, and turned the pages to chapter one. The author titled it, "The Mabinogion Myths". She devoured the fascinating legends until sleep finally claimed her.

The morning alarm woke her from a series of bizarre dreams stemming from the numerous myths read the night before. She shook away the final wispy images of demonic creatures hidden inside mountain caves and rose from her bed. She hurried through her morning routine, took hold of her work pack, and hefted it onto her shoulder. Then, for the first time as she exited her bedroom, she ran into Garreth as he left his.

"Don't tell me you slept in for once," she said as

they fell in step together.

He relieved her of her bag and shrugged. "Or, more likely, is it that you're up far earlier than normal in anticipation of our visit to the cemetery?"

"Well, perhaps it's a little bit of both."

After a quick breakfast, Garreth took her outside to the stables where the saddled horses awaited their arrival.

"Not that we couldn't have taken the car," he said as he assisted her onto the mare. "But our path is more direct and a bit faster if we take the horses."

"I prefer to ride anyway, and most especially, on a beautiful day like today." She patted her horse and then took hold of her reins while he mounted his own.

With Garreth at her side, the ride through the countryside invigorated her. So much so, that she met the sight of the cemetery with a slight twinge of regret. Still, the prospects of what they might find inside the tomb quashed it in the same instant.

Garreth led her through the iron gates and to the back of the cemetery. The three-sided mausoleum, with resplendent, ancient embellishments, protruded out of the hill that encased it.

"Ah, Garreth, dw i heb dy weld ti ers talwn," a male voice in close proximity said. She turned in the direction of the sound, but saw no one in the area. In fact, except for Garreth, she didn't see anyone after making a careful sweep of the entire cemetery.

Garreth returned a nod. "Bore da, Helyan, sut mae?"

Essie traced along her bottom lip with the tip of her tongue as she listened to Garreth speak to the breeze in his native tongue. For several minutes, the breeze responded. Her heart accelerated as the reason for that crashed into her mind. An actual ghost stood next to and spoke with Garreth. But how could he see the spirit when she couldn't?

Nonetheless, she forced a calm outward persona and while the conversation progressed, she looked over the individual gravestones behind the ghost. Many of them were simple in their design, others quite elaborate. Her gaze settled on the one just off to her right. She did a double take as she read the solitary name. Nia. A brief moment after the discovery, the door to the tomb appeared to open by itself and drew her attention away from the monument.

"Diolch yn fawr." Garreth extended his hand toward her, though his attention remained focused in the direction of the spirit. Once she placed her hand in his, he closed his fingers around it and drew her close to his side.

"Croeso," said the ghost.

The moment they entered the tomb, Garreth retrieved his powerful light and turned it on. She didn't know if the spirit accompanied them, so she didn't ask any questions as they traversed the stale, musty corridors that smelled of damp earth. Garreth turned right and then aimed for the ivory-colored sepulcher in the far back corner. Small portions of the coffin's protective casing along the top and sides had broken away, but it otherwise remained intact.

Garreth took her around to the side and pointed to the image inside the large oval in the center of the sepulcher. The man's face reflected the same image as found on the coin, just as he said. Etched symbols, identical to those in the cave, arced above the effigy.

Yet, as she dropped her gaze below the leaf-themed oval, a warm flush spread throughout her body. She stooped down to ensure the discovery. Her breathing accelerated and her heart all but burst through her chest. Her fingers trembled as she traced along the letters of the Latin alphabet. Did the words above the effigy match the words below? "Just like the Rosetta stone," she whispered.

Garreth drew his brows together. "Excuse me? What are you talking about?"

She tilted her chin upward as she fastened her gaze to his. "I think, and I truly hope, these words here are an exact replica of those written above. If they are, then we have the key to decipher the words in the cave. These words underneath the oval recite the greatest accomplishments, courage, and valor of your King Cadwr ap Brychan who died in the year 852, thus giving us almost an entire alphabet." She caught her lip between her teeth and shook her head as heady excitement all but consumed her. "Oh, Garreth! Do you realize what this means?"

Somehow, she quieted an exuberant yelp as she lunged to her feet, and in her elation threw her arms around him. In response, he crushed her to his chest where she could quite literally feel the rumble of his chuckles and the beat of his heart. She drew back just far enough to gaze into his eyes. The way he looked at her set her heart on fire. Just as she thought he might kiss her, he merely tightened his hold. He nuzzled his cheek against hers while he caressed the length of her back. She hid her disappointment behind an exuberant smile as she freed herself from his embrace and turned around. She took hold of her pack and withdrew her pencil and notebook. All the while, she hoped against hope, she appeared normal.

"I need to get all of this down before we leave," she rushed out in a single breath.

At once she turned to her work, copied each symbol, and then took photographs of the same. Finally, with her emotions under firm control, she turned around to face him. "All right, I think I'm done here. Let's head back to the castle and see if we finally have everything we need to read your inscription, shall we?"

****

Garreth could do nothing more than nod in reply. Her excitement, the rosy flush on her cheeks, and the dazzling smile she bestowed, enhanced her beauty. He took hold of her hand and turned toward the entrance as he sought to cool his ardor. The woman stirred his blood, more so than any other during the long years of his existence.

He had almost kissed her when he held her in his arms and would have—if not for the way she might perceive his kiss. Would she think it nothing but his joy over the shared moment of discovery? He would not have it so. No, when he kissed her for the first time, he would leave her without doubt as to the powerful feelings she had so effortlessly planted deep within his heart.

A part of him wanted to rush back to the castle in the hope this new information would provide a way to decipher the cave wall. Yet, in spite of that desire, the portion that wanted her undivided attention a while longer, held sway. He slowed the pace of their mounts as they chatted about the morning's events.

"So that brings me around to the ghost," she said after they had exhausted all conversation regarding Cadwr ap Brychan's sepulcher.

"Helyan?"

She nodded. "If that's his name, then yes."

"What would you like to know about the man?"

"Well, for one thing, why can you see him, when I can't?"

"He chose not to show himself to you because he didn't wish to cause you any fear."

"Oh." She drew her brows together as she considered his explanation. "Ghosts have the ability to appear to specific people regardless of the number of those around him?"

"Most of them acquire such a skill. Oh, and by the way, he wanted me to tell you that you are the most beautiful sight he has encountered in quite a while." That's not all the specter said, but he didn't choose to reveal any more than that. At least, not right now.

A blush splashed across her cheeks. "Oh, well— that's very kind of him. Thank him for me next time you see him."

"I'll do that."

She cleared her throat. "Did you know him while in his mortal state or did you meet him after his death?"

"We were well acquainted during his mortality. He served as one of the captains in our army. Unfortunately, we lost him during one of our more bloody battles and I must say, we mourned his loss."

A sideways glance accompanied the slight narrowing of her eyes. She paused for several seconds as at last, the stables loomed before them. "Just how many battles did you fight in, Lord Garreth?"

He shook his head and shrugged. "I've never had the occasion to number them, so I don't really know."

"Vague but safe enough answer, I suppose." She hesitated for a moment as she looked him over. "May I ask if one of your battles produced that attractive scar on your face?"

He reined his steed to a halt, dismounted, and somehow warded off a grin as he moseyed toward her. "Do you really find the scar attractive, Miss DeSpencer?"

Her eyes never once wandered away from his and right now, they revealed a trace of humor. "Um-hmm. Very."

Garreth took hold of her waist as he assisted her descent. Once she dropped her feet to the ground, he retained his hold far longer than necessary. He took pleasure in the fact that she didn't seem to mind. "Yes, I got the bloody thing in battle. I allowed my adversary to get a little too close, and he marked the error with the tip of his blade. Still, it served as a reminder not to make the same mistake again."

She shook her head and tsked. "I still find it so difficult to think of you in—well, in that way."

"In what way? Are you speaking of me as a man engaged in a battle using sharp, pointy, swords, while hacking at another with the sole intent of sending him to the devil himself? Or just living life in the thirteenth century?" He tucked her hand in the crook of his arm and then led her toward the castle.

A smile accompanied the slight shake of her head as she shot a glance skyward. "Both, but don't let it trouble you. If I'm here long enough, I'll eventually get over it, I'm sure."

Oh, one way or another, he would make sure she remained here long enough.

Less than thirty minutes later, Essie had her photographs downloaded to the computer, and printed out. They sat down next to each other with their collection of pictures, and drawings spread out before them.

"All right," she said. "I need the list you've compiled, as well."

He took hold of her notebook, flipped through to the page she desired, and set it alongside the drawings.

"Thank you. All right then—the first thing I'm going to do is translate the Latin text into English. I'll leave enough room beside each sentence for you. When I'm finished, I want you to translate each of the sentences into the old Welsh language as best you can. From there, we'll try to match the words with both the symbols on the cave and those on the sepulcher. Does that make sense?"

He propped his chin on top of his fisted hand and nodded. "Yes, it does."

She lifted her shoulders and gave him a smile. "Here we go."

Garreth chose not to interrupt as the minutes ticked off the clock. Nonetheless, he fastened his gaze on the notebook as she translated each of the words carved onto the stone of his ancestor's grave.

"If nothing else, the people over whom Cadwr ap Brychan ruled held the man in high esteem," she finally said.

He nodded in agreement. "A man that seeks to maintain peace, and uses wisdom in each decision he makes, is usually beloved by his people."

She tapped her pencil on the notebook while she scanned the translated paragraphs. "He died before Rhodri Mawr included most of Wales within his kingdom. Had he lived, I wonder what he would've thought of the man."

"I'm sure, just as everyone did, he would've celebrated the man's ability to unite most all the people of Wales."

Lowri opened the door at that moment and allowed Philip, who pushed a food cart, to enter the room ahead of her. Garreth glanced up at the clock, noted the lateness of the hour, and rose from his chair.

He inhaled a deep breath of the delectable aroma and raised a brow as he approached her. "Is that your famous oen cymreig melog?"

Lowri smiled. "Yes it is and made just as you like it."

"Smells delicious, Lo, thank you." He gave her a hug.

Essie raised a hand. "I'll echo that comment."

Garreth slid a hand inside his pocket and waited as the woman set about her task. "I must say—your timing is impeccable. I'm starving half to death, and I'm certain Essie is too."

"I thought you might be." Lowri placed the hot plates on the table alongside a basket of scones. Ice-cold beverages followed. "There. I'll leave you two to your work, but if you need anything else, give me a call."

"Thank you, Lowri, we will," he replied as he settled into his seat once more.

Essie waited until the pair vacated the room before she leaned close to his ear. "I half-way expected another reprimand, you know. I had no idea so much time had passed."

He cut off a piece of the savory meat and raised it to his lips. "I didn't either."

The light banter that passed between them finally waned as they finished their meal and returned to their work. An hour after Lowri served their dinner, Glenda and Bethann entered the library. On silent footsteps, they cleared away the plates and made their exit. About an hour later, he slanted his finished Welsh translation in her direction.

"I think that about does it."

"Then let's see what we have."

Essie assigned a letter to each of the unknown symbols. At the end of her task, only a handful of symbols remained without a corresponding letter.

"Now, let's put the letters into words and sentences. For these orphan symbols, I'll simply leave a space. In all likelihood, you'll guess the word without the letter anyway because the mind is quite adept at filling in the blanks. You, of course, will have to translate them into English for me."

He remained silent while she copied out the text. She slid the notebook in front of him, and with hope shining in her lovely eyes, fixed her gaze to his. "Your turn," she whispered.

In response to her anxiety, he took hold of her hand and raised the notebook off the table for a closer look. Just as she said, he could fill in the missing letters without undue hardship. Though a bit bewildered with the cryptic statement carved on Glodrydd's wall, he took a moment to fill in the gaps so they would have the complete text. Finally, he turned to face her. "This is in no way anything I expected. Nonetheless, the words more or less translate as follows: 'To quell the hunger, return the black dragon's heart.'" He let go of her hand, turned the notebook so she could see it, and shrugged.

A puzzled expression settled over her features as she raised a hand to her mouth. "That's it? That's all it says?"

"That's all it says."

"But, what on earth does it mean?"

He shook his head. "I wished I could tell you, Essie, but I'm afraid I don't have a clue."

Chapter Seven

Essie dropped her hands on top of the table and toyed with her fingers. "Then you're no further ahead in solving your dilemma, are you?"

"How can you say that? I now have the first piece of this puzzle. I couldn't very well move forward without it, right?"

"I suppose so." Now that he had solved his puzzle, it occurred to her that Garreth no longer needed her. She had accomplished the task he hired her to do. Should he find another such Ogham carving, he held the key to translate it.

Ridiculous as it seemed, tears threatened to surface and a lump formed in her throat at the mere prospect of consigning Garreth ap Daffyd to memory.

Pull it together, Essie. You had no doubt this day would come—and far better for it to arrive now, before your heart is lost completely to the Lord of Llys y Gwalch.

She lowered her head and fixed her gaze upon her restless hands. After a moment, she attempted a smile, and hoped it looked genuine. "Well, I guess you don't need me any longer, do you? So, if you want to schedule a return flight to New York, I'll pack first thing in the morning and let you all get back to some form of normalcy around here—"

At once, Garreth laid his hand on top of hers and

curled his fingers around them. With his free hand, he tilted her chin upward, forcing their eyes to meet. "No Essie, I cannot let you leave me just yet."

Something flared inside as he caressed her face with just his eyes. She drew in a breath and held on to it as she spoke. "Really? Now, why is that?"

A corner of his mouth curved upward. "For one thing, I've yet to discover your full name—"

"And you're not going to either," she cut in. "So you may just as well give up the quest."

He flashed a cocky grin. "We'll see who wins that contest in the days ahead. Two, it seems you've forgotten the importance of the palimpsest."

She shook her head as she glanced at her notebook. "No, I haven't forgotten. I thought that since you now have the key, you could just take—"

"Not my area of expertise as well you know. Therefore, I'm counting on you to make sense of those splotches. Last, but certainly not least, I do need you here. I want you here for as long as you're willing to stay. As I recall, you've already arranged your schedule so you might help me prevent the impending destruction. Am I correct?"

She lifted her brows and nodded. "Yes, but—"

"Then where is the harm in sticking around?"

"There's no harm, and I'm happy to help you however I can. You know that. But, I just didn't think I had anything else to contribute—"

He placed a gentle finger on top of her lips to halt her words. "Then it's settled. I'll hear no more talk of you leaving. All right?"

She rubbed her lips together and nodded. "All right. I guess you know that means you're going to have to be the one that kicks me out of here at the time of your choosing."

****

A hand wiped across his jaw to suppress the grin. He had an overwhelming desire to make her sign that oath in blood. Instead, he returned a firm nod of his head. "You have yourself a deal, Miss DeSpencer."

She appeared a bit confused as she gazed into his eyes. Did his own expression give away his intentions? He took hold of the notebook and hastened to move on before she questioned it.

"Let's see. To quell the hunger, return the black dragon's heart. I don't suppose in your study of myths and legends, you've read anything concerning black dragons, black-hearted dragons, crabby dragons, or just plain old dragons in general, have you?"

"No, I haven't, at least not yet. But that's a brilliant suggestion, Garreth."

He shrugged away the compliment. "I have my moments."

She leaned forward and laughed. "I'll spend a bit more time reading. However, I'll give the palimpsest the highest priority."

"Speaking of the parchment, you're of a mind to believe we can decipher it using this same key then?"

"I think so. So far, the symbols match both those in the cave and on Cadwr's sepulcher. However, at this point, I've only extracted the more distinct letters behind the topmost layer and they're in random places. Most of the underlying symbols are worn or smudged as you know. But don't worry, I'll get those figured out tomorrow, I promise."

He gave her a wink. "I've no doubt you will."

She glanced at the microscope and gave voice to a notion that had occurred to her earlier. "Garreth, do you think this style of Ogham might originate with the Tylwyth Teg?"

He gazed into her eyes for several moments as he considered the possibility. "I suppose it very well could have."

"If this *is* true, and they are in fact, responsible for bringing me the coin and the palimpsest—then I wonder if they also have any knowledge concerning the heart of the black dragon."

"My guess is they don't. The fact they gave you both items probably means they couldn't decipher the thing themselves. As you said, language changes over time. I'm also of a mind to believe that if they knew something about the heart or the dragon in connection with the catastrophic events, they would already have passed on that information."

"Not if they don't understand its significance." She glanced again at the notebook. "I wished we had a way to contact them so we could just ask."

"Perhaps they're keeping close watch over what we do. If they have something to add or can shed light on this thing, I'm sure they'll provide us with it."

****

That night she dreamed.

She walked along a sinister, foggy path, in a thicket filled with overgrown brambles that bloodied her skin and tore at her clothes. The light of the stars provided very little assistance as she headed straight for her destination with steadfast determination.

All the while, someone tracked her movements. She could hear the footfalls that echoed her own. Fear escalated with each step she took. Yet the overwhelming need to continue her journey, to obtain her goal, propelled her forward. Whispers assaulted her ears at every turn. She quickened her pace, for she didn't have much farther to go now.

Just then, a deep, deafening roar echoed around her. She couldn't tell from which direction it originated. Terror shot through her as she whirled around to face her adversary. Her heart pounded the moment her gaze settled upon the enormous, black dragon that stood no more than ten feet away. His blood-red gaze latched onto hers. He lowered his head and thundered toward her. She retreated backward until a rocky barrier halted her escape. In that same instant, she opened her mouth to scream, yet she couldn't force more than a whimper past her lips. The dragon sucked in a deep breath and reared back. He twisted his neck from side to side, flung his jaws wide open, and spat a massive, flaming ball of fire.

From out of nowhere, Garreth appeared at her side. He thrust her out of the dragon's path. She stumbled onto the damp earth just as the inferno enveloped him—

"No, Garreth, no," she screamed. She lunged to her feet and rushed toward him. Something took hold of her waist and yanked her out of the danger she so desired to enter. With all the strength she could muster, she fought against it for the overwhelming need to save him. Despite her struggle, the force held her bound.

"Shh, Essie, I have you. Everything is all right now. I'm here," he murmured. "You're safe."

Garreth cradled her in his arms and using the smallest of movements, rocked her from side to side.

She leaned back just enough to look at his face. Joy filled her heart the moment she realized that she'd experienced nothing more than a horrifying dream. She encircled his neck with her arms and hung onto him with all her strength. He cuddled her closer still, and she took comfort in and gloried in the feel of his arms around her. Yet, all the while, the vivid dream replayed in its entirety. Now, as Garreth held her with such tenderness, she realized she could blame the hellish nightmare on the pictograph's inscription. As her heartbeat finally resumed its normal pace, she inhaled a deep breath and took a moment to release it.

"Are you all right now, cariad?" he whispered against her ear.

Her hands slid down his chest as she locked her gaze to his. "Yes, I'm so sorry. I didn't mean to wake you, or cause alarm—"

"You didn't wake me, and I will not allow you to apologize for something over which you had no control. There's no need. Now tell me, what caused you so much distress?"

She closed her eyes, but visions of the dream compelled her to open them again. "Just a normal, ordinary, run-of-the-mill, vile, ugly, nightmare."

"Do you want to tell me about it?"

"There really isn't that much to tell." She lifted a shoulder as she shook her head. "I followed a path through a dense thicket at night—"

"Do you know why you followed this path?"

"I'm not sure. I think I did before I fully awakened, but I don't remember it now. The only thing I do remember is the intense need to reach my destination. All the while I could hear someone or something behind me. I'm still not sure as to his identity. Maybe the dragon, or you, or someone else altogether."

"You encountered a dragon in your dream?"

"Yes—and that massive, black dragon belched an enormous fireball right at me. As dreams tend to go, you showed up just in the nick of time and shoved me out of harm's way. But…you couldn't escape the flames yourself. I tried to get to you, but I just…" She stopped short as the memory engulfed her anew.

Garreth wrapped his arms a little tighter, drawing her even closer to the warmth of his body. "Not to worry; most dreams are just twisted, nonsensical reflections of the mind."

She rested her head against his chest and nodded. "I know, and I know the message we deciphered is to blame. Still—" Her eyes narrowed as the unintelligible whispers from the dream swirled around inside her mind. She sought to isolate those words. Words that repeated. Could she say them aloud? She would try.

"Garreth, just for my own peace of mind, does the phrase, tawel y ddraig du, or something close to it, mean anything to you?"

He loosened his hold just enough to gaze into her eyes. "Where did you hear that?"

"In my dream. A voice whispered the phrase over and over as I walked along the path."

"Did it come from the person that stalked you?"

"No—I don't know—maybe. The words spun around my head like a kind of ghostly whirlwind if that makes sense. Do you know what the words mean?"

She could see his reluctance to answer by expression alone. "Quiet the black dragon."

"Oh. Then the language *is* Welsh."

He nodded. "Yes, it is."

She took a moment to consider that. "I wonder if those are the same words my visitor spoke the night of my arrival. Perhaps my mind retained them and then spewed them out in my dream."

"That's always possible."

"If so, then our Fair friend, or friends, knows something about the reference to the dragon, don't you think? If they do, then why don't they just tell us what it is? I mean, we should be working together on this thing, shouldn't we?"

"They might not know any more than what they've given us. Perhaps the phrase, the coin, and the palimpsest are all the clues they have."

"Then it becomes all the more important to read the parchment." She shifted her gaze to the glass doors. The light of dawn now seeped in through the curtains. "I'm not going to get any more sleep. So maybe I'll just get dressed, head to the library, and work on it a little bit before breakfast."

He kissed the top of her head and then released her from his arms. "All right. I'll give you some privacy and meet you downstairs in a few minutes."

She tossed the blankets off to the side. "Okay—and Garreth? Thank you for coming to my rescue again."

****

With more reluctance than he had words to express, Garreth rose from the bed. He gave her hand a gentle squeeze and took a moment just to look at her before he gave her the privacy she sought. After he left the room, he made his way down the stairs and headed toward the library. All the while, he considered her nightmare. The dream didn't concern him until she recited the phrase in almost perfect Welsh. Could she really have retained such an expression over the weeks she had resided in his home? Or, more likely, did she have another late night visitor that produced the disturbing dream? But why would any member of the Tylwyth Teg seek to cause her such anguish? More important, what did they know concerning the dragon reference?

Essie had appeared quite distressed, imprisoned inside that nightmare. When she had called out his name with such horror, he'd been only too happy to awaken her—to take her into his arms and give her the comfort she needed. He loved the feel of her in his arms—

"You're up earlier than I expected considering the hour you and Essie retired for the evening," said Bran the moment he stepped off the stairs. "Nonetheless, I'm delighted to see you up and about, for I hardly slept a wink last night wondering what the two of you discovered yesterday."

Garreth raised a brow and feigned bewilderment. "Really? I thought when you placed Essie solely in my care it meant you didn't wish to be bothered with such insignificant things. As you might recall, you did have that interminable list of chores to take care of."

Bran lifted his nose and sniffed. "Don't be ridiculous. I made myself scarce for your benefit and you know it. From what I can see, the tactic worked like a charm if your arm-in-arm cruise down the hallway, heads bent close together, and shared laughter late last night, is any indication."

Garreth tilted his head to the side as he regarded his cocky chamberlain. "You think so?"

"Yes, I do." Bran looked knowingly into his eyes and smirked. "You could refute it if you'd like."

He said nothing in response, because he couldn't and wouldn't deny it.

The grin broadened. "Just as I thought. Oh, and, uh, to give you the heads up? Anne will pounce on you like some hideous spider the moment you least expect it in the hope she can extract all of the delicious details. Therefore, you might want to avoid the woman as you would the plague. Now then, will you answer my question, or do I have to find Essie and ask her?"

"Well, to begin with, you might like to know that Essie deciphered the inscription on the cave wall last night."

Bran's eyes widened. "Did she really? What does it say?"

"To quell the hunger, return the black dragon's heart."

A look of confusion beset the man. "What in heaven's name does that mean?"

Garreth shook his head, and shrugged. "We don't have a clue. We're hoping the palimpsest might reveal a bit more. However, she had a nightmare earlier this morning that concerns me more right now than the meaning of the inscription."

"How so?"

"Let me catch you up on all of our activities yesterday and some of our thoughts first, so the rest of it makes sense."

Garreth finished his account by reciting Essie's dream verbatim, and included the Welsh phrase she repeated with such distinction.

"That's very interesting," Bran said.

"Isn't it though? And honestly, I don't know what to make of it."

"Perhaps Essie's right. Maybe the Fair folk know far more about this situation than what they've revealed and as you suspect, they're responsible for conjuring the dream. As you know, they are a bit secretive when it comes to mortals."

"If that's true, wouldn't it be better for them just to show up at our door and discuss it with us? We're running out of precious time, and they know that just as well as I do."

"Wouldn't surprise me any if one or two of them did show up at your door. Perhaps you ought to prepare Essie for such an event."

Just as he made the comment, Essie appeared at the top of the stairs. "What are the two of you talking about in such serious tones?"

Garreth turned to face her. "I'm just giving Bran the updates as to all our latest discoveries."

Essie looked over at Bran. "That's good. So, I don't suppose you know anything about myths or ancient legends concerning black dragons, do you?"

"No, I'm afraid not. But I'll make a point of asking around today while I'm in the village. I usually stumble across an elder or two during my visits and if anyone knows of such things, it would be them."

"Yes, they probably would. Thank you," she replied.

He gave her a nod. "Well, if you'll both excuse me, I need to be on my way. I promised Roderick I would lend him a hand this morning with the repair of some of the walkways."

The moment Bran, who looked far too pleased with

himself for Garreth's liking, disappeared from view, Essie placed a hand on top of his arm. "Are you still coming or do you have errands of your own? I don't want to keep you from them if you do."

"Nothing is more important right now than you." He escorted her into the library, and helped her into her seat. She retrieved the parchment and flipped on the light to the microscope. After she situated the thing underneath the lenses, she took a deep breath and turned to face him. "All right, let's see what we can come up with this morning, shall we?"

Lowri served both breakfast and lunch with as little disturbance as she could manage. He succeeded in getting Essie to eat a bit, but she continued to work even as she ate. While she labored over the parchment, he read, he paced, stood over her shoulder, and offered what little support he could.

Finally, as the afternoon sun crept toward the hills, she rubbed her fingers between her brows and sighed "I don't know, Garreth. The remaining symbols are indecipherable. So, why don't you sit down and see if you can make some sense of what we have."

"Well, it's like you said, the mind fills in the missing pieces." Garreth took a seat beside her. He read the parchment twice to ensure accuracy. He turned then and looked at her. "I believe we're missing a few pages, but as near as I can tell, this is what it says. Are you ready?"

She closed her eyes and nodded. "Yes."

He lifted the notebook from off the table and cleared his throat in an exaggerated manner. "—cast their wicked spell. Just as they intended, the dragon grew lethargic and floundered. The creature dropped to his knees, and slumbered. While he slept, the evil wizards searched the cave until at last they discovered the hiding place of the dragon's heart, which they craved for their own villainous purpose. They whisked it far away and hid it so the dragon would never find it.

"After the passing of an age, the dragon awoke and discovered the theft. A terrible anger seized him. He stormed out of his cave and extracted a dreadful vengeance upon those around him, for the dragon destroyed all in his path. To those who survived, he left behind a dire warning—" Garreth shrugged and dropped the parchment onto the table.

Her mouth dropped. "That's all we have?"

He leaned his back against his chair and nodded. "That's all we have. But, in consideration of everything else we know, I would say the emblematic heart of whatever symbolizes the dragon needs restoration, or the destructive cycles will continue once every four hundred years. If nothing else, we now know what we need to accomplish. Well, sort of."

"How in the world will we figure this out in time, Garreth?"

"I don't know, but we will. We must."

They gazed at each other for several quiet moments. Finally, she glanced at the parchment and gave it a tap. "According to the palimpsest, the wizards entered a cave. Do you think it even remotely possible that Glodrydd's cave might be the one the author references, since that's where you found the inscription?"

"I don't know, Essie. We looked the cave over quite thoroughly many times in our quest to find something of significance and found nothing. However,

I suppose it's always possible we might've overlooked something."

Her lips curved into a mischievous smile as she shot a couple of quick nods in the direction of the hallway. "Is the lord of the castle game to find out?"

He rose from his chair and extended a hand. She instantly grasped it. "Do you want to get yourself a sweater before we go?"

She shook her head. "No, we shouldn't be gone long, so I think I'll be all right."

"Then come on." He led her out of the library, through the various hallways, and down into Glodrydd's room.

"Oh, wait a minute. Do you have small excavation tools in here, in case we need to poke around a bit or should I go back and get mine?"

"I think we still have some here inside the table drawer." He took hold of the handle and gave it a tug. After he extracted the leather bag, he fetched the flashlight and together, they exited the room.

Neither of them spoke as they traversed the winding path leading into the cave. Once inside, Garreth dropped the bag and placed the light on top of the large, flat boulder off to the right of the cave wall. He cast his gaze about the chamber. "So what are we looking for?"

Essie retrieved a spade from the bag, turned a slow circle, and approached the wall to the left of the pictograph. She brushed a hand against it. "Just look for anything out of the ordinary. Something that doesn't quite fit with its surroundings. Kind of like this area right here. Do you the see the difference in—"

An eerie tumultuous rumble and the sudden

shudder of the earth beneath their feet stopped her words mid-sentence. Her eyes widened as she stretched a hand toward him. Garreth bypassed the hand. He took hold of her waist, and drew her close to his body. The strength of the quake increased as each second that passed felt more like two. Portions of the rocky ceiling gave way and the cascading debris hurtled downward. He positioned Essie against the wall and sheltered her body as best he could with his own.

At that moment, a deep, resounding moan rose up from the earth. The unholy wail burst through an ever-widening chasm that headed straight for them. In less than a minute, they could tumble into the abyss!

"Hold on to me Essie," he whispered into her ear. "Hold on tight—and whatever you do, don't let go.

She peeked around his shoulder and fixed her horrified gaze on the breach. A gasp escaped her lips as she flung her arms around his neck. She didn't have a second to spare. For the moment she strengthened her grip, the ground gave way.

Chapter Eight

Essie squeezed her eyes shut and tucked her head against Garreth's neck as they spiraled downward. In response, he wrapped his arms even tighter around her waist. Yet, as they plunged into the ice-cold water below them, the force of the impact tore them apart. She thrust both arms and legs downward to find the surface before she ran out of breath. The powerful current hindered her ascent. But at last, she rose up out of the water and with a gasp, filled her lungs with some much-needed air. She blinked the water away from her eyes as she paddled in place and took in her surroundings. A river—they landed in a river below the cave.

She twisted her head from side to side seeking any sign of Garreth, but couldn't locate him regardless of direction. The lack of light made it even more difficult. Just as panic assailed her, he called out her name. She whirled around and swam in the direction of his voice. Still, she couldn't see him for all the shadows.

"Garreth?" she sputtered the name as the rushing water rose up and flooded her mouth. She spat it back out and wiped a hand across her face. The current spun her in circles, making her unsure of her path. She turned right and then left, gauging the distance between the riverbanks.

Suddenly, Garreth surfaced beside her. He grabbed

hold of her waist and towed her to the nearest shore. They crawled out of the water and onto dry ground. Once seated, he draped an arm about her shoulders and drew her close to his side, providing a bit of warmth. They both needed a few minutes to catch their breath.

"Are you all right?" he whispered as he brushed long strands of wet hair away from her face and swept them over her shoulder.

She nodded as the beat of her heart returned to its normal pace. "Yes, I'm fine, now—and you?"

He chuckled. "A little perplexed I think. In all honesty, I didn't expect to fall into a river."

"You didn't know a river existed beneath the cave?"

"No, I can't say that I did."

"Then you don't know where we are."

He elevated a brow as a slight, mischievous grin exposed the dimple next to his scar. "Of course I know where we are. We're sitting on the bank of a river that flows beneath Llys y Gwalch."

Soft laughter accompanied the shake of her head. "Now that's brilliant, Lord Garreth. Truly it is. But let's move a little bit beyond that keen observation. Do you know where said river leads?" A shiver coursed through her body and she clamped down on her teeth to stay the quiver of her chin.

"Not at the moment, but we'll find out soon enough. First things first, though. Perhaps we ought to build a fire, warm up a bit, and dry off as best we can. Then we'll explore the area and find a path that will take us home."

She rubbed her hands up and down the length of her bare arms to ward off the chill. "I'll go along with that."

He stood up then and turned his gaze to the dense forest of trees. "All right. Wait right here and I'll be back in a few minutes with some wood."

"No, wait. I'm coming with you," she said as she rose to her feet. "I can gather the kindling." While she spoke, Garreth's eyes never once wandered away from the woodland. Curious, she turned and focused her gaze in the same direction. Lights flickered through the foliage. The men or women carrying those lights steadily made their way toward them.

Garreth took hold of her hand, drew her close to his side, and waited for them to arrive. Essie could now hear the soft rustle of leaves, twigs, and footsteps in the distance. She shot Garreth a side-ways glance. He gave her hand a reassuring squeeze just as a dark silhouette emerged from the woods. Seconds later, a group of men holding their torches aloft, stepped into the clearing.

Essie could now see the faces of the tall, handsome, fair-haired men. In all, she counted six representatives of the Tylwyth Teg, for surely they could be no other. The one who emerged from the forest first, advanced toward them. With his light blue eyes fastened upon Garreth, he bowed and extended an upturned hand.

"Prince Garreth," he said, using a tone of respect.

Garreth placed a hand against his heart and inclined his head. "Cledwyn, it's nice to see you again."

Prince Garreth? Essie turned to face him and just stared. He spared her a brief glance, yet even then, his expression remained stoic. Why hadn't he, or anyone else for that matter, ever made mention of that particular title—a title that had never even once occurred to her? Did they not think it important or for some unknown reason, did they not trust her with the knowledge? The notion hurt her more than she cared to admit.

"If you'll follow us, we'll deem it an honor to see to your comfort." Without awaiting a reply, Cledwyn waved a hand in invitation and headed for the trees.

Garreth gave her a nod of reassurance and then shadowed the footsteps of their host. Soon they arrived at a shimmering lake where a large boat, worthy of any fairytale one could ever imagine, awaited them. The men helped her board and after providing them both a warm blanket, directed them to cushioned seats along the side of the boat. Moments later, the craft set sail.

No one spoke during the entire voyage, nor did she have any idea how long they sailed before they docked at a pier and disembarked. Cledwyn and his company led them all the way through the corridor of a cave and into an exquisite garden filled with a vast array of unusual, colorful flowers. Among them, she spied the same blue roses that daily adorned her bedroom. A delightful mix of delicate perfumes permeated all around as they traversed the cobblestone path that led to a grand, palatial structure, built of blue glass and ivory-colored stone.

Once they entered the structure, Cledwyn led them through the grand hall and into a richly furnished study. A roaring fire blazed in the fireplace, providing additional warmth. Four men waited inside. One of them stepped forward, fixed his gaze to hers, and bowed low at the waist.

"We bid you welcome to Llys y Helig, my lady, I am Afon, the king's chief attendant," he said.

"Essie DeSpencer," she replied as he took hold of her hand, raised it to his lips, and kissed it. The handsome man made no move to release her from his grasp as his gaze penetrated every portion of her being. His inspection made her a bit uncomfortable.

Garreth took possession of her waist then and offered Afon his hand. "Afon—it's been quite some time," he said with a slight edge to his tone.

Amusement filled the man's eyes as he finally released her and took hold of Garreth's offered hand. "Yes, it has. I trust all is well in your kingdom?"

"At the moment, yes."

The soft knock at the door interrupted the conversation.

"Please forgive the intrusion, but if you will come with me, my dear, we will get you into some dry clothes."

She looked over her shoulder and faced the owner of the melodious voice. A lovely golden-haired woman, with delicate features even more refined than the men, extended a hand while giving her a gracious smile. Essie shifted her gaze to Garreth who didn't look the least bit concerned.

"You needn't look so worried, Essie. Our queen will take good care of you," said Afon.

The Queen?

"I'll have you back in no time at all," she replied. "I promise."

The woman draped an arm about her shoulder as she led her out of the room, down a small hallway, and up two flights of stairs. She offered another smile as they stepped onto the landing. "My name is Hefina and I believe they call you Essie, am I correct?"

"Yes. But how did you know that?"

She laughed. "Didn't you know? Those in my realm can hear all the whispers carried by the winds. They reveal many things to those who are willing to listen. Of course, as you might suspect, not everyone listens."

"Now why doesn't that surprise me," she murmured.

"Ah, here we are now." Hefina opened the door and with a sweep of her arm, invited her to enter the room. "The door to your right leads to the lavatory. You'll find a robe on the hook. Take off your wet things and leave them in the basket. We'll launder them and have them ready for you in the morning."

Essie glanced at the designated door. "Thank you, you're most kind."

"The pleasure is ours." Hefina drew her attention toward bed. An exquisite sapphire gown, and all the accessories to go with it, lay across the magnificent, white quilt. "For you to wear to dinner. Would you like me to send someone to help you dress?"

"No, I think I can manage."

Hefina inclined her head. "As you wish."

She opened her mouth to thank her hostess again, but Hefina raised a hand to stop her words. "Please, your gratitude isn't at all necessary. We are the ones who need to thank you for your selfless service in our urgent matter. I'll return for you shortly."

After she vacated the room, Essie took a moment to absorb the glorious beauty of the white and gold bedroom. But then again, everything inside the realm of the Tylwyth Teg possessed the same enchanting artistry.

After she finished her shower, she slipped into the dress that fit as though custom made. As she stepped in front of the mirror to admire the gown, a soft knock sounded against the door. "Come in."

Hefina again deigned to act as her escort—and that surprised her. "Are you ready?"

"Yes, I am and thank you for the use of the dress, it's quite beautiful."

Hefina tilted her head to the side and placed a finger against her cheek as she looked her over. "As are you my dear."

Essie clasped her hands in front of her and smiled. "Thank you."

Hefina made small talk as they made their way back to the study where Garreth, refreshed, and dressed in a white poet-styled shirt and black trousers, awaited her arrival. From across the room, their eyes met and held. The result of that moment didn't surprise her in the least. For the man never failed to take away her breath—

****

Garreth retained Essie's gaze as he made his way to her side. He took hold of both her hands, lifted them to his lips and kissed them. "You look absolutely beautiful," he whispered. He meant what he said. No other woman on this earth matched both her inner and outer beauty, and tonight, the cut and color of her gown enhanced her comeliness.

A pretty blush stained her cheeks as she briefly dropped her gaze. "Thank you. You look pretty nice, yourself, *Prince* Garreth."

He shook his head. "Naught but a meaningless title. Don't let it trouble you."

At that moment, Afon approached them and placed a hand on top of his shoulder. "Garreth, the king would like to meet your lovely companion."

He gave Afon a nod and then turned to face her. "Are you ready for this?"

"Yes, I think so."

Garreth escorted Essie to the back of the room where the ruler of the Tylwyth Teg, seated in a resplendent chair by the fire, awaited them. "Essie may I present Gwynn ap Nudd, king of the Tylwyth Teg. In turn, Gwynn, may I introduce you to Dr. Essie DeSpencer."

Essie bowed her head in a show of respect. "I'm pleased to meet you."

Gwynn gazed into her eyes for a small moment and then smiled. "As I am pleased to meet you, for we have much to discuss."

A mixture of curiosity and anticipation filled her lovely eyes over the comment. Yet, the moment she took in a breath to speak, one of the king's attendants entered the room.

"Sire? Dinner is served."

Gwynn nodded, rose from his chair, and waved his fingers forward. "Come."

Garreth tucked her hand into the crook of his arm and followed the king and his council into the dining room.

He assisted Essie into her chair and then settled into the seat beside her. Gwynn insisted on keeping the conversation pleasant all throughout dinner and it annoyed him no end. For it gave the company of men every opportunity to vie for Essie's attention. In fact, he half expected Afon to leap across the table and sit in her lap, not that he would've allowed it. Currish lout.

Once they moved the party back into the study, the king took his seat, bade them sit on the small sofa across from him, and though the man included him with a glance, he fixed his gaze upon Essie.

"You have interpreted the writing on the cave wall," said Gwynn.

Essie shot him a fleeting look before she focused her gaze on the king. He sought her hand, and at once, his fingers closed around hers.

"Yes, though it took us awhile, Garreth and I finally deciphered it," she said.

"Afon thought you most capable of the task. Tell me, have you made any headway with the parchment?"

"*You're* the one responsible for the gift?"

Gwynn dismissed her surprise with a wave of his hand. "We hoped it might be of some use."

Essie leaned forward. "You don't have any more such pieces, do you?"

"No, we discovered only the one."

"Pity. Could you tell me where you found it?"

"We found it amongst Nia's possessions long after my beloved daughter's death. Why do you ask?"

Color drained from her face and it took Garreth a moment to understand the reason for that. No doubt, someone told her about his betrothal to Nia. However, until this moment, she didn't know of the woman's relation to the Tylwyth Teg. It seemed she had difficulty reconciling the two, as well as understanding the reason for the omission. In response to the unexpected revelation, she leaned away from him and attempted to withdraw her hand from his. Despite her subtle struggle, he didn't allow its escape. Not when her thoughts traveled a very wrong path.

She gulped, put a couple of fingers to her brow, and nodded. "I…um…hoped we might find the…uh missing pages. But—"

"Then you've already deciphered the document?"

"Yes," she breathed out. "Just this afternoon, in fact. But it's only a portion of the…uh… chronicle."

Garreth gave her hand a little squeeze and stepped in to provide the details of the palimpsest since he found it obvious she couldn't keep her mind on the task. A look of confusion beset the king at the end of his narrative. "You seem just as baffled as we feel."

"I'm afraid so, Garreth, I'm afraid so." Gwynn drummed his fingers against the top of his desk.

"I take it then that you know nothing concerning the black dragon referenced on both cave wall and palimpsest?"

"No, nothing at all, I'm afraid. Nonetheless, you can rest assured we'll put all our efforts and resources into discovering its meaning from this point forward."

"As will we," he replied.

Essie looked over at him for a moment, and then returned her gaze to the king. "What about the coin? Did you find that amongst Nia's possessions as well?"

Gwynn drew his brows together. "Coin? What coin?"

"The coin I found in my sweater pocket. The one that led us to Cadwr ap Brychan's sepulcher. Without it, we wouldn't have deciphered either the pictograph or the palimpsest."

The king glanced at Afon who shrugged in return. "I'm afraid we don't know anything at all about a coin."

Her puzzled gaze returned to him. "Then who do you suppose put that coin in my pocket, Garreth?"

He shook his head. "I don't know."

Soon thereafter, Gwynn concluded their conversation and dismissed them to their beds citing the lateness of the hour. He promised to provide them an escort home first thing in the morning. The dawn didn't arrive fast enough to suit Garreth. Essie needed an explanation about his relationship with Nia and he wanted to give it.

All throughout the early morning hours and the breakfast that followed, Essie remained cordial, but aloof. Afon took advantage of that fact. The man sorely tried his fortitude. Yet, until he and his companions bade them farewell at the pier, he had no choice but to endure his foolish banter.

For the need to speak with Essie alone, the voyage across the lake seemed far longer than the first, as did their trek over the mountain and to the river. Their guides followed the river east, to a large fissure in the rock that led to a passageway. Finally, the darkness of the tunnel gave way to light as they approached the waterfall in the realm of Llys y Gwalch.

"We'll leave you now, but watch your step as you pass behind the cascade and onto dry ground. The moss-covered rocks can pose a danger," said Cledwyn.

Garreth glanced at the rocks and nodded. "We will."

Cledwyn took hold of his arm and clasped it. "Then I bid you farewell, my friend. I'm sure we'll see you soon."

"Thanks for the escort, and please pass along my gratitude to Gwynn. We missed him at breakfast."

"I'll give him your message." With that, Cledwyn and his men turned and walked away.

By the time he turned around himself, Essie had already made her way beyond the waterfall. He expelled an exasperated sigh and followed.

"Essie, would you please wait a minute," he said as he walked out into the clearing.

She halted her steps, wrapped her hands around her arms, and awaited his arrival. After a moment, she turned around to face him and fixed her troubled gaze to his.

He placed a hand against her cheek and caressed the length of her jaw. "Essie, you don't have to—" He shook his head as he shot a glance skyward. "Look, just ask me your questions. I'll gladly answer all of them."

She lowered her eyes and gulped. "You don't owe me anything, Garreth," she whispered, her pain obvious in both voice and tone. "You are my employer and I am your employee. Have you forgotten that little fact? I have no right to expect—"

"No, Essie," he cut in. "We've gone far beyond the relationship of employer and employee and well you know it."

"Where in heaven's name have the two of you been?" bellowed Bran. "You had us worried sick."

Essie looked out over the group of men in the glade, waved her hand, and gave them a smile. "On quite an adventure," she called back.

Though she appeared relieved over the unexpected interruption, Garreth took advantage of the hand she released and hastened to claim it. "We're not finished with this discussion, Essie," he said, turning her to face him.

She didn't have time to reply. For in that same moment, Bran approached, wrapped his arms around her shoulders, and gave her a hug.

"We discovered the calamity inside the cave this morning. Were you inside when the ground gave way?" Bran directed the question to him. "We saw the torch and thought the worst—"

"Yes, but the river beneath the cave floor cushioned our fall," he said. "Then Cledwyn promptly rescued us, offered their hospitality, and escorted us to the realm of the Fair folk."

"Yes, we saw that river," he said. "Well, let's get you back to the castle before Lowri has another fit of the vapors. I'll call off the hunt and let everyone know you're home safe and sound. Then my friend, you and Essie will have to sit down and give us all the details concerning your adventure."

"Tell me, Bran," said Essie as they headed for the castle. "Did the pictograph survive the quake?"

Bran shook his head. "No, I'm afraid there is but bits and pieces left of the carving. In fact, there isn't much left of the cave at all and rocky debris has consumed most of what does remain. We'll probably just need to seal it off."

Lowri ambushed them the moment they entered the hall, just as he expected. A mountain of food followed. Garreth then waded through endless hours of unnecessary fuss and repeated explanations. All throughout the tiresome episode, Essie avoided his gaze. Finally, he had enough.

Garreth rose to his feet, strode across the room, took hold of her hand, and all but yanked her to her feet despite the ongoing conversation. He swept his gaze about the suddenly silent room. "Excuse us, please." Though he didn't really care if they excused him or not.

No one uttered a word as they vacated the room. Garreth led her to the side door of the castle. He escorted her outside to the garden, and over to a comfortable curved bench beneath the shelter of the trees. This particular area would give them the privacy he sought.

"This isn't necessary, Garreth," she said as he sat down beside her.

He ignored the comment. "What troubles you the most, Essie? My insignificant title that no one ever bothered to mention? My association with the Tylwyth Teg? Or is it my past relationship with Nia?"

She shook her head and looked away. "Your title and your relationships are none of my business, Garreth."

He claimed her stubborn chin, forcing her to meet his gaze. "Now how is that fair, when I've made the details of your life and any future relationship you might have, mine?"

Although his comment obviously surprised her, she said nothing in return.

"So, let's start with the title shall we? In answer to the natural question you *might* have, my father served as king of Llys y Gwalch at the time our symbolic "black dragon" destroyed it. In my *royal* opinion, the need for a monarch ended in that same moment and so decreed it."

She mulled that over for a time. "Did your people feel the same way?"

"I don't know and in truth, I didn't care or bother to ask anyone. Nonetheless, throughout the centuries we've formed a workable government that satisfies most everyone. However, I do have to admit, there are some, who out of respect for the circumstances surrounding my birth, continue to use the title that means nothing to me."

"Tell me something, Garreth; did your people readily appoint you as the leader of this workable government?"

He hesitated for only a moment. "Yes, they did. But that doesn't make me their king."

She returned a slow nod. "I see."

Garreth took hold of her hand and twined his fingers through hers. He took a deep breath and slowly released it as he sought to put a bit of order to his thoughts. "So, do you want me to expound my various experiences with the Tylwyth Teg, which truly are not that impressive, first? Or would you rather discuss the reasons I agreed to marry a woman I loathed?"

Chapter Nine

Essie stared. She couldn't help it really. For of all the things she expected to fly out of his mouth, his emphatic statement about the woman she assumed he loved, and loved deeply, didn't appear anywhere on the list.

He cocked his head to the side as he studied her face. "Does the remark surprise you? Do you find it callous?"

A hand traveled to the necklace she wore. "I don't know—I mean—I don't know what you expect me to—"

"I don't expect anything," he cut in. "However, what I don't *want* is for you to have any false assumptions about a distasteful situation that occurred almost four centuries ago. One, I might add, I would just as soon forget ever happened. However, since someone obviously mentioned the incident to you, I want you to have an accurate, full account of what transpired during that brief period of my life."

She shook her head. "Please, Garreth, you don't have to explain—"

"Oh, but I want to explain," he replied. "Are you willing to hear me out or are you not?"

Essie focused her gaze on the spectacular sunset, long enough to swallow past the knot in her throat and gain a bit of control over her emotions. "Yes, I'm willing to listen."

"Thank you—and I must ask that you bear with me. I've never put my thoughts into words for anyone else, so this might come off sounding a bit disjointed."

"I think I can deal with that."

He paused for a moment and then shrugged "We've already discussed my first four centuries following the sinking of Llys y Gwalch. You know I spent most of the time rebuilding what the devastation destroyed and discovering alternative ways to become self-sufficient in a vastly different environment. No one paid much attention to the passing of time or the fact we aged very little along the way. I can't remember whom or even the year someone pointed it out. We all just took it in our stride and continued living our lives one day at a time."

"Do you think your extended life span has something to do with the Tylwyth Teg?"

He shook his head. "Why would you think that?"

"Oh, I don't know. I suppose because every book you own on the topic mentions the longevity of their race. Perhaps by using an enchantment of some sort they passed the gift on to those in your province once you dropped into the sea."

"Enchantments, hmm." For a minute, he considered the notion. "Out of curiosity, what else do the books tell you about their people?"

"Well, the authors all agree they possess magical powers of one kind or another. They can make themselves invisible to the eyes of man and turn themselves into various animal forms. The books say that most are quite benevolent while others are just the opposite in nature and those who aren't can be quite dangerous."

He lifted his brows and nodded. "All true. But I don't think they're responsible for our prolonged existence. Magic ability they have, but I don't believe they have the capacity to extend a person's life."

"Why not?"

"Because there were times, rare though they may have been, one of them fell in love with a mortal and married him or her. The mortal lived out a normal life span and then died, leaving the Fair spouse to grieve. If they had the power to prolong life, don't you think they would've applied it to the person they loved?"

"Yes, I suppose so." She dropped her gaze as she mulled over the complexities of the issue.

"I can see you have a question. Go ahead and ask it."

"A while ago you told me that some of your people have elected to leave this realm and join those of us on the surface. Do they continue to live an innumerable number of years? If so, how do they explain their lack of—"

While she struggled to put the rest of her thought into words, he shook his head. "For whatever the scientific reason, whether the obvious change in atmospheric pressure, food, water, pollution, or a combination of any number of things, once a person leaves this realm for any length of time, they return to a normal aging cycle."

"Oh—and what about those who leave the surface and choose to stay in your realm?"

For a moment he said nothing. He just looked at her and that simple gaze somehow had the power to wreak havoc inside her belly. A slight grin emerged in obvious response to the blush that colored her cheeks. "They age as we do, cariad."

She closed her eyes as she gave her head a little shake. "I'm sorry. I didn't mean to derail your thoughts. I believe you were leading up to the second catastrophe."

"Ah, yes. By the time I arrived at the conclusion I would indeed live to see the approaching apocalypse, I could do nothing to stop it. I didn't even know where to begin the monumental task. Then, just as Glodrydd warned, the event happened again and right on schedule. A vast number of our people died that day— men, women, and children. As you know, the destruction devastated me, and I vowed to do all in my power to prevent the next. Shortly thereafter, various members of the Tylwyth Teg deigned to visit us. Cledwyn, Afon, Aneirin, and Urbgen to name a few. From time to time, they helped us plant a variety of crops suited to our new climate and showed us how to rebuild our structures to withstand nature's calamities a little better.

"Then, a few decades or so after the second destruction, Nia appeared in our realm for the first time. She sought me out, introduced herself, and offered her assistance as a daughter and emissary of king Gwynn. Yet, despite the offer, she never once lifted a finger to help anyone with the most basic task. I don't think it ever even occurred to her to bestow the simplest act or word of kindness upon those who may have needed it.

"The woman, admittedly beautiful to look upon, wore that beauty like a trophy. However, her physical beauty never extended into her eyes or into her heart. She never once uttered a single word that endeared her to me. Quite the contrary."

Garreth's voice trailed off as a far away expression entered his eyes. His free hand caressed the top of hers for a few quiet moments. The contact sent shivers through her spine and filled her heart with liquid warmth. Did he know that?

"Needless to say, the king's daughter didn't interest me in the least and I avoided her whenever possible. Somewhere along the way, she finally understood that fact. This didn't set at all well with her vanity or her self-centered scheming I knew nothing about at the time. Then, one night she appeared inside my bedroom, citing a need to speak with me privately. I told her I didn't have any desire to listen to anything she had to say. Since I didn't invite her to enter, I asked her if she'd be so kind as to leave me in peace."

She produced a smug little smile that did naught but irritate. "Not even if my purpose has something to do with preventing the next calamity?"

"As you can imagine, that grabbed my attention. I had no choice but to hear her out. She told me she possessed something that, along with the carving on the cave, might give me all I needed to halt the destructive cycles. However, she wanted something in return for this gift." His narrowed eyes filled with disgust.

"This gift—do you think she spoke of the palimpsest?"

He responded with a slow nod. "After what Gwynn said last night, I'm beginning to think so. But at the time, I had no idea what she possessed. Nonetheless, visions of the deaths and destruction flooded my mind. Once again, I could see the lifeless bodies of women and children strewn about the landscape." He dropped his gaze for a moment, lost in his thoughts.

"So I asked her what she wanted," he continued. "Nia indulged in a bit of triumphant laughter and then said she wanted a very simple thing—something I could give without undue hardship. I asked her to clarify. She said she wanted to be the wife of *King* Garreth ap Daffyd. The item in her possession would be my wedding gift if I complied. However, before the wedding ceremony, she demanded that I submit to a royal coronation in which I would take my rightful place as king of Llys y Gwalch. She would plan everything down to the smallest detail. I need only show up at the designated times and places."

"So to save your people, you agreed to her conditions, I take it."

"I had no other choice. The whole affair made me sick to my stomach, and I made myself just as scarce as I could in the days that followed. I vowed to follow the same pattern after our marriage. Then, during one of my more lengthy absences, and just shy of the approaching nuptials, Nia had an accident. She, along with her usual and favored entourage, rode off on horseback during one of our torrential rainstorms. Those that survived the mishap told me she wanted to oversee some minor detail concerning the upcoming nuptials. I understand several people advised her not to go. But Nia cared only for Nia and for what Nia wanted, so off she went.

"Somewhere along the way, the water-soaked earth gave way beneath the weight of the horses. She and two others plummeted off the side of a cliff and lost their lives." Garreth fixed his gaze to hers. "I didn't mourn her death, Essie. I only mourned the loss of the item she promised to give me. Does that make me a horrible person?"

She shook her head. "No, it doesn't make you a horrible person."

"Anyway, there you have it. My one and only brush with the state of matrimony."

"Why? Why didn't you ever choose someone to spend your life with, Garreth? Eight hundred years is a very long time to wander alone."

"There are several reasons. My highest priority throughout the centuries and to this day, is to end the destructive cycles. I didn't think it fair to submit a wife to the conditions under which I lived. The intensity of my searches, and the hours I spend in this endeavor is not conducive to the kind of marriage I desired to have. In all honesty, none of the women in my *past* ever managed to capture my heart or even my attention for more than a few months at any given time. If any of them had, I might've rethought my position much earlier."

The way he looked at her right now caused the beat of her heart to accelerate and the heat from her belly to rise to her cheeks. Again. Unsure if she understood his words in a way he didn't intend, she hastened to move on. "Did anyone else know the details of this arrangement you had with Nia?"

"Not that I'm aware of. I never had any desire to disclose it myself. I don't think her pride would have allowed her to do so either. In fact, she went out of her way to make people believe I deeply loved her. If you can imagine that."

"Then that's probably why no one inside her realm ever gave you the palimpsest after her death. Without the details, no one would know she promised it to you or that it held any kind of significance as to the apocalypse."

"Since he didn't tell us, we have no way of knowing how long it took Gwynn to discover its existence," he added. "For all we know, he passed the thing off to you, soon after he found it."

She nibbled at a nail and then dropped her hand into her lap. "The real question here is where did she find it?"

"I don't know and in all likelihood, there's no way of finding out now."

"Perhaps, but, that brings us around to the mystery of the coin. If no one inside the realm of Llys y Helig is responsible for dropping the thing inside my pocket, how do you suppose it got there?"

"We cannot discount the Fair folk completely, Essie. Just because Gwynn is not aware of the coin, doesn't mean someone else from his realm is. We might find there is someone inside the King's realm with his or her own agenda."

"But what would they hope to gain?"

"At this point, I'm not sure. We'll only be able to answer that question when we have solved the entire puzzle. However, there is one other thing we need to keep in mind, as well."

"What's that?"

"The image on the coin is that of Cadwr ap Brychan. That means the piece originated here, not in Llys y Helig."

"You think someone from your own realm snuck the coin inside my pocket?"

"I think we need to consider the possibility, along

with all the others."

"If that person understood its importance, why wouldn't he or she have just given it to you before now?"

"I don't know."

Her thoughts raced ahead. "You said at times, the Fair folk would choose mortals for their mates, correct?"

He nodded. "Yes, I did."

"Did any of them ever marry someone from your realm?"

"Yes. A handful of times, I would say."

"Once married, do they choose to live in the realm of the Tylwyth Teg or do they live here?"

"Some stay, some leave. Why do you ask?"

"Just trying to get everything straight in my head." She paused for a moment. "I suppose these couples have children?"

"Certainly."

"Do these children inherit the power of their Fair parent?"

He nodded. "Some of them, yes, but not all."

"So then the possibility exists that our nameless shadow not only lives here, but has Fair blood to boot. And, in consideration of the Welsh phrase I could hear in my nightmare, this person must know something about the black dragon."

"I suppose those are all possible conclusions."

"Unless—what if this person didn't realize the writing on the coin matched the writing in the cave *until* they saw the photographs on our work table?" Just then, Hefina's off-handed comment tumbled into her mind. "Or—maybe that's all he or she knows because *we* mentioned no more than that when we talked about it in the library. Hefina said her people can listen to all the whispers carried by the winds and in this way learn many things. So if our shadow—"

"Really?" He tilted his head to the side. "When did she tell you this?"

"Last night, after she introduced herself and then asked me to confirm that she had my name correct."

"And did she?"

"Yes, she did."

Humor filled his eyes as he held her gaze. "What name did she call you?"

She brushed the wind-blown hair away from her face and shrugged. "Just Essie."

He rubbed a hand over his mouth in a much too obvious bid to keep his expression stoic. "Just Essie, hmm. Are you certain she didn't say something like, Saudi E-rabia DeSpencer? Or—how about Sardinia Erie, as in that quaint little town and county in the state of New York from whence you hail?"

She rolled her eyes, shook her head, and huffed out a breath.

"No? Well, let's see then—"

"Oh for goodness sake," she turned her head to the side, refusing to meet his gaze. "Just let it go, Garreth."

Garreth placed a hand against her cheek and gently turned her face toward his. "No, I can't do that. Therefore, you might just as well tell me. I'll find out eventually. In fact, I might pay Hefina a call and see if she can fill in those two little blanks."

"Won't do you any good. She said she hears the whispers of the wind, and those winds have yet to hear the name themselves. Trust me."

"Are you so sure about that?"

She lifted her nose and nodded. "Yep. Pretty sure."

"You've dismissed the fact that you talk in your sleep."

She opened her mouth to make a retort. But just then, the fleeting movement of a shadowy figure inside the castle captured her full attention. She fixed her gaze on the glass doors with the sheer curtains—her balcony doors, in fact.

Garreth turned around and followed the direction of her gaze. "What's wrong, Essie? Do you see something?"

She stood up and dragging him along beside her, took a step forward. "I think someone is in my room."

He shot her a quick glance and then shifted his attention to the balcony. "Wait here."

"No, I'm coming with you." She ignored Garreth's sigh as he gripped her hand a little tighter. They made all haste back inside the castle and then hurried up the stairs. He shoved her behind him just as he opened the door and hit the light switch.

The empty room didn't look at all disturbed. Nonetheless, Garreth checked under the bed and inside the wardrobe. He then inspected her bathroom. She didn't see anything out of place and neither did he. But as they made their way back inside the bedroom, a small gust of wind toyed with the balcony doors now standing slightly ajar.

Garreth strode toward it and thrust the doors all the way open. She remained but a step behind as he walked out onto the balcony and cast his gaze upon the ground.

"Well, whoever visited your room is gone now." He ushered her back inside and latched the doors.

"So, why doesn't that surprise me? Of course, now we have to wonder if he or she left something else behind before they skittered out of here," she said as her eyes examined every corner of the room.

"We might've disturbed him before he had the opportunity." He turned around to face her, locked his gaze to hers, and just looked at her for several quiet moments before he spoke. "Perhaps we ought to switch bedrooms for a night or two."

"I don't see where that's necessary, Garreth. Whoever my visitor is, he or she has never hurt me."

"I know that. But the fact remains you don't recognize this person. Perhaps I will."

"I really don't think he'll come back tonight and even if he does, he would surely note the difference between the two of us."

A slight grin emerged. "Most assuredly, but he would still have to enter your bedroom to note it." He traced a gentle finger up and down the length of her jaw. "Humor me, hmm?"

She dropped a sigh of resignation and shrugged. Part of Garreth's charm was his old-world chivalrous nature. Though maddening at times, she had no desire to remove it. "Do you mind if I take a shower first?"

"Not at all. If it's all right with you, I'll wait here while you bathe, though."

Essie waved a hand as she opened a dresser drawer. "Please yourself, this is your castle, after all."

He flashed a grin. "So it is."

"All right, I promise not to dawdle. Just let me get my things and I'll be back before you know it—"

"Take all the time you need. I'm in no hurry."

As the warm water cascaded over her skin, a host

of thoughts clamored for her attention. She found it a bit difficult to sort through the chaos. The shadowy presence in her bedroom—did he leave something for her to find this time? Unfortunately, the answer to that question would have to wait for the morning. She couldn't conduct a thorough search until then.

Though the question continued to nag, Garreth's betrothal to Nia demanded a portion of her solitude as well. His explanation filled her with a curious mixture of joy and relief, as did his comments regarding his marital status. Yet, doubt plagued there, too. The heady attraction between the two of them escalated a little more each day. No doubt about that. For she could see it in his eyes and feel it in his touch. But a big difference existed between simple physical attraction and love. She had no idea what place she held in his heart, if any at all, and she truly didn't want hers broken by the lord of Llys y Gwalch. She didn't want to be just another woman that drifted in and out of his life.

At length she turned off the faucet, took hold of her towel, and exited the shower. Though she hurried to dress, she took additional time to dry her hair. Afterward, she donned her robe and then headed back to her bedroom.

Garreth turned around, just as he set one of the books down and took hold of the newest volume she borrowed from his library. He held it up for her inspection. Yet all the while, she couldn't miss the appreciation that filled his eyes as he looked at her. He glanced at the title. "Anything interesting in this one?"

"I've yet to crack the cover on that one. I plan to read a chapter or two of it tonight, unless you want to take a look at it yourself. I can find another."

"No, I still have a book in the library I want to finish." He gave her the book and then offered his hand. "Come, Miss DeSpencer; allow me to escort you to the door."

"That really isn't necessary, Garreth," she said. "Your room is just down and across the hall."

He said nothing in return, but simply waited for her to comply. After a moment, she shrugged off the inevitable. She slipped her hand in his as they made the short walk to his bedroom.

"I'll inform Lowri of the exchange so should you need anything, she'll know where to find you," he said.

"Thank you, Garreth. But no one need make a fuss. I'm sure I'll be just fine."

"I'm sure you will. Good night, Essie, sweet dreams." Despite his whispered words, he made no move to leave her side. For a few moments, he simply gazed into her eyes. She drew in a quiet breath as he let go of her hand, took hold of her waist, and drew her closer to his body. Deliquescent warmth consumed her. Without doubt, he intended to kiss her and she wanted nothing more than to experience that kiss. Without thought, her hands found their way from his chest and then up and around the breadth of his shoulders. Yet, just before their lips touched, the voices ascending the top of the steps shattered the intimate moment.

Garreth muttered a curse underneath his breath. He dropped his hands from around her waist as they turned around and faced the sound of the approaching footsteps. Anne and Lowri, each carrying a tea tray, looked relieved to see them as they rounded the corner.

"Oh, there you are," said Lowri. "I couldn't imagine to where the two of you disappeared. No one witnessed your return to the castle and I thought perhaps—"

"All is well," Garreth cut in with a slight edge to his tone. "You needn't worry, Lo. I'm quite capable of taking care of both Essie and myself."

Lowri put a hand to her hip and wagged her head. "Well, I wouldn't have worried if not for your disappearance last night. Now, what are the two of you doing standing out here in the middle of the hallway? Is something amiss?"

Garreth caressed her face with nothing more than a simple gaze before he shifted his attention to Lowri and her question. "No, nothing is amiss. I simply decided to trade bedrooms with Essie for the night."

"Oh." The woman looked puzzled. "All right. I'll just take Essie's tray to your room then."

She found Garreth's reluctance to leave her in the hands of Lowri quite obvious. Nonetheless, she answered his smile with one of her own, bid him goodnight, and followed Lowri through the door.

No more than ten minutes ticked off the clock before she stood inside Garreth's very masculine bedroom all by herself, with book in hand. Lowri had left the tea tray on top of the table, turned the bedcovers down, and vacated the room.

Essie stood for a moment in indecision as she studied the massive bed and then cast her gaze on the big leather chair in front of the fireplace. Both chair and fire beckoned, and at once, she heeded the call. She settled into the comfortable cushions, swung her legs up off the floor, and gazed at the various hues within the dancing flames. For a while, her thoughts lingered on the kiss she and Garreth almost shared. She bemoaned the loss. How long would she have to wait for another such moment?

She released a sigh and opened the book. The pages fluttered of their own accord and then stopped at a thick sheet of folded vellum tucked inside the middle of the book. She picked up the page with the utmost care, unfolded it to her view, and examined the details of the hand-drawn illustration.

Did this drawing, which looked like a map of sorts, originate from her elusive, late-night visitor? Or did someone slip it inside the book decades—maybe even as much as a century ago? She didn't recognize the location of point A, of course. Yet if one could find it, the mountainous trail promised to lead to a blazing ball of fire.

Chapter Ten

Garreth had awakened far earlier than he had anticipated. Perhaps he could place the blame on the unfamiliar bed in a bedroom he had never slept in. But more likely, the delicate scent of Essie's perfume wafting up from the pillows lured him away from his sleep. Again, his thoughts traveled to the previous evening and to the kiss Lowri and Anne interrupted. A kiss he wanted to have and one Essie didn't seek to avoid. He let go of a heavy breath and again cursed his luck over the untimely interruption.

Meddlesome women—

Just then, a soft knock at the door interrupted his silent reflections.

"Garreth," whispered Essie. "Are you awake?"

She sounded agitated. He bolted for the door and flung it open. "Is everything all right?"

She glanced down at the book she held to her breast "I need you to see something. Tell me if you've ever seen it before or if it means anything to you."

"What did you find?"

She made her way inside the room and sat down on the edge of the bed. She opened the book, extracted a sheet of paper, unfolded it, and then handed it over to him. He sat down beside her as he made careful study of the antiquated page.

"I found that last night inside the book before I

went to bed. I hardly slept a wink wondering what it might mean, but I didn't want to disturb you."

He glanced up from the parchment. "You needn't ever worry about disturbing me, Essie. Especially if you believe you have something important to share with me. All right?"

"All right."

He returned his gaze to the faded drawing. "No, I've never laid eyes on this diagram before."

"The thing looks as if could've been stuck inside your book for quite some time. On the other hand, I suppose it's also possible the illustration is another gift from my elusive visitor. What do you think?"

"I suppose either one is possible."

"You wouldn't have any idea as to the locations of the depicted areas, would you?"

He lifted a shoulder as he shook his head. "No, I'm afraid I don't."

"I wonder if there is some way we can find out."

Though it seemed she asked herself the question, he answered anyway. "Most of the time, and with enough perseverance, one can find a way to do almost anything one desires. However, the length of time it takes to discover the answer is the real question."

She raised her brows a tad. "Yes—well, let's hope it doesn't take as long as it did to decipher the pictograph."

"Even then, we really don't know how relevant this illustration is to our task. Of course we have to take a close look at it because we don't know if your visitor left it behind or not. However, as you've just pointed out, someone could've slipped the page inside the book at any given time over the countless decades I've had it on the bookshelf. I'm sure if we made careful study of each volume I own, we'd find dragon references and illustrations aplenty."

"I know. I've already seen quite a few of them. But none of the others will concern me as will this one."

"No doubt. Therefore, we'll put forth every effort to make sense of it, all right?"

Though her gaze never once wandered away from his, she said nothing in return. He could see her sorting through a plethora of thoughts that troubled her just by expression alone.

"So, what are you thinking now?"

She took on a far away expression. "A variety of things, I suppose. One—it makes sense we would need to know where to find the dragon in order to return the heart. So then, as if by magic, a map appears that just *might* take us to his lair. Of course, in order to conduct our search, we first needed to know about the dragon and his heart. So *voila*, we receive a coin and palimpsest that help us do just that—and after centuries of fruitless search.

"Now, I'm aware the parchment, having its origin amongst Nia's possession, is a gift from Gwynn ap Nudd. But he has nothing to do with the coin or this map, should we find the latter relevant. That means someone else has had possession of these things and for quite some time. Right?"

"Yes, I suppose I would have to agree with that."

"So, where did he or she get them, Garreth? Does he or she have anything else we need in order to solve the riddle? And the question that nags me most? Why all of the secrecy and the peek-a-boo, hide-and-seek? Why not just *hand* all of these things to us at one time

145

and tell us what it is he knows face to face?"

Garreth couldn't answer any of the questions he had asked himself at least a dozen times already. Perhaps because of his distasteful experience with Nia, he also wondered over their benefactor's objective. Did he have his own agenda concerning the heart of the dragon? Did he hope to stay one step ahead of them in their quest to find and return the object so he could take the object himself? If so, for what purpose? Whatever that purpose, be it good or bad, it now involved Essie, and that changed his perspective on just about everything.

"Garreth?" She peeked up at him through her lashes.

"Hmm? I'm sorry, did you say something?"

A slight smile touched her lips and for a moment, he allowed his gaze to tarry there as the memory of last night's interruption entered his mind. An attractive blush followed his perusal.

"I asked you if you thought it even remotely possible that Nia once had possession of all these things," she said without taking a breath.

He cocked his head to the side as he considered her query. "What gave rise to that question?"

"Just the fact that she had the palimpsest. What if at one time she had everything we now have in our possession and someone filched all but the parchment?"

"If that be the case, why would this person leave the palimpsest behind? Why not take everything?"

"Perhaps she separated the document from the rest herself, because that's all she intended to give you. Or—better yet—what if she wanted to give you everything *but* the palimpsest? What if she transported the coin and the map to the castle in preparation for the wedding?"

Garreth returned a slow nod. A scenario like that made sense. "Very possible. Nia would do something like that."

"You told me on the day of her accident, she traveled with her favorite attendants. Did she always travel with them?"

"Yes, she did."

"Then perhaps a survivor of the accident also had knowledge of these things."

The notion didn't sit well. If one of her confidants had such knowledge, then he or she intentionally withheld the information from him until now. Why?

Then, as if she could hear his thoughts, she said, "Perhaps that person, despite the passage of time, couldn't make sense of the artifacts himself, and finally gave them to us just to see if we could."

"Again—quite possible and perhaps even probable."

She paused for a moment. "Did Nia have her own room here in the castle?"

"Yes, she did." He understood the reason behind the question and so stated it aloud. "You wish to conduct a search in the room she used to see if anything else is hidden away inside it."

She gave him a nod. "Is anyone using it right now?"

"No, it's empty and but for the occasional visitor, usually is. I gave her use of that particular room, which is located on the other side of the castle, because I wanted her as far away from me as I could get her."

"I see." She glanced at the doorway. "Well, can we

go and take a look, if just to satisfy my curiosity?"

"Yes, we can. I'm curious now myself. So, why don't you get dressed while I fetch a key? I should have one in my room," he said as he rose from the bed.

"All right, it'll only take me a minute."

Ten minutes later, he thrust the key inside the lock and opened the door. He switched on the light, placed a hand against the small of her back, and escorted her inside the chamber.

"I'm not sure what we're looking for," he said as his gaze swept across the room.

She exaggerated the clearing of her throat. "Well, the last time I told you to look for something that didn't quite mesh with its surroundings—" Essie let the sentence hang as she studied the wall across from the door.

Garreth dipped his head and chuckled. "I remember."

"How could you possibly forget?"

He and Essie conducted a thorough search of the entire chamber. They searched behind the portraits and under tables and chairs. They even checked the casing around the windows and doors.

Finally, she brushed the wayward strands of hair away from her face and tossed them behind her shoulder. "I need you to help me move the wardrobe away from the wall."

"No, step aside. I can get it." A careful search of the stones underneath and along the wall behind the wardrobe yielded them nothing. Garreth turned his gaze to the bed. "The only thing left to move is the bed, but the massive canopied frame is too heavy for me to lift alone. So, I'm going to need a little help to haul it."

She placed a hand on top of his arm to halt his steps. "No, wait. The bed is fairly high off the floor. I think I can slide underneath it well enough to check."

Just as she knelt beside the bed and flipped the coverlet on top of the mattress, an icy gust of wind shot through the room and thrust her backward. A deep, guttural growl accompanied the blast. Before they had the chance to react, a huge, mangy, wolf, with teeth bared, emerged from underneath the frame.

Garreth hunkered down, yanked Essie into his arms, and shielded her with his body as the animal lunged. The beast leaped over the top of them and disappeared into thin air before his paws hit the floor. Essie stared with mouth agape before she turned her rounded eyes toward him.

****

He could feel her heart race against his chest as he combed his hands through her tousled hair. "Are you all right, cariad?"

She stared at him for a moment, and then swallowed hard. "There is no way a *real* wolf could've fit underneath the bed or go through a closed door, much less one that size."

"No, a real wolf wouldn't even have been able to get inside this room."

"One of the Tylwyth Teg or some other type of otherworldly—werewolf-type—creature?"

"I would almost have to think so," he said as he loosened his grip.

"Then there must be something vital underneath the bed." A look of determination filled her eyes as she moved to escape his arms.

He tightened his hold once again and held her

captive. "No, let me get someone in here, and we'll move the bed out of the way, all right? We don't need any more surprises."

She let go of a breath and nodded. "All right."

As he stood, he helped her to her feet and then with his arm about her waist, they made their way to the intercom. Vaughn answered his call. "Vaughn? Could you get Bran for me and send him to Nia's old room? I need a hand in here."

"Anything I or Gerald can do to help you?"

"No, just find Bran. We can take care of it."

"Will do."

Within a few short minutes, Bran entered the room. He shot a glance back and forth between their faces and raised a brow. "Is something wrong?"

"Not unless you want to count the Fair shifter we just encountered hiding beneath the bed," said Garreth. He gave Bran the details of the morning's events and the reason for the visit to Nia's chamber.

Bran flicked his thumb at the bed. "Well, let's get the bloody thing moved and see what we find then," he said.

Essie watched as the men took hold of the frame and hefted the bed into the middle of the room. While Garreth and Bran searched the area behind the bed, she focused on the string of corded leather snaking out beneath the front of the pleated canopy curtains. The dark brown cord clashed with the delicate rose-colored hues of the heavy linen drapes and bedding.

She made her way to the braided strip, stooped down beside it and gave it a tug. The cord refused to give way. She dropped her back to the floor, took hold of the railing, and scooted underneath the bed.

"What are you doing?" Garreth sounded a bit perturbed.

She ignored the question as she traced the leather tie to its point of origin. The quest didn't take her long. Someone had entwined a leather bag between the timbers. She hastened to untie the network of knots, took hold of the bag with both hands, and with a grunt, yanked it free.

"Essie," called Garreth yet again. This time she noted exasperation in his tone.

"I'm coming, I'm coming." She inched her way out from underneath the bed holding onto her prize. Garreth offered her his hand and helped her to her feet. She gave him the bag and while she dusted off her jeans, he peeked inside.

Bran moved a step closer. "Anything in it?"

Garreth withdrew his hand, and held up a ripped fragment from a piece of parchment. "Just this."

Essie took the section from Garreth and turned it over. "This looks like a piece of another palimpsest. Well, what's left of one, anyway. Do you see the faint underwriting here?"

"Yes, I can see it. Do you think it's part of the chronicle we already have?"

"Under the circumstances I would bet that it is. But, we'll have to look at it under the microscope and make sure."

He then pointed out a jagged slash down the middle of the sack. "Looks like our phantom wolf just shredded the bag."

"Do you think he did it deliberately?" asked Essie.

Garreth shrugged. "It sure looks like it to me. If that's the case, he probably carried away the remainder of the document and anything else the bag might've contained when he escaped the room."

Essie dropped a hand to her side. "This just keeps getting more and more complicated."

Garreth fixed his gaze to hers as he considered her comment. "No, not if we don't allow it to. All we need do is work with what we have, what we know, and then collaborate—"

Bran pinched his brows. "What are you thinking, Garreth?"

"I'm thinking we need to pay Gwynn ap Nudd another visit and the sooner the better."

Bran smoothed the corners of his mustache. "Do you think it wise to show up at his doorstep without an invitation and so soon after the first?"

"Why not? He made no attempt to keep the pathway secret and not a soul from his realm ever once waited for an invitation to show up at mine," he replied.

"True enough—"

"The morning's events make the visit necessary, Bran. I think we need to take everything we've collected this far, including this bag, and see if Gwynn can identify the owner or provide insight in regards to the wolf."

"All right," said Bran. "When do you want to go and whom do you wish to take along on this little outing?"

"Just as soon as we can get a few supplies together and I think just the three of us this time around," Garreth replied. "We don't want to overwhelm them with too many guests."

"But Garreth," she interrupted. "How are we going to cross the lake if we don't run into anyone from their realm?"

"I recall seeing several canoes tethered near the pier. I'm sure Gwynn won't mind if we use one."

Bran nodded. "I'll see to gathering a few supplies. I need to let Anne know we're going, and I should probably let Lowri know, as well. The woman will throw a major fit if she isn't allowed to get us some food together."

Garreth placed a hand on his shoulder. "And, Bran—would you mention that it's just the three of us and not a whole army, hmm?"

Bran glanced at the door and shrugged. "I'll tell her if you think it'll do any good."

"In the meantime, Essie and I will take a quick peek at this fragment underneath the scope. If the symbols match those we have, it won't take us long to figure out what it says."

Twenty minutes later, Essie handed Garreth the Welsh words that coincided with the discernible symbols beneath the topmost text. He drew his brows together as he studied what they had of the message.

"Well, if you ask me, I'd say the thing is definitely connected to the palimpsest we have. However, there is always room for doubt. Now, having provided the disclaimer, this is the sum total of what our fragment says." He dropped his gaze to the parchment. "—crystal, its inestimable power, created by the magic of the—"

Essie huffed out an irritated breath. "Are you kidding me? That's all we have?"

"That's the entire fragment."

She closed her eyes, and placed a hand to her brow. "I should've just brought you the map when I found it.

Maybe if we had searched Nia's room a bit earlier we'd have found the bag with contents intact."

"No, I don't think the time would've made any difference. I'm confident our "wolf" guards, or did guard, the room. And Essie, I don't think I want to share this particular piece of parchment with Gwynn just yet."

"Why? Don't you trust him?"

"I believe Gwynn is very trustworthy. I know, he too, is putting forth a great deal of effort in the prevention of another apocalypse. But I don't know how far we can trust those within his realm. So, until we figure this out, just don't mention the fragment, all right?"

"I won't say a word—"

Bran stepped just inside the doorway. "Are you both about ready?"

"Not quite," she said as she turned to face him. "Let me gather a few things together in case the king compels us to stay the night again."

"No hurry," said Garreth. "Just come down to the hall when you're ready. We'll meet you there."

Essie collected the few things she needed and dropped them inside her nylon backpack. She spied her notebook then, and reluctant to leave it with a devious wolf on the loose, decided to take that along as well. The notion led to one other thought.

She hurried down the steps and made her way to the hall where Bran and Garreth awaited her.

"Garreth? I'm a little worried. Do you think we need to gather all of our research and take it with us? For safe-keeping, I mean."

He shook his head and as he approached, he

relieved her of her backpack and offered his hand. "You needn't worry. I already have everything secured and hidden away."

"That's good." She placed her hand on top of his and at once, his fingers curved around it.

"Are you ready to go then?"

"Yes, I am."

Garreth led the way from the castle to the glade and then around the lake to the waterfall. "Careful now, be mindful of the moss," he said as she made her way behind it and entered the corridor.

"You know, throughout all of the centuries, I never had a clue that this tunnel existed," Bran said, heading up the rear.

"Neither did I." Garreth once again claimed her hand. "But the path does explain the abrupt appearances from the various members of the Fair folk. So, Essie wasn't far wrong when she wondered if they used the lake to travel from their realm into ours."

Throughout the morning hours, Garreth made sure to keep all conversations light. Essie wondered if he did so just in case their wraithlike wolf dogged their trail and listened. Then, just as Garreth suggested they stop and have a bite to eat, Afon, Cledwyn, Urbgen, and Aneirin emerged from the surrounding trees.

Afon headed straight for her. He took hold of her hand, drew it to his lips, and planted a kiss on top of it. All the while, he retained her gaze. "How nice to see you again, Essie," he said and then added, "You too, Garreth—Bran."

Garreth huffed out a breath as he stepped forward. He placed a hand about her waist and drew her close to his side. "Afon."

Afon smirked as he finally shifted his gaze to Garreth and bowed. "Come, the king is anxiously awaiting your arrival."

Chapter Eleven

Yet again, Afon pushed the level of his tolerance to the limit. If not for the need to speak with Gwynn, he would already have vacated the king's palace, and his realm, with Essie firmly in hand. Not that she seemed taken by the man's overbearing, blatant advances. Quite the contrary, actually. Still, he refused to give up his quest and that fact irritated him no end. Even more annoying, he knew it.

"Garreth, I hope I didn't keep you waiting," said Gwynn as he entered the study and strode toward his desk.

"Not at all," he replied. "Afon has provided suitable entertainment to while away the time."

Afon chuckled in response to the comment. He shot a glance heavenward as he bounced on his heels. "Didn't you know? Providing you such entertainment fills me with the utmost pleasure, Garreth."

"I bet."

Gwynn ignored the combined laughter of those in the room as he took his seat, leaned back in the chair, and gazed at each member of his personal staff. "Would you all excuse us, please? I crave a private moment with my guests." His eyes remained fixed on the procession until the last man walked out of the study and shut the door behind him. Only then, did he give them his full attention. "You have news for me."

Garreth nodded. "Some, but more importantly, we're hoping you can give us some insight and perhaps a little bit of assistance. Bran, show Gwynn the chart."

Bran withdrew the parchment from the bag and handed it to the king. Gwynn placed a fisted hand against his cheek as he studied the illustration at length. "Where did you find this?"

He and Essie looked at each other for a moment before he related the events preceding and following the discovery of the chart, save revealing the existence of the torn fragment. At the end of his narrative, Gwynn leaned forward, clasped his hands on top of his desk, and fixed his gaze upon the wall behind him. Garreth used the lull in conversation to retrieve the shredded bag.

He placed it on top of the desk and slid it toward the king. "I don't suppose you recognize this satchel or know its owner, do you?"

Gwynn picked up the sack and examined both sides. He traced along the jagged slit with his index finger and then handed it back. "I'm afraid I can't identify this particular bag or its owner. Now, having said that, I must also tell you that I believe it originated here in Llys y Helig. The braiding that stitches the sides together is unique to my realm. That means, it's also quite possible, your spectral wolf resides right here."

"We've not discounted the possibility he resides in my province, Gwynn," Garreth replied. "I know you're aware we have many citizens that have a portion of Fair blood running through their veins. Our phantom wolf could be any one of them. Nonetheless, Essie and I have tossed around the idea that the bag might have once belonged to either Nia or one of her personal attendants. Hence the reason we paid you this visit."

The king said nothing for several moments. "What would bring you around to such a notion?"

"We discovered the bag inside the room she used at the castle. I can assure you, very few people have occupied it since her death. There is something else I think you should know, for it might have something to do with the palimpsest and the chart." Garreth leaned forward. He then recounted the events and the subsequent agreement leading to his and Nia's betrothal. The king of the Tylwyth Teg didn't seem the least bit surprised to hear it.

Gwynn shifted his gaze to his hands and focused on the play of his thumbs for a time. Finally, he shook his head and tsked. "I must apologize for the pain and suffering she caused you Garreth, but unfortunately, Nia always did things her way. I don't think I could have stopped her purpose even had I known the details of your arrangement, which I assure you, I did not. The child was headstrong and self-centered all the days of her life. No amount of discipline ever eradicated it, I'm sorry to say."

"You've nothing to apologize for, Gwynn. You have no control over the actions of an adult child and as far as I'm concerned, that which is past is past."

"Thank you for that, Garreth. Now the questions we must ask ourselves is why this person retained these items for so long, and what motivated him to share them now. Of course, the most obvious question is whether or not any of Nia's surviving staff is involved."

Garreth shrugged. "Essie thought perhaps our wolf grew weary of his efforts to make sense of the puzzle himself and turned it over to us to see if we could make sense of the thing."

"A reasonable assumption—a reasonable assumption indeed. Therefore, we must ever remain on our guard, for if such is the case, our wolf has his own agenda apart from ours." He drummed his fingers on top of his desk. "Let me think on this tonight. You will of course, stay until the morning?"

"If you wish," said Garreth.

"The request is more than just a simple wish, Garreth. I think it crucial if we're to make progress on our current dilemma and do so before the next apocalypse. I'm hoping, that come the morning, we'll have more to discuss. Especially, if you will allow me to retain possession of the chart?"

Garreth gave him a nod as he dismissed the document with a wave of his hand. "Be my guest."

Once the king rose from his seat with parchment in hand, they followed suit. "Then in the meantime, I invite you to enjoy the hospitality of Llys y Helig. However, I would ask that you refrain from speaking about the details of our discussion outside of this room, for in this room our words cannot be overheard. Such is not the case elsewhere."

The remainder of the day, dinner, and the evening's entertainment helped while away the tedious hours. But now that he lay in the darkness of his silent bedchamber, the last vestiges of fitful sleep fled altogether. Right now, a breath of fresh air sounded good.

Garreth rose from the bed, dressed for the day, and wandered outside his bedroom doors to the connecting veranda. He leaned against the balustrade, propped an elbow on top of it, and turned his gaze to the scattered lights that caused the hills to sparkle. Dawn had yet to touch the sky, though the sun would make its appearance soon enough. He took in that deep breath of fresh air he craved, held it for a moment, and then released it as he wondered what the day would bring.

"Now tell me something Garreth, why am I not surprised to see you wide awake, fully dressed, and outside in the dark all by yourself?"

Garreth turned around in response to the sound of Essie's voice and fastened his gaze to hers. She looked so beautiful dressed in blue and bathed in glorious moonlight. He took a moment to drink in the image she presented. With her hands behind her back, she shut her balcony doors, and then strolled toward him. Didn't she understand the peril in which she had placed herself with each advancing step she took?

By heaven—he sincerely hoped not.

He remained silent as she approached. Once she arrived at his side, she rested a hip against the railing, and turned to face him. She lifted a brow and waited for him to speak.

He didn't intend to speak.

As his only response to her question, he slipped a hand around her waist, and pulled her into his arms. His other hand glided along the contours of her cheek and then cupped the side of her face. She inhaled a sharp breath, just as he brushed his lips against hers for the simple pleasure it gave him to do so. She shivered in response. He then deepened the kiss he could no longer hold at bay. Within that momentous kiss, he expressed every emotion she had ever inspired.

The hands she had placed against his chest traveled upward and then encircled his neck. He broke away from the first kiss, just for the desire to experience another, and then another before he lost count. The powerful love he had for this woman ran deep and right now, he wanted her to know that.

"Dw i'n dy garu di, Essie," he whispered, before he kissed her yet again.

Essie didn't understand the words he spoke in his native tongue, but she could feel the fiery passion and the strength of emotion behind them. In return, she brushed her fingers through his hair and used the next kiss to express the profound love she had for the lord of Llys y Gwalch. He dropped his hand from her face, wrapped both arms around her waist, and strengthened his hold during the duration of the kiss.

At its end, he inhaled a ragged breath and rested his forehead against hers as a shudder coursed through his body. "By all the saints, woman—"

Just as she opened her mouth to speak, to tell him that she loved him without condition or fear of the life-changing consequences that might follow, a deliberate clearing of the throat shattered the moment. Garreth muttered a curse as he relaxed his hold, released a heavy sigh, and turned his head in the direction of the sound.

"Good morning Gwynn," he said.

"I'm so sorry," the monarch said as he motioned them to his side. "I didn't mean to intrude on your privacy. Nonetheless, I must say I'm pleased to see you both awake. I ran into Bran in the hallway. He's now awaiting us in the study. If you please, I need you to follow me right now."

Essie glanced at Garreth. Alongside an almost imperceptible shake of his head, he gave her an apologetic grin. He took hold of her hand as they followed behind the king. They stopped at the study just long enough to collect Bran. From there, Gwynn led them down a continuous flight of stairs that took them deep inside the earth. A series of flaming torches along the wall lit the path.

Finally, they arrived at the bottom step. Before she could take in her surroundings, the king ushered them down a wide hallway off to the right. A large wooden door loomed at the end of the corridor. As they approached, she could see a brass colored inlay, in the shape of a multi-pointed star, centering the door. Gwynn halted his steps, withdrew a chain from around his neck, and placed the heptagonal pendant into the depressed center of the star. Mysterious lights, appearing from out of nowhere, illuminated all points. A click sounded, and the door swung open of its own accord.

She and Garreth exchanged a glance as they entered the room. At first glimpse, the chamber resembled a cross between an antiquated library and an ancient alchemist's burrow. Stacks of parchment and scrolls littered the shelves that lined the walls. Several tables appeared haphazardly placed about the floor. A vast assortment of vials, filled with an array of colorful liquids, sat on top of a solitary table. The musty smell of stale air, stagnant water, and damp earth permeated all around them.

At the back of the room stood Cledwyn. In turn, he stood next to Merlin the magician, or at least the persona her imagination conjured when she read the tales of King Arthur—sans the pointy hat. Even his dark brown robe looked of ancient origin. His light blue eyes studied each of them in turn.

"My friends, this is, Uvan, my personal advisor, and my father's before me." Gwynn gave the man a respectful nod. "And Uvan, this is Lord Garreth, Bran, and Essie DeSpencer, the gifted woman who finally deciphered the pictograph."

Uvan bowed his head, but said nothing in return.

Gwynn turned and gave them his full attention. "I want you all to know that Uvan is also making every effort to avoid the coming disaster. Last night I shared our latest discussion with him and showed him the illustration you discovered in your book. Because of the scroll there on the table, he is familiar with the places noted on the map. Therefore, he can provide you with the directions you need to find the cave."

"Do you know what's inside the cave?" asked Garreth.

"According to the legend recorded on the scroll, a dragon resides within," said Uvan in all seriousness. "The scenario fits with the Ogham writing on the pictograph, as well as the palimpsest, does it not?"

Essie's heart accelerated as her nightmare flooded her mind. She glanced at the scroll on top of the table and then looked at Garreth. He took hold of her hand and gave it a reassuring squeeze.

"You don't mean to say you believe there is an *actual* fire-breathing dragon inside the thing, do you?" Garreth scoffed.

Uvan shook his head and shrugged. "I don't know, but I wouldn't discount it."

"Tell me something, Uvan. Have you ever seen a real dragon?"

Amusement filled the ancient eyes as he shook his

head in response to the question. "No, Prince Garreth, I can't say that I have. Nonetheless, I merely want to point out that you should prepare yourself for all things."

"Then, you have never visited this cave yourself."

"No, I haven't. But the scroll gives precise directions from a location known to our people. I daresay you shall not have trouble finding it."

"Given the recent events surrounding our mission, Garreth," said Gwynn, "we thought it might be prudent to take an extra precaution, if you're willing to agree with our judgment."

"An extra precaution?"

"Yes, there is no time like the present to explore this lead. No one in your realm will know you're gone until it's far too late to follow. The people in mine will simply believe you've returned to your home. You can begin your journey from a passageway between our realms, known to only a few. This passageway will take you to the surface. I will assign both Cledwyn and Aneirin to act as your guides. They are both loyal and trustworthy."

Garreth spared Cledwyn a glance. "How long do you think it will take us to arrive at our destination?"

Uvan approached the scroll and turned it so they could see. "According to our historian, your journey will take you very near the Snowdon Mountain."

Garreth shifted his gaze to the wall and scraped his fingers across the scruff on his chin. "Then depending on our mode of travel, we could be gone several days."

"I think we'll need some horses if we're going to take a trip to the mountain," Bran cut in. "And, if we want to shorten the journey, we'll need to drive as far as we can first."

Garreth shook his head. "I can't ask you to go on this one, Bran. Not with Anne being as close to delivery as she is. Right now, your place is at her side, and I'll need someone I can trust to watch over the place while I'm gone. I also think it prudent to keep an eye out for our elusive wolf."

Bran seemed a bit relieved. "If that's your wish."

"Then it's settled," said the king. "In the hope you would concur with this plan, I've already taken the liberty of supplying you with everything you'll need for your adventure, including the horses for the final leg of your journey. All you need do is locate and explore the cave. Hopefully what you find therein, will lead us to the next needful step. In the meantime, I'll discover if either Ceri or Eleri is in any way involved with this intrigue."

Essie shifted her gaze to Garreth. "Ceri and Eleri?"

"Nia's attendants who survived the accident," he said.

She returned a slow nod. "Oh."

Gwynn waved a hand toward the door. "Then if you're ready?"

****

In less than two hours, they bid the king of the Tylwyth Teg goodbye and boarded the boat that would sail them across the water. Garreth had the detailed map Uvan created, tucked inside his pocket. Several times during the voyage, Essie gazed out at the woodland on either side of the lake.

"What are you looking for?" asked Garreth.

She turned her head to the side and shrugged. "Oh, I don't know. I suppose I'm just making sure a wolf isn't following us. Gwynn's comments made me a little jittery, I think."

Cledwyn's wink accompanied a grin. "If someone of that ilk followed us, we would know. So, don't worry, Essie. For the time being, all is well."

They parted ways with Bran at the entrance to the passageway leading to the waterfall within their realm. From there, Cledwyn turned back. They walked about a half mile before he slipped through another crevice she had overlooked, and from the glance she exchanged with Garreth, so had he.

Cledwyn guided them through a maze of corridors inside the mountain. Along the way, they stopped for lunch and then again for dinner. Finally, well after the sun dipped below the horizon, they emerged from the passageway and entered a forest, illuminated by glimmering stars and a full moon.

"We'll stay here for the night," said Cledwyn as he turned his gaze and gave a nod to the left of where they stood.

Only then did Essie notice the small, antiquated cottage all but hidden by the shadow of trees. Ivy covered the stone face. A single chimney rose up from the thatched roof and a weathered, wooden door separated two large, square-paned windows. Four horses grazed in a small fenced pasture next to the house. Cledwyn led them to the door, opened it, and bade them enter first. The furnishings found within looked just as archaic as the outside structure and the sight instantly charmed her.

Cledwyn had a fire going in no time at all. Aneirin set about unpacking the supplies that sat against the wall in the corner. Those supplies included food, bedding, and changes of clothing for her and Garreth. She had no idea how they got there and decided not to ask. Aneirin tossed a sleeping bag at Cledwyn and then gave one to Garreth.

"Essie, you get the feather bed," said Aneirin as he thrust a thumb behind him to the bed in the corner. "And I'd advise you to make use of it sooner rather than later. We leave at first light."

He didn't have to ask her twice. Sleep eluded her most of last night and the journey this far added to her exhaustion. She made quick use of the somewhat primitive bathroom facilities and while the men packed for the morning, she slipped into the comfortable bed.

Sometime later, a persistent noise disturbed her sleep. Fatigue wouldn't allow her eyes to open as she assessed the sound. Something scraped up and down the window next to the bed.

No, not a scrape—

The clatter sounded more like a series of taps. What would cause that? Finally, when she couldn't take another minute of the irritating sound, she turned toward the window and opened her eyes. A large hawk, the largest she had ever seen, tapped mercilessly at the window. He fluttered his wings in a most frantic way as his bright red eyes gazed into hers. She had the most bizarre notion he wanted her to lift the window and let him inside. Even more bizarre, she couldn't stop herself from doing it, no matter how hard she tried. A gust of air accompanied the lifting of the casement.

With the window wide open, the hawk flew inside and circled the room. Essie shifted her gaze to the roaring fireplace, seeking her companions. None of them were there. All of the furnishings and all of her companions had disappeared. She didn't have time to ponder the reasons for this oddity. For at that very moment, the bathroom door at the back of the room creaked opened. The hawk made a mad dash for the exposed passageway.

Essie leaped from the bed to follow. The bathroom had also disappeared, leaving a long dark hallway in its stead. She placed a hand against the wall to guide her steps. Minutes passed before darkness gave way to diffused light. She could just barely hear the sound of the hawk's flapping wings. Despite her fear, she moved forward.

Then, without warning, a flaming burst of fire lit up the stone chamber in which she now stood. She faced the point of origin just in time to see the head of a dragon emerging from a hollow in the wall. She drew in a breath. The hawk, which had hovered just above her head, flew at the creature's gaping jaws. Her heartbeat accelerated the same instant her hands flew to her mouth and smothered a scream. She squeezed her eyes shut as the dragon ravaged the hawk. Despair and sorrow consumed her, though for the life of her, she couldn't say why. Nonetheless, she fell to her knees and sobbed.

"Essie—it's all right," whispered Garreth. "Everything is all right now. You simply had a dream."

He had her in his arms and held her close. She gulped, drew in a sharp breath, and then gazed into his eyes. He brushed the tears away from her face and dropped a comforting kiss against her lips. She glanced all about the room as she combed her fingers through her hair. The cottage looked just as did when they entered it last night.

"I'm sorry, did I wake you up?"

"No, we were already awake," he said. "In fact, Cledwyn and Aneirin are outside saddling the horses. Are you all right now?"

"Yes. I'm fine. I just had another ridiculous nightmare, that's all." She dabbed at the corner of her eye and shrugged.

"What about this time?"

"Nothing really. Nothing about it made any real sense. I'm sure all of the events over the past couple of days had something to do with producing the thing."

"Oh come on, tell me about it," he said as he rubbed his hand along the contours of her back. "Talking about it will make you feel better."

"All right—I dreamed this very large hawk wanted in through that window," she said as she inclined her head toward it. "I've never seen such a gorgeous bird. His feathers were gray, white, and black, and he had these piercing red eyes that penetrated my soul. Anyway, long story short—I let the hawk in and followed him into some sort of round chamber made of stone that suddenly connected to this cottage. A dragon emerged from his lair and devoured the hawk. I don't know why, but the whole thing devastated me."

She expected Garreth to laugh or make light of the dream. But he didn't. Instead, she caught a fleeting glimpse of recognition before he hastened to drop his gaze. She wouldn't have it. Not now. She placed her hands against his chest, forced him to back away, and looked into his eyes.

"Don't, Garreth. Don't keep secrets from me. Our cause is too important for you to shield me from something you think might worry or upset me. I need

170

all of the facts if we're to succeed, just as you do."

He loosened his hold and blew out a breath of resignation. "All right. Has anyone ever told you what Llys y Gwalch means in English?"

"No. I've never thought to ask."

Garreth paused, placed a hand against her cheek, and caressed lightly against it with his thumb. "It means Court of the Hawk, Essie."

Chapter Twelve

Dread took control over her emotions and refused to let up or let go. She shook her head as both dreams stormed her mind with raging ferocity. Two very different dreams, yet each of them ended with Garreth's destruction.

"No..." She choked back a sob as she lifted a trembling hand away from his chest and covered her mouth. "No. We can't do this, Garreth. We need to turn back. Right now. We'll find another way. Please."

"Look, you needn't put too much stock in the reality of those dreams. They're just dreams and nothing more. You know this."

"How can you say that? Those dreams have revealed truth of things I didn't even know existed."

"To a certain degree that's true. But you're a very intuitive woman, Essie. Perhaps that intuitiveness simply revealed itself in your dreams. No, don't shake that beautiful stubborn head of yours. You know it's possible. Might I also add that it's quite possible your subconscious mind overheard the reference to the hawk from a member of my staff? Mayhap you might even have seen the carved image on one of the graves inside the cemetery. Such is not an uncommon sight, I assure you."

"I don't care where it came from. All I know is that I can't proceed with this quest if there's even the smallest chance the thing results in your death. I can't do that, Garreth. I can't. You can't ask me to do that."

"Many people have died during each apocalypse, Essie. There's no guarantee I or any other person inside my realm will live through another. Therefore, don't you think it best for all concerned to make a concerted effort to prevent the next one from taking place?"

Before she could reply to his sound reasoning, the latch clicked and the sturdy hinges moaned against the weight of the door.

"Oh good," said Cledwyn as he entered the cottage and fixed his gaze to hers. "You're awake. Can you make do with some bread and cheese for breakfast and eat as we travel? I'd like to cross as many miles as we can today."

Essie took in a deep breath and returned his smile as best she could. She suppressed her reluctance and tossed her quilt off to the side. As she and Garreth rose from the bed, they exchanged a glance. He filled his with calm assurance and somehow, it filled her with a small portion of the same. In all reality, they couldn't abandon their journey. Not now. She knew that. "Yes, that'll be fine. I'll hurry and get dressed."

Ten minutes later, they turned their horses in a southeasterly direction. Within the hour, they emerged from the forest that sheltered the cottage. Garreth pointed at the mountain range, now in line of sight.

"That's Snowdon, the tallest mountain in Wales," he said.

"Is that where we're going?" She gazed upon the highest peaks in the distance.

"Not exactly, but we'll get close enough for you to get a good look." Then as an afterthought he added, "I hope the ride won't be too much for you."

"You needn't worry about that issue. My uncle Eli and I traveled by horseback more often than not during his endless expeditions. Most of the time he required me to pony one of the mules that carried our supplies. As you can imagine, sometimes that got a bit dicey when said mule didn't wish to cooperate. Therefore, I can assure you, this ride will be a piece of cake."

Garreth chuckled. "Tell me, how long would you and he be gone on these various expeditions of his?"

"Oh, I don't know—anywhere between a couple of weeks to almost the entire summer." As she made the comment, her mind traveled backward in time and briefly relived some of those experiences. Experiences that were delightful as well as those that tested her skill and mettle. "The length of time always depended upon the project."

"Your parents didn't mind the fact you were gone so long?"

"First of all, you have to understand my parents were—and still are—tree-hugging environmentalists. They had their own agendas concerning conservation, preservation, and the restoration of our damaged planet. So, not only did they think these expeditions were good for my personal growth, education, and development, it also gave them a bit more freedom to travel to the places they didn't deem safe enough for a child to go."

"Hmm," he said as he rubbed a hand across his mouth to cover a grin. "Environmentalists, huh? Now, let me think. What would a pair of "tree-hugging" environmentalists, name their precious daughter?"

"Here we go again," she murmured under her breath.

"How about SkyAnne Earth DeSpencer?" he asked.

She turned to face him and lifted a disdainful brow. "Sky—Anne—Earth—DeSpencer," she repeated each word in a slow, distinct, monotonous tone. "Are you serious?"

"Not quite right? Well then, how about SeaAnne Earth DeSpencer?"

"Oh, for heaven's sake," she huffed. "How long did it take you to come up with those?"

Garreth feigned indignation. "Are you making fun of me, Miss S.E. DeSpencer? I issued the question in all dead seriousness."

Cledwyn laughed over their play. "Are you telling me, Lord Garreth, that you don't know Miss DeSpencer's full name?"

He put a hand to his heart and shook his head. "Alas, despite all my best efforts to gain that information, Miss S. E. DeSpencer refuses to divulge the name given her at birth," said Garreth. "I can't imagine any name being as hideous as all that can you?"

"Will she tell us if we guess it?" asked Aneirin, getting into the game.

"She says not, but I should think expression alone would give away the secret should we happen across it," he said. "A pale, greenish, hue would be a dead giveaway, wouldn't you agree?"

"Yes, I think you just might be right about that." Cledwyn rested a finger against his bottom lip and then gave it a little rub. "S.E.—hmm. Perhaps they named her for the stars or even the constellations, then. They are part of our atmospheric view, are they not? If pollution worsens here on the surface, the haze would prevent those who dwell here from seeing them with the naked eye. Her parents would surely be concerned about this tragedy. So, how about Sagitta Equuleus or Sagittarius Eridanus?"

"The same thing could be said for the great rivers of the earth," Aneirin said. "Perhaps they chose one of those. Let's see, what about Sungari Euphrates or Salween Euphrates?"

Essie laughed. She gazed first at Cledwyn and pointed a finger in his direction. "No and no," she said and then shifted both gaze and finger toward Aneirin. "No, and definitely not."

The guesses grew ever more ridiculous. Along with those guesses, the banter and light-hearted conversation continued throughout most of the day. Without doubt, they did so in a deliberate effort to keep all conversation away from their true purpose. A wise decision on their part, for in all likelihood, the wind carried their words to iniquitous ears that strained to eavesdrop. A couple of times along the way, Garreth withdrew his map, and without a word of discussion, adjusted their course.

By the time night fell, Garreth had led them up through the hills, traversed the ever-changing terrain of another magnificent forest, and then halted near the banks of a beautiful blue lake, nestled by the surrounding hills. The sight took away her breath.

Cledwyn gazed out over the water. "How much longer do you think it'll take us to reach our destination, Garreth?"

"I'm not sure. Depending on the terrain, we might be looking at another full day," he replied.

"Perhaps then we ought to camp here for the night, and get a good night's sleep, so we're alert and refreshed when we face tomorrow's challenge."

"I wholeheartedly agree with that. I think Essie's had enough for one day," Garreth said as he dismounted and then ambled to her side.

Garreth, ever the charming, chivalrous gentleman, took hold of her waist, and assisted her descent despite the fact she could dismount from her own horse without undue hardship. Not that she minded—quite the contrary actually.

"How are you holding up, cariad? Are you all right?"

"Yes, I'm fine. However, I must admit, I'm happy to be out of the saddle for awhile," she said as she found her footing. "I need to stretch my legs for a bit, I think."

"Then Garreth, why don't you take Essie for a walk while Aneirin and I prepare a fire and set up camp," said Cledwyn.

"Sounds like a good idea," said Garreth as he turned to face her and offered his arm. "Essie?"

He led her to the thick cover of trees, which surrounded the north side of the lake. While they strolled along the grassy banks, she took delight in the play of moonlight as it danced on top of the gentle swell of the water. Then, as they approached the edge of the headland, Garreth turned her around and tugged her into his arms.

As his lips teased just above hers, he whispered, "Just so you know? I've hungered for this moment ever since Gwynn interrupted the last."

The singular kiss following the comment displaced

the trepidation and concern she'd carried since waking from her dream. Delicious warmth that began somewhere deep inside her body, took its place. That warmth gushed forth, overflowing all possible limits, and she wanted nothing more than for the mesmeric moment to go on forever. She slipped her arms around his neck and melted a little deeper into his embrace.

Essie responded to each successive kiss just as she did before and never before had a woman's kisses affected him so deeply. The fierce passion erupting between them threatened his reason as well as his resolve. But then the subtle whispers located somewhere in the back of his mind reminded him that above all else, he needed to protect her from the ominous forces that lurked in the shadows. Forces she didn't truly understand. He couldn't do that unless he maintained his wits. Yet, despite his dogged determination to remain ever vigilant, he kissed her twice more before he mustered the strength to rein in his desire.

She took a much-needed breath then and melded her soft, golden brown eyes to his. "Much more of that, Lord Garreth, and you'll make me forget the reason we're here."

"I can return the same compliment to you, cariad." Garreth brushed his fingers through her hair and paused for a moment just for the pleasure it gave him to look at her. He shook his head and released a ragged breath. "I don't think you know what you do to me, woman."

In response to his comment, she took in a shallow breath and blushed. "A compliment I can return as well," she whispered.

That earned her another kiss, and then another.

Good job, Garreth.

He flashed a self-deprecating grin and then cocked his head in the direction of the encampment. "Come on, we'd better get back before I lose all self-control."

The night passed without incident and just as the dawn touched the sky, they mounted their horses and continued east. The final leg of this journey gave him the most concern. Not that he believed anyone followed them at this point. Cledwyn and Aneirin would have perceived it if they had. No, the hidden cave itself worried him far more than any tangible threat from man or beast. They had no idea what awaited them inside the cavern, and Essie would plunge headlong into the danger without a second thought. The very thought of something terrible happening to her, devastated him.

About three hours later, he reined his mount to a halt, withdrew the map, and compared it to their current surroundings. The large, jagged rock protruding from the ground matched the illustration he held in his hand. His gaze traveled upward as he assessed the steep, rocky hill that loomed before them. They would need to get to the other side. "We'll need to journey the rest of the way on foot."

"If such is the case, then we should also take a moment to refresh ourselves," said Cledwyn as he gave his horse a gentle pat and then dismounted. "After we've eaten, we'll take only what we need to complete our journey and leave the rest behind. Agreed?"

Once they secured the horses in a cloistered area suitable for grazing and with plenty of water from a nearby stream, they donned their lightened packs. Garreth claimed Essie's hand, and drew her near to his side. "Stay close to me. I need you to promise me that, all right?"

She simply nodded as he turned and headed for the northern side of the hill. The steep, winding twists and turns of the climb didn't show them any mercy. The higher their ascent, the more perilous the climb. The surrounding trees and dense foliage darkened their trail. The waning light of the setting sun didn't help their cause, either. Unfamiliar sounds of forest creatures heightened his senses as he traveled along the designated path.

Finally, just up ahead, he spied the remains of an ancient, petrified tree noted in the illustration. They should find the entrance to the cave just to the left of the gnarled branch. He motioned his companions forward as he maneuvered through the overhang of thick vegetation and stepped through the tapered fissure. The moment they entered the dark cavern, Cledwyn withdrew a length of uniquely sculpted quartz crystal. He waved a hand over the rock and in the instant, brilliant light emanated from it. The light revealed a plethora of eerily shaped stalactites, in various colors, which cluttered the cave.

"From here, we're on our own," Garreth said as his gaze roamed about the chamber that contained two distinctive passageways. "I have no idea what we're looking for. So, keep your eyes open for anything unusual."

"Well, at least we weren't accosted by a dragon the moment we entered his lair," said Essie.

Garreth chuckled. "Indeed, and I suppose we can be grateful for that."

Aneirin perused the area and shrugged. "I don't see anything out of the ordinary in here. So, unless you see something I've missed, we need to choose one of those paths and move on."

"Let's start with the one on the right, and see where it leads," Garreth said.

"All right, everyone stay together and watch the placement of your feet." Cledwyn gave a nod as he lifted the torch aloft. "Let's go."

The long, dank passageway led them down a steep grade to another cavern, larger and far warmer than the first. Water dripped from a rocky ledge at the top of the wall opposite from where they now stood. Aneirin drew their attention to the crevice behind them and to the left of the chamber.

"Looks as if our initial choice didn't matter, for it appears both passageways converge right here."

"So it seems. Does anyone see anything that needs further examination inside this cavity?" Cledwyn extended the crystal torch and made a slow, thorough sweep of the surrounding area. "I only see a smattering of stalactites and nothing more."

"Better to ask Essie that question," Garreth replied. "She has a better eye for that sort of thing."

She met the comment with laughter. "Need I remind you yet again of what happened the last time we searched a cave looking for something out of place—not to mention the fiasco inside Nia's bedroom."

Cledwyn's eyes darted back and forth between Essie and him. "May I ask what happened inside the cave the last time?"

"One of our earthquakes occurred and the ground gave way beneath our feet," he replied. "As fate would have it, we ended up in the river below after which you and your men promptly rescued us."

"Ah. I wondered how you got wet."

Garreth turned to face Essie. From all appearances, she had shifted her attention away from the conversation and placed it on the wall of the cavity. "Is something wrong?"

"I'm trying to figure out where the water is going," she said. "The ground below looks dry."

"Let's go find out." He took hold of her hand and headed for the ledge. The familiar, slick, loose pebbles along the way drew his gaze upward to assess the damaged ceiling. Over the centuries, quakes had affected the stability of this cavern just as it had inside Glodrydd's cave. They needed to discover the secrets within and quit the place before the fragile stalactites crumbled down around them in response to their mere presence.

"Look Garreth," said Essie pointing at the dark chasm that ran parallel to the wall. "That looks like a set of steps leading downward, crude though they may be, don't you think?"

"Yes, it does. Cledwyn, can you cast some light on the thing?"

In answer, Cledwyn picked his way to the edge, stooped down, and made a slow sweep of the area with his torch. "I'm guessing that someone from a far distant time fashioned these ancient stairs out of the rock."

"Ancient indeed and they don't look very stable at present," Aneirin replied.

"Stable or not, we're going to have to see where they take us," Garreth said.

"You're right, of course. I'll go ahead and lead the way. However, if I plummet off the side, you might want to stop and retrace your steps." Cledwyn took in a deep breath and motioned them forward with a wave of his hand.

"I'll bring up the rear in the event someone needs to grab hold of Essie," said Aneirin.

Garreth didn't intend to let Essie fall, nor would he allow any harm to come to her. He firmed his grip on her hand as they followed Cledwyn's slow, careful, footsteps. Aneirin remained close behind. The stairs, secure enough to hold their weight, dropped them at least twenty feet into the earth, maybe more. A narrow corridor met them at the bottom. They followed its continuous, sloping curve until it broadened. Moonlight filtered in through a crevice at the top of the mountain and lit up the grotto they now entered.

Garreth looked over Cledwyn's shoulder. He focused his gaze in the center of the chamber on the large, round rock that rested on top of a stone platform made by human hands. The light of the moon and stars illuminated the smooth, flat surface. In that same moment, Cledwyn halted in his tracks.

"Would you look at that," he said as he aimed the light at the ground in front of the rock.

Aneirin leaned forward, straining to see. "What is that thing?"

"I don't know," whispered Cledwyn. "I can, however, tell you the creature is dead."

"I compliment you on your perceptive examination of the beast." Aneirin quipped.

Garreth, with Essie in hand, moved around Cledwyn, and knelt beside a set of massive bones that circled the entire dais. He ran a hand across the gaping jaws from which protruded several sharp teeth. His gaze then swept over the portion of skeletal remains they could see from their vantage point.

"These bones right here look like they might've once formed wings," he said, indicating them with a nod. "And very large wings, at that."

Essie drew her brows together as she shook her head. "You surely aren't suggesting this is the skeleton of a dragon, are you?"

"I didn't suggest anything," he said. "I merely pointed out the facts."

"Why would such a notion trouble you anyway, Essie?" asked Aneirin. "There are countless stories of dragons from all over the world."

"That's right," she said. "They're just *stories*— stories meant to delight children, nothing more."

"Are you so sure about that? Many myths are based in truth," Cledwyn reminded her. "So if not a dragon, exactly what kind of creature do you think this is?"

"Oh, I don't know." She sought a reasonable explanation. "Perhaps it's a pterosaur. They're known to have wing spans in excess of thirty feet."

"Very possible," said Garreth as he stood to his feet and wiped the dust from his hands.

Aneirin let loose a derisive snort. "That doesn't make sense. How would you explain the presence of a pterosaur inside this cave and how would it have come to wrap itself around a dais made by human hands?"

"Perhaps those responsible for the structure found the bones. After the discovery they fashioned the dais and stone in the center of its deathbed, and all in deference to what they *thought* was a dragon," she said.

Aneirin put a hand to his hip, the look on his face, skeptical. "I don't know. Do pterosaurs even have teeth such as those? I thought they had beaks like a bird."

"Well, here," said Essie as she shrugged off her pack and retrieved her notebook and pencil. "Let me make a drawing of the bones and we'll compare it to the drawings of pterosaurs on the internet when we get home."

"If you wish," Garreth said and while Essie set about her task, he and his companions walked a complete circle around the stone. The body and tail of the creature wrapped around the entire dais and touched the jaw.

Aneirin hopped over the skeleton and stepped onto the polished platform. He focused his gaze on the flat surface of the circular stone. He studied it for a moment, and then beckoned him forward with a wave of his hand. "Garreth, what do you make of this?"

Essie lifted her pencil off the page and tracked his progress as he made his way to Aneirin's side. Cledwyn tagged along behind him. He spared Essie a quick glance before he dropped his gaze to the round, black iron surface, set inside the lip of the stone. The surprise must have registered on his face, for Essie rose to her feet and fused her gaze to his.

"What is it Garreth? What's up there?"

Garreth took in a deep breath and lifted his brows. He didn't want to tell her. But already she picked her way across the bones on her way to his side. She would see it for herself. He cleared his throat. "We have, inlaid in brass, the depiction of a black dragon. Within the dragon, on the left side of his chest where his heart would be located if alive, is a hollow—in the form of a hawk."

Chapter Thirteen

Essie swallowed past the lump in her throat as she gazed at the European style dragon, exactly like the one in her dream. The etching of the creature, situated on the inner iron plate on top of the altar, measured about eighteen inches in height. He sat on his haunches with his neck arched and wings subdued. A one-inch band of brass outlined the body and highlighted the prominent features. The deep hollow within the cavity of the dragon's chest, in the defined shape of a hawk, sent shivers down her spine. Her dreams, the message of the Ogham writing on Glodrydd's cave, and the words of the palimpsests coursed through her mind in a tangled, chaotic mess. Visions of Garreth's death returned to haunt her. Did those visions serve as an omen of some kind or a devastating statement of fact, which nothing could amend? No, she wouldn't accept the latter. She couldn't. Her love for Garreth ran too deep. She couldn't lose him now—not now.

She opened a new page of her notebook and copied the depiction simply because it gave her something to occupy her hands while she struggled for control over her emotions. The seven peculiar symbols spaced evenly within the outer rim, provided additional time and she needed every minute she could find to compose herself. Garreth tilted his head to the side, and fixed his concerned gaze to her face. She didn't want to address that concern right now. While she made her sketch, no one spoke. Finally, after she completed the drawing, giving it as many details as she could possibly think to give, she finished sketching the bones. Then, with nothing more to do, she closed the book, turned to face her companions, and gulped.

In a bid for normalcy, she scrunched her shoulders together and took in the faces of her companions. "Well, I think we now know the shape and size of the dragon's heart. Now all we need do is find the piece, return it to its proper place, and do it in time to stop the disaster."

Garreth brushed her hair away from her face and swept it behind her shoulder. Obviously he could see right through her pitiful facade. He took hold of her hand. "A task more daunting than finding the location of the dragon's lair, for this time, we have no clues to aid our search."

"At least not yet," said Cledwyn.

Aneirin turned to face them and paused for a moment. "Do you think our mongrel knows where the heart is?"

"Better yet, I wonder if he already has the thing in his possession," said Cledwyn.

"If he does, that would certainly hasten a successful conclusion to our quest," Garreth replied. "All we'd have to do then is relieve him of the thing and bring it back here."

"But how do we discover who *he* is?" asked Essie. "I've never seen anything more than a shadow and the ghostly apparition of a wolf."

"There are ways to ferret him out, Essie," said Cledwyn. "But those ways will include time, patience, and a bit of cunning on our part."

Garreth lifted a brow. "Do you have something in mind?"

Cledwyn took on a contemplative expression. "No, not yet. Well, at least not the details. But I should think that rather than allowing him to guide our path with the crumbs he throws our way, we should throw a few crumbs of our own."

Garreth grinned. "Excellent plan, Cledwyn. Once we return, we can make him believe we've attained far more knowledge than what we actually have. Such a ruse just might make him careless."

"And that will surely lead to his exposure," said Cledwyn. "If the fates are willing to assist us in our mission, we'll be there when it happens. Once we uncover his identity, we'll have access to all he has regarding this mystery. The key is—we want him to remain ignorant of that fact *until* we have collected everything we need."

"Yes, but we should also keep in mind that our wolf may not have the heart in his possession," Essie said. "Perhaps he's hoping we'll find it for him. If such is the case, then we have no choice but to keep looking. Time is growing ever shorter."

"I know. Don't worry. I have every intention of continuing our search," Garreth replied.

Soon thereafter, they made their way out of the interior cavern and up the crumbling stairs. The instant they returned to the outer chamber, Garreth glanced at the passageway they still needed to explore.

"Let's make our exit through the opposite corridor," he said. "I want to make sure there's nothing there we need to discover before we quit this place."

Cledwyn directed the crystal to the opening, scanned the terrain in search of the least troublesome path, and waved a hand. "All right, follow me."

They picked their way through the clutter of rocky debris and around the fragile stalactites. Once inside the uncharted passageway, Cledwyn slowed his steps and made a thorough search on each side of the stony walls while they traversed the path back to the mountain fissure. Then, just as faint moonlight gleamed from the other end, Essie gasped and halted her steps.

"Cledwyn, wait. I need you to bring the light back here again. Right here in this area, please," she said pointing to the left hand side of the wall, shoulder high. The light from the crystal torch revealed a cluster of faint markings.

First she used her fingertips and then the palms of her hands to brush away the buildup that had attached to the carving over the centuries. She shook her head and huffed out an impatient breath. "Does anyone have any water left? I'm going to need more than what I have," she said as she dug around inside her pack, extracted her water bottle and pocketknife.

"Here, you can take mine," said Garreth. "If you need more, we can go back and fill the bottles."

She merely nodded in response as she doused the wall with the water everyone handed her at once and painstakingly removed the silt from each symbol, one at a time. Finally, she exposed the entire carving to their view. She traced each character with the tip of her knife in order to define it.

"This style of Ogham is far different from what we found inside Glodrydd's cave, Garreth," she said.

"Is it a style you recognize?"

She closed her eyes and released a sigh. "No, I'm afraid not."

"Do you think you can find a way to interpret the thing?"

"Of course. You're the one that told me there is always a way. As you know, our first task is to look for small similarities in the writing we already have."

Aneirin put a hand on her shoulder. "Perhaps Uvan can help with the task. He's one of the ancients. There's a chance he can read it or at the very least, provide a bit of assistance in deciphering it."

Cledwyn nodded. "He might at that."

"That would be a blessing," said Essie as she dropped her knife inside her pack and withdrew her notebook. "I didn't bring my camera, so give me a minute to copy this down and then we can go."

Just before they vacated the cave, Cledwyn turned to face them. He gazed into each of their faces. "Remember Uvan's warning, the knowledge of what's inside this cave must not be uttered aloud once we're out in the open."

The comment gave her pause. "He's right, Garreth. So, how are we going to figure this out if we can't discuss it once we're home?"

"Not to worry, Essie," Cledwyn cut in. He gave her a confident wink. "Uvan can provide a safe haven if you desire one. All you have to do is ask him."

She recalled then, the words of King Gwynn and his admonishment not to discuss the purpose of their visit outside his study. "Perfect. I think we're going to need such a place."

"All right, let's get a move on," said Garreth. "I'd like to get just as far down the mountain as we can possibly manage tonight."

The climb down seemed even more daunting than the climb up. After a couple of hours, they found a suitable niche in which to pass the remainder of the night. At once, their Fair companions made a thorough sweep of the surrounding area. They deemed it clear of phantom wolves or any other ethereal creature that might pose a threat and immediately set up a makeshift camp.

"Hey, Essie," said Aneirin, the moment he produced a roaring fire with nothing more than a few dead tree branches. "I just had another thought."

"Another thought?" she repeated with a slight shake of her head. Her mind traveled to the bones inside the cave, the carving on top of the altar, and even the mysterious symbols on the wall.

"Yes, and it's a brilliant one if I do say so myself." He raised a hand and swept the heavens. "Starry Evening DeSpencer. Am I right?"

Cledwyn all but doubled over with laughter. "You think that's brilliant, Aneirin? I have one so much better than that. I've been saving it. Is everyone ready? Solar Eclipse—Solar Eclipse DeSpencer. Just picture her parents, waiting for the celestial moment to happen. They gaze deeply into each other's eyes and then suddenly, Mr. DeSpencer smiles at Mrs. DeSpencer—"

Essie put a hand on her hip, focused on the ground beneath her feet, and sighed. "Oh boy, here we go again."

****

The return journey to the realm of the Tylwyth Teg didn't seem nearly as long as the journey to the dragon's lair. Once again, the King, somehow already expecting their arrival, awaited them inside his study. His smile broadened as they entered. With an impatient hand, he waved them forward.

"Come in my friends, come in. Aneirin, make sure the door is closed."

Once they settled into their seats, Gwynn placed clasped hands on top of the desk. "Now then, Garreth, tell me what you found."

Garreth propped a booted foot across his knee as he gazed at the king. "We found an intricate etching of a black iron dragon, missing a heart. The hollow cavity is in the shape of a hawk, approximately four inches in length, and three in both width, and depth. We now know the shape of what we need to find and where to place it once we have it in our possession. All we have to do is find it."

"Excellent," he said. "Tell me all about your experience. I want all of the details from start to finish."

Garreth ended his report by handing Gwynn Essie's sketches of the dragon, the bones surrounding the altar, and the Ogham carving. He paused, giving the king ample time to study them.

"We're hoping that perhaps Uvan can help us decipher the message on the cave wall," he said once the man finished his study of the illustrations.

"No better time than right now to ask." Gwynn replied as he rose from his seat, took hold of the notebook, and motioned them toward the door. "Shall we? Oh by the way, I have eliminated Ceri and Eleri from our list of suspects. I am quite certain neither of them have anything to do with this intrigue."

The moment they entered Uvan's private sanctuary, the king approached the ancient wizard and handed him the sketches. "What do you make of these?"

Uvan glanced at the sketch of the bones first. After a moment, he fixed his mirthful gaze upon Garreth. "Ah, it looks like we have us a dragon after all, wouldn't you say?"

Garreth hooked a thumb inside his pocket and shrugged. "Essie would like to do some comparisons before we name the creature."

Uvan merely laughed as he turned the page. He examined the drawings of the altar and the Ogham carving at length before he lifted his eyes from the pages. He looked about the room with slow deliberation, taking in his vast stocks of scrolls and parchment as he did so. He put a hand to his beard and gave it a gentle tug as he finally shifted his attention to her.

"I'm afraid I don't know the meaning of all these symbols, Essie," he said. "But I might have something that will help you uncover the complete message."

"You do?"

Uvan nodded while he handed her the notebook. "Yes, I have in my possession, a piece of parchment that Glodrydd found a few months before the second catastrophe took his life."

Garreth seemed surprised. "Is that right?"

"Yes, indeed. You see, at that particular time, Glodrydd stumbled across what he believed to be an omen concerning the disastrous cycles. Since we were working together on this dilemma, he presented the piece to me, desiring my thoughts. I'm sorry to say he never returned to collect it."

Gwynn looked every bit as surprised as Garreth.

"You never told me that, Uvan."

Uvan returned a guilty shrug. "No, I didn't. At the time he presented it, we couldn't make sense of it. We wanted to have proof of its worth before we disclosed it. Glodrydd died shortly thereafter and any hope to translate it, died with him. After the passing of so many centuries, I must confess that I had quite forgotten about it until now."

The king nodded. "I see. So, can you tell us anything at all about this parchment?"

"Only that Glodrydd found it encased in a tiny stone cavity within the cave in Garreth's kingdom."

Essie pounced over the revelation. "He did? Did he find anything else inside the cave?"

"Not to my knowledge," Uvan said as he toddled over to his shelves and began sorting through the vast number of dusty manuscripts. "I know he spent years searching the thing in its entirety."

"You said that Glodrydd believed the parchment spoke of an omen concerning the apocalypse. Why would he think that since you couldn't decipher the text?" asked Garreth.

"Though we couldn't identify the text, we could identify the number symbols, for these have changed very little over time. Also, the symbols for the basic elements, earth, wind, fire, and water have also remained constant."

"The parchment speaks of the elements?" asked Essie.

Uvan nodded alongside a grunt as he yanked a sheet from near the bottom of a stack. "Yes it does, but the specific connotation contained in the message escaped us. However, the numbers indicated the four hundred year intervals we've witnessed three times this far, and in each apocalypse, we've witnessed the destruction caused by each of the elements. I must also tell you, there's a depiction of a hawk much like the one in your drawing, Essie. This, of course, is what led to Glodrydd's quest and for understandable reasons."

Essie made her way to the table in response to Uvan's unspoken invitation. He smoothed out the parchment and then pointed to the specific symbols he could decipher. "This one here represents the number four, this one represents one hundred. These here are the symbols for the elements. The first is wind, followed by water. You must decipher all of the words before and in between them for them to make any real sense, I suspect. The second line shows the symbols for earth, located here and fire, which our author placed here. Of course, the hawk's placement is obvious."

Though Uvan gave fair warning, the illustration of the hawk caused a slow thud in the beat of her heart. What did Garreth's kingdom have to do with all this madness? Coincidence alone couldn't possibly be a factor, could it? The troubling thoughts plagued her mind as she copied each of the known symbols into her book and identified them for future use.

Finally, she shifted her gaze to Uvan. "You wouldn't happen to have any other examples of this particular style in your possession, would you?"

"I don't really know, Essie. I've accumulated my library over the course of many centuries. Some of the books and scrolls, I must admit, I've never even glanced at. But, you're welcome to muddle through them if you wish."

Essie cast her gaze about the cluttered shelves and

blew out a breath. Still, the daunting task needed doing if she had any hope of deciphering the scroll and the pictograph in a timely manner. "Then I suppose I should get started right now, because it looks like it's going to take two or three days to go through everything you have."

"I wonder, Garreth, if you should return to your realm while Essie examines the scrolls," said Cledwyn.

A twinge of unease set in the moment he made the suggestion. She whirled around to face Garreth.

He briefly met her gaze before giving Cledwyn his full attention. "Why would you think something like that would work to our advantage, Cledwyn? Our wolf, whether from your realm or mine, would know she's here without me. That poses a possible danger I don't intend to risk."

"The risk won't exist if we make it appear we're taking her to the airport. If we can get our wolf to follow us there, we can unmask him," he said.

"How will you make it appear she's leaving this realm when she is not?"

Gwynn took a step forward and placed a hand on top of his shoulder. "My wife can make herself look very similar. I'll ask her to dress in Essie's clothing and simply put you both in the car about dusk and make a trip to the airport. She'll board a plane and before it takes off, she can disappear and return home with no one the wiser. You needn't worry. I give you my solemn word that we'll take very good care of Essie while she's our guest. Once she's completed her task, we'll get in contact with you."

"Yes," said Cledwyn. "At that point we can cloak Essie's presence, take her to the airport, and you can make the pretense of picking her up and taking her home."

The more detailed the plan, the more reasonable it sounded to her, even though it meant that she wouldn't see Garreth at all during the length of her stay. "You know, our ruse would take on a little more credibility if I actually went somewhere and returned with something we—or at least the wolf—might deem significant."

"I don't think that's necessary, Essie," said Garreth. "The plan here is to catch him during our first trip to the airport."

"Yes, but what if he doesn't take the bait right away? What if he wants to wait until I return when it's just you picking me up without any member of the Fair folk around?"

"She's right about that, Garreth," said Cledwyn. "Our wolf just might want to wait until you're alone."

Garreth cast his gaze downward and paused as he considered their arguments. His heart sank over the mere thought of Essie's absence. Yet, if they could bring a quick end to the approaching disaster, then he would make the sacrifice. "All right, should our wolf elude us the first time around, we'll include such a trip in the final stages of our plan. But only if we can think of a credible place for her to go."

"I already have one," said Essie. "Since our wolf knows about the references to the black dragon, I can visit the Hunterian Museum in Glasgow. They have several pterosaur wing fossils I can examine and compare to our creature in the cave. I could purchase a couple of books on the subject of dragons and then come home. I need only be gone for a day."

Garreth returned a slow nod. "All right. If that's

your wish, I'll arrange a ticket and a car rental."

"Don't look so glum, Garreth," said Aneirin. "This is only going to take a few days and I promise we'll take good care of your lady while she's with us."

"I'm counting on that," he said. "See to it that you don't disappoint me."

Shortly before dusk, Gwynn escorted Hefina into the small bedchamber across from Uvan's, where Essie waited. The queen smiled as she approached and then offered her the bag she held in her hand. "This is filled with a few changes of clothing and personal items in case you need them during your stay."

"Thank you. As always you're very kind," Essie replied. She turned her gaze toward the bed, swept a hand over the jeans and T-shirt, and shrugged. "I'm afraid these are only clean clothes I have to offer in return."

"They're perfect," she said.

Once Hefina donned her clothes, she took in a breath, tilted her chin upward, and closed her eyes. Within minutes the queen completed her transformation. The spectacle fascinated her no end.

"How do I look?" The queen twirled a full circle.

Essie rubbed her lips together and lifted her brows a tad. "Almost like I'm looking into a mirror."

Hefina laughed as she headed to the door and grasped the latch. "I'll send Garreth in. I'm sure he wants to bid you farewell before we leave."

Garreth must have lurked in the hallway, for the instant the door opened, he stepped inside. A moment later, he had her in his arms. "I'm not sure I like this little arrangement," he said.

"Well, if my stay unmasks our wolf, then it'll be

worth the risk, don't you think?"

"The risk isn't what I'm talking about, Essie, though that is a concern, of course. No, what I'm referring to is the time I have to spend without you. Whether you realize it or not, I've grown quite accustomed to having you at my side. The days will be far too long without you—far too long."

He didn't give her the chance to respond to his comment, nor did she have any desire to say anything in return once his lips took possession of hers. A gentle knock at the door ended the kisses that professed his tender sentiments and left her breathless.

"Are you ready?" Cledwyn called out from the other side of the door. "We need to get going."

Garreth shook his head, and released a breath of resignation. "Don't be gone long Essie," he whispered huskily. "Get your work done and please, for my sake, hurry home."

Chapter Fourteen

Essie wound the final scroll, secured the leather strip around it, and returned it to its proper place on the shelf. She turned around to face the table and settled her gaze on her notebook. For all the long, tedious, hours she spent examining each piece of parchment and every scroll Uvan owned, she had very little to show for it. In fact, she had less than three sparse pages to account for her time. Would those few pages be enough?

"Why the solemn sigh, Essie?" Uvan asked, without diverting his attention away from his microscope and boiling bottles of colorful liquids.

"Oh, I don't know. I suppose for one, I just finished going through everything your library has to offer and two, I found very little that matches the writing on Glodrydd's parchment."

He glanced up then and she found his ancient eyes filled with humor. "Still, some is far better than none, I should think."

"Yes, I suppose you're right about that," she said as she returned to her table. "And, if I'm lucky, what I have will be sufficient to decipher the symbols. If it is, then all I have to do is put it together and hope it makes sense."

"I wished I could be of more help to you, but alas, my talents and interests have always been and are now, firmly entrenched in the science of alchemy and the metaphysical—" Uvan shrugged away the remainder of his sentence.

"Actually, there might be a way you can help me, if you're willing." Essie closed her notebook and then shifted her gaze to meet with his.

He turned and faced her head on, giving her his undivided attention. "My dear Essie, you've but to ask."

"Let's see. How shall I put this?" She nibbled at a fingernail for a moment as she gazed at her companion. "Cledwyn mentioned that you have the ability to create a safe place inside Garreth's castle—a library perhaps—closed to those who might seek to eavesdrop on conversations or examine things, which are none of their concern."

A slight grin tugged at the corners of his mouth. "I believe I can take care of that for you and what's more, I'll have it done before you return from Glasgow. Will that please you?"

"Very much so. Thank you."

"Oh, and speaking of that trip to Scotland? If you find yourself feeling a bit perplexed while you're there, pay a visit to a man named Ian Penrose. He isn't at all hard to find, and I'm sure he can answer all of the questions you'll surely have at the end of the day."

"All right, I'll keep that in mind."

Just as she made the remark, Gwynn entered the chamber and fastened his gaze to hers. "Are you close to finishing your task?"

"I am finished. I placed the very last scroll back on the shelf a few minutes ago," she said.

"Excellent. I've just received word from Garreth. He's arranged your ticket, a car, and a hotel room.

Therefore, we'll whisk you off to the airport a little later this evening, and then he'll pick you up at the same time tomorrow. Is that satisfactory?"

The very mention of seeing Garreth again stirred the embers in her heart and gave them life. Oh, how she longed for that moment. She breathed out a sigh, and nodded. "Yes, that sounds really good."

****

Garreth gazed out at the view from his library window. Yet, he truly didn't take note of what it had to offer. His thoughts remained firmly centered on Essie. He missed her far more than he thought possible, and he wanted her home.

Home.

Did she know how many times she referred to Llys y Gwalch as home while they searched for the dragon's lair? The memory of each instance filled him with a sense of contentment and pleasure. If he had anything to say about it, this would be her home. Permanently— for the rest of their very long lives.

"Begging your pardon, Prince Garreth," said the voice behind him.

Garreth whirled around to face his unexpected companion. A companion he didn't hear come in. Nonetheless, Uvan stood in the center of the room. He bowed his head as their gazes met. "Hello, Uvan."

A slight grin emerged on the wizard's face. "Sorry, I didn't mean to startle you or intrude upon your thoughts. But, I'm here to fulfill a promise."

He approached his guest. "A promise?"

"Yes, indeed and I always keep my promises." He lifted a finger to his lips, to stay further questions.

For the next several minutes, Uvan traversed every

inch of the room, paying close attention to the windows and doors. He sprinkled some sort of substance that sparkled as it scattered and then disappeared. All the while, the man whispered words he didn't quite hear. Finally, the wizard turned away from his task and met his gaze.

"I'm finished here. This room is now secure from all outside forces wishing to intrude on your privacy. Anything you say or do will remain inside these walls unless the witnesses disclose it either by design or accident. I'm afraid there's nothing I can do about that should the incident occur."

"Thank you, Uvan. I appreciate your help more than you know."

"Your gratitude is unnecessary. I'm happy to assist you any way I can. Such a thing makes an old man feel useful. Now then, before I go, do you have any other rooms you wish to secure?"

Essie's late night visitor popped into his mind, as did her disturbing nightmares, and the fact she copied relevant references into her notebook after she retired for the night. Since they didn't catch their wolf at the airport as they'd hoped, the man could still pose a threat to his lady. Especially if desperation set in. "If you don't mind I would appreciate it if you would secure Essie's bedroom as well as my own."

A short while later, Uvan finished his task and disappeared from the castle as silently as he had entered it. Immediately thereafter, Garreth sought Bran out, and with a slight tilt of his head, invited him to follow. This far, he hadn't mentioned anything of importance to his chamberlain, save the fact he put Essie on a plane. Bran understood the silence without his having to give an explanation. Once inside the library, he shut the door firmly behind them.

"Gwynn's advisor has just paid a visit to the castle and left us a gift. We are now free to speak of confidential things inside this room, but in this room only, Bran. Please keep that in mind."

"You needn't worry, and you have no idea how relieved I am to hear we finally have a place to speak openly. Because I have a few things I need to share with you."

"All right, have a seat. But I'd like to catch you up on our latest adventure first, if you don't mind." Garreth offered the chair in front of his desk as he sat in the one behind it.

At the end of his narrative, Bran scratched a finger across his brow. "All very interesting. You know, Garreth, we've gained a great deal of knowledge since Essie's arrival."

"Yes we have and right now, I can't tell you how grateful I am we chose to ignore our inaccurate perception as to her age and physical ability."

Bran laughed over the hours they debated the issue. "That among other things. Looking back on it now, I wonder what made us so certain we'd greet a woman elderly and infirm."

"I don't know. Perhaps her vast experience in the field, which, by the way, began in her childhood. Or maybe we thought her old and feeble because she uses her initials."

"Speaking of those initials, has she ever revealed the names that go along with them?"

"Not yet, but don't worry. I'll have that information in due course. You can count on it."

"I've no doubt you will. The question is—which will you solve first? The mystery of Essie's initials or the location of and mystery surrounding the heart of that bloody dragon."

"At this point, the location of the heart and the part it plays is far more important than the name Essie's parents gave her at birth. And in regards to that heart—" Garreth opened the topmost right hand drawer and withdrew his father's ring. He placed it on his index finger. For a few quiet moments, he twirled it around with his thumb as he fixed his gaze to the golden goshawk that centered the piece. "The heart we seek is identical to the image of this hawk right here, save its size."

"Do you think the dragon's heart is made of gold then?"

"I don't know. The relic could be made of anything. All I know is the shape of the hollow matches the insignia on my father's ring with exactness. Yet, given Essie's nightmares, especially the last one inside the cottage, I'd like to keep this information from her as long as possible."

Bran nodded. "I'd have to agree with you there. Such a thing would probably cause her undue worry and stress. Right now, she needs to concentrate all her efforts on deciphering the message inside the dragon's lair."

"You know, I've wondered, ever since Essie discovered that particular pictograph, if it might contain some kind of instruction, or, as ridiculous as it sounds, some incantation that corresponds with the placement of the heart. The problem is we only have one shot to do this right."

"Well, I'm sure if anyone can figure that out, it will be Essie." Bran combed through his mustache with the tips of his fingers as he took on a thoughtful expression. "Speaking of Essie, you say she didn't truly leave for Scotland until yesterday?"

Garreth shook his head, tugged the ring off his finger, and tossed it back inside the drawer. "No, she didn't."

"And neither Cledwyn nor Aneirin sensed the presence of anyone with Fair blood the day you escorted Hefina to the airport in her place?"

"No, I'm afraid they didn't. That in itself gives credence to the notion that our wolf lives here in Llys y Gwalch. If he does, then he'll surely believe that I did in fact put Essie on a plane for Scotland, and therefore, will be watching for my trip to the airport."

"Well, if he does live here, that will surely narrow down his or her identity."

"Yes, it will. We already know those who carry Fair blood make up a small portion of our residents. That alone should assist us in unmasking him."

"Perhaps we should compile a list."

"Might not hurt and if you don't mind, I'll go ahead and let you take on that duty."

"Consider it done." He paused. "Essie is coming home this evening you say?"

"She is. In implementing this portion of our plan, Essie and I will give our wolf a couple of false leads to whet his appetite if he follows me to the airport. Perhaps in so doing, he'll grow careless enough to expose himself in some way."

"Speaking of our elusive shifter, I had quite an interesting conversation with Helyan while you and

Essie were off on your expedition to the dragon's lair."

Garreth leaned forward as he clasped his hands on top of the desk. "Oh?"

"According to our ghostly comrade, a rather large wolf paid a midnight visit to the cemetery the same day you encountered a wolf of like description inside Nia's bedchamber."

"Is that right?"

"Yes, and according to Helyan, the wolf made a straight path to Nia's grave. He sniffed around a bit and then dug a sizeable hole off to the side of her stone."

"Did he put something in the hole or did he take something out?"

"Neither, for during the dig, the wolf appeared to sense the presence of the ghosts. According to Helyan, he looked right at them and then tore off. Helyan and a few of his companions followed, of course. However, just outside the cemetery, the wolf vanished into thin air. They investigated the hole directly afterward, but found nothing inside."

"Did you ask him if the wolf carried anything in his mouth?"

"No, I didn't. I didn't want to give away any information out there in the open where my words might be overheard. Therefore, I shrugged the whole thing off as if it held no great importance. However, I did ask Helyan if he saw anything else out of the ordinary and unfortunately, he said no."

"Good man." Garreth took a few minutes to organize his thoughts. "The way I see it, our wolf didn't dig for the sake of digging. So either he intended to bury something, like a torn palimpsest, or he intended to dig something out, like a heart in the shape of a hawk. Somehow, we need to discover his intent."

"I don't believe Helyan or any of his ghostly companions possess the skill to dig into the earth," said Bran. "That will take physical labor by a pair of tangible hands. However, we can assign him to watch for the wolf's return—*if* the wolf returns at all."

"If he has something in the ground he wants out, he'll have to return. However, please keep in mind the ghosts can't stop him from retrieving whatever might be buried."

"Then we need to get there first."

"Yes, but I'd rather do it when he's not there to watch our every move," he said.

"How do you figure on doing that since the Fair folk can make themselves invisible to our eyes?"

"I think I can get Cledwyn or Aneirin to help us."

"Better not wait too long—"

"Did I hear someone mention our names?"

Bran twirled around in his chair the moment Cledwyn uttered his first word. Garreth shifted his gaze from his chamberlain's startled face, to acknowledge the presence of his guests.

Aneirin looked about the room and nodded his approval. "Uvan did a good job. We didn't even suspect you were here, but thought we'd check anyway."

Garreth flashed a grin and nodded. "Good to know."

"In light of Essie's return later this evening, we decided to pay you a visit now and devise something to gain the attention of our ethereal friend—if he's watching," Cledwyn said.

"Do you have something in mind?"

"Considering what you've revealed already, two

things come to mind," he said. "First, we can search Nia's bedchamber, and then pay a visit to the tomb of the kings. I think our wolf expects you to ask for our help in examining these areas a little more thoroughly. Of course, we already know we aren't going to find anything in Nia's room because he will already have removed it. However, once we visit the tomb, we can make him believe we've discovered something of significance inside it."

"The plan is a good one," Garreth said. "But before we leave this room, I think there's something else you should know about our phantom wolf. Bran, why don't you tell them what you've just told me?"

Cledwyn and Aneirin listened without interruption as Bran related the details of the wolf's visit to Nia's grave.

"Well," said Cledwyn at the end of the tale, "we'll need to find an opportune time to scan this area ourselves. If he buried the heart, we need to collect it before he moves it elsewhere."

"We'll also need you to let us know the exact moment that opportune moment arrives," Bran replied.

"Will do," he said. "So, are we ready for this phase of our plan?"

In response to his question, Garreth rose from his chair, withdrew a large ring of keys from his desk drawer, and made his way to the door. As he opened it and stepped into the hall, he said for the benefit of anyone who might be listening, "Thank you both for coming. I appreciate any help you can give me in this matter and please be sure to pass along my gratitude to Gwynn."

"Of course. We're happy to help in any way we

can, Prince Garreth," said Cledwyn as he bowed at the waist in a show of respect. "The king is pleased we're finally working together on this issue."

"Come, the room Nia used is this way." Garreth led them to the other side of the castle, and down the hall to her doorway. He stuck the key into the lock and turned the latch. Cledwyn and Aneirin entered first.

"Essie found the pouch underneath the bed," he said. "We didn't find anything else, but perhaps we might've overlooked something."

"All right," said Aneirin. "Give us a moment to conduct our search and see if we can come up with anything else."

Though in all likelihood quite unnecessary, their Fair companions made a thorough sweep of the entire chamber. At the end of their inspection, they turned toward him and shrugged their apology.

"We're sorry, but we didn't find anything of significance, Lord Garreth," said Aneirin.

"I thought not," he replied. "But I wanted to make certain."

"Of course," Cledwyn replied. "So, off to the tomb of the kings then?"

About an hour later, they reined their horses to a halt just outside the iron gates and dismounted. Garreth led them through the entrance, to the back of the cemetery. Helyan, alongside a few of his companions, manifested themselves as they approached the tomb. They greeted them in their native tongue.

"Good morning, Lord Garreth," said Helyan. "Fine day for a visit to a quiet, serene cemetery, wouldn't you agree?"

Garreth understood his underlying meaning. The

wolf hadn't returned. "Fine day, indeed. How are you doing?"

"Oh, can't complain—"

While Garreth chatted with Helyan and his friends, Cledwyn and Aneirin scoured the surrounding area. Upon his return Cledwyn fastened his gaze on Nia's place of burial. "Now is a good time to explore the earth beside the grave. Aneirin will alert us if that should change."

Helyan sauntered over to the stone monument, turned around, and leaned a shoulder against the left side of the grave. Without saying a word, he shot a glance at the telltale signs of disturbed earth.

Yet, before Cledwyn could kneel beside the stone to conduct his investigation, Aneirin returned. He gave an almost imperceptible shake of his head.

Cledwyn placed one hand on his companion's shoulder, gave it a friendly shake, and gazed pointedly at the tomb entrance. "Shall we?"

Garreth led them inside the vault. He pointed out the sepulcher of Cadwr ap Brychan. "Our coin led us to that crypt there in the corner. Therefore, perhaps you might find something else of value inside the chamber."

"Rest assured, we'll spare no effort to do just that, Lord Garreth," said Aneirin.

Garreth made small talk with the ghosts and Bran, while Aneirin and Cledwyn inspected every inch of the sizeable cavern. Finally, they turned their attention to Cadwr's grave. In a movement slow and steady, Cledwyn swept a hand over the top of the sepulcher. He paused midway and cast his gaze upon Aneirin. Aneirin placed his hand alongside Cledwyn's and nodded.

"Something is inside the crypt, Garreth," said

Cledwyn. "Care to give us a hand?"

Garreth could see by expression alone that he meant what he said. At once, he and Bran assisted in the partial removal of the heavy lid. Cledwyn slipped a hand inside the sepulcher, withdrew a tattered scroll, and handed it to him. He tucked the artifact inside his shirt while they replaced the lid. The moment they had the grave secure, he retrieved the scroll. Everyone gathered around him as he untied the leather cord and unwound it.

"This looks very much like the parchment already in our possession," he said. "I wonder if it's part of our chronicle or something all together different."

"I don't know, but if the writing is the same, then Essie can decipher the thing without any trouble whatsoever," said Bran as they exited the tomb.

"True enough. But before she can accomplish that, I need to bring her home," Garreth replied.

"Yes, well, in the meantime, don't let that parchment out of your sight," said Aneirin.

"You needn't worry about that, my friend, I don't intend to."

Chapter Fifteen

Immersed deep in her troubled thoughts, Essie cast her gaze toward the ground as she made her way out of the museum and over to her car. Her visit created questions no one inside the building could answer. The depository didn't own so much as a single fossil that mirrored her drawing. They didn't even own one that resembled it. She couldn't find anything in the multitude of books either and surely they depicted every pterosaur fossil known to mankind. The highly respected paleontologist she spoke with after hours of searching scoffed at the illustration she showed him.

He rolled his eyes heavenward and released a derisive snort. "Don't tell me—Ian Penrose's work again?"

She lifted a shoulder as she gave her head a little shake and feigned ignorance as to the name. "I'm sorry. Ian Penrose?"

The man squeezed the bridge of his nose as he closed his eyes, and released an aggravated sigh. "Where did you get this drawing?"

His question caught her off-guard. "Well—uh, from—from a book in the library."

"In the science section no doubt," he sneered. "I don't know why librarians even allow his books on the same shelves. Look, you can't take any of the man's works seriously. He's a nut."

She had murmured some kind of an apology then and left the building soon after. But now that she stood here on the sidewalk, with the rain pouring down on her head, she didn't quite know what to do or where to go. Perhaps she should go ahead and pay a visit to this Ian Penrose. Uvan said she could find him easily enough. Might she find his address in one of his books? She supposed she could at least give it a try. After all, she did have a couple of hours to kill before she headed off to the airport.

Essie got into her car and drove to the bookshop that she had passed on the way to the museum. Thirty minutes later, she walked out of the building with her purchases tucked inside the sturdy shopping bag, feeling a little befuddled, and a whole lot ridiculous. 'The Science and Study of *Dragonology*?' He couldn't really be serious, could he?

Still—the books would serve as fodder for their phantom wolf. Right? Despite her misgivings, she returned to her rented car, copied Penrose's business address from volume one, and drove off. If nothing else, this fool's errand would take her close to the airport. Once she pulled up in front of his gate, which looked more like a residence than a business, she inhaled a deep breath of courage, and exited the car. Her legs carried her to the door without mishap. She knocked, stepped back, and then waited for the man to answer. Part of her prayed that he wouldn't.

He did.

An elderly gentleman opened the door a crack.

She wiped the raindrops away from her face and forced a smile as their gazes met through the small opening. "Hello, Mr. Penrose?"

"Yes, is there something I can do for you?"

"I hope so. My name is Essie DeSpencer. A friend of mine said you might be able to answer some questions I have."

He cocked his head to the side. "Does this friend of yours have a name?"

"Uvan—" she stopped short. For it occurred to her then, she had no other name to give. She certainly couldn't add, "one of the Fair folk."

Ian gazed at her for several long moments, as if assessing her character. "Ah, Uvan. I think I remember him now. The little round gentleman with dark brown hair and receding hairline, am I correct?"

"No, gray," she replied without giving it any thought. "And he's tall and slim."

Penrose smiled at her then, opened the door wide, and beckoned her inside with a wave of his fingers. "Come in, child, you're getting soaked to the skin."

He seated her in a comfortable but tattered tweed chair and then fastened his gaze to hers. "Can I get you some hot tea or some sort of refreshment to warm you up? Americans like chocolate, don't they? I could offer you some hot chocolate if you'd rather."

She shook her head as she pulled her notebook out of her bag and flipped it open. "That's very kind, but no thank you. I have a plane to catch, so I can't stay long. However, before I go, I wanted to know if you could shed some light on a particular illustration of mine."

Ian sat down opposite her, accepted the notebook she offered, and made careful study of her drawing. "Where did you get this?"

"Well, I—uh, found a replica inside a cave and made a copy for myself. Do you know what it is?" A

215

lengthy, awkward silence followed her question. She waited it out.

"All right, Miss DeSpencer, I'll give you the information you seek. These bones belong to what those of us in the dragonology field call a magnus Occidentalis draconis, or a great dragon hailing from the region surrounding the Francia Occidentalis kingdom. Furthermore, don't let anyone tell you these creatures are nothing more than a fanciful myth. I too, have seen detailed pictographs of these dragons. In truth, there are drawings in numerous caves all over the world. So at one time, man was well acquainted with these animals. They are not pterosaurs, as some scientists would have you believe. However, I do believe they evolved from the species." He traced the outline of her sketch with his fingertip. "This particular dragon generally chooses remote mountain or sea caves for their lair, and they are quite partial to the treasures of the earth, especially gold."

Did an expression of shock or disbelief register on her face? She didn't know. But she did know her expression made Ian laugh.

He rose to his feet and extended his hand. "Come with me, child. I think I'd like to share something with you that I normally don't share with unbelievers. But since you're a friend of Uvan's and he sent you my way—" He let the rest of his sentence drop as he took hold of her hand, helped her to her feet, and then escorted her down a darkened hallway.

They descended a flight of stairs and approached the steel door at the bottom, offset to the right. He withdrew a set of keys from his pocket, unlocked the numerous locks, and opened the door.

The enormous room housed a plethora of ancient fossil bones on the tables and abundant shelves. Elaborate color illustrations of various dragons from all over the world papered the walls. She gulped as he led her to the large table in the back corner of the lab.

"This is my evolutionary table," he said with a hint of pride to his tone. "The first three sets of wing bones at the top are indeed common pterosaur fossils. But if you examine these fossils in their order, you'll see the distinct changes in the humerus, pteroid, and sternum bones, taking place over time. Now then, in the last three sets of fossils here, we see the changes in the wing carpus, metacarpus, and radius. Not only do they look far different from our bones at the top of the table, they are far heavier in order to carry a far heavier species. Do you see the resemblance to your sketch?"

Essie did see it and what's more, she didn't see any of these "dragon" fossils, in any form, in the museum. "Yes. Where on earth did you get all of these specimens?"

"In various places all over the world."

"You didn't choose to share them with other scientists?"

A tired, faraway look appeared in his eyes as he shook his head. "No, not for quite some time now."

Her gaze strolled about the room. "You must have collected them over a long period of time."

He laughed as he dipped his head downward. "Yes, a very long time."

She met his gaze, and finally noted the ancient eyes that gazed back. A breath of soft laughter escaped her lips. Oh why not—"You're one of the Tylwyth Teg, aren't you."

A slight smile emerged, but he said nothing in response.

"Of course, I should've known." She tsked as she gave her head a little shake. "So tell me, have you ever actually seen a living dragon?"

"No, but my grandfather did once. As a very young man, he happened across one in its final death throes, and remained with the beast until it died. Over the years, he often spoke of the creature's nobility and magnificence. I suppose his tale is what instilled my lifelong interest in the science of Dragonology. I always hoped that one day, somewhere on this earth; I would find one yet alive. But alas, as of this moment—"

She placed a gentle hand on top of his shoulder. "Who knows, maybe one day you will."

A broad smile emerged as he gave her a wink. "In all likelihood, Miss Essie, that very hope is what keeps me going. I've a notion that in this ever-changing world of ours, if dragons still exist, they prefer solitude and a bit of quiet peace from all the noise and chaos caused by modern man—as do I."

Essie wanted so much to tell Ian about the bones and the mountain cave he could find them in. But she couldn't. Not right now anyway. Perhaps after she and Garreth completed their task, she could ask Uvan to pay him a visit. After an extensive tour of his impressive lab, she bid him goodbye and headed for the airport.

Yet, all of the interesting things they discussed fled her mind the moment she exited the plane in London, navigated through the building, and finally caught sight of Garreth, striding toward her. He had her engulfed in his arms mere seconds later. The searing kiss that followed told her just how much he missed her. She used the second to return the sentiment. The third stole away what little breath she had left and made her forget they stood inside a crowded airport with a host of enthralled onlookers passing them by. She wouldn't have cared anyway.

"Ah, I've missed you, Essie," he whispered against her ear.

"And I have missed you—far more than you know." He gazed at her then as if nothing in his life equaled her importance, not even the approaching disaster. She hoped her eyes reflected the same.

The grin that emerged said she succeeded. He caressed the side of her face. "Are you ready to go home, cariad?"

"Yes I am." Only then did she remember her part in their ruse. "I have so much to tell you. Oh—and I bought a book that contains thousands of dragon legends from around the world. I'm hoping one of them can shed a bit of light on our palimpsest. I even found a factual book on dragons, if you can believe that. At least the author treated the subject as if the creature existed at one point in time. I can't wait to show you that one."

Garreth relieved her of her cumbersome bag, laced his fingers through hers, and then headed for the exit doors. "We'll have to take a look at them as soon as we arrive at the castle then. While we're on the subject of the palimpsest, Gwynn sent Cledwyn and Aneirin to help us in our search to find more pages. They tell me the Fair folk are capable of seeing things we would most likely overlook with our human eyes."

"That's good. Did they find anything of significance?"

"Yes they did find something they deemed significant, though they didn't find the piece inside Nia's room. Therefore, I don't know if it relates to our task or not."

"Where did they find it?"

"They discovered this particular item in the tomb of the kings—inside Cadwr's sepulcher."

Essie stopped and fixed her gaze to his. "What exactly did they unearth?"

"They found a scroll, Essie—and if I'm not mistaken, it matches the writing found in Glodrydd's cave."

Her mouth dropped. "Really?"

He merely nodded in answer to her question. Yet, the expression in his eyes and on his face said he related his experience just as it occurred, with no embellishments to lure the wolf. In all likelihood, their phantom shifter already knew about the scroll, because he too, witnessed the event.

"I can't wait to see it."

He gave her hand a gentle squeeze and cocked his head toward the parking lot. "Then let's get a move on. We have a long drive ahead of us."

With all the light-hearted conversation they shared along the way, the miles didn't seem all that long. But then again, time always flew while in Garreth's company. She met the sight of the castle with a curious mix of regret and anticipation, knowing her private time with Garreth had ended for now.

Bran, a still very pregnant Anne, and Lowri met them at the door. No surprise there.

"Are you hungry?" asked Lowri within fifteen seconds of arrival.

Garreth shifted his gaze to her and raised a brow in silent question. Not wanting to commit an unpardonable sin, she merely shrugged in return.

"We'll have something light, if you don't mind. And Lo, could you bring the tray to the library?"

"I'll have it ready in no time at all," Lowri replied.

Anne linked her arm with Lowri's. "Here, let me help you with that. I need to feel useful. *If* I can still waddle out to the kitchen, that is."

"Thanks, ladies," Garreth called out over his shoulder. "Bran, care to join us?"

The moment they entered the library, he shut the door and fastened his gaze to hers. "Uvan paid us a visit early this morning. So, we're free to discuss whatever we will without fear in this room. I also asked him to secure your bedchamber as well as mine, should something arise in the night we need to discuss—such as visits from hobgoblins, nightmares, and unexpected gifts."

"That's good, thank you. So tell me all about the discovery of the scroll. I'm so anxious to hear about it."

He settled her into one of the leather chairs opposite the fireplace and then sat in the one to her right. Bran took the left. He propped a foot on top of his knee. "Well, in keeping with our plans to lure our phantom wolf out into the open, Cledwyn and Aneirin showed up shortly after Uvan's departure. We decided to visit Nia's chamber first since that's the most logical place to begin such a search. From there, we made a run out to the cemetery."

The comment surprised her. "Why did you choose the cemetery of all places?"

"Well, Cadwr's tomb did provide the key to

decipher the pictograph, so again our ethereal visitor would expect us to perform a search there as well. However, the fact that our wolf paid a visit to the cemetery in our absence and dug a hole beside Nia's grave fueled the need. We hoped we might find the opportunity to explore the area, but while we spoke with Helyan, who witnessed the initial event, Aneirin detected a pair of watchful eyes. We gave the cause up for lost for the time being and moved into the tomb."

"So, Helyan is watching for the wolf's return, then?"

Garreth nodded. "Helyan is standing guard. If the wolf returns, our ghostly friend will take note of everything he does and look for anything he might remove. In the meantime, Cledwyn and Aneirin are seeking the first opportunity to search the area themselves."

"Can I see the scroll?" she asked.

Garreth rose from his seat, made his way to the desk, and unlocked the bottom drawer. He extracted the parchment, handed it off to her, and then returned to his seat. "Please keep in mind this might not have anything to do with our quest. The parchment may have been buried with the man at the time of his death and simply extols his virtues."

"I know." She untied the cord and unwound the scroll in its entirety. "Still, we need to make sure—"

Just as she made the comment, a knock sounded on the door. Before they had the chance to respond, Cledwyn opened it with food-laden tray in hand. Aneirin followed with another. They both entered with broad grins on their faces.

"Thought we'd help the ladies out and bring the

trays in for them," said Aneirin as he placed his heavy burden on top of the worktable. "Poor Anne looked as if she would topple over at any moment with this tray stuck clear out in front of her. Now tell me, Garreth, are the three of you really going to eat all this stuff?"

"I'd think I'd like to hang around and watch them give it a go," said Cledwyn with a slight shake of his head.

"We could do a much better job and appease Lowri if you both would join us in the effort," said Garreth. He rose from his chair, helped her to her feet, and led her to the table. "As you can see, the woman has a tendency to overdo it."

Aneirin picked up a scone the same time as Cledwyn, and just before he took his first bite, he inhaled a bit of the aroma. "Don't mind if we do."

"Umm—this is good. Give my compliments to the cook." Cledwyn finished his off, wiped the crumbs from his mouth, and took another as they approached the table. Once she neared his side, he leaned down and kissed her on the cheek. "Hello, Essie, it's good to see you."

She returned his smile. "Nice to see you too."

He finished off his second scone and then turned toward Garreth. "Anyway, we just stopped by to let you all know we found an opportunity to investigate the entire cemetery, paying particular attention to the perimeter around Nia's grave. Unfortunately, we didn't detect a thing. Since our wolf has never returned, we can only assume he wanted to hide something or—"

"That means he probably hid his item or items elsewhere." Bran cut in. He let out an exasperated sigh.

"We're not so sure about that Bran," said Aneirin.

"You see, the thing is, Helyan didn't see the wolf carry anything in his mouth, nor did he carry anything around his neck, or use his feet to drag his burden."

"Then why would he dig a hole?" asked Essie.

"That's what we've come to discuss," he replied. "Many things come to mind. For instance, mayhap our mangy mutt hoped to throw insignificant crumbs *our* way in order to throw *us* off the proper trail."

"That makes sense," said Garreth. "Such an act would cause us to spend valuable time in a fruitless search."

Aneirin nodded. "Yes. On the other hand, perhaps he's conducting a search of his own and what better place to begin such a search, than at Nia's grave since, at one time, she possessed something of significance?"

Essie drew her brows together. "Who prepared Nia's body for burial?"

"Ceri and Eleri," Garreth replied. "As we have said before, they were part of her favored entourage and the only two who survived the accident."

"Could they have placed something of importance inside her clothes or on her person before burial?" she asked.

"Possible, but not probable," Garreth replied. "Lowri and her staff assisted the effort. If Ceri or Eleri slipped something in her clothes or on her body, they would have noticed, I'm sure. As you might recall, they had more than one body to attend at that time."

"We didn't waste any time in burying them either, Essie." Bran said. "The raging storm only looked to worsen and everyone thought it best to get them into the ground that same day. So, truly, they didn't have a whole lot of time to prepare."

"Don't forget, Gwynn absolved the ladies of anything to do with this intrigue after we returned from our journey," Garreth reminded her.

"So he did."

"I think the best thing we can do right now is let Helyan and his friends do their job, and we'll do ours," Garreth said.

Essie placed the scroll next to the microscope. She would examine it later. "That brings us back to the dragon and his hawk-shaped heart."

"And the message inside his lair," replied Garreth. "Did you find anything at Llys y Helig that will help us figure that part out?"

"Just bits and pieces that might help us decipher the symbols. Uvan didn't have nearly as many examples inside his library as I'd hoped."

"Some is better than none," he said.

She breathed out a laugh. "That's just what Uvan said."

"What did you find out about the bones?" asked Aneirin.

"On top of every other impossible thing I've had to—" Essie waved a hand, shook her head, and tsked. "From all appearances, it looks as if we have us a real, honest-to-goodness, dragon. The bones didn't resemble the known pterosaurs in any way. Uvan understood the futility of my search and so he suggested I look up a friend of his after I visited the museum." She gazed first at Cledwyn and then at Aneirin. "Perhaps you know the man—Ian Penrose?"

Cledwyn grinned the moment the name left her mouth. "Yes, indeed. He's a resident of our realm, though he visits the surface from time to time."

"Often enough to have gathered quite a collection," she said. "The man has more dragon fossils in his basement than you could possibly imagine."

"Did he give you any knowledge as to our particular specimen?" asked Garreth.

"According to Ian, he's a magnus Occidentalis draconis. The beast originates here in western Europe and likes to collect treasure."

"Then perhaps the ancient order that first discovered the bones inside the cave found his hoard as well, and decided then and there to fashion the altar around the beast."

"Possible," said Cledwyn. "Do either of you have any ideas as to the significance of the heart in the shape of a hawk?"

"I suppose they could've discovered such a piece within the treasure trove itself," Essie replied. "A hawk made of gold, or one fashioned from precious gems—such as a diamond, ruby, or sapphire—"

"Or mayhap a hawk fashioned from crystal," Garreth cut in, as he locked his gaze with hers. "Created by magic."

Chapter Sixteen

The light of the early morning dawn filtered into her bedroom and teased her awake. In response to the gentle nudge, Essie's eyes fluttered open. She placed a hand against her mouth and covered a yawn. A slow stretch and a deep intake of breath followed. While she gathered the courage to abandon her warm, comfortable bed, her thoughts drifted toward Garreth, just as they always did. The private moment she craved last night eluded her. Discussions surrounding the coded messages contained on the scroll and the pictograph found inside the dragon's lair prevented it.

The men talked so long last night that she didn't have the chance to study the scroll herself. She would do that today and before breakfast if possible. But in order for that to happen, she had to get up. So get up, she silently commanded her stubborn body. Just as she coerced her legs to swing over the mattress and forced her toes to sweep against the Persian rug, a soft knock sounded against the door.

"Essie, are you awake?" Garreth called out in a low voice.

The skittish butterflies resting deep inside took flight. "Yes—you can come in."

She rose from the bed just as he stepped inside her room. At once he strode toward her, and gathered her into his arms. The action caught her off guard. "Are you all right?"

"I am now." The toe-curling kisses that followed contained just a hint of disquiet.

The moment he gave her leave to breathe she fastened her gaze to his. "Are you sure you're all right?"

The slight grin that curved one side of his mouth accompanied an almost imperceptible shake of his head. "How to answer the worry that has filled those beautiful eyes?" He paused for a moment and then shrugged. "Well—let's just say you aren't the only one plagued by nightmares."

"You had a nightmare?"

He took in a slow breath and released it in like fashion. His fingers brushed through her tousled hair, as he gazed deeply into her eyes. "Not important at the moment. We can discuss that later. Right now, I need you to promise that you won't leave—not for any reason. Not for *any* reason, Essie."

His request puzzled her. "I've already made you that promise, Garreth. I told you weeks and weeks ago that I wouldn't leave until you kicked me out, remember?"

"I know you did. Just promise me again. I need you to do that."

"All right, I promise, upon my word of honor, that I will not leave Llys y Gwalch until you invite me to leave."

"You may be waiting around a long time for such an invitation—a very long time, cariad." Garreth kissed her again, many times in fact, before he released her from his arms. At length he gave his head a shake and stepped away to cool his ardor. "I think I better let you get dressed before I get us both in trouble."

A winsome smile touched her beautiful face as she accompanied him to her door. "All right, my chivalrous lord, I'll meet you downstairs in a few minutes."

****

The task he had just given himself proved far more difficult than what he had first thought and not because he wanted nothing more than to hold her captive in his arms. No, the nightmare that bolted him into awareness held its fair share of the blame, and its recollection haunted him.

The seduction of a thick, dark, swirling mist, a mist that exuded pure evil, had compelled Essie to enter its depths. Somehow, that mist denied him entrance when he sought to reclaim her. He called to her, many times over, but either she didn't hear him or she chose not to answer. Mayhap the mist even prevented her return. Whatever the cause, the dream shattered him and that feeling didn't lessen even after he had fully awakened. At that moment, he had to seek her out, make her promise to stay. Yet, how could he offer forever unless he put an end to the recurring disasters?

Garreth shook away the dream and directed his focus to the here and now. He and Essie had far more important things to do to today than dwell on nightmares. As he entered the library, his thoughts settled on the mysterious scroll found inside Cadwr's sepulcher. He retrieved the relic from his locked desk drawer, carried it over to the worktable, and sat down in his usual place. A brief moment later he had the cord untied and the scroll opened to his view. He propped an elbow on the table and rested his chin on top of his fisted hand as he studied the symbols in depth. A short while later, the click of the door latch drew his gaze upward. Essie entered the room. She met his gaze as she made her way to his side.

"Oh good, you have it out," she said.

"Ready and waiting." He rose to his feet and held her chair while she sat down.

"All right then, let's take a look at what we have, shall we?" she murmured as she scooted her chair forward. She took hold of her notebook and flipped it open to her page of deciphered symbols.

Garreth silently interpreted each word as she placed the letters beneath them. The moment she finished her task, she fastened her gaze to his, and waited for the translation.

He didn't keep her waiting. "Behold, when the sun grows dark and the black cloud threatens to destroy, the great noble hawk will rise. His mighty hand will restore the fragile balance, and end the chain of chaos that rules the world of man."

They simply looked at each other while she processed this information. Finally, she said, "I'd have to say it's connected to the apocalypse."

Garreth nodded. "Yes, I believe I'd have to agree with you there."

"I wonder who wrote this prophecy."

He shook his head. "I don't know. I can tell you I've never heard it spoken before. But just the fact that Cledwyn detected it says the scroll must contain Fair magic. I suppose I should also mention the Tylwyth Teg are quite prolific when it comes to spouting prophecies."

"Then perhaps Uvan knows its author." She dropped her gaze to the scroll and placed a finger at the bottom left-hand corner. "There is just this—this extra little thing down here. Do you see it?"

"Yes, I see it. But I have to tell you, the splotch looks like nothing more than a smudge from a wayward drop of ink to me."

"Oh, I don't know—look closer. The line here and the connecting one below it appear a little more deliberate. If so, then perhaps this is the personal mark of the person who created the scroll."

"I suppose it's possible. But that doesn't necessarily mean he's the one who made the prediction. He might simply be a scribe. Nevertheless, whether we give Uvan the scroll ourselves or send it back with Cledwyn, we'll make sure Gwynn's advisor takes a look at the thing."

"Did Cledwyn and Aneirin finally agree to stay overnight then?"

"That they did, though Lowri gets the credit for managing the feat. The woman simply refused to take no for an answer. You know how she can be."

"Yes, I know, and this time I'll have to thank her because it works to our advantage to give them the scroll now. That way we can stay here and work on deciphering the pictograph. If Uvan thinks the scroll is important, or can shed any light on the thing, I'm certain he'll let us know."

"All right, I'll make sure they take it with them when they leave."

Essie merely nodded while she made a copy of the translation for Uvan in both languages. She then placed the copied sheet on top of the parchment, wound the scroll, and fastened the leather cord around it. "You know, I find it interesting that someone placed the scroll on Cadwr's body. I mean, do you think whoever foretold this event actually believes the man will come back from the dead?"

"I don't know, perhaps. The memorandum carved on the sides of his tomb make it clear his people believed him an extraordinary leader. Think of the tales of King Arthur, a man also held in high esteem among the people of the British Isles. There are many who believed and some who continue to believe, he'll return from the dead the moment Britain needs him again."

She caught the bottom of her lip with her teeth for a moment and nodded. "Yes, you're right about that. But if that were really the case, you think he'd have made an appearance long ago. I can think of many instances during British history, her people could have used his help."

"Indeed. We can say the very same thing for Cadwr. He missed out on a couple of catastrophic events, did he not?"

A couple of rapid knocks at the door interrupted any reply she might've made. Lowri retained her possession of the knob as she opened the door. She glanced at him first and then at Essie. "I thought I'd find the two of you in here. Now come along, breakfast is ready and in case you've forgotten, we have guests that should not be neglected by their host."

Garreth chuckled as he rose from his chair and took hold of the scroll. "I can assure you, Lo, we haven't forgotten our friends. In point of fact, we were just discussing them."

A little over an hour later, they accompanied Cledwyn and Aneirin to the lake and bid them goodbye. Cledwyn tucked the scroll safely inside his vest and promised to hand it over to Uvan upon their arrival. With a vow to return, they disappeared behind the waterfall. Garreth then turned to face Essie. "So, are you ready to tackle the pictograph?"

"That I am—ready and anxious."

He claimed her hand and drew her close to his side. He shrugged away his reluctance. "Then I suppose the responsible thing for us to do is return to the castle."

The walk took twice as long as it should have. He had no one to blame but himself for the lackadaisical pace. But he just found himself enjoying her company and her laughter. For both eased the torment of the nightmare that still haunted him.

As they approached the library door, he spied an agitated Vaughn, rattling the handle in a vigorous attempt to open the door. The current attempt didn't look like his first. "Looking for me?"

Vaughn whirled around to face him. His startled look changed to one of instant relief. "Yes, I am. I need to get a key to one of the cars. Bran has asked me to fetch the doctor. Anne is in heavy labor and everyone is in an uproar over the announcement."

"Didn't anyone tell you? For easier access, I moved all the keys to the carriage house, save the one to my personal vehicle."

"No, no one said a word. But trust me, I'm heading there now." He bobbed his head and hurried down the hall.

The moment he disappeared from view, Essie turned to face him. Excitement had filled her eyes. "Dare we go see how our expectant parents are doing or do you think they would rather be alone right now?"

"I don't think it would hurt to make a brief visit. In

fact, Bran just might need a steady hand to calm him down. Come on." He led her through the great hall, down the northeast corridor, and into the bedchamber prepared for Anne's labor and delivery. The door stood wide open. Some of his staff hovered around the bed, engaged in various duties in preparation for the upcoming birth. Of course, Lowri led the charge.

Anne beamed at them as they entered. She extended a hand toward Essie. "Oh, I'm so glad you're here. I need someone to help me ignore the contractions when they come. Everyone else is too busy to chat right now, and Bran is useless. One would think he's having the baby instead of me."

Essie laughed as she sat down on the edge of the mattress. "All things considered, how are you feeling?"

"In between the pains, I feel absolutely marvelous. They're coming about every three minutes now, so if I grimace, moan or groan, pay me no mind and keep right on talking."

"Hmm. Well, maybe I can take your mind off those pesky contractions if I gather the staff and ask them to do a little karaoke sing along for you while I prattle on about nothing in particular—all to the beat of the music."

Anne squeezed her eyes shut as she laughed outright. "Oh, that would be a lark and believe it or not, I think Garreth actually has one of those crazy machines around here somewhere. It's been ages since we've had it out though. Oh dear—here comes another one—"

Garreth turned his attention away from the girls as Bran approached, eyes glazed, and looking quite frazzled. Truly, the sight almost made him laugh. He quashed the desire though, at least for now. Instead, he grabbed hold of Bran's shoulder and gave it a shake. "How are you holding up, old man?"

Bran shook his head and blew out a snort. "I feel like I haven't had a wink of sleep all night. Poor Anne tossed and turned from the moment she laid down. She just couldn't get comfortable regardless of position. Then the pains started about three o'clock this morning and we've been awake ever since—"

"Well, not to worry," he replied. "The doctor will be here shortly. We ran into Vaughn in the hallway, frantically yanking on the handle of the library door, searching for a car key. I pointed him to the carriage house, so they should be along almost any time now."

Bran appeared puzzled. "I told him the keys were all in the carriage house the moment I sent him on his errand. Well, no matter. Perhaps he's just as rattled as the rest of us and didn't pay close attention to what I said."

Garreth chuckled as he returned a nod. "No doubt. After all, it has been awhile since we've experienced a birth inside the castle."

"That's about to change and sooner rather than later," Lowri said her no-nonsense tone of voice. "Let's hope the doctor is here to witness it."

Once the doctor arrived and entered the room, he shooed them all out, save Bran and Lowri. Garreth turned his gaze away from the closed door and then gave Essie a wink. "I suppose we could while away the time in the library, pondering over a pictograph, if you'd like."

She flashed a smile. "Sounds like a wonderful plan. I'm not sure—but I think I even hear the thing calling to me."

He chuckled over the comment. "Male voice or female?"

"Male—definitely, male."

"I don't know if I like that."

They spent the rest of the morning hours as well as the entire afternoon laboring over the mysterious symbols. Essie isolated the ones used frequently, while he made a list of common words to fit them.

"That's about it," she finally said. "I don't have anything else to use for comparison, so we're just going to have to figure this out with what we have."

"All right." He slanted his notebook to the side so she could see his lists a little better. "I still have a ways to go before I'm finished, but this is what I have produced so far, in both Welsh and English."

"That's a very good start. I can begin working with what you have now and we'll just go from there. Keep in mind, this one is going to be like a complicated jigsaw puzzle. We're going to have to find the pieces that fit together on all sides until the thing makes sense, and that could take quite a bit of time."

Just then a rap sounded at the door, the handle clicked, and Lowri entered grinning from ear-to-ear. "Important though it may be—that work can keep for the rest of the evening. Right now, we have an impromptu dinner celebration to attend."

"And just what are we celebrating, Lo?"

Lowri lifted her brows, swayed from side to side as a secretive little smile lit up her face. "I believe I'll leave that announcement to Bran and Anne. So, if you don't want to miss hearing the news first-hand, I suggest you hurry along."

"All right, we'll be there in just a minute. Don't start without us." He rose from his chair as Essie closed the notebooks and stacked them together.

"Then don't keep us waiting," Lowri called back in the same moment she shut the door behind her.

After the woman vacated the room, he took hold of the notebooks and locked them away in his desk drawer. Essie met his gaze as he extended a hand in invitation. "Are you ready to meet our newest resident then?"

Excitement filled her eyes. "Yes I am."

He escorted her into the already crowded hall, settled her onto the sofa, and then sat down beside her. Excited chatter surrounded them as they waited for Bran to make his appearance. They didn't have long to wait. Within minutes, Bran, carrying his precious bundle in one arm, with Anne hanging onto the other, strolled into the room. The new mother looked radiant. He couldn't remember a time, during all the years of their long lives that he'd seen Bran's smile any broader. The man's joy gave him a great deal of pleasure. Essie looked at him then and locked her eager gaze to his. In response, he took hold of her hand and twined his fingers through hers.

Bran's eyes twinkled as he cast his gaze around the room. "Now lest anyone think I'm an ogre, I tried my best to keep Anne in bed. She wasn't having any of it."

Anne stuck her nose in the air and gave her head a little shake. "You have that one right, beloved husband. I'm not about to miss this presentation."

He gave her an affectionate smile, leaned down, and kissed her on the cheek. "Nor would I want you to, my dear. So—do I have everyone's undivided attention then?"

Laughter met the comment as he and Anne exchanged a mischievous glance. He turned the babe around for all to see. Inch by inch, he peeled back the blankets until he revealed a frilly pink gown, with matching booties.

"Ladies and gentlemen, I'd like to introduce you to my daughter, Rhosyn." A series of oohs, ahhs, and applause met the announcement. "She looks just like her beautiful mother, don't you think? Just look at all that reddish-blonde hair."

As the comment left his mouth, the sound of a baby cry echoed from out of the northeast hallway. Bran turned in the direction of the sound, as they all did. A broad smile emerged as he gave his bewildered audience a wink. "Ah! That would be my son, Rhodri, spoiling our surprise. Can't blame him though. I think he's feeling a little left out of the festivities. What say you?"

Whistles and cheers erupted all around as Lowri entered the great hall pushing a pram. She leaned down and picked up the tiny infant, dressed in blue. Bran made a quick exchange and then held his son aloft. "Anne thinks this one looks like me." He cocked his head to the side as he paused, regarded the babe for a moment, and then shook his head. "I'm not sure that's a compliment."

As laughter filled the hall, Bran turned around and handed the still fussy Rhodri to Lowri. She laid him next to his sister who at once joined her brother in his protest.

Anne breathed out a laugh and headed for the buggy. "Sounds like the twins might want a little private time with their mama," she called over her shoulder.

Lowri wrapped an arm around Anne's waist as she turned to face the crowd. "In the meantime, don't let all of this food go to waste."

Bran gave his wife and babies a kiss before Lowri escorted them back down the hallway to the sound of cheers and applause. The moment his family disappeared from view, the proud papa turned around, bounced his brows, and grinned. Garreth rose to his feet, tugging Essie alongside him as Bran made his way through the throng of well-wishers.

"Looks like you might've forgot to tell me something, Bran," he said.

He shrugged away the remark. "Sorry about that. But when we found out we were having twins, Anne swore me to secrecy. She said she wanted to keep it a surprise."

"A feat well managed. I didn't suspect a thing. Congratulations, you have some fine children there, my friend."

"Yes," said Essie. "They're just beautiful and you tell Anne that motherhood becomes her. I can't believe how good she looks after having given birth earlier today. Most of the women I know remained in bed for at least a day or two and looked quite frazzled during the whole of it."

Bran shook his head. "Not Anne. Right from the beginning, she said she intended to follow in the footsteps of both her mother and her grandmother. Those women worked the family farm there in Ireland all throughout their pregnancies, went into the house and gave birth when the time came, and still put dinner on the table that night—or so she tells me." He winked.

The look on Essie's face almost made Garreth laugh outright. She still wore that bemused expression as he escorted her to her bedroom door later that evening. Just as he took hold of the doorknob, she turned to face him.

"How long has Anne been a resident of Llys y Gwalch?"

He shrugged. "Oh, I don't know. Well over a century, I should think."

"Well—where did she and Bran meet?"

"At that farm in Ireland he spoke of just now," he said. He pulled her into his arms and brushed his lips against hers. "The man went to buy a horse and returned instead, with a wife. He looked just as joyful then as he did today. At the time, I envied the man. But I'm not the least bit envious anymore—"

Chapter Seventeen

Essie studied the two sets of paper she had spread out across the table. Each set put Garreth's list of possible words in their systematic placement within the five pages she had meticulously created. One set represented the carving inside the dragon's lair. The other, the parchment Glodrydd gave Uvan. She had also placed the symbols for the elements in their designated place on the second set. Two pages of each set looked far less garbled than the other three. Still, she didn't want to eliminate any of them before Garreth gave his opinion.

She let go of a deep breath as she rose from her chair and made her way to the large, floor-to-ceiling window. Thick, dark clouds dominated the sky for as far as the eye could see, and the rain continued its merciless hammering upon the water drenched earth. Puddles of water were everywhere. Did Nia lose her life on a day such as this?

Nia.

She shook her head as the saga of the Tylwyth Teg princess crashed into her mind. What knowledge might she have taken to her grave? Did the woman hide away any more of the parchment pages they needed or did she just have the one? Most important? Where did she get it, and how did she know of its connection to Glodrydd's wall? If only they had those pieces of the puzzle.

A pair of strong arms encircled her waist and at once, startled her out of her reverie. Before she could react to the unexpected embrace, Garreth nuzzled the side of her neck and then placed a gentle kiss against her cheek. Delicious shivers traveled up and down her spine in response to his touch.

"Tell me, what subject has you so lost in thought, that you didn't hear me come in?" he murmured against her ear.

"Oh, I don't know." She turned around to face him and placed her hands on top of his forearms. "A million things I suppose. But they all boil down to the fact that our resources are few and we're running out of time." She paused for a moment. "What are we going to do if we fail, Garreth? What if we can't stop the apocalypse from taking place?"

"I don't think that's going to happen, Essie. I really don't. We're close. I can feel it. But if by some small, remote chance we should miss our deadline, we'll simply pick up the pieces and rebuild. We've done it twice before and we can do it again. From there, we'll continue our quest until we put an end to the destruction."

"But the deaths that will surely occur—I don't know if I can handle that. I've come to love your people, Garreth. Especially Lowri, Bran, Anne, and the twins. I know it would destroy my heart and my very soul if something happened to—"

He placed a finger against her lips. "Listen now, it doesn't do any of us any good to dwell on the 'what ifs'. You need to get those kinds of thoughts out of your mind or they'll drive you crazy. Trust me, I know firsthand. What you need to focus on instead, is the fact that we're doing everything in our collective power to prevent them."

She nodded as she glanced at the table. "I know that. Really I do. But—"

"Good. Then let's keep our concentration on finding a solution to our puzzle, agreed?"

"Agreed." She swept a hand toward the table. "So, come on then. Let me show you what I have so far. Maybe you can see something my tired eyes keep missing."

Just as she finished making the suggestion, Garreth shifted his focus to the window. He seemed intrigued by something. She turned her head to follow his gaze. A small but lavish carriage, drawn by two horses, halted in front of the castle entrance. A short, horse driven, two-wheeled, tarp-covered wagon followed the carriage. Afon, Urbgen, Cledwyn, and Aneirin rode behind the wagon. The four Fair men dismounted, while the two men occupying the wagon vacated the cart and made all haste to open the carriage door. Immediately thereafter, Gwynn, Hefina, and Uvan stepped out.

"I suppose we need to put our work on hold for the time being and greet our guests," he murmured as he placed his arm around her waist.

"What on earth would bring them all the way here on a day like this?"

"Well, for Uvan to have accompanied them, I would think they must've discovered something important they need to share with us. Whatever it is, I'm sure they'll reveal it at the time of their choosing. When they do, I think we'll go ahead and share the fragment we found inside the pouch. We've yet to do that."

"Do you think their visit has something to do with the scroll?" She gave him a sideways glance as they made their way to the door.

"I think it's quite probable."

She and Garreth arrived inside the great hall just as Rhys opened the door and stepped aside to allow the Fair folk entrance. Garreth offered his hand to Gwynn, which the king grasped in the instant. He then gazed at each person in the royal entourage while giving them a respectful nod. "Welcome to Llys Y Gwalch."

"Thank you, Garreth," said Gwynn. "I hope you don't mind our dropping in on you unannounced, but my dear wife got wind of your recent additions, and nothing would do, but that we offer a gift. Today. Right now, in fact—the storm notwithstanding."

Hefina laughed as she drew her shoulders together in silent apology. "Yes, you must forgive me. But twins are a rare treat regardless of realm. Therefore, I think you can understand my desire to see them once we had the gifts finished."

"I can indeed. Please make yourselves comfortable, and Rhys? Would you let Lowri know about the arrival of our guests and ask her to provide refreshments for them? In the meantime, I'll ask Bran and his family to join us, if you'll excuse us for a brief moment?"

"Of course," Gwynn said as he settled in next to his wife.

Within minutes they returned with Bran's family following close behind.

Lowri had already produced an impressive afternoon tea as well as an invitation to dinner, which their guests readily accepted. In that same moment, a very proud Anne delivered a sleeping Rhosyn into the waiting arms of the queen.

"Oh, she is just so precious," murmured Hefina as she gazed at the babe and cuddled her close to her breast.

"Yes, we think so," said Anne. "She's especially precious when she's asleep. We find it even more precious when they're *both* sleeping at the same time."

"I'll testify to that," said Bran as he handed his son off to his wife. "Seems to me, we no sooner get one fed, changed and back to sleep when the other one decides to get up."

Hefina laughed as she tucked the blanket a little more securely around the tiny body. "I remember those days. At times, I didn't think they would ever end. But trust me, in no time at all it will be nothing more than a fond memory, and you'll wish for their return."

"That's exactly what my mother used to say," Anne replied as a faraway look entered her eye. "Alongside her admonition to take time to rock each of my babies and sing them lullabies for as long as they allowed it. For a time would surely come when they wouldn't."

"Wise woman," Hefina replied, "and speaking of that wisdom, Olwen, Twedwr—would you be kind enough to bring in our gifts?"

"Certainly, Majesty," said Olwen as he and Twedwr rose from their seats.

The Fair men returned with an exquisite rocking chair, ivory in color and trimmed in gold paint. Intricately carved daffodils, painted yellow with green leaves, adorned the top rail and arms of the chair.

Anne gasped when she saw it. "Oh, my—why, it's the most beautiful thing I have ever seen." With Rhodri still in her arms, she vacated the sofa and settled into the soft cushions of the rocker. The moment she set it in motion, soft, lyrical music rose up and filled the room with its enchanting lullabies.

The expression on her face must've matched Anne's, for Garreth turned and met her gaze. He simply looked at her for a moment and then his own expression softened. The way he gazed at her right now took away her breath and somehow held her captive for several quiet moments. Only the queen, retrieving two additional gifts from her bag, managed to break the spell that held them bound. Anne handed Rhodri to his father, so she could accept her lavishly wrapped boxes. The little outfits with matching blankets, made by the artisans of the Tylwyth Teg, were something to behold. She'd never before seen anything to equal them.

Pleasant conversation filled the remainder of the day and accompanied them throughout dinner. Finally then, as Lowri offered to show Garreth's guests to their rooms, citing the weather as an excuse to keep them, Gwynn and Uvan elected to remain behind. Cledwyn and Aneirin echoed the sentiment.

"Don't keep Garreth up too late," Hefina warned. "We've taken up most of his day. Therefore, we needn't take up most of his evening."

The king chuckled. "Don't worry, I won't. I promise I'll join you shortly.

Cledwyn, Aneirin and I, just need to discuss a few minor things with Garreth and Bran concerning the causeway that connects our realms. Essie, you're welcome to join us if you wish, since Garreth doesn't look of a mind to part with you. Can't say I blame him for that, though."

Laughter accompanied them into the library. Yet, once Garreth shut the door, Gwynn raised his brows and released a heavy sigh. "I'm sorry, Garreth. I didn't intend for this day to drag on as long as it did, or extend ourselves an overnight invitation, but we had an uninvited guest in close proximity all throughout our visit. We could feel him lurking in the shadows. Therefore, we didn't want him, or her, to know our visit was two-fold in nature."

"That's quite all right," he replied. "Cledwyn and Aneirin can confirm that Lowri would have finagled a way to keep you overnight anyway, and we certainly don't mind having you here. Indeed, we find it a pleasure."

Aneirin and Cledwyn glanced at each other and laughed.

"Yes we can attest to that fact, your highness. We found it far easier to agree with the woman, than go against her wishes," said Aneirin.

Garreth returned his attention to the king. "So, I take it then, you have something you wish to discuss with us?"

"That we do," he replied. "Uvan thought it important to sit down together and discuss all of the bits and pieces we've collected this far, up to and including the scroll you discovered."

Garreth glanced at his desk. "Why don't we sit at the table, then? I'll put everything out that we've gathered, including a fragment of a palimpsest you've yet to see."

Gwynn lifted a brow as he approached the table

and selected a chair. "You found a fragment from another piece of parchment?"

"Yes, we did—inside the leather pouch, actually, and on the day the wolf revealed himself." He unlocked the drawer, removed the bundle, and returned to the table. "But at the time we brought you the bag, we didn't know you had a study secure from outside forces. We didn't want to give away the discovery should the shifter have followed us to your realm. Therefore, we left the piece behind."

"Understandable as well as wise," said the king, who then turned his gaze toward Essie. "Were you able to decipher it?"

She nodded as Garreth settled in beside her and claimed possession of her hand. "Yes we did. The piece simply says, and I quote, 'crystal, its inestimable power, created by the magic of the—.' Garreth thought it possible this portion of the palimpsest spoke of the heart itself and I believe he's right."

Uvan twiddled his thumbs as he fixed his gaze upon Essie. Yet it seemed he looked straight through her rather than at her. After a lengthy pause, in which no one spoke, he said, "Yes, indeed. Garreth *is* right. There is no doubt of that. You see, this small discovery has unearthed a distant memory I had all but forgotten until you jarred it. I know now that the heart we seek *is* fashioned from crystal. As I recall, the piece is dark green in color, and extracted from deep within the Halkyn Mountain, almost two millennia ago. The man who discovered it became a most powerful, but benevolent wizard. Legend states the rock resembled a great bird of prey even from the moment he removed it from its rocky nest. After years of working, shaping, and polishing the piece, the distinctive features evolved into its present form. I should think from the information we now have, we can assume the form duplicates the hawk in your insignia ring, Garreth. Of course, Essie's illustration confirms that as well, wouldn't you agree?"

Essie's mouth dropped and for a brief moment, their eyes connected. She seemed hurt that Uvan provided the knowledge of his ring, rather than him. An instant later, an expression of fear overtook all other emotions she now experienced. A slight shudder coursed throughout her body as she returned her attention to Uvan.

"Yes," Garreth said. "I suppose you're right."

"Do you have any idea who might've taken the heart and when the theft occurred?" asked Essie.

Uvan clasped his hands on top of the table and shrugged. "Nothing more than what you have already discovered within the chronicle and passed on to us. As you recall, the palimpsest states that three wizards stole into the dragon's lair and seized the heart. I have no idea as to the identities of those wizards or their purpose for desiring it. As to the time of occurrence? Certainly prior to the first calamity, for that is what triggered the incident. But I've no idea how much time lapsed between the two events. Could be years, decades, even centuries for all we know."

"I don't suppose any of your legends speak concerning the purpose of the heart, do they? I mean, just exactly what is this crystal supposed to do?"

Uvan lifted a hand in concert with his brows. "Though I'm not certain, I recall the legend speaking of the natural magic found within the crystal at the time of its discovery, Essie. In fact, the relic contained a powerful magic, which the wizard magnified over the ages, thereby making it even more powerful. In consideration of Glodrydd's parchment, and everything we've discovered this far, I'm now of a mind to believe the magic has something to do with controlling earth, wind, fire, and water."

The moment he made the statement, it made perfect sense. Garreth leaned forward. "I think you're right, Uvan. These are the very elements that come into play during the cycles of annihilation."

"The notion also fits with the partial chronicle we have," said Essie. "Perhaps the missing warning that follows, speaks of the destruction."

"I think we can safely assume it does," said Uvan.

"If that's the case, then all we need do is find and replace the thing in order to keep it from recurring," said Garreth. "Correct?"

Uvan fixed his gaze with his as a small grin turned a corner of his mouth. "Yes, I should think so. But I'm not at all convinced it's a *we*—rather, I believe it's a *you*."

Essie's mouth dropped. "What do you mean by that?"

"The scroll," said Uvan. "I think the message makes it clear that Garreth must be the one to replace the heart. No one else will have the power to accomplish the feat."

Essie unknowingly gripped his hand a little tighter as she shook her head, "No, that can't be right. They found the scroll on top of Cadwr's remains. The scroll said King Cadwr ap Brychan would rise—"

Uvan lifted his chin and laughed outright. "Oh

come on, Essie. Surely you don't honestly believe a dead man is going to rise, do you?"

"You think that's such a stretch for me right now? Before I accepted this assignment I considered myself a well-grounded woman. Yet, since my arrival, fairies, ghosts, dragons, and magic have become part of my reality."

"Yes, well, be that as it may, no magic on this earth that I know of can bring someone back from the dead. No—as you might recall, the prophecy made no mention of a specific name. The scroll simply states the "noble hawk" will rise to the occasion. Right now, the noblest hawk in this realm, or any other for that matter, is Prince Garreth. He is, after all, the direct descendent of the first and rightful ruler of Llys y Gwalch. Though you may not know this, Lord Garreth's nobility is legendary in its own right and far exceeds that of Cadwr."

"But that doesn't mean he needs to face his task alone, Essie," Cledwyn cut in. "Both Aneirin and I will certainly accompany Garreth back to the dragon's cave. Have no fear."

She lifted her chin and firmed her jaw. "So will I."

The moment she made the statement, Garreth's nightmare flooded his mind with an unyielding force that gripped his heart. Once again, he could see the dark, evil cloud engulfing her—consuming her. A menacing mist that somehow imprisoned her inside its foul belly. He clenched a fist as he resolved in that same moment to prevent her from making that journey, even if he had to send her away on some fabricated errand in order to accomplish it. For he wouldn't permit a single minion of hell, or all its minions combined, to steal her away from him.

Somewhere then, in the back of his mind, he could hear Uvan speaking. He shook away his troubled thoughts and focused instead on the conversation at hand. Essie drew her brows together as they exchanged a glance. She sensed his uneasiness. He could see it in her eyes. In silent reply, he simply shook his head and gave her hand a gentle press meant to reassure them both.

"The deciphering of the message inside the dragon's lair is just as important as locating the heart, Essie. For in most cases, an exact order of words or exact actions must accompany a specific ritual in order to complete it," said Uvan. "I think we're going to find Garreth has more to do than simply dropping the crystal into the hollow cavity of our dragon and exit the cave."

Essie released the ragged breath she unknowingly held and nodded. "I know, and we're working with all diligence to interpret the symbols. I promise you, I will have it done with time to spare. Setting the translations aside, I believe the more difficult task is finding the heart. That crystal could be anywhere on this planet, right?"

"No, I don't think so," Uvan replied. "You have to remember the period of time in which the wizards removed it. World travel didn't exist. Man walked, or if lucky enough, rode on horseback. I think we're going to find the heart is somewhere here in Wales or along the western boundaries of England. In all probability, the crystal rests within a two hundred mile radius of the dragon's cave."

"Still, even that's daunting," she replied.

Uvan tilted his head to the side as he considered

her statement. "Yes and no. Keep in mind the power of the magic within the crystal. That's something the people of the Tylwyth Teg can feel when in close proximity to the item emitting it."

"How close is close?"

"Oh, probably within a range of about three miles we can detect the presence of strong magic. Of course, the closer we get, the stronger the vibration. So don't worry, Essie, we're using every skill we collectively possess as we plan what I believe to be an achievable strategy. Rest assured, we'll locate the heart in a timely manner."

Much later that evening, when he and Essie finally had the library to themselves, she turned to face him, wrapped her hands around her arms, and rubbed away the evening chill. "Why didn't you tell me about the ring?"

He shook his head as he approached her. "No deception intended. I just couldn't bring myself to add an additional worry to the heavy burden you already carry."

She mulled that over for a moment and then nodded. "Thank you for your concern, Garreth. But now that I know about it, may I see it?"

In response to her request, he placed a hand against the small of her back. Together they made their way to his desk. He opened the tiny drawer, retrieved the ring, and held it up for her inspection, all without saying a word. She took hold of it then and made careful study of its design.

"I wonder if this hawk is an identical replica of the dragon's heart by coincidence or by intent."

"I don't know. In truth, I can't even tell you how

old this ring is, or even how many kings wore the piece before I, as a very small lad, noticed it for the first time on the hand of my own grandfather."

She released a shuddered breath as she returned the ring to the drawer, closed it, and then fastened her gaze to his. "You know it seems the more we learn, the more questions we have. I can't help but think if we even knew half of those answers, we might already have solved this thing."

He gathered her into his arms then and held her close to his heart. "Don't worry, Essie. I have a very strong feeling we're going to solve this thing much sooner than either of us anticipates and without a single loss of life."

"I hope you're right, Garreth," she murmured as she rested her head against his chest. "I really hope you're right."

Chapter Eighteen

Essie propped her elbow on the library table, dropped her cheek onto her curled fingers, and closed her eyes. Another week gone. Despite all her efforts, the symbols refused to make sense, regardless of placement. In truth, she just didn't have enough common letters to decipher either the pictograph or Glodrydd's parchment in the time they had left, and she didn't know where to get any more.

Or did she—

The thought gave her pause. She opened her eyes, leaned back against the chair, and focused her gaze outside the window. She and Garreth found what they needed once before in the tomb of the kings. Dare she hope that luck would smile down on her twice and in the same place? She glanced down at her watch. Garreth's duties would keep him another two hours at least. Due to the hour of his expected return, he would probably postpone the trip until the morning. She didn't want to wait that long. Not when every minute counted.

The decision made, she cleaned off the table and locked away everything pertaining to their quest inside the desk drawer. She contacted the stable via the intercom and asked for a horse. Just before she exited the room, she scribbled a quick note for Garreth that made him privy to her plans. Minutes later, she headed straight for the cemetery, carrying her tools, a flashlight, and a bit of hopeful anticipation. Her eyes scanned the cemetery as she approached the gate. She didn't see anyone in the vicinity. At least not anyone alive. Would the spirits allow her entrance without Garreth?

Essie dismounted, tethered the mare beneath the tree, and left her to graze. She shook off her trepidation and made her way to the fence. The gate swung open of its own accord just as she extended a hand toward the latch. A sudden breeze toyed with her hair in an impossible sort of way the moment she walked through the gate. She halted her steps, took in a breath, and held it.

"Helyan? Is that you?" she whispered, feeling more than a little foolish as she awaited a response. Just when she gave up the wait, a voice answered.

"At your service, Lady DeSpencer."

In that same instant, a very attractive spirit dressed in ancient knight's apparel, appeared just off to her right. The man who fastened his dark brown eyes to hers looked mortal in every sense of the word. Somehow, she didn't expect that in a ghost. She swallowed past the dryness in her throat and responded to his subtle bow with an equally subtle nod of her head.

"What brings you to our little cemetery on this fine day?"

"You speak English," she said, stating the obvious.

Helyan took a step forward, broadened his stance, and folded his arms against his chest. "Among other languages. But then again, I've had time aplenty to acquire them, have I not?"

"Yes, I suppose you have." She lifted her clasped

hands to her chin while she sought to reconcile her preconceived notions concerning ghosts with the spirit that stood before her. He had his head tilted to the side as if he waited—oh. She released her breath. "I'm sorry, you asked me a question. I—um—I wanted to see if I could find some other examples of writing, similar to that found on King Cadwr ap Brychan's sepulcher."

A slight smile curved the corners of his bearded mouth. "Then allow me to act as your escort. One can get lost inside the catacombs if one is not familiar with them."

"Thank you, Helyan, you're very kind."

He shook his head and his shoulder-length dark brown hair actually moved in concert with the motion. She found herself staring again.

"Kindness has nothing to do with the offer, Lady DeSpencer. For the opportunity to attend such a beautiful woman is naught but a pleasure."

A breath of laughter accompanied the slight shake of her head. This ghost made it quite clear that not even death interfered with a man's ability to flirt. At least, not with *this* man's ability, anyway. "Thank you. The symbols I'm looking for would predate King Cadwr's death. I don't suppose you know right off hand if such carvings exist?"

Helyan dropped an arm about her shoulder and surprisingly, she could feel it. He then conducted her to the entrance of the tomb. "Such marks exist indeed. But you'll have to determine if they are what you seek. Come. I'll show you where they are."

Once inside the tomb, she turned on her flashlight. He then led her in the opposite direction of Cadwr's crypt. They made several turns before Helyan took her inside a rectangular chamber that housed six separate sepulchers. Four large ones sat in the front, while two smaller ones sat in the back.

"These graves belong to the earliest kings buried inside this tomb and of course, they all precede Cadwr in death. Those two," he said pointing to the tombs against the back wall, are queens."

Essie made a slow even sweep of the cavity with her flashlight. "I wished I could see a little better," she murmured, wishing she had grabbed a more powerful light.

Helyan waved a hand and in that same instant, four torches lining the walls burst into flame, and lit up the chamber.

Her mouth dropped as she whirled around to face him. "How did you do that?"

He clasped his hands behind his back, lifted a brow, and shrugged. "A mortal would find it difficult to understand."

"Try me."

"All right, then. I simply divert the full power of atmospheric energy to a specific place in order to use it for a specific purpose."

She gave him a smile. "You're right. The explanation *is* difficult for a mortal to understand."

Her ghostly companion chuckled in response. She made her way to the first of the graves and thoroughly examined the top and sides of each. Time had diminished the carving and in this light, she couldn't tell if the markings were relevant to her cause or not. Nonetheless, she made a rubbing of each symbol and then photographed the entire surface using the infrared setting. She followed suit with each sepulcher within the chamber. All the while, she and Helyan chatted about a great many things. The longer they spoke, the more comfortable he made her feel in his presence. In fact, he almost made her forget that he no longer housed his mortal body. Almost.

"Would you mind if I asked you a personal question? I won't be offended if you don't want to answer it."

"I don't mind answering your questions. Feel free to ask me anything you'd like."

"Why did you choose to remain here, rather than move on to wherever it is most spirits go after death?"

Helyan dropped his gaze downward and for several moments, he said nothing. Then just as she opened her mouth to apologize for delving into things that were none of her concern, he took a step toward her. "If you will allow me, I would like to answer your question by telling you a story."

"By all means."

"Many centuries ago, against the threat of invasion, a king called all of his able-bodied men to arms. A young man, the only son of a crippled father who could've chosen otherwise, heeded the call. Though this father relied on his son for a great many things, he didn't begrudge his decision or course of action. Nay, the resolution did naught but fill the man with pride. Many times over the years, he said his son's service to the king brought honor to his name and family.

"The son fought many battles over the course of his lifetime. But one in particular, he would never forget. Once again, an enemy bent on invasion and conquest, stormed into the realm of the king. The king's army fought valiantly and repulsed their adversaries with very little loss of life. Yet, in the face of defeat, the enemy sought to annihilate the land. As they retreated to the hell from whence they came, they burned every home and field they passed in a misguided sense of vengeance."

Helyan paused in his story and a distant look entered his eye. Essie said nothing to disturb his thoughts. She couldn't. The massive lump growing inside her throat didn't allow it.

"The king's son, a man of great renown despite his tender years, caught sight of the smoke and flames licking the sky. He turned his mount and rode with all haste toward the destruction. Along the way, he organized his troops into several small units, sending each in a different direction. Their assignment? Save what they could and tend to those in need. He took a few of his men and rode south. The first farm he happened upon belonged to the man with the crippled father. Fire had all but destroyed the house." Helyan knotted his brows together as he shook his head and conjured a sigh.

"Every soldier, including the crippled man's son, gave the cause up for lost. But not the king's son. No one else would've dared enter that house. The heat, too hot, the flames, too high. The men in attendance called out to the king's son in warning. They begged him not to enter the structure. He went in anyway. A few minutes later, he returned, carrying the crippled man in his arms. Miraculously, the man still lived. He placed the crippled man into his son's waiting arms. Without any hesitation whatsoever, he ordered the son to take his father to the castle and see to it that his staff looked after his injuries and any need he might have during his recovery. The old man remained a privileged guest for the rest of his life."

Tears threatened to surface, and at that precise moment, Uvan's declaration tumbled into her mind. The noblest hawk, indeed. Yet, the story didn't surprise her in the least. Essie stated the obvious. "You're speaking of your own father and Garreth, aren't you."

Helyan slowly nodded. "In return for his selfless gift, I vowed then and there to watch over the prince of Llys y Gwalch for as long as he drew breath. In my estimation, my death didn't absolve me of that vow."

She shook her head as she fought off the urge to take hold of his hand. "I understand that, but I'm sure Garreth wouldn't expect you to—"

"No, he wouldn't," Helyan cut in. "And that very thing in itself, earns my respect and my loyalty, Lady DeSpencer. So, as long as Prince Garreth draws breath, I'll remain right here."

"Please, it's just Essie," she said as she released a breath and fixed her gaze to his. "You're a good man, Helyan, and just so you know? You have earned *my* deepest respect. As far as my friendship goes? You have that without any strings attached."

His flirty grin returned. "I'll treasure both, m'lady." He then dipped his head in the direction of the crypts. "Are you finished with your task?"

She cast her gaze about the room and nodded. "I am for now. However, if I find my rubbings and photographs are inadequate, I'll have to return with some tools and see if I can enhance the symbols."

"Then I shall hope you find such a need, for I have truly enjoyed your company far more than you know."

"You don't have to wait for my return, Helyan. I'm not hard to find if you really want to talk to me."

"Mayhap I might take you up on that offer, Lady Essie."

"Yes, well, just make sure I'm in the same room while you do the conversing, hmm?" said Garreth.

Essie whirled toward the sound of the unexpected voice. Garreth, with arms folded, leaned a shoulder against the wall, the toe of his boot rested against the ground. The moment their eyes connected, he gave her a wink, hoisted himself away from the partition, and made his way to her side.

Helyan's laughter filled the chamber the moment Garreth dropped a possessive hand around her waist. Her ghostly friend then said something in Welsh. Garreth responded in kind. An apparent brief, light-hearted conversation followed the exchange. At the end of it, Garreth fused his mirthful gaze with hers and cocked his head toward the entrance.

"Are you ready to go home?"

"Yep, I'm finished here—at least for now."

Just as the words left her mouth, Helyan stepped forward. He took hold of her hand, drew it to his lips, and gave it a kiss. Again she could feel it as though the man were mortal.

Garreth tugged on her waist. "Let's go. The sun is just about to set, and I'd like to get you home before dark."

She resisted the tug for a small moment as she turned her gaze toward her ghostly friend. "Thank you for your help, Helyan, and I meant what I said. Any time you want to talk to me—" She let the sentence hang as Garreth escorted her out of the chamber.

They traversed the maze of corridors without speaking. But once they exited the tomb, Garreth gave her a side-ways glance. "Now that he's introduced himself, what do you think of Helyan?"

A smile emerged in response to the question. "He's very sweet, and we got along quite well together. I can see why you mourned his loss."

Garreth chuckled as he assisted her onto her horse. "Yes, well, we didn't have to mourn it very long."

"Really? How long did it take for him to make his presence known after his death?"

He shrugged as he handed her the reins. "About two—maybe three months. I don't mind telling you his sudden appearance set me back on my heels the first time I saw him."

Essie laughed. "I bet so.

"Especially since the man didn't have full control over the ability and he kind of flickered in and out of focus." Garreth swung up on his horse, slowed the stallion's pace, and fell into step beside her. "Didn't take him all that long to master the feat, though. Speaking aloud followed. We celebrated the moment he mastered that particular skill, and we could have normal conversations with him again."

"I don't doubt that for a single minute." Her mind imagined a simple version of the scene and it made her wonder. "Garreth, at the time of Helyan's death did his father still live?"

"He told you about his father?"

Essie gazed into his eyes and nodded. "Yes, he did—and about the noble prince who saved him from the slow, agonizing death of a burning fire."

Garreth shrugged as if the incident held no great

importance. "You should know that Helyan is famous for embellishing his tales."

"Perhaps," she said. "But I don't think he embellished a thing about this one, and you still need to answer my question."

"Did his father still live? No, and we can thank the heavens for their mercy, for his father could not have borne such a loss. Helyan didn't outlive him by much, though. I think we only had about six months or so between their deaths."

"Did Helyan leave a wife or any children behind?"

He responded to the question with a quiet chuckle. "I don't think Helyan ever considered marriage. That's not to say he didn't leave a string of broken hearts behind. The man did have a way, and had his way, with countless women during his mortality. A number of them vied for his attention and I can tell you they were all quite distraught when each learned of his death."

"I'm not surprised to hear it. However, I am surprised none of them hung around after their own deaths."

"Many of them did, actually. Trust me, the man *still* has no lack of female companionship when he so desires it, and even now they vie for his attention."

Essie shook her head and released a breathy laugh as she considered the totality of Helyan's existence. "Does he always keep to the cemetery? I mean, what kind of an afterlife can one have in such a creepy place?"

"He would probably take exception to your calling the place *creepy*. However, he doesn't dwell in the cemetery at all, at least not in the way you mean. More often than not, one can find him as well as all of his ghostly companions inside the pub, stirring up quite a ruckus during the wee hours of the morning."

"Really? Interesting then, that both times I've visited the cemetery he happened to be there."

"That's only because he took note of the visit, and your presence intrigued him. You see, within a mile or so of whatever his current location happens to be, he can hear the slightest noise, movement, or conversation by the living. If he's interested, he'll go see what they're up to."

"I see."

"So, tell me, while you poked about the chamber, did you find anything significant to our cause?"

"I'm not sure. I hope so. But, I won't know until I download the photographs. The erosion made the symbols difficult to see, especially in that light. So, I'm hoping the infrared defined them enough to make sense of them."

Of course, Lowri pounced the moment they returned. The woman insisted they eat dinner before they closeted themselves inside the library. Should that have surprised her? Nonetheless, in less than twenty minutes, she had the enlargements of her newest photographs spread out across the table. She studied, eliminated, and discarded them one by one. At least she did until she arrived at the last set, bearing the markings from the sepulcher of the first king buried inside the tomb. Her heartbeat accelerated as she took hold of her magnifying glass and compared the symbols with those inside the dragon's lair and upon Glodrydd's parchment.

"We have a match," she whispered. Essie could hear the excitement in her voice. She whirled around to face him as her smile broadened. He shifted his focus from his growing list of words to meet her gaze. "Garreth, we have a match!"

He slid his chair over, dropped an arm over her shoulder, and gazed at the photographs. "Do you think this will give us the key we need?"

She nodded as her eyes swept over the remaining photographs. "Yes, I believe so. They just have to."

They worked on the puzzle well past midnight. Finally then, after she isolated all of the common symbols within the text, she slid the notebook away from herself and in front of him.

"Now it's your turn to find the words," she said, fastening her gaze to his.

He glanced at the clock. "Why don't you go up to bed and get some sleep then? As you can see, it's very late and right now, there's nothing else you can do here."

She shook her head. "No, I want to stay, and I can work at the word placements while you create your lists."

"That can wait until the morning," he argued.

"I beg to differ, Lord Garreth. If I stop now, I won't sleep a wink for the combination of worry and anticipation." She lifted a brow and flashed a smile. "On the other hand, think of how well I'll sleep if I have all of this figured out *before* I go to bed."

Despite the resolve, as the clock neared the two a.m. hour, she could feel the strain on her weary eyes. Essie stifled another yawn as she juggled assigned letters, words, and orphaned symbols underneath the text found inside the dragon's cave. Again. How many times had she done this very same thing? A sigh escaped. She needed to clear her head, and get a bit of blood pumping. With that need uppermost in mind, she rose from her chair. But then just as she turned away, Garreth took hold of her hand to halt her progress. She turned to face him, yet he had his gaze fixed on her notebook. For several moments, he studied her latest efforts. He picked up the pencil, erased a symbol here and there only to replace it with another. Finally, a small nod accompanied another eternal pause.

Just as she opened her mouth to speak, he raised the notebook from off the table as he fastened his eyes to the page. "Nyu lies in peaceful rest. Thrice the circle passes. The yellow sun shines. Thrice more, the sun sets over the blue horizon. Retreat twice and the deep dark brown will bury the vibrant red, but only upon the fourth forward pass will Nyu restore the balance."

The moment he finished reading the inscription, he dropped the notebook onto the table. He then gave her his full attention and grinned. "We have the instructions I'm going to need to replace the heart. It seems that I just have to drop the crystal into its designated spot, and turn the outer rim the number of specified times in the appropriate directions."

"You know what? That also agrees with something I read in one of your books this past week. The author said the druids spoke of the fifth element. An element they named the Spirit of Nyu. This element dominates the center of the magic circle. According to tradition, it's Nyu that brings balance to all other elements."

"Then all we need do is find the bloody thing and return it to its proper place."

Chapter Nineteen

"I just talked to Lowri. She said so far as she is aware, Essie hasn't stirred," said Bran as they strolled down the hallway in the direction of the library. "But no surprise there, considering the time she went to bed last night—or rather should I say this morning?"

Garreth placed a hand upon the doorknob, turned the handle and freed the latch. "All right, let's get to it then. Everyone is inside and I don't want to keep them waiting."

He entered the room two steps ahead of Bran, who shut the door behind him as he made his way to the table. Garreth greeted Gwynn, Uvan, Cledwyn, and Aneirin with a courteous nod. "I must confess I didn't know if Hefina could hear me or not. I'm glad the message got through and that you were all willing to come on such short notice."

"Hefina doesn't miss much," said Gwynn. "She said if she understood your message correctly, then you have translated both the parchment and inscription found inside the dragon's lair. Is that right?"

Garreth settled into his chair. "Yes, it is. She's very perceptive."

The king clasped his hands together, set them on top of the table, and leaned forward. "Excellent. We're quite anxious to hear what they reveal."

"I'll read the translations of Glodrydd's parchment

first. The declaration confirms what we already know concerning the cycles of destruction and the part the elements play in that destruction." He picked up the notebook from off the table and dropped his gaze to the open page. "Henceforth, take heed and beware the four hundred year awakenings. Following the morning's darkest hour, tumultuous winds trouble the water. Furious waters disturb the peace of the slumbering earth. Once the venomous fire of the black dragon smolders… Beg for mercy and pray for the return of the hawk."

Uvan broke the silence first. "I believe the pronouncement also confirms the part you must play in our quest, Garreth."

Garreth dropped the notebook off to his side. "Yes, I couldn't help but notice that too."

"But again, Garreth," said Cledwyn. "Know that you're not alone in this task. Aneirin and I will attend you every step of the way."

"I know, and I appreciate your willingness to lend a hand. But, before we worry about that step of our mission, we need to find the dragon's heart," he replied. "Are you having any luck on that front and is there anything we can do to help speed things up? I have several good men who could help you."

"This far our luck has arrived in the process of elimination," Gwynn replied. "We're narrowing our search each day by hundreds of acres, beginning in the south of Wales and moving northward. We have several teams engaged in this effort, so I think we can handle it by ourselves. At least for the time being."

Bran extended the finger that supported his cheek. "Yes, but can we harbor any hopes of finding the thing in time?"

"With absolute certainty," said Uvan. "We've covered far more ground than what you might think, Bran. As I said before, I'm convinced we'll find our heart in either Wales or somewhere along the far western borders of England. My only concern right now, is in knowing precisely what to do with the heart once we have it in our possession."

"I believe the pictograph gives us that information." He slid the notebook in front of him. "The inscription reads, and I quote, "Nyu lies in peaceful rest. Thrice the circle passes. The yellow sun shines. Thrice more, the sun sets over the blue horizon. Retreat twice and the deep dark brown will bury the vibrant red, but only upon the fourth forward pass will Nyu restore the balance." I'm of a mind to believe these are the complete instructions for placing the heart within the hollow of our black dragon," Garreth said as he leaned back against his chair. "Do you agree with me or do you think we need to look for additional directions?"

Uvan shook his head. "No, I think you're right. I'm sure there is nothing more to find. Whoever wrote those instructions wouldn't just give us a portion. In addition, the inscription mentions all the assigned colors of the elements and in their correct order. As you have already surmised, all you need do is replace the crystal, turn the altar's outer rim the designated number of times and in the proper direction. The inscription makes it clear the crystal represents Nyu, which is the element that restores the order of nature."

"Yes, Essie told me about that last night. She said the Druids referred to Nyu as the element that dominates the center of the circle, bringing balance to all others. That makes sense in regards to our current dilemma," he said.

"Speaking of Essie, is there a reason she decided not to join us this morning?" asked Cledwyn. "She's not ill, is she?"

Bran's growing smirk ended in a chuckle. "At least to this point, she isn't aware we are having this discussion. She and Garreth worked rather late last night on the translations and right now, she is sound asleep. Garreth didn't want to wake her."

Gwynn lifted a brow as his gaze flitted between him and Bran. "Oh? Is there a reason for the exclusion beside the need to sleep?"

Garreth cleared his throat and nodded. "Yes, there is, actually. If you don't mind, I need a favor from all of you. Once we find the heart, and for many reasons, I would prefer that Essie remain unaware of its discovery until after we've replaced it."

"Ah," said Cledwyn. "You don't want her to accompany us on our return journey."

"Not if I can help it." Laugher met his emphatic statement. "The thing is, she's had a couple of troubling nightmares concerning this quest that end in my death, and they concern her far more than they should. I don't need or want her doing something foolish in a misguided attempt to protect me from something that doesn't exist and thereby, endanger herself."

A grin tugged at the corners of Uvan's mouth as he rubbed a finger down the side of his nose. "We'll do all in our power to help you, Lord Garreth, of course. But be aware, a woman's determination is not easily overcome."

Uvan's statement haunted him long after the Fair folk took their leave. Nonetheless, he had determination as well, and his will in this matter would prevail. He would make sure of it. Essie meant far too much to him to risk losing her now. Far too much—

"Bore da, Garreth."

Garreth turned in the direction of the unexpected voice. Helyan hadn't paid a visit to the castle for quite some time. Yet, he couldn't say it surprised him to see the man now. "Good morning, Helyan."

Helyan looked about the room. "The lovely Lady Essie is not around?"

He shook his head as he approached him. "Sorry to disappoint you, but she's still sleeping."

"Ah, it's probably just as well." The ghost shrugged. "You are the one I need to speak with anyway. I wanted to let you know that our beslubbering, fen-sucked wolf paid another visit to the cemetery late last night."

"Is that so?" He paused. "Did he head straight for Nia's grave again?"

"Yes, he did. But this time he didn't dig around the stone. He merely circled the thing a couple of times with the same slow, unhurried thoroughness Cledwyn gave it. He then investigated the graves of Nia's attendants in like manner. Once he finished that particular task, he went inside the mausoleum and poked around a bit."

"Did he really? Did he take note of your presence this time?"

Helyan shook his head. "No, I stayed out of range."

"Excellent. He didn't, by chance, unearth anything, did he?"

"Not a thing. After he finished snooping around, I decided to follow him—at a respectable distance, of course."

"Good man. Where did he go?"

"Here," said Helyan. "He entered the castle through the back entrance. By the time I made it through the wall myself, he had disappeared without a trace."

Garreth cocked his head to the side and as he scrubbed a hand back and forth across his mouth, he considered the reasons for that. One stood out far more prominently than did the others. "Perhaps he no longer needed his wolf persona then, because this is where he dwells. If that's the case then in all likelihood, he is a trusted member of my staff."

"The thought crossed my mind as well. If such proves true, how will you discover his identity?"

"Don't worry, I'll find a way. That you can count on. In the meantime, I need you to do me a favor, if you will."

"You know you've but to ask."

"I appreciate that more than you know. What I need is for you to watch over Essie until such a need no longer exists. Most especially, I need you to watch over her well-being if there comes a time that I can't do it myself," he said.

"Ah. You're planning a journey of some kind that doesn't include Essie," Helyan said.

"If things work out the way we hope, then yes. I think—at least I hope—we're very close to ending the catastrophic cycles. If we have uncovered everything there is to uncover then we just have to find a crystal stolen centuries ago from a dragon's cave, and return it to its proper place."

Helyan considered that for a moment. "You know where this place is?"

"Very near the Snowdon Mountain."

"So, after all this time, the whole thing comes down to a piece of crystal pillaged from a cave. I find that very interesting," he said.

"Indeed, and quite unexpected to say the least. If you have a minute, I'll tell you all about it," Garreth replied.

Helyan chuckled as he shot a glance heavenward. "I've got naught but time on my hands, m'lord. Please feel free to provide an explanation to all of this madness."

Garreth launched into the details of all they had discovered and all that had transpired to date. The moment he finished the narrative he gave the ghost a sideways glance. "None of what I've told you can leave this room, Helyan. For this is the only place our words are secure from outside forces. If anyone should discuss the details aloud, our wolf will surely get wind of it. Should you find a need to speak with me about any of this, for any reason, you'll need to return here to the library."

"Understood. In the meantime, I think I can have a word with some of our ancient spirits and see if they know anything concerning legends of wizards and pilfered hearts. In addition, you needn't worry about my charge concerning Essie, for it's a charge I take seriously. I'll attune myself to her presence this instant and make her my priority from this moment forward."

"Thank you, Helyan. You don't know how much I appreciate that."

"What do you appreciate?" Essie met his gaze first and then turned toward Helyan, who looked at her with an intensity that obviously made her uncomfortable. Nonetheless, she gave him a smile. "Good morning, Helyan."

The ghostly knight bowed low at the waist. "Good morn, m'lady. How are you this fine day?"

"Very well, thank you. How about yourself?"

"Can't complain," he replied.

Her gaze flickered back and forth between the two of them. "So what did I miss?"

"Nothing really. I just filled Helyan in on everything we've discovered this far. He's offered to ask some of the old spirits if they know of any legends concerning the heart."

She shot him a worried glance before she returned her full attention to Helyan. "How are you going to do that without our wolf knowing about it?"

Helyan winked. "A spirit doesn't need to speak aloud in order to converse with another spirit, Lady Essie. Speaking aloud is a skill we attain over time and solely for the benefit of those still living."

Essie breathed out a quiet laugh and nodded. "Yes, of course, I forgot about that and—thanks for the offer to assist. We need all the help we can get, right now."

Helyan returned her smile and then gave them both a nod. "I'll get right to task then. If I should find something I deem important, you'll be the first to know."

The moment the ghost took his leave, Essie turned to face him. "We should probably contact the Tylwyth Teg and let them know we deciphered the pictograph."

"News travels fast in their realm. They already paid

us a visit early this morning."

"They did? Why didn't you wake me up?"

"I didn't see any need. Due to time constraints, they only stopped by long enough to hear the translations and of course, that only served to fuel their desire to resume their hunt for the heart. They feel they're getting close."

"I can understand that." She let go of a sigh and tsked. "I just wish I could do something to aid the search."

"Don't let it trouble you. I have every confidence they'll find the crystal with time to spare. From all reports, they have things well under control."

Her gaze lit upon the bookshelves. "I suppose they do. Even so, it might help if I immerse myself in the ancient legends of Great Britain for the next little while. You have several books in your library I've yet to touch and perhaps the answer to our riddle is in one of them."

He shook his head ever so slightly as he gathered her into his arms and drew her close. "You could do that. But right now, we're going to put everything concerning the crystal, the heart, and anything else concerning diabolical wizards, magic, and black dragons on hold for a little while. After all the long hours you've put into this project, you need a break and so do I."

A brow lifted as a mischievous smile emerged. "A break? Sounds irresponsible, Lord Garreth."

He nodded. "Perhaps it is, but we're going to take one anyway."

Her fingers slid down his chest. "And do what?"

He grinned in response to the innocent question. "Now *that*, Miss S. E. DeSpencer, is a loaded question, and in all likelihood could get me into a whole lot of trouble if I answered it. Therefore, I think it best if I let you choose the activity."

A lovely blush proved his shameless comment flustered her a bit. She bit down on her lip and shrugged. "Oh…well, I've yet to visit the village and I'd really like to see it."

He turned his head to the side and looked at her askance. "I've never taken you to see the village?"

She shook her head. "Nope, you haven't."

"How neglectful. All right then, the village it is."

Fifteen minutes later, she and Garreth exited the castle grounds and turned their horses east. Farmland and lush landscapes abounded on either side of the cobblestone road upon which they traveled. Hidden amidst the majestic trees stood a smattering of ancient houses made of stone and covered with ivy. Contented horses, sheep, and cows grazed in the fields.

"This feels so much like I have stepped into another time and another place. Nothing looks modern—at least not on the outside," she said.

"Nothing is. We haven't had to build any new houses or buildings since the last destructive cycle."

"Really?"

He nodded. "We've only had to modernize what we already had."

"Well, where do the couples live that have married since that time? Surely you have them."

"Most certainly. But either they have moved into the empty houses or apartments, which we built plenty of the first time around, or they simply added a level or a wing to existing family structures."

"That's very interesting." She paused for a

moment. "Just how many people live here, Garreth?"

"Oh, probably a little over twenty thousand give or take a few. Now that I think on it, it's been a while since we've conducted any kind of census, so that number might be off a bit."

"Do you know all of them by name?"

"Yes, I think so. But you have to remember I've had a number of centuries to learn them."

"I suppose you have at that. But such a task seems a bit daunting to me."

"Not when you take just a few people at a time and as you might expect, you'll meet a handful of our residents today while we're in the village." He cleared his throat as he assumed a serious expression. "There is just one problem with that, though."

"A problem? What kind of problem?"

"I don't know quite how to introduce you. Shall I say, let me present Dr. Sirona Edula DeSpencer? Or mayhap it might be better if I said, Salacia Epona DeSpencer?"

Essie laughed as she turned her gaze heavenward. "You're desperate enough to delve into the mythological goddesses now, are you?"

He cocked his head to the side and shrugged. "Why not? I can see where such a theme fits you quite well, and you're blushing. So, perhaps that means I'm getting close to the mark. If not the first two then, how about Salus Egeria or Secia Empanda?"

She leaned toward him. "How about you just introduce me to the villagers as "Essie" and leave it at that?"

Garreth chuckled, bridged the span between them with an extended arm, and took hold of her hand. "If you wish, but just so you know, I'll not give up my quest."

She flicked a length of hair behind her shoulder. "Far be it from me to deprive you of the pleasure."

At first glance, the medieval village looked like something from off a movie set. Especially the row of buildings that made up the market place. But when they stepped inside the various buildings along the cobblestone street, she could see the same modern conveniences the castle possessed. She took just as much pleasure in exploring them as she did in meeting the people attached to them. Above all else, she delighted in meeting the children that persisted in tagging along beside them during her visit.

Then finally, at the end of a delightful day, Garreth escorted her inside the quaint, Tudor-style tavern for a bite to eat. Her gaze slowly explored the room. Metal hanging-wheel candelabras and metal wall sconces provided diffused light. Two-thirds of the way to the ceiling, the stonework connected with the plastered walls, trimmed in half-timber. Fireplaces roared on both sides of the large room and offered its guests a cozy welcome. A host of tables crowded one side of the room. The other provided plenty of space for the musicians and those who danced to the music that sounded far more modern than what she expected. Wall decorations consisted of a couple of tavern signs, a coat-of-arms, and various depictions of the hawk. One stood out from the rest, for it looked identical to the one in her dream.

Just as she opened her mouth to ask about that hawk in particular, one of the men behind the bar made all haste to their side.

"Lord Garreth," he said with a respectful nod of his head. The short, rotund, middle-aged man then said something in Welsh. Garreth responded in kind.

At the end of their brief conversation, Garreth turned toward her. "Lloyd, I'd like to introduce you to Essie DeSpencer and Essie, this is Lloyd, the owner of the tavern."

Essie returned the man's broad smile. "Hello Lloyd, it's nice to meet you."

He placed a hand against his heart and bowed at the waist. "Oh no, the honor is mine Lady Essie."

The man looked her over with the same unmasked curiosity every other person that Garreth introduced her today did. She took in a breath and slowly released it as he made his perusal. Finally, he escorted them to a table, made more private than the others by a knotwork lattice panel. Garreth held her chair as she sat down.

"I hope you don't mind," he said as he settled into the chair opposite hers. "But I took the liberty of ordering our meal. The menu is in Welsh."

"No, I don't mind at all, thank you."

"So, what do you think of our village?"

"I think it's wonderful. You have everything here a person could ever want or need. Do the proprietors get their supplies from the surface or do you make everything yourselves?"

"A little bit of both."

She leaned back in her chair as Lloyd served their drinks and placed a basket of scones on the table. "Thank you."

"You're welcome, Lady Essie," he said and then shifted his gaze to Garreth. "I'll have your meal ready in just a few minutes."

While they waited, Garreth entertained her with humorous stories about several of the boisterous patrons. By the time they finished both dinner and dessert, she could easily put a name and a face to each of those stories.

Garreth shoved his dessert plate off to the side and cocked his head in the direction of the dance floor. "Would you like to dance?"

An apologetic shrug accompanied the slight shake of her head. "You know—I'd like nothing more than to dance with you right now, but I think if we were to dance, everyone else would leave the floor and take the opportunity to gawk at the woman dancing with the Lord of Llys y Gwalch. Quite honestly, I think I've had enough attention for one day, if you don't mind."

He laughed outright as he took possession of her hand and rubbed his thumb across the top of it. "You have caused quite a stir today, haven't you? Well, all right then, are you ready to return to the castle or is there something else you'd like to do first?"

She dropped her napkin onto her plate. "No, I'm ready to go home, if you are."

The ride back to the castle took far less time than she desired. For she truly didn't want this magical day to end. Neither did Garreth it seemed, for he led her into the garden, rather than inside the castle. Then, under the light of the full moon and the brilliance of the stars, he took her into his arms and held her close to his heart. He fastened his gaze to hers and the way he looked at her at this moment, caused her pulse to race and a flush to splash onto her cheeks.

"If you don't mind, I don't think I'm ready for the day to end quite yet."

A warm, delicious flush crept over her body. "I don't mind."

He strengthened his hold and gazed deeply into her eyes. "Dw i'n dy garu di, Essie," he whispered huskily.

He said those very words just before he kissed her in the home of the Tylwyth Teg. Just as before, he didn't give her the time to ask what they meant. As her hand dropped around his shoulder while the other weaved through his hair, their lips met. The all consuming passion that erupted between them silenced her question. She would wait for a far better time to ask for a translation of those words—a far better time.

For right now, she and Garreth danced to the tune only they could hear.

Chapter Twenty

"The list of those with Fair blood living inside the castle is quite short," said Bran. He rested the side of his face between his finger and thumb as he gazed at the names on the page. "We have but seven. The thing is—I can't believe any one of them would be our wolf."

Garreth dropped his hands on top of his desk and leaned back in his chair. "Who do we have?"

"We have Rhys, Vaughn, Glenda, Philip, Aeron, Bethann, and Gerald."

He took a moment to consider each individual as Bran read the name. Yet, throughout all the days of his life, he believed every one of them loyal to him and to Llys y Gwalch. For they had served his father with like devotion. Nonetheless, he had a conspirator residing inside his home, and that conspirator had his own agenda. He wouldn't rest until he discovered his identity as well as his purpose.

Bran tossed him the notepad. "So, now what?"

"Now we concentrate our efforts on finding him or her out." He picked up the pad and tucked it away inside the bottom drawer.

"How do you propose we do that?"

"By a process of elimination, and I think we'll go ahead and start with the women right now." He rose from his seat at the desk, made his way to the intercom, and pressed the button assigned to Lowri.

"Yes?"

"Lo, could you bring a tea tray into the library for me and Bran, please?"

"I'll be right there."

Bran huffed out a breath and shook his head. "A tea tray, Garreth? Pray tell, what're you going to do with that?"

"I can't very well ask Lowri to send both Glenda and Bethann in here to clean up a mess unless there is a mess to clean, now can I? Once they arrive, we're going to talk about the interesting carving we found on Cyhelin's sepulcher." He settled into his chair and scooted it forward.

Bran's lips curved into a smile as understanding took hold. "Oh, you mean the carving that resembles a heart. Or, do you think a depiction of a dragon would be more effective?"

Garreth dipped his head to the side and shrugged. "I don't think it matters. After the women overhear our conversation, I'll ask Helyan to monitor the tomb and see if either of them takes the bait. If neither of them shows up in a reasonable amount of time, we'll work on the names of those men."

Minutes later, a knock sounded against the door just as Lowri entered carrying her tray. He lifted a hand to halt her progress. "You can stop right there."

She glanced down at the tray filled to capacity. "Did I forget something?"

"No. I just want you to drop the tray where you stand, if you please." The look on her face almost made him laugh out right. "Don't worry. The mess won't spoil the rug. Not from where you're standing, anyway." The woman stared at him as if he'd suddenly sprouted a set of horns or something else equally offensive. "Come now, don't be afraid. The task isn't all that difficult, I assure you."

Lowri shrugged, sucked in a breath, and then let go of her burden. She squeezed an eye shut as the china slammed onto the stone floor and shattered. "Whoops."

"Think nothing of it," he said with tongue-in-cheek. "Accidents happen. Just send Glenda and Bethann into clean the mess while you make us another tray, please."

The woman looked more than a little puzzled, yet somehow refrained from asking the questions he could see she had. "All right. I'll send them in right away."

They didn't have long to wait. The sound of footsteps and the hum from the wheels of the cleaning cart alerted them to the women's approach. Bran turned around to face him and propped an arm on top of the desk.

"That being said, I think Cledwyn's discovery is quite significant," said Garreth as the women entered the room.

"Yes, I agree. But do you think we can discover the location of the cave from the pictograph alone? There are some distinctive markings that should help us out a bit, I know, but—"

"That's a good very question, Bran. However, if Essie can translate the symbols beneath the carving on Cyhelin's sepulcher, perhaps we'll have everything we need."

"And then at long last, we can finally put an end to the destruction."

Just as Bran made the comment, Lowri returned to the room with the second tray in hand. She sidestepped the shards the ladies had swept into a pile. "Let's try this again, shall we? And this time, without the mishap."

He hid a grin behind his hand. "Thanks, Lo."

"Thanks?" She focused her attention upon the mess. "Oh. You're thanking me for breaking the tea set, of course. You never really liked that pattern, did you."

"You have to admit, the pink posies were a bit much."

She laughed as she made her way to the desk. "Well maybe when I look for replacements, I can find something with a skull and dagger motif, if that makes you more comfortable."

He gave her a wink. "Perfect."

The moment the women exited the room and closed the door, he rose from his seat. He made his way to the side window and cracked it open. Garreth spoke but a single word before he closed it again. He needed no more than that. "Helyan?"

By the time he reclaimed his chair, Helyan stood inside the room.

His ghostly friend dipped his head in greeting. "At your service, m'lord."

Garreth returned the nod. "I need you, or one of your trusted companions, to do me one more favor if you will."

"Just name it and it will be done."

"Keep an eye on the tomb of the kings over the course of the next several days and without revealing your presence. I need to know if anyone goes inside the mausoleum. In particular, I need to know if anyone examines Cyhelin's crypt."

A slight grin emerged. "You've laid a trap for our

wolf."

Garreth nodded. "I hope so. Now we just have to wait and see if he wanders into it."

Helyan's smile broadened. "Brilliant."

"Well—we'll at least hope the plan is brilliant," he replied.

****

The moment Garreth called her name, Essie stuck her bookmark alongside the current page, and closed the book. From under the shade of the garden tree, she turned to face the cobblestone path that led to the back entrance of the castle. She sat up a little straighter in anticipation of his company. "I'm over here."

In less than a minute, he had settled into the bench beside her and dropped an arm around her shoulders. Then, after a kiss that left her quite witless, he took hold of her book, and glanced at the title. "Are you finding anything helpful in this one?"

A disappointed sigh accompanied the shake of her head. "No, not so far."

"Looks like you're almost finished with it. Perhaps there is nothing to find in this particular book."

"I wouldn't be surprised. But then again, we can't let a stone go unturned as they say."

"Well, even if you do find something, you need to keep in mind the author might speak of myths and legends that may or may not have a foundation in truth. After all, it's quite possible the author made everything up."

"I know that. But, so far this book contains various legends concerning the Tylwyth Teg, an assortment of other fairy types, shape shifters, ghosts, and mythical realms, to name a few. On top of all that, I can't tell you

287

how many times he has mentioned the sinking of Llys y Helig. So, what do you think of all that?"

"Well, I guess you have me there," he said as he handed the book back. "How many more such books do you have left to read?"

"Only one more after I finish this one." She fanned the pages of the few remaining chapters and then gave voice to her thoughts. "After that, I might have to make a trip to the surface, visit a couple of book shops and see if they have something you don't."

He paused for a moment while he toyed with the notion. "You know, that might be a very good idea."

She snapped the book shut as she fastened her gaze to his. "I don't suppose you searched me out because you have some fabulous news to share with me that would make such a trip unnecessary?"

"No, I'm afraid not. Well, at least not yet. But then again, we haven't heard from our Fair friends for a couple of days now. That just might mean they're getting close."

"I hope so. Our deadline is a little less than a month away."

He caressed her face as he gave her a confident smile. "Don't let it worry you, cariad. I'm sure we'll have everything set to right in plenty of time."

"So everyone keeps saying."

"Then how can everyone be wrong?" he teased.

Just as the words left his mouth, the earth bellowed her rage from deep within the ground. Her heart dropped as the terrifying sound invaded her ears. She sucked in a breath and held it. A vicious trembling accompanied some kind of deep, guttural reverberation that scared her half to death. In that same instant,

Garreth engulfed her in the protection of his arms. He held her tight against his chest while the ground shook violently beneath their feet. Just as she wondered if it would ever stop, it finally did.

Garreth drew back just enough to look into her eyes. "Are you all right?"

"Yes—I'm fine. Are you?"

"Couldn't be any better."

She turned her gaze to the castle, looking for any signs of damage to the structure. She didn't see any. But then concern for the welfare of those inside took hold. "We need to check on everyone else."

In silent agreement, he tugged her to her feet and together, they returned to the castle. Her eyes darted about the great hall, looking for damage and found nothing major to cause alarm. Garreth's staff, taking everything in stride, busied themselves with the cleanup in their usual, efficient manner.

He approached and then placed a hand on top of Aeron's shoulder. "Is everyone accounted for?"

The steward righted the small end table and nodded. "Yes, Lord Garreth. Everyone is well and accounted for."

Bran emerged from the hallway and made his way toward them. "I just spoke with Rhys. No one has reported any major damage within the castle or in the village—just a few broken trinkets, easily replaced, is all."

Essie took her first deep breath and fastened her gaze to his. "Anne and the twins?"

"The twins slept right through the event, if you can believe that," he said. "However, as you might expect, the trembler shook Anne up a bit, simply over worry for

289

her children. Of course, the moment Lowri burst into the room with her no-nonsense attitude, she calmed right down."

Garreth flashed a grin and nodded. "Lowri does have that gift."

"That she does. Now that I've left my family in her very capable hands, do you want to go out and check for structural damage or would you rather do that later?"

Before answering his chamberlain, Garreth turned toward her and fastened his gaze to hers. "Will you be all right for a little while?"

"I'll be just fine, Garreth. You needn't worry." She glanced at the book she wanted to finish and at once, her mind traveled to a comfortable chair, situated in front of a cozy fire. She tilted her head toward the staircase. "But while you're gone, would you mind if I made use of that great big papa bear chair inside your bedroom for an hour or two? Up there I'll be able to stay out of everyone's way. Well, at least I will for a little while."

"I don't mind at all. I'll see you shortly." He dropped a sweet, unhurried kiss onto her lips, and then he and Bran exited the castle.

Once he disappeared from view, she turned around, made her way up the stairs, and slipped quietly into Garreth's room. She took a moment to pick up the things that had fallen onto the floor before she settled into the comfort of his plush chair. She tucked her legs underneath her and then opened the page to her bookmark. An hour or so later she arrived at the final chapter. The author entitled the section, "The Many Legends Concerning the Hidden Gold of Powys." She fastened her eyes on the page.

"Our story takes place in Ystradgynlais, which translates into English as 'vale of the river Cynlais.' Now, for those unfamiliar with this particular region, Ystradgynlais is a town, situated along the River Tawe, and is the second largest town in Powys, Wales. The watch, iron, and coal-mining industries are responsible for the growth of this area. These facts are well known to most. However, not so well known is the local legend concerning a hoard of gold, hidden somewhere inside a hill cave near Y Garn Goch, on the summit of Mynydd y Drum, or the Drum Mountain. A rich hoard protected to this day by three demonic entities or so the fable goes. According to the legend, these entities will not allow anyone near the treasure. Whispers abound that many have tried over the centuries and all have failed. A failure, I might add, that ended in each person's agonizing, violent, death.

"There are several variations to this legend. One variation, and the most popular from among them, reveals the existence of three cauldrons, teeming with gold, buried inside the hill cave spoken of previously, on the summit of the Drum Mountain, each protected by a powerful demon. Other legends speak of just one cauldron, yet the treasure it contains surpasses all others. Whether one cauldron or three, the fable most always concludes with the same prophecy. This prophecy states that a young girl will one day climb the summit and claim the treasure for her own. It further decrees that the demons will be powerless against the magic she carries within herself. But until that fateful day arrives, the demonic spirits will protect their hoard at all cost. For those determined to seek this treasure, consider yourselves duly warned."

Essie read the entire chapter twice. The third time around, her heart began a slow rhythmic hammering inside her chest. Her lips parted in response to each shallow breath she took. She peeled her eyes away from the book. While focusing instead on the dance of the waning flames, a barrage of chaotic thoughts swirled around inside her mind, seeking a smidgen of logic and truth behind the legend. Each of those thoughts concluded with one simple fact. Three demons, or more likely three *wizards*, guarded a priceless treasure somewhere inside a hill cave on the peak of Mynydd y Drum. Somehow—*somehow*, she had absolute knowledge that those wizards staunchly guarded the heart of the dragon for they considered that heart priceless treasure, indeed. That knowledge filled her with a curious mixture of exhilaration and trepidation.

Nonetheless, she would share this information with Garreth the minute he returned to the castle. From there they could travel to Llys y Helig and present this newfound knowledge to Gwynn and Uvan. They could then collect Cledwyn and Aneirin and set out immediately for the summit spoken of in the book. Surely it wouldn't take the Fair men long to discover the heart's resting place. Finally then, they could put an end to the destructive cycles. She could then offer Garreth her heart, mind, and soul for as long as he wanted her to stay—for she loved him far too deeply to consider any other choice. At long last, she could tell him that. She fixed her gaze upon the pages one more time, needing final confirmation before she shared her discovery.

At the same time, the doorknob turned and the

hinges moaned against the weight of the door, which meant that Garreth had already returned. Though she could hear the distinctive sounds, she refused to look away from the book. Her excitement escalated. She offered him her hand and while engrossed on the final paragraph, she said, "Garreth, I know where the heart is."

"Excellent. You have no idea how long I have waited to hear someone say that."

She slammed the book shut and bounded to her feet to confront the intruder. Vaughn, not Garreth, stood in the doorway with push broom in hand. Fear gripped her heart the moment their gazes met. A maniacal sneer had settled across his features, and she could feel the evil he exuded from where she stood.

He abandoned his broom, closed the door, and locked it. The sound of the click echoed loud in her ears. The shifter stepped slowly as he approached her. His crazed eyes darted between her face and the book she cradled in her arms. In that same instant, her mind screamed out a warning—*No matter what, he mustn't get possession of the book*. In response to the silent directive, she opened the book and flung it into the fire. Flames devoured the pages.

An animalistic growl rumbled deep within his chest. "Now look what you've done." He paused for a moment and for the look on his face, that pause made her blood run cold. In an instant, he replaced his anger with indifference. "Well, I'm afraid we're going to have to retrieve the heart of the dragon together. After all, I can't kill you now, can I? And I can't have you alerting anyone else as to the heart's location, or my identity."

She shook her head and gulped. "No, I'm afraid

not. I'm not going anywhere with you, Vaughn. Have you forgotten? You're inside Garreth's castle. I've only to call out and everyone within hearing distance will come to my aid."

He shot a glance at the ceiling and laughed. "Oh, I think you'll cooperate easily enough."

"What makes you think I'd do something like that?"

"Because if you don't, people you care about will die. Despite what you might think, it's not at all difficult to take the life of those who dwell beneath the sea. At least, not for someone with my unique set of skills. Perhaps I'll begin with Garreth or Bran, or how about those innocent little twins." He wiped a hand across his nose and shrugged. "You know, maybe I would find the greatest satisfaction in ripping all their throats out at once."

Her heart fell into the pit of her stomach as she envisioned such a bloody scene. "No—"

Vaughn dipped his chin as his eyes drilled through hers. "No? Does that mean you agree to accompany me and assist my quest without undue fuss or incident?"

"Only if you give me your word that you, or any cohort you might have working with you, will not harm a single resident that belongs to this province."

He stared at her for several very long seconds. "All right. In exchange for the terms I lay out, I'll give you my unbreakable bond that no one within the realm of Llys y Gwalch will be harmed in any way."

She huffed out a derisive breath. "Your terms?"

He moved a little closer and nodded. "Oh, yes. I will *not* have anyone inside this castle believe you are leaving against your will. Therefore, you'll pack all your belongings like a good little girl. You'll tell Lowri that you're leaving and that you have asked me to take you to the airport. When she asks you why, you can tell her the last quake unnerved you—that you fear for your safety."

"She's not going to believe that."

His features hardened. He leaned toward her and growled, "Make her believe."

She didn't miss the threat in his tone of voice. With a bit of reluctance, she released a breath and nodded.

"After that, you'll guide me to the heart. Do we have an agreement?"

She closed her eyes. "Yes, we have an agreement."

"Then come, Miss DeSpencer. I'll escort you to your bedchamber so you can pack."

He accompanied her all the way inside her bedroom, closed the door, and then leaned against it. Tears threatened to spill down her cheeks as she retrieved her luggage from the wardrobe. *Garreth*, her heart sobbed. *On, Garreth, I'm so sorry.* What would he think once he returned? Would he think her a coward? Would he ever forgive her for breaking her promise?

Don't think of such things, Essie.

Nothing matters right now, but keeping him and the inhabitants of this castle safe from the clutches of the putrid wolf and his vicious threats.

Despite the quandary, her mind sought for a means of escape all the while she packed her things. She just couldn't find one that guaranteed the lives of those she loved. Not right now, anyway. But once she arrived at the surface, she would find a way to thwart Vaughn's plans. She had to, or the cycles of destruction would continue. That very fact threatened the lives of those she loved every bit as much as Vaughn did. If she could get the heart first, she could somehow defeat her captor. Then she could make her way to the dragon's cave and—No, she couldn't do that. According to the prophecy, the noble hawk had to replace the heart, not her.

Her mind raced ahead of the thought and gave birth to an idea that took root and sprouted in a reckless direction. Because if Vaughn found her out—

"You're not trying to stall, or do something stupid, are you?"

"No, I'm ready." She zipped up the last of her bags and took hold of the handle. A deep sigh escaped as she turned away from the bed. She took a couple of steps on her way to the door and then glanced down at her clothing. "Wait a minute. I can't trudge through the wilderness dressed like this. I need to change my pants for some jeans and my shoes for some boots or we'll never get there."

His eyes traveled the length of her form and his slow lecherous perusal made her sick to her stomach. He folded his arms against his chest. "Go ahead if you feel the need."

Her mouth dropped. "I am *not* going to change my clothes in front of you," she ground out between clenched teeth.

He chuckled. "All right. Hurry up and change. I'll take the first of your bags down the stairs and get us a car. By the time I return, you had better be ready or everyone inside this castle dies."

She handed him the bag in her hand and nodded. That gave her less than five minutes to prepare.

Chapter Twenty-One

Garreth returned to the castle just as Essie made her way down the stairs with a suitcase in hand. Vaughn followed a step behind, burdened with additional pieces of her luggage. She halted mid-step as her eyes widened and then connected with his. She looked like a cornered hare. Try as he might, he couldn't make sense of the unfolding scene.

"Essie, what are you doing?" She had trouble meeting his gaze and that alarmed him.

"I...uh...I'm leaving, Garreth," she stammered.

"I can see that, but where are you going?" Her heartbeat accelerated as he asked the question. He could see it in the rapid rise and fall of her chest.

She bit down on her lip and gulped. "A...home. I'm...I'm going home."

His gut gave way, and it took him a moment to absorb the horrendous pain her simple statement caused him. Her eyes now refused to meet his altogether.

He swallowed past the knot forming in his throat. "Why?"

She peeked at him from beneath her lashes as she resumed her slow journey down the stairway. Each step caused her a great deal of anguish. Not only could he see it, he could feel it. That made her actions even more bewildering. She sniffed a couple of times. "Because I can't stay here and wait for the approaching disaster to happen. I…I don't have the strength to watch people die. You can't ask me to do that, Garreth. You can't."

He paused for several long moments as he sought control over his emotions. Never before had the task been this difficult to achieve. "But you said you would stay until the last possible moment. We still have several weeks before—"

"I know, and I thought I could stay," she whispered. "I'm so sorry…so very sorry. But I just can't. Please…"

Please? Please, what?

Countless scenarios stormed his mind. None of them made any sense. Nothing she *said* made any sense. Nevertheless, right now, at this moment, only one thing remained certain. He couldn't let her go. Not yet. Not without a fight. He approached the staircase and as she descended the final step he took gentle hold of her chin and tilted it upward, forcing their gazes to meet.

"I need you Essie."

She squeezed her eyes shut, just as a tear spilled down her cheek. Another followed. He wiped them away. She took in a ragged breath, opened her eyes, and shook her head. "There is nothing more I can do for you, Garreth. All of the translations are complete. You'll have to figure the rest of the puzzle out yourself."

"Essie, you can't—"

"I gave you my blue notebook weeks ago," she cut in. "Everything I have to offer is inside that notebook. Should you find the need, you can refer to all my notes in the days ahead." She wiped a hand across her mouth and nose. "Please…I've got to go now, or I'll miss my plane."

Panic and desperation took hold. In a last ditch effort to keep her at his side, he took her rigid body into his arms. Then just as he would kiss her, she dropped her head and pushed against his chest with her hand. A small wail escaped her lips.

"Don't…"

In response to the pitiful word, he dropped his arms to his side and stepped away. She swept past him and all but ran to the door. Vaughn met his gaze. He could see the pity in the man's eyes. He didn't want it.

"I'll be back in a while," said Vaughn.

Garreth nodded and just as he would pass, he grabbed hold of his shirtsleeve. "Before you leave her, make sure she boards her plane safely, Vaughn."

He bobbed his head. "Yes, Lord Garreth. I'll do that. Don't you worry; I'll take good care of her."

"See that you do."

The instant the door put a barrier between him and the woman he loved, Bran approached from behind and placed a hand on top of his shoulder. "I'm sorry Garreth."

He stiffened. Until that moment, he had quite forgotten Bran's presence. Though, just as well he witnessed the event for himself—for he wouldn't need to answer any question, he'd rather not answer. He firmed his jaw and turned around to face his chamberlain. "I want to be alone for awhile if you don't mind. See to it that I'm not disturbed."

Bran merely nodded as he turned and made his way to the library. He locked the door and took a moment to gaze about the room. But no matter where he looked, he could see Essie. He could see her working at the table with her books and stacks of photographs spread out all over the place—making phone calls at his desk. He could see her standing at the window, gazing out at the rain or the sunshine. He could see her lounging in the chair in front of the fireplace where they shared countless, pleasurable conversations.

A quiet, derisive laugh escaped his lips as he completed the thought. Pleasurable conversations, yes. But now that he brought each to mind and relived them, he could see the glaring omission. Never once, in all the time they spent together, did he hear her say that she loved him. Did he ever inspire such an emotion? He scoffed over the very notion. If she loved him, she would never have left him. She would have allowed him to silence her fears. His eyes closed for a moment. Then, for a very long while, he did naught but pace, and deal with the pain of her loss.

By the time dawn colored the sky the innumerable questions for which he had no answers, finally quieted. For now, he would cling to the one thing that provided a small amount of comfort. Essie would stay safe from the all dangers surrounding his quest. He wouldn't have to think of a clever way to send her away while he embarked on his journey to replace the crystal. Perhaps now, he could even assist in looking for the thing—

A knock at the door interrupted his somber thoughts. He took in a deep breath and slowly released it. "Yes?"

"Garreth, I need to talk to you. I need to talk to you right now," said Lowri. "It's urgent."

The woman sounded distressed. Had something happened to Essie? He strode to the door and flung it open. "What is it?"

She wrung her hands and then lifted them to her face. "Something's terribly wrong…terribly, terribly, wrong."

"What do you mean?"

"Most of Essie's things are still inside her room," she blurted out.

His insides churned as the beat of his heart accelerated. "What are you talking about? She had all her luggage with her—"

"I know that. But when I went into her room to change the linens, I couldn't find any of the sheets in the cupboard. Most of the towels are missing too. I thought perhaps for one reason or another she moved them to the wardrobe." Her eyes bore into his as she dropped a hand against her throat. "I opened the door to take a look, and Garreth—most of her clothes are still hanging in the closet. I couldn't imagine why she would leave them behind. Call it simple curiosity if you will, but on a hunch, I decided to check the drawers to see if she left any of her belongings there as well. She had."

In response to the revelation, he punched on the staff's intercom button with his fisted hand.

"Yes?"

"Rhys? I need you to send Vaughn to the library right now."

"Yes, Lord Garreth."

He returned his attention to Lowri. "Did she leave anything else?"

Lowri chewed on her lip and offered a helpless shrug. "I don't know. I didn't take the time to check everything—I thought it more important to find you."

"Lord Garreth?" Rhys interrupted.

"Yes?"

"Vaughn isn't here and the car is still gone. From all reports, he never returned to the castle last night."

His heart dropped into the pit of his gut. Garreth hit the button to Bran's room. "Bran I need you to come to the library, right now."

"I'm already here."

He whirled around just as Bran entered the room from the hallway. "Good. Call the authorities and see if they have any accident reports involving the car. If one doesn't exist, report the bloody thing stolen."

"What's going on?"

"I'm not sure, Bran. All I know at this point is that Vaughn didn't return to the castle after his supposed trip to the airport."

Bran drew his brows together and shook his head. "Supposed trip?"

"I'll explain everything after you've made your calls." He placed a hand against Lowri's back. "Come on; let's go see what else she might've left behind."

They traversed the hallways and climbed the stairs in silence. All the while, his thoughts raced over every possible scenario. None of them provided peace of mind. Lowri entered Essie's room just ahead of him and then stood off to the side to let him through. The wardrobe doors, still opened, revealed several pieces of Essie's wardrobe.

"They look very hastily hung, don't they," he said as he sought a plausible reason to explain the wild disarray. "But perhaps they only appear that way because of the recent quake."

Lowri followed his gaze as she bit down on her lip. "I don't have an answer for that. The clothes inside the drawers look just as chaotic. Do you see? She has her underthings mixed with some of her T-shirts. The drawer on the right has socks intermixed with her jeans. I can tell you, she is far more organized than that."

"And you never found the missing linens?"

"No, but I didn't look in every nook and cranny either." She turned around then and made a thorough search of the bedroom. After a few minutes inside the bathroom, she returned, shaking her head. "The linens just aren't here. However, some of her personal toiletries are, and I can't think of a woman on this earth who would leave her perfume behind."

Bran burst into the room just in time to hear the comment. His gaze flitted about the chamber. "No accidents of any kind have been reported during the past forty-eight hours."

A memory stirred. He now recalled with clarity, the day the twins were born and Vaughn stood outside the locked library door with a look of intense agitation, yanking at the handle. Bran said the man knew where to find the keys. Why didn't he see it before?

"That can only mean one thing, Bran. Vaughn has revealed himself as our wolf, and now he has Essie."

"But why would he take her?"

Garreth could think of only one reason. He whirled around, strode out of Essie's bedroom and into his own with his entourage following close at his heels. The broom, leaning against the wall screamed for attention. He gave it a curt nod. "Looks like Vaughn did indeed, pay a visit to my room after the quake, and more than likely, while Essie occupied it," he said as he continued his journey to the fireplace.

Nothing seemed out of place on or around his chair. His gaze drifted to the mantel. Then a burgundy fragment in the far corner of the grate caught his eye—a fragment that matched the cover of the book Essie held in her hand just before she asked to use his bedroom. He leaned down, retrieved it from the ashes, and dusted it off.

"I believe he took her because she discovered something important inside this book. Somehow Vaughn became aware of that fact when he entered the room. I'm assuming that in order to keep him from the full knowledge, she did the only thing she could. She tossed the book into the fire."

"That in turn would require her prompt removal from the castle, for how else could he gain the information he seeks without interference?" Bran balled his hands into tight fists. "The weedy maggot forced her to leave this castle against her will and beneath our very noses."

Garreth nodded as he chucked the fragment back into the fireplace. "I believe the linens stuffed inside her luggage is proof enough of that."

"We've got to find her, Garreth," wailed Lowri. "We have to find her before he does something awful to her."

"The problem is, they could be anywhere by now," said Bran.

The moment Bran made the comment, something Essie said just before she walked out the door thundered into his mind.

I gave you my blue notebook weeks ago. Everything I have to offer is inside that notebook. You can refer to all my notes in the days ahead, should you find the need.

He turned around to face Lowri and Bran. "She

never gave me her notebook. Why didn't I catch that when she said it?"

"What?" Bran seemed truly perplexed. "What are you talking about?"

Garreth shook head. "Before she left yesterday, she said she gave me her blue notebook. She said she gave it to me weeks ago. Do you remember?"

A slow nod followed the question. "Yes, I do, now that you mention it."

"She never gave me that book, Bran. We need to find it, and we need to find it now. There's something in it she wants me to know."

"Well, it has to be inside her bedroom," said Lowri. "She wouldn't have had the opportunity to go anywhere else, would she? Not with Vaughn standing guard over her."

"You're probably right. Let's go see if we can find the bloody thing." Garreth led the way. He rifled through each of the drawers while Bran ransacked the drawers and cabinets in the bathroom. Lowri searched the wardrobe from top to bottom. The blue notebook remained elusive. Then, just before they vacated the bedroom, he glanced at the pillow, peeking out from the blanket. He yanked back the covers on the bed and tossed the pillow aside.

"You found it," said Bran.

Garreth exhaled a sigh of relief as he retrieved the book from under the sheet and flipped through the pages. There, at the very bottom of the final page she had used, he found what he sought. He tapped at the passage. "Looks like she only had time to write a few words. But they're enough." He snapped the book shut and headed for the door.

Bran shadowed his steps. "What did she say?"

"She's telling us the heart of the dragon is buried in a cave situated somewhere on the southern peak of Mynydd y Drum." He paused for a moment in consideration of the clue she left behind. "Knowing Essie, she'll probably lead Vaughn only in the general area, in the hope we arrive before he forces the issue."

"Then we need to get going," he said. "Vaughn is hours ahead of us."

"You can rest assured, I'll find a way to catch up, even if I have to hire a helicopter," he shot back as he strode down the hallways, bolted down the stairs, and exited the castle through the side door. Bran remained a step behind. Once outside he made ready to address Hefina, knowing the slight possibility existed that Vaughn could hear him as well.

He looked at Bran, gave him a nod, and assumed a somber tone. "All things considered, I think it's a good thing Essie decided to go home. Knowing she's out of danger makes my mind rest easier. However, we need to let Cledwyn and Aneirin know that we're on own from here on out and I suppose the sooner we give them that message, the better. That way they can make any needed adjustments."

"Yes, you're right about that. Nonetheless, I think they'll be quite disappointed she didn't give them the opportunity to say goodbye."

"If not for our timely arrival, we wouldn't have had the opportunity either." Garreth put a finger to his lips to stay further comment.

He returned to the side door, and just as he entered the castle, he called for Helyan. By the time he stepped inside the library, he found Oswallt, not Helyan, awaiting his arrival.

The ghost dipped his head in both greeting and respect. "Lord Garreth, I'm afraid Helyan is not here."

He sucked in a breath filled with rising alarm. "Not here? Where is he?"

The ghost shifted his gaze to the west. "He is attending Lady Essie."

Tremendous relief washed over him the minute the words left his mouth. Helyan would watch over and protect her. He nodded. "Thank you, Oswallt. That's the best news I've heard all day. If you can get word to him or if you hear from him, let him know we're heading in their direction."

Oswallt returned his nod and disappeared.

"I wonder how long we'll have to wait for Cledwyn and Aneirin," said Bran as he turned his gaze to the window.

"Not long, I should think," said Cledwyn as he entered the room with Aneirin at his side. "We were already on our way here and therefore, could hear your message loud and clear. Now what's all this nonsense about Essie leaving?"

"She's gone, and we've just discovered that she didn't leave of her own choice," Garreth replied.

"What do you mean?" asked Aneirin.

"Just that." Garreth briefly closed his eyes as he rubbed a hand against his forehead. "Yesterday, Bran, and I set out to look for structural damage following the quake. Essie said she would read while we were gone. But, upon our return, we met up with her as she descended the stairs with luggage in hand and Vaughn a step behind. When I asked for an explanation, she told me she couldn't stay here any longer. She said she couldn't take the trauma of watching people die should we fail to stop the apocalypse in time. Therefore, she wanted to go home." He shrugged. "I believed her."

"What changed your mind?" asked Cledwyn.

"Early this morning Lo stopped by Essie's room to change the linens and give it a thorough cleaning. In so doing, she discovered that Essie didn't fill her suitcases with all of her clothes, instead she filled them with sheets and towels."

"I don't understand," said Aneirin.

"Neither did I at first." He gazed at Aneirin for a moment and then made Cledwyn his focus. "I'll fill you in on all of the details later, but it boils down to this. Essie believes the heart of the dragon is located inside a cave at the top of or near Mynydd y Drum. There is now no doubt in my mind that Vaughn somehow gleaned a small portion of Essie's discovery." He shook his head and shrugged. "Perhaps, thinking I had entered the room instead of Vaughn, she made some kind of statement regarding that fact and that's when our devious wolf finally revealed himself. He then forced her to leave the castle."

"You're sure Vaughn is our shifter?" asked Aneirin.

"Without a doubt. The man never returned to the castle after they left and most importantly, before she walked out of the door, Essie made sure I would look for her notebook. Unfortunately, I didn't pick up on that fact until this morning. That notebook provides the location of the heart."

"Then we need to go now if we hope to catch up with them," said Cledwyn. "How long will it take you to pack your things?"

"About five minutes." Garreth took a step forward, halted and then turned toward Bran. "This is your call Bran, you can come along if you'd like, but since we have no idea how long we'll be gone, if you want to stay and watch over your family and Llys y Gwalch, that's fine by me. For those things are equally important."

Bran never wavered. "The man has Essie, Garreth. Of course I'm going with you."

"Then go get your stuff together," he said as he continued his journey to the door.

Bran fell into step beside him. "All right. I'll order up a few supplies while we pack and then—"

"We'll take care of the supplies," Cledwyn cut in. "Just gather whatever you need, and let's get out of here. For each minute takes them farther away."

"Indeed it does. If we head for the surface, I can hire a helicopter. That should cut the distance with great efficiency."

"I think we can get there faster by boat. Besides, a helicopter would only alert Vaughn as to our presence," said Cledwyn.

In less than ten minutes, they passed through the waterfall on their way to Llys y Helig. By the time they arrived in the realm of the Tylwyth Teg, Cledwyn and Aneirin had amassed all of the details. Garreth recited those same details to both Gwynn and Uvan while Cledwyn and Aneirin prepared their fastest ship with all necessary supplies.

At the end of his report, Gwynn shook his head. "I'm sorry, Garreth. I'm sure it disappoints you to discover that Vaughn is the one who betrayed your trust."

Garreth nodded. "In truth, he would've been the last man I suspected. All the years he stood at my side and ate at my table, never once did his loyalty come into question."

Uvan turned his gaze to the king. "If you don't mind, I believe I'll go along with them this time around. Perhaps I can assist you in some small way."

Gwynn nodded as he rose from his chair. "Yes, you might at that."

"If nothing else, I can keep the wolf deaf to our words while we search them out," Uvan replied.

Both Gwynn and Hefina stood on the pier as they set sail for the shores of Swansea. From there they would travel inland, toward the Drum Mountain. The journey across the waters didn't take long. The craft, invisible to mortal eyes, flew over the ocean waves at great speed. Before the sun cast an afternoon shadow, they dropped anchor, disembarked, and with supplies in hand, made their way to shore. Garreth turned his gaze to the hills. Somewhere out there, Vaughn held Essie captive. But not for much longer and once he caught up with them, the wolf would pay dearly for taking her against her will. He would see to it.

"This way," said Cledwyn as he waved them forward. "We know a bit of a short cut. If all goes as planned, we'll catch up with them well before the sun sets. If luck remains our ally, he'll never see us coming."

Chapter Twenty-Two

Would that she could scream. Instead, Essie clenched her teeth and turned her gaze to the car door window. She had uttered but one word to Vaughn since they drove away from the castle. The moment they exited the tunnel and hit the surface, he asked for a destination.

In return, she simply said, "Powys."

He made a few distasteful jokes along the way, which she refused to acknowledge. She didn't respond to any of his attempts to make conversation, either. He gave up his efforts after a time and they just traveled the endless miles in silence. That suited her just fine. She needed every single minute to devise a plan of escape should Garreth fail to find and read her notebook.

Garreth…

She closed her eyes against the agony caused by the memory of their last moments together. He looked so hurt when she announced her departure and refused his kiss. She could see the pain in his eyes. In that moment, she had to call up every ounce of strength and will she possessed to walk over the threshold, and get into the car. A strength and will that would've altogether evaporated if she had allowed their lips to touch.

The remark concerning her notebook didn't even

faze him. She didn't see so much as a spark of understanding in his eyes. Would he call the comment to mind once someone discovered the clothing she left behind? She hoped so. For if he did, it wouldn't take him long to put everything together. He would immediately contact Cledwyn and Aneirin and seek their help. Together they would surely have the power to defeat the wolf. They could then turn their full attention to retrieving and replacing the heart.

"We're entering Powys County, Miss DeSpencer," said Vaughn, breaking into her thoughts. "Where do we go from here?"

"On a bit of journey," she replied.

He huffed out a derisive snort. "A bit of a journey."

"Yes. All I'm going to tell you is that we'll begin our little expedition at the town of Ystradgynlais and then head for Mynydd y Drum."

He slammed on the brake, screeched to a halt, and whirled around to face her. "All you're going to tell me?" he snarled.

She met his menacing gaze with boldness. "Do you really think I'm stupid, Vaughn? If you do, let me set you straight here and now. I'm not going to answer another question or say another word about where we're going, the direction I'll follow, or the landmarks I need to find. I'll simply lead you to our destination and surely, someone with Fair blood flowing through his veins can feel the powerful magic of the heart in close proximity. Right?"

Vaughn just stared at her. Hatred emanated from his very soul and that gave her a curious mix of apprehension and audacity. Right now, she clung to the audacity.

She turned her head and gave him a side-ways glance. "What's the matter? You aren't sure of your abilities? You don't know if you have enough Fair blood flowing in your veins to do the job? After all, you couldn't feel the scroll inside King Brychan's tomb, could you now," she taunted. "Well you better hope you're up to the task. Because the piece is *buried* somewhere out there, and I can only lead you in the general direction. You see the book didn't provide a map—no "x" marks the magic spot. If you can't feel it, you're going to need to do a whole lot of digging in order to obtain it. Oh, yes, that reminds me, you did bring a shovel along on this journey, didn't you?"

A harsh glint appeared in his eyes. He gnashed his teeth in a fit of rage. "I ought to kill you right now."

"Well go ahead and do it then. Let's see where that gets you." She held his gaze for several tense moments. He didn't respond. "I'm not afraid of you Vaughn."

"You should be," he snapped. Without waiting for a response, he jerked his shoulder forward and tramped on the gas.

Essie took great care as she slowly released the breath she had held throughout the confrontation and closed her eyes. She curled her fingers into her palms to quiet the tremble. Vaughn would take great pleasure in killing her if he got the chance. She had to make sure he didn't get that chance.

Minutes passed, or maybe hours. She couldn't tell. All she could really say is that darkness still pervaded the skies. A waning moon and the brilliance of stars provided the only light along the dusty lonely road Vaughn now followed. Then, without any kind of warning, he swerved to the side of the road and stopped the car. Dread settled in the moment he turned off the engine. He turned his gaze toward the covering of trees and vegetation. In that moment, she had no idea what he had planned. Visions of her lifeless abandoned body filled her mind. She shivered.

"Get out," he said.

She tugged on the handle and exited the vehicle as he made his way to the boot of the car and raised the lid. Her heart dropped. Would he rummage through her luggage and discover the stolen sheets and towels? If he did, in all likelihood he would not wait for the cover of trees. He would kill her on the spot. She studied the forest in a bid to gauge the distance from the car. But how ridiculous even to consider such a thing, she couldn't possibly outrun a wolf.

"Get yourself together one bag and make sure it's a bag you can carry yourself," he snarled. "I'll give you two minutes to find what you need."

Essie took hold of the nylon bag she hastily prepared at the castle and stepped away. In turn, he grabbed the large backpack, some rope, tossed a couple sleeping bags onto the ground, and then slammed the lid shut.

"If you don't want to sleep on the bare ground, I suggest you pick up one of those bedrolls." Without waiting for a response, he snatched the bag closest to his position, turned around, and headed into the trees.

They walked quite a distance and just as fatigue took its toll, he whirled around to face her. "This is as good a place as any. We'll camp here for the night."

He dropped to a knee, rummaged around inside his pack, and tossed her a couple protein bars. She didn't thank him. In fact, if she didn't need to keep up her strength, she wouldn't even eat them.

"Don't think of trying to escape," he said. "You won't make it past the first tree should you try anything so foolish, and then for your trouble, you can spend the rest of the night tied to a tree. Decision's yours."

She said nothing in reply, but brushed the crumbs from off her hands, shook out her sleeping bag, and crawled inside. Her gaze swept the heavens for a brief moment as she called Garreth to mind. *You do know I love you, don't you Garreth, even though I didn't get the chance to say it?* Then, of their own volition, her eyelids closed and though she fought them, the tears fell anyway.

****

An unexpected thump against her thigh awakened her at the break of dawn. She peeked through the slit of her eyelids and found Vaughn standing over her.

"Get up."

She sat upright and as she wiped at the corner of her eyes, Vaughn dropped a granola bar and a bottle of water into her lap.

"Hurry up and eat that," he said as he turned a squinted gaze east, toward the rising sun.

She ripped the top off the wrapper, extracted the bar, and took a bite. The thing tasted just as stale as the one she ate last night. Nonetheless, hunger compelled her to eat it.

While Vaughn chewed on his own, he fastened his eyes to hers. His silent scrutiny made her most uncomfortable. Finally, he said, "I'm afraid I'm going to have to tie you up for awhile, Miss DeSpencer. I need to go into Ystradgynlais, obtain a *shovel*, a few supplies, and some food. You understand why I can't take you with me, and I can't leave you to wander free. You might get lost."

She refused a response of any kind and that made him laugh. He twisted his features into an expression of mock sympathy.

"Aw—now isn't that pathetic? I can see the hope of a grand rescue shining within your lovely eyes." He wiped his mouth against his sleeve and laughed. "What a crock. Do you really think Garreth is somehow going to find you out here? Do you think he's even going to try since you were the one that did the leaving? I mean, you don't really think he harbored any great affection for you, do you? Didn't anyone bother to tell you the man has collected and then discarded an endless stream of women throughout his very long life? You're no different from any of the others. If he hasn't replaced you already, he will soon enough, I assure you. In a few months time, he won't even remember your name."

Despite the intense pain his callous words inflicted, Essie took hold of her water bottle and drained it. She picked up the wrapper and then stuffed it, and the bottle, inside the side pouch of her bag. All the while, she endured the sound of his malicious laughter with cool indifference worthy of any dramatic performance.

A short while later, he bound her hands and feet with the rope he extracted from the car and then tethered her to the tree. Satisfied with his network of knots, he flashed a sardonic smile and disappeared into the brush.

All the tension she had carried inside these past eighteen or so hours, oozed out of her body. She took a moment to revel in the relief generated by his absence. She leaned her head against the tree, and closed her eyes. Yet, in so doing, a deluge of disjointed thoughts assailed her. At what point would Vaughn rid himself of her? Did she make a mistake in mentioning Mynydd y Drum? Had Lowri, or anyone else for that matter, discovered her clothing or the missing linens? Did they understand the reason behind the theft? She clung to the belief that somehow they did. What about her notebook? If Garreth found it and looked through the pages, he would know she didn't willingly break her promise. More importantly, he would know where to begin his search—if not for her, as Vaughn suggested, then at least for the heart.

"Lady Essie? Are you all right?"

Startled over the unexpected voice, her eyes shot open and as she heaved herself forward, she gasped with both surprise and delight. "Helyan! What are you doing here?" Her hand flew to her mouth and covered it. She shouldn't have spoken, for Vaughn could surely hear her.

A grin curved a corner of his mouth upward as he knelt beside her and placed a hand underneath her chin. "Making sure that vermin doesn't lay a hand on you. Though it brings you no comfort now, I will have you know that I've been with you, every step of the way. You're not now, nor have you ever been alone. Oh, and you needn't worry about speaking aloud. I have the ability to absorb your words as long as I'm beside you."

Tears threatened to surface as she raised her bound hands toward his face. "Oh Helyan, you don't know how happy I am to see you. But, why did you wait so long to show yourself to me? I could've used you last night."

"I know and I'm sorry. But I'm sure you would

agree that revealing my presence to Vaughn would be most unwise. Therefore, the moment you exited the castle, I followed at a distance he couldn't detect."

"Oh." She dropped her gaze as disappointment beset her. "Then Garreth didn't send you."

Once again he tilted her chin upward until their gazes met. "Now, how could he? He didn't know you were going to leave Llys y Gwalch, did he?"

She met the reminder with a slight shake of her head. "No, I guess he didn't."

"But that doesn't mean he's ignorant as to my presence at your side. I suspect Garreth knows I'm with you."

"You do? But how could he possibly know?"

"Because he charged me with watching over you, should something occur that would prevent him from doing it himself, and it's a charge I take very seriously. He knows this. Now let me loosen that rope a bit, so you're a little more comfortable while we await Vaughn's return."

"Thank you." She watched in fascination as the ghost merely focused his attention on the cords. In a matter of seconds she could slip her hands through the ties if she so desired. "How did you do that?"

"I simply willed it so." He gave her a wink as he settled in beside her with legs inclined and his arms resting on top of his knees. "We don't want Vaughn to know I'm here, so just leave the ropes on. However, when he returns and unties you, don't forget to pull them taut."

"Don't worry, I won't forget."

His gaze shifted briefly to the cords that wrapped around her wrists. "Believe me, I would rather just get you out of here right now, but you simply don't have the ability to outrun Vaughn's wolf persona. Even with a head start, he could still detect your scent and follow. I think it far better for us to wait until Garreth arrives."

"Then you think he'll come?" She shot a glance skyward and tsked. "Silly question. He has to come, else how would he obtain the heart?"

"He's not coming for the heart, Lady Essie, I assure you. He's coming for the woman he loves."

The comment brought Vaughn's taunts to the forefront of her mind. "The woman he loves—"

"Oh come now," he gently chided. "You surely didn't allow Vaughn's childish temper tantrum to cast a pall over Garreth's feelings for you, did you? The man loves you Essie—from the very depths of his soul. The love he feels for you is an amazing thing, and I've waited centuries for him to find it. You know, I almost gave up hope until the day he escorted you into the cemetery. I knew then, that at long last, he found his soul mate and even told him so."

She shook her head and laughed. "His soul mate, Helyan? Do you really believe in such a thing?"

Helyan nodded. "Indeed I do. A man can have many loves over the course of his lifetime. Don't let anyone tell you any different. However, he has but one soul mate. And when he finds her, it's like a raging bolt of lightning exploding inside his heart with tremendous force. The heat consumes him, and he is never the same again. No other woman will ever do, compare, come close, or take her place in his heart."

She searched his eyes for a moment as she considered his words. "Those are some very lovely sentiments. Are you speaking from experience?"

He lifted his chin and laughed. "No, I'm still waiting around to find mine. She's still out there somewhere."

A smile manifested itself in response to his declaration. "Well, I hope you never stop looking for her."

"I don't intend to. Now enough of me. We've more important things to discuss."

"All right, what would you like to talk about?"

"Vaughn said something about your hope for a rescue before he blessed us with his absence. Dare I give some credence to the notion that Garreth already knows your destination? I'm only asking because if he doesn't, I'll need to leave you for a time, find him, and give him directions."

Essie fixed her gaze on the distant hills and nodded. "If he found my notebook, then he knows the general direction. But, I suppose if this is to make any sense, I need to tell you that I discovered the location of the heart in one of Garreth's library books."

The remark stunned him. "You unraveled the mystery inside the pages of a book?"

"Yes, I did. Yesterday, during his absence, I made use of Garreth's room in order to read while the staff tidied up after the quake. I found the passage just before I heard his door open. I didn't turn around to look—I should have—but I just assumed he had returned. I assumed wrong. Therefore, I made Vaughn, not Garreth, privy to my discovery."

She lifted her face to the sun and briefly closed her eyes. "You don't know how thankful I am that I didn't blurt out the location. If I had, I believe Vaughn would've killed me then and there. Instead, he merely threatened to slaughter Garreth, Anne, Bran and the twins if I didn't leave the castle with him and lead him to the heart. So, while he stood there and watched every move I made, I packed my things. I didn't know what else to do."

Helyan took hold of her hand and gave it a gentle squeeze. "You couldn't have done anything else, Essie. You did the right thing."

"Yes, well then I got this idea. I thought if I could just get rid of Vaughn for a few minutes I could leave behind some clues. So, just before we left my bedroom I looked down at my clothes and said that I needed to change into something more appropriate for hiking. He gave me five minutes. I never changed clothes so fast in my life. I think I had it done in about thirty seconds. Anyway, I used my remaining time to toss as many pieces of clothing as I could, back inside the drawers, hung some of my things inside the closet, and exchanged them for sheets and towels. With only seconds to go, I took my notebook, scribbled the heart's location on one of the pages, and shoved it underneath my sheets. Vaughn returned just as I zipped up the last of my suitcases."

She paused as emotion overcame her. "I didn't expect to see Garreth, but as fate would have it, I did." Tears welled up in her eyes as a lump rose in her throat in response to the pain of the recollected memory. She gazed into his eyes. "Helyan, he just looked so hurt."

Her ghostly companion wiped away the tear that streamed down her cheek. "Garreth had the strength to bear it, m'lady, and from what you tell me, he didn't have to bear it long."

"I hope not. I sincerely hope not," she whispered.

"So, I take it your plan is to lead Vaughn in the proper direction, but not close enough for him to feel any trace of the heart, am I right?"

"Yes and only because time is growing short. I thought if Garreth found me, we would be all the closer to the heart. But right now, I don't have a clue as to where I'm going. I don't even know the direction I'm supposed to be heading from here, other than the cave rests somewhere on the southeast side of the mountain."

Helyan rubbed a hand along his mouth, and then pointed at the hills. "Those are the peaks of Mynydd y Drum—there in the distance. Vaughn knows this as well, so you can't lead him in the opposite direction, but you can turn more to the north, rather than south. Just try to slow your steps a bit—make as if you're looking for those landmarks you mentioned. If you do that, I think Garreth will arrive well before we need to worry. Once we take care of Vaughn, we can turn in the proper direction and send Garreth in to retrieve the heart."

"No, we can't do that."

"Why not? The man will be right there as you said, and the task is simple enough."

"You don't understand. *I'm* the one that has to do it."

He paused for several seconds before he spoke and all the while, he retained her gaze. "What makes you think that?"

"The legend in the book is very specific. Three wizards—whether in the flesh or not—guard the treasure and they have jealously guarded it from the day they stole it. History speaks of the countless men who have died in the attempt to claim it over the centuries.

But, according to the ancient prophecy, a girl is destined to climb the summit and take possession of this treasure, which I now know is the heart of the dragon. The prophecy states the demons have no power to stop her. So you see—a man can't do it. Only a female can accomplish the feat."

"Legends are just that Lady Essie. You can't take every word as truth."

"I know that, truly I do. But something deep inside me *knows,* beyond any doubt whatsoever, this part of the legend is fact. If we are to have any hope of reclaiming the heart, I'm the one that has to go inside the cave and get it," she said, calling her nightmare to mind.

"I don't know if Garreth will go along with directives that are naught but a legend."

"He has to, Helyan—he just has to. You need to help me convince him of that. Please?"

His expression softened. "I can't make you any promises. The man has his own way of doing things and sometimes it isn't easy to get him to change his mind on how those things are done. That especially applies when it comes to you—"

"We might only have one opportunity to get this right, Helyan. Therefore, don't you think we ought to follow the instructions, be they right or wrong?"

He cast his gaze to the ground and conjured a sigh. "I'll see what I can do once he arrives."

"Garreth told me once that you can hear people's voices and their movements up to a mile away. So, you'll know the moment he's near, right?"

A slight smile tugged at the corners of his mouth. "I'll know."

"Is there some way you can let me know, without giving your presence away to Vaughn?"

He flashed a full-fledged grin. "Don't worry, m'lady. When the time comes, I'll let you know that rescue is imminent. In the meantime, keep in mind that I'm close and I'll not allow Vaughn to hurt you. Indeed, I'll not even allow him the pleasure of touching you. You have my solemn oath on that."

The lump in her throat returned. "Thank you, Helyan. I can't begin to tell you how much it means to me that you're here."

"You flatter me, Lady Essie."

She shook her head. "Not at all, for from the moment I first met you, I counted you among my dearest, most special friends and I always will. Therefore, who better to provide comfort when that comfort is needed?" She leaned over then and placed a light kiss against his ghostly cheek.

Amusement filled his eyes. "Mind doing me a personal favor?"

"Ask and it's yours."

"Tell Garreth you gave me that kiss."

She laughed. "All right, I'll do that."

In a matter of seconds, his humor fled. He turned his gaze west and studied the landscape. "The wolf approaches."

Chapter Twenty-Three

Because of Helyan's presence, Vaughn's attempt to intimidate by bounding toward her in his wolf persona didn't so much as cause a flutter in the beat of her heart. If anything, it only served to fuel her contempt. She hid a yawn behind her hand as he dropped his over-burdened bag from his mouth, skulked into the bushes, and shifted to human form. Her indifference and lack of fear irritated him. She could see it all over his face the moment he emerged, and it gave her a measure of satisfaction. He yanked off her ropes. All the while, he avoided her gaze.

"Let's get going," he said, using the same gruff tone he had assumed the moment they vacated the realm of Llys y Gwalch.

Essie rolled up her sleeping bag and gathered her things, taking just as much time off the clock as she could. Finally, after his third and most exasperated sigh, she stood and faced northeast.

She slung her bag onto her shoulder and took hold of her bedroll. "This way."

They traipsed through the trees and over the rough terrain for well over an hour before Vaughn broke the silence. "How long do you think it will take us to arrive at our destination?"

She cast her gaze at the mountain that loomed in the distance. "I really don't know. As you might recall,

I'm not a native of Wales, nor do I pretend to know the details of its geography. All I can do is look for the particular landmarks noted in the book. How far apart they are is anyone's guess."

Nothing more passed between them until the noon hour approached and Vaughn raised a fisted hand skyward. "We'll stop here and get a bite to eat. I don't need you fainting on me now."

Essie merely nodded in response. She didn't know if the incessant growling of her stomach compelled him to stop, or if the man hungered himself. His reason didn't matter. She simply found some solace in knowing that a lunch break would give Garreth additional time to catch up—*if* he found her notebook. She dropped both bag and bedroll, fashioned herself a seat underneath the shade of a tree, and sat down.

He tossed her some fruit, a couple of scones, and another bottle of water. "Let's hope we make our destination soon. Because if we don't, you're going to get mighty hungry."

"I think I can manage to take care of myself if the need arises and if given the opportunity to do so unfettered by you."

He returned a dubious chuckle. "Oh, is that right?"

She rubbed the pain at the back of her neck and closed her eyes. "Yes, that's right."

"Well, if nothing else, you've got spunk, I'll give you that much," he said as he stuffed the remaining portion of his Welsh cake inside his mouth. "Still, I think it would benefit you all the way around to complete your task before nightfall."

"Why? Will I turn into a rock when the sun sets or do the sands of my hourglass run out?"

Sardonic humor filled his eyes, yet he didn't condescend to answer.

She suppressed a shiver of apprehension. "I can't make you any guarantees, Vaughn. We've already discussed this."

He stopped chewing for a moment and then swallowed down the bite he had in his mouth. A stony glint appeared in his eye as he leaned forward and clenched his teeth. "I *want* that heart, Miss DeSpencer."

She stared back, boldly meeting his gaze. "I think you've made that quite clear already. But I want to know why. Why do you want it so badly? Do you get some sort of perverse pleasure out of watching people die and their lands destroyed? Or—or do you think the piece is somehow valuable enough that—that—" While she floundered for the word she wanted to use, Vaughn threw back his head and roared with laughter.

"I wondered how much you and Garreth figured out after you closed off access to the library and refused to speak of it anywhere else." He huffed out a derisive breath. "You don't have a clue. But, since it won't matter in the *outcome* of things, let me enlighten you a little bit. The heart is *priceless*, for it does far more than bring balance to the elements. You might've discovered that fact if you had just looked beyond the need to replace it. You see, the magic of the heart can also *detect* things of great worth that are hidden deep within the elements of earth, water and fire—things like gold, silver, diamonds, and other precious metals and stones. All the treasures of the earth are mine for the taking, once I have the heart in my possession."

The comment served to fuel her annoyance. She shook her head. "And what will all those treasures give you?"

He flashed a grin meant to taunt. "Anything I want, for the infinite power that comes with such treasure. For that, I thank you for your unwavering determination to put all of the pieces together for me. The endless waiting for someone with your skills to come along seemed nigh on unbearable at times."

"Such a pity then, you couldn't figure it out for yourself centuries ago."

"Wasn't for lack of trying, I assure you." A faraway look entered his eyes as he focused his gaze somewhere above her head. "But then, besides having certain knowledge of the crystal's existence, and its power over the elements, we had little else to go on— with even fewer resources at our disposal. We couldn't find anyone who had the knowledge to decipher the writing on the parchment or—"

She pounced on the word. "We?"

He stared at her for a time without answering. In the very moment she didn't think he would, he said, "All that happened a long time ago. She's no longer among the living, so it doesn't matter."

"Nia?" she pressed.

A disdainful chuckled accompanied a skyward glance. "No, certainly not Nia."

"Really? But then how did you know about and gain possession of the coin and the parchment hidden inside her bedroom underneath her bed?"

"Does any of that really matter?"

She combed her fingers through her tangled hair as she lifted a shoulder. "No, I suppose it doesn't. But it would serve to satisfy my curiosity."

He paused for a time and then shrugged, "Let me

just put it this way—Nia didn't have the same priorities we did. First and foremost, she set her heart on elevating her status from the insignificant title of princess to queen. She craved the power of ruling a kingdom and that is something she never would've achieved in the realm of Llys y Helig. Amassing the wealth remained ever secondary to her goal. Therefore, she thought it in *her* best interest to offer Garreth a piece of our collected puzzle. I'll leave it at that."

"Ah. So the cohort you speak of was one of Nia's personal attendants then. If I were to hazard a guess, I'd say she met her death alongside Nia, and is—in all likelihood—buried beside her in Garreth's cemetery. Was it her grave you actually visited the night you dug that hole in the soil next to Nia's stone?"

Vaughn narrowed his eyes as he rose to his feet. "I liked you better when you kept your mouth shut. Now, let's go."

Essie rose to her feet and then took a quick peek behind her shoulder. Nothing but endless landscape returned her gaze. A sigh she didn't intend to release escaped her lips. In response, her vile companion shook his mangy head and laughed.

"You still aren't hoping that Garreth's coming to your rescue, are you?"

"Tell me something, Vaughn, do you really think he's so thick that he hasn't figured out who you are and what you're about by now?" she countered.

He shrugged. "Oh, I give him full credit for all that. The man isn't stupid—far from it. But what good does the knowledge do him now? You left him of your own accord, isn't that right? He saw that much with his own eyes. Now, should he go so far as to call your New

329

York residence seeking confirmation of your arrival, he'll not find you at home, correct? He'll then have to give credence to the idea that you and I are working together. Even should he dismiss that notion as impossible, he still won't know where to look for you. The United Kingdom comprises well over two hundred thousand square kilometers. So, you tell me, where will he begin his search, Miss DeSpencer?"

He met her stubborn silence with another bout of malicious laughter.

****

Garreth wiped the sweat from off his forehead with the back of his forearm and gazed up at the afternoon sun. The dank bypass Cledwyn led them through had shaved a considerable number of miles off their journey. Yet, any evidence as to either Essie or Vaughn's presence eluded them. Did they, perchance, travel the wrong path or were the pair so far ahead they'd never catch them in time? The questions troubled his mind. He had to find her. He just had to.

"You think we would've seen something of them by now," Bran groused as Aneirin inspected the surrounding area for any telltale signs of their presence.

"I should be quite surprised if we did," Cledwyn replied. "You must understand—a person can make their way to the mountain's summit in a great variety of ways. Following the same route is remote at best. Don't forget, Vaughn used a car and traveled the various roads and highways, while we chose the sea. Nonetheless, sooner or later, all paths will finally converge in the very area we are headed. You needn't worry. We'll find them."

"Well, let's hope we find them in time," Bran

muttered.

"That's no longer a consideration, Bran. We *have* found them, or at least we've picked up their trail," said Aneirin. He rose to his feet and with a broad grin on his face, wiped the dust from his hands. "I believe they stopped right here for a bite to eat and not all that long ago."

"Indeed they did."

At the sound of the unexpected voice, Garreth whirled around to face it. Relief flooded into every particle of his body and soul. "Where are they, Helyan? Is Essie all right? He hasn't hurt her, has he?"

Everyone simultaneously converged upon the ghost with a host of questions. He stepped back and held up a hand. "Essie is fine at the moment. She's doing an admirable job of rebuffing all of Vaughn's taunts and threats with cool indifference. I can also tell you, her courage and pluck is driving the man to distraction.

"Right now, they're about four miles ahead of you, heading in a northerly direction on open plain. I detected your presence a while ago. Since I can still maintain my connection to Lady Essie without undue hardship, I decided to pay you a brief visit and let you know all is well. Don't look so worried, Garreth, I can still hear every move she makes, and I'll rejoin her shortly."

"They're headed north, you say?" Cledwyn cut in.

"Yes, and she's deliberately taking her time." Helyan nodded as he shifted his gaze to the northern side of the mountain. "By so doing, she gives you time to catch up. At the same time, the maneuver keeps Vaughn from detecting the heart."

"She'll not get away with that for long," Uvan said,

taking a step forward. "Once they arrive at the foothills, Vaughn will expect to feel the presence of the magic. The lack may provoke him."

"Then we need to make sure we intercept them well before they get there," Garreth replied.

"The problem I see," said Bran, as his gaze darted between each of their companions, "is that instead of the heart's magic, he'll sense *your* presence once we close in. That doesn't bode well for Essie, either."

Uvan stroked his beard while he considered the quandary. "Point well taken, Bran. Therefore, it falls to you and Garreth to remove Essie from Vaughn's grasp."

"No." Garreth shook his head. "I'll go in and get her myself. I believe one has a far better chance of catching our wolf unaware, than two."

"Well now, wait a minute," said Bran. "How are we going to find her if Cledwyn and Aneirin fall behind? We have no way of tracking them ourselves."

"That won't pose a problem," said Cledwyn. "We can lead you close enough to catch a glimpse of them without Vaughn detecting our presence. He's only half-blood. Therefore, his senses are not as strong as ours. We also have the element of surprise as our ally. Since he's not expecting us, he won't expend needless energy looking for us."

"You're right about that, Cledwyn," Helyan said. "Vaughn *isn't* expecting you. Although he's sure you've uncovered his identity and purpose, he's of a mind to believe you've no hope of discovering his whereabouts. He's also quite certain that finding Essie is the least of your concerns, since she voluntarily left Llys y Gwalch."

"That works to our advantage," said Aneirin, returning his attention to Garreth. "Once we find them, we'll keep them just in sight and simply follow them for a time. Then when the sun sets, you can use the shadows of early evening to conceal your presence until you're upon them. That's when you make your move."

Cledwyn nodded in agreement. "Yes, and if you can find a way to do it, grasp Vaughn from behind, rather than confront him head on. Once you have him about the neck, hold on tight. Should he still have the ability to transform, you'll not be near his jaws. If you can just hold onto him long enough for us to join you, we can take control—"

"No!"

The single word, reverberating with both alarm and dismay ended the discussion. All eyes shifted to Helyan who disappeared even as the word spewed out of his mouth. Dread paralyzed each of them for one infinite moment. Something terrible had just happened and it involved Essie. A shot of adrenalin coursed through Garreth's veins, displacing all else. At once, he tore off running, paying no heed to the thick, barbed vegetation that conspired to slow him down or block his way. He had but one thought as he muscled through the bramble—he had to find his lady, for he could not live without her. The thunderous footsteps of his companions echoed behind his as he sprinted toward the foothills of Mynydd y Drum. He ran until exhaustion bade him stop for breath. Until that instant, he didn't consider whether he followed the correct path or not. He leaned down, placed his hands on top of his thighs, and inhaled a series of deep breaths before any of the others caught up to him.

Cledwyn grasped his shoulder. He gave his head a shake and panted as he sought to replenish his air supply. "Slow down a bit, Garreth," he finally huffed out. "We're picking up traces of the wolf's scent now. That means we're nearing his position and must proceed with caution from this point forward. They're not moving as fast as we are. In fact, they may have even stopped for one reason or another."

The comment unnerved him. He didn't want to consider the reason. "The wolf's scent?"

"Yes, Vaughn has shifted into his wolf persona."

Garreth exhaled a final lengthy breath and stood erect. Visions he didn't want plowed through his mind. "In which direction are they headed?"

Cledwyn's eyes swept the horizon as Aneirin, Bran and Uvan approached them. "They are headed south."

"They changed course then," he said.

"Yes, I'm afraid they have."

"Do you suppose that means he somehow found out that Essie was leading him in the opposite direction?" asked Bran.

"I suppose the possibility exists," Cledwyn replied.

Bran dropped his gaze as he blew out a sigh. "If that's the case, then he must've detected the magic of the heart."

"No, I don't think that's the reason for the change," said Aneirin. "For we have yet to feel any trace of it ourselves. More likely, since he'd yet to detect the presence of magic, he grew suspicious and simply changed course."

"His reason doesn't matter right now," Garreth said. "Right now our priority is finding Essie."

Cledwyn cocked his head to the side. "You're

right. So, now that we've caught our breath, let's get going. But watch where you place your feet and keep your footsteps as quiet as you can. We don't want Vaughn noting our presence."

Garreth remained but a step behind as Cledwyn and Aneirin cut a jagged path leading to the foothills. The setting sun deepened the shadows in which they concealed themselves. Though he welcomed the darkness, it also curtailed their ability to observe their environment without hindrance.

Just then, Cledwyn and Aneirin halted their steps and stooped low to the ground. Cledwyn waved a hand in silent command for the rest of the company to follow suit. Each obeyed the directive. Garreth strained to see beyond the deepening gloom that surrounded them. The sounds of nocturnal creatures assailed his ears, yet he didn't hear a single errant noise that indicated Essie or the wolf moved in close proximity.

Aneirin turned a puzzled gaze to his comrade. Cledwyn shrugged in response. In unison then, they crept forward. With deliberation, they kept their movements both silent and small. An overwhelming need to discover the reason for this behavior consumed Garreth. Yet, to keep Essie safe, he stifled the need to ask and inched forward in the same manner. They maneuvered through the trees, around several large boulders, and into a small clearing. His Fair companions dropped to a knee and explored the ground that lay before them.

Aneirin pinched a piece of the earth and drew it to his nose while he and Cledwyn exchanged a glance. "Vaughn's blood."

"*Vaughn's* blood?" Garreth hissed. "What are you

talking about?"

Cledwyn gave him his full attention. "From what we can see, it appears that a struggle took place here and it involved Vaughn. The struggle left him injured. The amount of blood on the ground indicates he lay here for a time, perhaps unconscious—"

"Essie?" he cut in.

Aneirin shook his head. "There's no trace of her here. The blood belongs to Vaughn and to Vaughn alone."

"So you think Essie somehow managed to get away from him then?"

"I think we can safely say she did at least for a time. But since Vaughn is no longer here—" Aneirin shrugged and let the rest of his sentence take them where it might.

Garreth didn't need him to finish it. "We must close the distance, and we must close it now. Which way did he go?"

Cledwyn said nothing, but turned toward the hills and took off at great speed. In less than ten minutes, the Fair men once again halted their steps. Garreth followed their pointed gaze. He could now see the wolf in the distance, creeping forward. His gaze then fell upon Essie, no more than a few paces ahead. Vaughn skulked along the hilly terrain, keeping to the shadows, while silently stalking his victim. Any minute now, he would find an opportunity, and strike her. Though Helyan stood at Essie's side, he didn't know if the ghost had sufficient power to thwart the full force of Vaughn's attack.

He wouldn't chance it. Garreth snaked past Cledwyn and Aneirin. So intent on his victim, Vaughn didn't hear him approach until the very last moment. Just as he propelled his body forward, Vaughn whirled around, and with teeth bared, lunged for his throat. Garreth dropped to the ground, wrapped his arms around the wolf's neck, and yanked him down. He encircled the creature's body with his legs and held tight. All the while, he struggled to keep Vaughn's teeth away from his face by increasing the strength of his grip around his neck. The sound of approaching footsteps intermingled with the sound of Essie's voice. She screamed his name in the same instant he wrenched his knife from out of his boot sheath. Unable to position the weapon at the wolf's throat for a clean kill, he plunged it into his side. Vaughn yelped and frantically struggled for freedom. Garreth withdrew the blade and using all his might, thrust it in again. This time, the knife found its mark. The wolf fell limp. Garreth rolled the carcass off his body in the same moment his comrades converged upon the scene and surrounded the lifeless wolf.

He rose to his feet and wiped the dirt from his face with the back of his hand. Rather than focusing his attention on the grisly work of his companions, his eyes sought for and then settled upon Essie. She closed the distance between them and flung her arms around his neck. He snatched her to into his arms and held her close to his chest. He reveled in the feeling. If he had his way, he would keep her locked in his arms for a very long while. A very long while—

"Essie—"

"I'm sorry, Garreth," she whispered brokenly. "I'm so sorry. I didn't mean for any of this to happen. I didn't mean to cause you any pain."

337

"Shh, you have nothing to apologize for. None of this is your fault." He drew back just far enough to gaze into her eyes and wipe the tears away from her face.

"But it is—I shouldn't have said anything until I made sure—but oh, Garreth! I couldn't let him hurt you. I just love you so much and when he—"

He silenced the rest of her comment with an ardent kiss that grew in intensity and passion, for he didn't need anything more than that simple, heartfelt, pronouncement.

Chapter Twenty-Four

Essie stood on top of the grassy hill sheltered in the strength of Garreth's arms, with Helyan still at her side. Just below them, Uvan, Cledwyn, and Aneirin disposed of Vaughn's remains in the manner demanded by the Tylwyth Teg for one of his ilk—or so they said. A shiver coursed throughout her body as the tense hours spent in the shifter's company flooded her mind. In response, Garreth cuddled her closer still, offering even more of the comfort she found in his embrace. She dropped her head against his shoulder—and that's when she noticed the blood.

She drew in a deep breath, bolted upright, and wrenched herself free of his grasp. "You're hurt!" she said pointing at the blatant evidence with her index finger.

Garreth looked down at his shoulder. He studied the stain that marred the sleeve of his shirt with an expression of indifference and then shook his head. "Don't let it trouble you. I didn't feel any pain when it happened, and I don't feel any pain now. I'm sure the wound is not as bad as it looks."

"No. Let me see it." She unbuttoned his shirt and lifted the sleeve away from his shoulder. Angry welts surrounded a series of dark red puncture marks from which blood oozed. She wrinkled her nose. "Looks like Vaughn sank his teeth into you pretty good. We need to get this cleaned up. Just give me a minute. I've got some water in my bag and something that surely resembles a cloth."

He grabbed hold of her hand just as she turned away and wheeled her back around to face him. "Not necessary, Essie. I'm all right."

"I'm going to clean it anyway," she said as she withdrew her hand and crossed the short distance to where she had abandoned her pack.

Helyan chuckled. "Better just let her do it, Garreth. You know as well I, it always makes a woman feel better to fuss."

Essie rolled her eyes as she extracted her water bottle and a clean pair of socks. Fussing had nothing to do with it. The possibility of infection did. She eyed the large boulder off to her right. "Come sit here, Garreth and take off your shirt," she said as she made her way over to the rock.

Once she had him seated, she doused a sock with water and dabbed at the wound. The thing looked even nastier after she cleaned it. She raked her fingers through her hair and shook her head. "I wished I had some peroxide or something," she murmured. "Who knows what kind of foul, disgusting, bacteria Vaughn had floating around inside his mouth."

"Don't worry about it Essie," said Garreth. "I've recovered from far worse."

The various scars on the back and chest of her battle-hardened warrior testified to that.

Uvan approached them then and halted his steps just behind her. He peered over her shoulder and without saying a word, headed into the dense foliage. She tracked his progress until he disappeared. Her gaze then shifted to Cledwyn and Aneirin, and the roaring fire that consumed what remained of Vaughn's repulsive body. Cledwyn picked up another piece of wood and tossed it on top of the flames. In response, the fire hissed and belched eerie shapes and colors, sending them skyward. The memories of the past few days returned.

"Do you want to tell me about it, cariad?" Garreth used a tone meant to soothe.

A slow breath passed through her lips as she closed her eyes. Did she want to tell him about her experience? He took hold of her hand and tugged her onto his lap. He fastened his gaze to hers and waited for her to speak. Perhaps he needed to know the details after all—

"As you know, after you and Bran left, I went up to your room to read."

Essie recited the details as they unfolded without any interruption from either Garreth or Helyan. She paused in her narrative at the point Vaughn grew suspicious, angry, and weary of her presence. Her words trailed off as she recalled the event.

"What made him suspect that you were leading him in the opposite direction?" Garreth prodded.

"Because we were close to the mountain and he didn't feel even the slightest twinge of magic emitting from our surroundings. I told him I couldn't help it— that I followed the directions in the book as best I could. Nonetheless, I could see the skepticism in his eyes. He forced a change of course then and in the direction we truly needed to go. We traveled south for a time and that unnerved me. Yet, thankfully, he still couldn't detect any sign of the heart." She took in a deep breath and shrugged. "He bellowed his rage. I told him that I couldn't help what he could or couldn't feel. I suggested that either he didn't carry enough Fair blood to sense the magic or that the legend in the book was just that and it contained no bearing in fact. That made him even angrier."

Indeed, it had. Very angry. His eyes blazed with hatred. They turned fiery red as he glared at her and then, after an incalculable amount of time, they turned coal black. So much so that his pupils disappeared completely. He clenched his teeth as he twisted his head to the side. Veins popped out from his neck and then right in front of her eyes, he shifted from his human form to his wolf persona. An indescribable fear consumed her as he inched his way toward her just so he could savor the moment. By then, the brilliant red had returned to his eyes. She tried to scream, but only managed a quiet whimper—

Just as she recalled the event, Uvan returned, carrying a large leaf that held some kind of dark green slimy mush. She welcomed the disruption.

"I don't mean to interrupt, but you need to apply this poultice to Garreth's shoulder and the sooner, the better," he said. "The pulp contains a mixture of healing herbs that work quite well on an injury of this sort."

"Thank you, Uvan." She gave him a smile as she rose to her feet. He handed her the moist, pulpy substance and at once, she busied herself with its application. Their task finished, Cledwyn and Aneirin chose that moment to join them.

Garreth took hold of her hand and gave it a gentle press. "What happened then?"

She dipped her head to the side and shrugged. "Vaughn shifted his form and then with his jaws gaping wide open, he lunged at me. The force and weight knocked me to the ground. I rolled onto my side. Without taking my eyes off him, I sought for a weapon of some kind. My hand closed around the remnants of a dried-out, jagged tree branch." Her gaze shifted to Helyan for a moment. He winked in response. "I thrust the stick into his ribs just as Helyan bashed the back of his head with a rock—a very large rock. Vaughn's body fell limp to the ground—I couldn't tell if the blow killed him or just rendered him unconscious. Helyan yanked me to my feet. We didn't waste any time at all in assessing Vaughn's injuries—we simply took off and you know the rest."

Garreth's fingers brushed through her wind-tousled hair. He shook his head. "I'm so sorry, Essie. If I had only paid attention to what you tried to tell me there on the stairs instead of feeling sorry for myself, you wouldn't have had to endure everything you did. Indeed, Vaughn would never have made it outside our realm."

"No, I prayed for the delay. Don't you see? Keeping Vaughn busy kept everyone in Llys y Gwalch safe."

"I could argue that point and probably will at a later time, but right now, I think you need some rest. You've endured far more than you should have at the hands of Vaughn, and you've endured the ordeal with very little sleep. I think we'll just camp here for the night and get an early start in the morning."

She shook her head. "I couldn't possibly sleep now. Especially not here," she said as she fixed her gaze upon the diminishing fire. "Now that we've come this far, I would much rather continue our journey to the cave. You must understand the legend only gives us a direction. As a result, it might take a while to find the crystal and even longer to obtain it."

"Even longer to obtain it?" Cledwyn repeated. "What do you mean by that?"

She hesitated as she sought a coherent explanation. "Well, according to the legend, the hill cave is eternally guarded by three demons, or more likely, by the magic of the three wizards who stole the piece in the first place. Over the centuries, countless men have searched for the treasure only to die a gruesome, hideous death in the process. Added to this legend, the author provided another. He said that long ago, a warlock once residing in Ystradgynlais discovered the location of the hill cave. This warlock discovered there was but one way to acquire the treasure—a mortal needed to spend an entire night on the mountain and survive the terrors he would surely encounter."

Uvan narrowed his eyes. "Did your book mention any specifics as to what these terrors entailed?"

"Yes. The author mentioned powerful phantom spirits appearing in the guise of a bull, a goat, boar, and lion, each meant to terrorize the intruder. If the mortal withstood the spirits, he would then encounter a blazing wheel of fire with the power to tear the mortal in two."

"Sounds brutal," said Aneirin. "I can see where an unsuspecting man probably wouldn't survive the night."

"Like I said, according to the legend, no *man* has survived it." Essie paused for a moment and exchanged a glance with Helyan. "However, there is a prophecy connected to this legend that provides a better ending. I think we should pay attention to it."

Garreth narrowed his eyes as his gaze penetrated every corner of her soul. She could now see the suspicion in his eyes. Did her expression give her away? She licked across the bottom of her lip. "This fable states that one day a girl will climb the mountain. She and she alone will have the power to claim the treasure within."

Garreth bounded to his feet while shaking his head. "No, Essie. We're not even going to discuss this. You're *not* going in there."

"The legend states differently, Garreth. If you want that heart, then I'm the only one in this group that can go in there and get it."

"It's just a *legend*, Essie," he ground out between clenched teeth.

She nodded. "Yes, and so is the lost realm of Llys y Helig, the Tylwyth Teg, the Tuatha de Danann and let us not forget the absurd notion of *dragons*," she shot back.

Helyan spared her a glance before he shifted his attention to the Lord of Llys y Gwalch. "She does have a point, Garreth."

Garreth dropped his forehead onto his elevated hand and gave it a rub. "Oh, Helyan, not you too."

"Well, just wait a minute," he said. "The legend doesn't prohibit a spirit from entering the cave alongside this female. Essie will not go in there alone and you have my personal guarantee, I'll not allow anyone or any *phantom* in any form, to harm her in any way. You know I have the power to do that."

Essie thanked her ghostly friend with a slight dip of her head. He acknowledged in like manner.

Uvan took a step forward and cleared his throat. "I

believe this story needs to be taken just as seriously as all others we have uncovered this far, Garreth. Keep in mind if we fail to collect the crystal, we fail to end the destructive cycles. The legend states a woman will have the power to claim the heart. I believe this is so. But, as an extra precaution, I can also provide Essie with additional protection against demonic entities."

"Can you look me in the eye, Uvan, and tell me the risk of injury or death doesn't exist in this venture?"

Uvan put a hand on his shoulder. "I can look you in the eye and tell you the risk is so miniscule, that we needn't seriously consider it."

"We'll all be standing right there at the entrance, Garreth," said Cledwyn. "Should something unexpected occur, that threatens Essie in any way whatsoever, we'll simply go in and remove her from the threat."

He firmed his jaw. "What if we're not in time to save her?"

"Garreth," said Aneirin. "We'll not allow Essie any harm."

"Yes, indeed, you're right about that," he stated with a sudden look of determination filling his eyes.

****

Much later that night, Essie fell asleep nestled in his arms. Exhaustion had finally won the day and her long dark lashes pulled the cover over her golden brown eyes. He brushed the long strands of hair away from her face and then dropped a kiss against her cheek. She stirred, but did not awaken. Though he took comfort in the tranquility she found in sleep, the same had eluded him for much of the night. For each time he closed his eyes, his nightmare concerning Essie and the thick, swirling mist that stole her away, plagued his mind.

Trust. Helyan, his Fair companions and even Essie had asked for his trust in regards to their judgment. He found it difficult to give. The love he had for Essie consumed him and he simply could not face life without her. Nonetheless, his lady insisted on going inside that cave, with or without his consent. She had to, she said. Now, for the first time since he had begun his quest to halt the destructive cycles, he wished for a delay.

Finally, as dawn approached, he eased her out of his arms, covered her with the top of her bedroll, and rose to his feet. He replenished the dwindling fire with the few remaining pieces of collected wood, and then turned his gaze toward the summit of Mynydd y Drum.

"She'll be all right, Garreth. I give you my word."

Garreth shifted his focus from the mountain to Helyan who now stood at his side. "I'll hold you to it, my friend." He paused for a moment and then said, "I never did thank you for watching over her while Vaughn held her captive and for keeping her safe. I'd like to remedy that now."

"You needn't thank me for something I considered an honor. Lady Essie is quite a woman. You're lucky to have her."

"Yes, I am." He shifted his gaze to her sleeping form. "Tell me something, Helyan; did she know you were there the whole time?"

Helyan shook his head. "Not at first. Vaughn didn't let her wander far. So, I didn't get the opportunity to speak to her until he tied her up and went for supplies."

His heart dropped as his mind instantly conjured such a scene. "He tied her up?"

Helyan slapped him on the back and grinned. "Not to worry, I loosened the ties the moment the vermin disappeared."

"You're a good man, Helyan, and you know what? I'm glad you decided to hang around for awhile."

The ghost waved a hand in dismissal. "Ah, I can't imagine myself being content to strum a golden harp on top of a billowy cloud—should that be my ultimate destination. If it isn't? Well, then I'm happy to have cheated the devil out of his due."

The laughter they shared roused Bran, Cledwyn and Aneirin from their slumber. Uvan followed soon thereafter. But not until Aneirin announced breakfast, did he have the heart to awaken Essie. Nonetheless, she seemed well rested and more than a little anxious to resume the journey. Would that he could postpone it. Despite the desire, they broke camp less than thirty minutes later.

Cledwyn approached her. "Now tell me Essie, what specific information did the book give concerning the location of the treasure?"

"Well, according to the author, the treasure is hidden somewhere inside a hill cave near Y Garn Goch, on the southern summit of Mynydd y Drum."

He flashed a broad smile. "If that's the case, then we should feel the presence of magic well before the midday sun touches the sky."

The prediction proved accurate. Uvan could feel the power of the crystal ahead of both Cledwyn and Aneirin. He adjusted their course twice as they moved over the rough terrain and toward the mysterious hidden hill cave mentioned in the pages of the book. After they stopped for a bite to eat, Cledwyn took over the lead.

They climbed upward, moving south and all the while, Garreth retained possession of Essie's hand for the need to keep her close to his side for as long as he could. He found it obvious the same need had taken hold of her as well. Within the hour, they dropped down inside a narrow gorge, and followed its course for several minutes. Without warning, their Fair companions abruptly halted their steps. The men exchanged glances and then simultaneously approached a rocky wall with an overhang of dense vegetation.

"The piece is somewhere behind these rocks, right here," said Aneirin. He waved a hand in a circular motion along the wall, as did Cledwyn and Uvan.

"Here," said Uvan beckoning the men with a wave of his fingers. "Essie should enter straight through here. Do you feel it?"

"Yes, I do." Cledwyn placed his shoulder and hip against the wall, and thrust his weight against it. The rock wobbled a fraction in response. "I don't think it will take much to expose the original opening."

"Then let's get to it," said Aneirin. "I'd like to get Essie in and out of there before the sun sets. After all the legend says, "one day" doesn't it?"

"And day it is," said Bran as he rolled up his sleeves and approached the wall.

The apprehension Garreth carried inside intensified the moment the first rock tumbled to the ground. He faced Essie and gave her hand a gentle squeeze. "Care to spend a few minutes with me while our companions open the door?"

She gave him a dazzling smile. "I'd love to spend a few minutes with you, Lord Garreth."

"Don't wander far," Aneirin warned. "We'll have

this open in no time at all."

"You needn't worry. We'll not go any farther than what we can hear you call."

They followed the gorge around the bend and encountered a brook that meandered down the mountain. The lush vegetation following its path would give them the privacy he sought. He led her into the shadows of the trees, turned her around toward him, and tugged her into his arms.

"Promise me you'll take every precaution while you're inside that bloody cave," he said.

She crossed her heart. "I promise I'll take every precaution."

"And promise me, that you'll not allow anything, anyone, or any power created by the demons or wizards of hell, to hamper your return."

Her hands moved up from his chest and encircled his neck. "Garreth, I promise you everything is going to be all right. I'm going to go in there, find the crystal, take it from its nest, bring it out, and hand it to you. All the while, Helyan will stand right by my side and ensure my success. You know as well I do, that should we find ourselves in a bad situation—something we don't expect or can deal with ourselves—he'll sound the alarm."

"I can't lose you again, Essie," he murmured. "I don't have the strength to suffer through that kind of pain again."

"You're not going to lose me, Garreth. I love you, you know. And I love you too much to let such a grievous thing happen."

In response to the declaration, he held her closer still and lowered his lips to hers. The soft, tender kiss they shared yielded another and then another that grew in both passion and intensity. The kisses that followed left them both without breath and at last, he reluctantly loosened his hold.

"Dw i'n dy garu di, Essie," he whispered as he brushed his fingers through the length of her hair. He shook his head. "Dw i'n dy garu di."

She stepped back just enough to search his eyes. A look of bemusement settled over her beautiful face. She tilted her head to the side and smiled. "You know, that's the third time you've said that to me—well, fourth, and I still don't know what it means."

Her comment startled him a bit. Had he never uttered the sentiment in English? But then again, mayhap his heart had a tendency to speak those words in his native tongue. A quiet chuckle accompanied the slight shake of his head. Once again, he held her body just as close to his as he could possibly get it. He brushed his lips against hers and just before he kissed her a final time, he murmured, "It means, I love you, Essie—and I do love you—with my whole heart and soul."

Chapter Twenty-Five

Essie dutifully drank the potent brew Uvan concocted and insisted she drink. She didn't have a clue as to its purpose, nor did she ask. For right now, the dark dank opening of the hill cave commanded her full attention. The beat of her heart accelerated as she peered into the inky black shadows through which she'd have to pass. Garreth gripped her hand a little tighter as he followed her gaze.

Uvan placed a hand against her back and pointed toward the entrance. "Now, Essie, I believe you'll indeed encounter the specters spoken of in the legend and in their proper order. Their main function is to cause fear and drive you away. They cannot hurt you unless you allow it. Do you understand? The mind is a powerful thing. If you believe they can injure you in some way, then injure you they will."

Essie nodded. "Yes, I understand. Do you think I'm allowed to carry some kind of light in there?"

"We wouldn't allow you to go in without one," said Cledwyn. He cocked his head to the side and swept a hand toward Aneirin.

In that same moment, Aneirin approached her with a lighted torch. "Deep chasms do exist inside caves. Therefore, watch the placement of your feet, Essie. We don't want you falling down a hole or injuring yourself."

"I'll be careful." She shifted her gaze to Helyan. "So, are you ready then?"

He returned a courtly bow. "Ever at your side, Lady Essie."

Though she pivoted in the direction of the crevice, Garreth refused to release her from his grasp. She turned around and for one precious moment, they just looked at each other. His reluctance to let her go made her task all the more difficult. She didn't know what to say that would make him feel any better.

He let out a sigh of resignation and then placed a gentle kiss on top of her lips. "Make sure you come back to me, Essie."

She gave him a smile and hoped it didn't show any signs of worry. "Nothing could keep me away, so don't worry."

The moment he let go of her hand, she took in a deep breath and made her way to the mouth of the cave. Yet, just short of her destination, a swirling dark mist rose up from the ground, barring the entrance. She would have to pass through it. Garreth sucked in a breath and started toward her. Bran took hold of his shoulder, halting his progress.

"No, Garreth," he said. "Let her go. She'll be all right."

Essie glanced at Garreth a final time, and entered the cave. Even with the brilliant light of the crystal, she could barely see two feet in front of her face. She paused for a moment so that she could give her eyes time to adjust. A narrow path loomed before them. But then, just as she stepped forward, what sounded like a thousand blood-curdling screams burst forth from the interior of that corridor. She cemented her feet to the floor and swallowed the yelp that sought release. Her insides burned from the effort. Garreth called her name as the shrieks subsided, but she didn't have the power to answer or give him the reassurance he needed at that moment.

"Don't be afraid," whispered Helyan. "You're not in any danger, m'lady. I'll not allow anything to harm you."

She simply nodded, gathered a bit of courage, and resumed her journey.

"The bull will appear shortly. No matter how he chooses to appear, just keep moving. He can't hurt you," whispered her ghostly companion.

Within minutes, heavy hooves pounding against the ground alerted her to the specter's presence. She looked in every possible direction but couldn't find him. Nonetheless, the farther she walked the louder and more distinct the noise became. A snort and then a deep bellow sounded in close proximity. She could feel the moisture of his breath on the back of her neck. The beat of her heart increased twofold as she cast her gaze round about in search of the creature. He remained elusive. Perhaps he wouldn't show himself. Maybe she need only endure the sounds and sensations the specter created. Then, just as she convinced herself that it must be so, the beast with blood red eyes stood right before her, blocking her path. Enormous. Hulking. Terrifying.

"Keep walking," Helyan instructed. "He's not solid."

She closed her eyes and plowed right though the phantom. Ice-cold air burst from somewhere deep inside her soul and shot outward through her limbs. She shuddered for the chill that gripped her body. The bull disappeared in the instant.

"Now, that wasn't so bad, was it?" Helyan teased.

"I suppose it could have been worse," she whispered. "After all, I *am* still alive, even if completely unhinged, right?"

He chuckled. "That's right. The goat is next. When you see him, just keep walking. You needn't even pause."

Good advice. So why then, did the simple bleat cause such inner turmoil? Her dry mouth lacked the necessary spit to swallow. She took in a shallow breath and slowly let it go. The bleat sounded again, much closer this time. She banished her fear. Just how hideous could a goat be after all?

More so than she thought possible.

The rancid, rotting corpse *leered* at her. A thick gooey substance eked from his gaping jawbone and dripped to the floor. A moment later, without any warning whatsoever, it lowered its head and lunged with its horns projected toward her. At once Helyan placed a hand on the small of her back and urged her forward. She complied. Again, the frigid temperatures filtered in and traveled throughout her body. Just as the spirit dissipated from view, the grunting of the boar announced his presence, not giving her any recovery time. The sound echoed all around, coming first in front, moving around to the sides, and finally behind her. The apparition now stalked her, and it *wanted* her to know that.

"Don't turn around, and don't look back," said Helyan. "Just keep moving forward."

The boar matched each step she took, yet somehow he gained. The moment he closed the distance between them, the deep, ferocious roar of a lion assaulted her from the front. The creatures worked together to pen her in. She had nowhere to go. No place to run. She didn't know what to do.

"Don't turn either to the left or the right," said Helyan, "and don't look over your shoulder. You're almost there. Keep your feet moving forward."

In the instant the words left his mouth, a frosty gust of swirling wind circled around her like a tornado, tearing at her hair, skin, and clothes. Within the torrent, she could hear the fierce guttural growls of all the phantom beasts next to her ears. Together the specters created some kind of barrier. Invisible anchors hung around her feet. They wouldn't budge, despite all her efforts.

"Hel-yaan?" She could hear the rising panic in her voice as she called his name.

"Keep walking, Essie," he commanded.

She shook her head. "I'm trying. I just can't do it."

"Yes you can. Thrust your body forward and I'll give you an assist," he said as he placed a hand around her waist.

Essie summoned all her strength. She squeezed her eyes shut, heaved herself forward, and hoped all the while that she wouldn't land on her face. The spirits disappeared the moment she broke through the thick, vaporous whirlpool. She exhaled a breath as she turned her head and fixed her gaze upon Helyan. Her ghostly companion flashed a smug "I told you so" grin and opened his mouth to speak.

She held up a hand to stay his words. "Better that you don't make that comment aloud—at least, not right now."

He merely chuckled as they moved down the passageway. They rounded a curve that arced to the left and then followed another bend to the right. Dim light grew brighter with each forward step. Then a final right hand turn led them into a rounded chamber that housed the massive fire wheel spoken of in the legend. Eerie hums and clicks groaned inside the cavern. The circular apparatus spanned at least eight feet in height and diameter. Colorful, mesmerizing flames spewed forth from both sides of the rim, shooting upwards of four feet. She gaped at them in awe. Nothing in the book prepared her for seeing the device with her own eyes. The wheel twisted, turned, and then sped up and down and back and forth inside the chamber. Without question, those dancing flames served as sentinel, guarding the magnificent heart that rested against the wall. One couldn't help but admire the hawk's ethereal beauty. She found it nigh on impossible to tear her eyes away from the shimmering crystal.

"Do you see the heart, Helyan?" she pointed to the small niche against the back wall. The green crystal pulsated with light.

"Yes, I can see it."

"How am I going to get it?" she murmured aloud. She paused for a moment as she considered the quandary. "There is nothing ghostly about those flames and in all likelihood, can burn one to a crisp if one wanders to close."

"No doubt at all. Still, according to the legend, a woman will attain the thing. Therefore, I'm certain you'll find the means to do it."

She studied the movement that appeared chaotic at first. But after a time, the movement slowed down—at least it did in her mind's eye. Somehow, she could view the complex pattern in slow motion and decipher it. A gift from Uvan's brew perhaps that provided *the magic she carried within?* Right now, the reason didn't matter. If she timed it right, she could slip through the side of the wheel as it bounced off the wall, and take the crystal from the cavity. Twice more she counted the seconds between the most advantageous intervals. She marked her path, and waited.

Four, five six, she took a deep breath and turning her body sideways, skittered forward. Without any thought of possible consequences, she snatched the crystal, and clutched it to her breast.

"Stay right where you are, Essie," Helyan called out. "The thing has changed its pattern."

Essie inched back against the wall. The fire wheel pitched from side to side and spun wildly in circles. One would almost believe the thing detected and searched for an intruder. Perhaps it did. She stood very still. Again, she waited and this time, the wait seemed endless. Finally, another pattern established itself. She counted it twice to make sure she had it right. On the third go round, she counted the twenty-eight agonizing seconds, prayed she counted them accurately, and made a mad dash to Helyan's side.

Rather than on her, he fixed his gaze upon the wheel and then his expression changed—to one of concern. "Run, Essie, run—and don't stop until you're outside the cavern."

Instinct alone drove her out of the inner chamber and through the twists and turns of the passageway. The hums and clicks grew louder, deeper, and more ominous. They sounded close to her heels now. Still, she didn't look back nor did she stop until she arrived at the mouth of the cave. She only paused then, to search for her companion.

"No! Get out of the cave, Essie. Now!"

She swiveled her body back around and plunged through the mist, straight into Garreth's arms. Though she could hear his relief as he held her close and whispered her name, he didn't look at her. Instead, his gaze remained fixed on the cave. Curiosity compelled her to look behind her shoulder. In that same instant, a massive ball of fire shot through the mist. He dropped to a knee, taking her along with him, and then shielded her with his body. Visions of the nightmare in which the flames consumed him barged into her mind. She struggled for release in a frenzied desire to look after his welfare since he ignored it himself. But he held her tight. The flames shot just over his head, slammed into the rock on the opposite side of the gorge, and dissipated.

Then, as if in response to the affront, the earth shook. The violent quake loosened rocks, flung them onto the floor of the gorge, and then obliterated the cave. While the dust settled, Garreth leaned back, his hands traveled up the length of her arms, to her face, and then weaved through her hair. Throughout the process, his eyes, filled with so much love and concern, searched every inch of her body.

"I'm all right, Garreth," she said as he stood and helped her to her feet.

"Are you sure you're not hurt? We heard those horrific howls right after you walked in. You didn't answer when I called out to you and I thought—" He stopped short and shook his head. "Despite all my efforts I couldn't penetrate the mist."

She placed a hand against his jaw. "I'm sorry, Garreth. I tried to answer you. Really I did. But for the panic that beset me, I just couldn't get the words to come out of my mouth." Essie turned her gaze toward her ghostly attendant. "If not for Helyan, I probably would have failed at my task."

Garreth gave his friend a nod. "I'll be forever indebted to you."

Helyan shook his head. "I won't hear a word of that. Again, the honor and the pleasure belonged to me, Lord Garreth. However, I must say your lady had scarce need of my services."

"There isn't so much as a smidgen of truth to that, Helyan. Still, we got what we came for." Essie dropped her gaze to the crystal she clutched in her hand and then offered the piece to Garreth. "So now it's your turn, my love."

"We'll need to return to Llys y Helig and replenish our supplies before we begin that leg of our journey," said Cledwyn as he approached them.

"Yes, that is a must," Uvan replied. "But I think the first order of business is to allow Essie a few days rest while we prepare for the final phase of this mission. We have the time, and I believe she's earned it, wouldn't you all agree?"

Essie didn't know how badly she needed the rest until she got it. Sleep claimed fourteen hours of the first day she spent in the realm of the Tylwyth Teg and ten of the second. The third morning she slid out of bed well before the sun peeked over the horizon. A luxurious shower followed. For the journey ahead, she donned her favorite stonewashed jeans and her navy blue, long-sleeved T-shirt—all freshly laundered, courtesy of the Fair folk. She laced up her hiking boots and vacated the room. Perhaps, if she could find Garreth, they could take a stroll in the garden before they called them to breakfast. With that goal in mind, she headed down the stairs.

"Ah, the lovely Essie DeSpencer has arisen," said Afon as he ambled toward her.

"So it seems," she replied.

"You know, Garreth didn't want us to disturb you for at least another half hour." He leaned in close and grinned. "So the way I see it, that would give you and me a bit of private time together to—catch up, if you will. Perhaps we could go for a walk and watch the sun rise."

"Now what makes you think a woman like Essie, would deign to accompany a lecherous man like you?" Garreth countered to the sound of the man's laughter. In an obvious bid to dismiss his presence, he dropped a hand to her waist, and placed a sweet kiss on top of her lips. "Good morning, cariad. How are you feeling today?"

"I'm feeling well-rested, well-fed, and a whole lot mollycoddled."

"That's as it should be." He glanced at Afon and lifted a brow. "You'll excuse us?"

Afon smirked. "If you insist."

Garreth led her out into the courtyard. The rising sun danced through both water and clouds, creating a spectacular display in the sky above them. Rich floral aroma from the countless flowers drifted toward them on the gentle flight of the wind, and the music of birds filled her ears. In knowing what lay ahead of them, she took a moment to savor the tranquil moment.

Garreth turned her around to face him. The expression in his eyes gave away his intentions long before he opened his mouth. "Essie—"

"No." She raised a hand. "Don't ask me to stay behind, Garreth, because I won't do it. No matter what you say, I'm coming with you—even if I have to make my way to the dragon's lair by myself."

He heaved a deep breath and closed his eyes while his fingers rubbed against his forehead. "You've had enough, Essie. More than your fair share and far more than what you bargained for when you accepted my first invitation. Between the terrors endured inside the wizard's cave, and what Vaughn put you through, you needn't endure any more. Right after breakfast, I'm sending Bran home to his family while I finish this quest. Please, for my sake, go with him. Please, Essie."

A knot formed in her throat. Didn't he know how difficult he made it for her to deny his request when he looked at her like that? But she just couldn't comply. Not this time. Her hands traveled over the breadth of his broad chest and around his shoulders. In the same moment, his arms looped around her waist and drew her close. His gaze pleaded with hers with an intensity that gripped her heart. She squeezed her eyes shut and for a small moment, she rested her head against his chest.

Once in control of her emotions, she fastened her gaze to his. "Tell me something, Garreth. If our positions were reversed and I asked you to leave me now—asked you to wait at home for my return—would you do it?"

He didn't expect such a question and for a moment, he just stared at her. "No, but that's an entirely different matter altogether. I—"

"How so?" she interrupted. She could see his struggle to find an answer that downplayed the danger he faced. He couldn't find one.

"I just don't want to put you through anymore. You've had enough."

"If you truly mean that, then don't ask me to stay behind."

"Essie, please."

"A long time ago, I promised you I would stay by your side until the last possible moment. Do you remember that?"

"Yes, of course, I remember. How could I forget?"

"Then don't ask me to break that promise—*twice*."

The words found their intended mark. A ragged sigh escaped his lips. His hand caressed the length of her back as he dipped his head and nuzzled his lips against her neck. The very action sent shivers up and down her spine. "All right, I'll comply with your wishes, but on one condition and on one condition only."

She pulled slightly away. "No, I am not putting any conditions on this—"

He placed a gentle finger against her lips. "At least hear me out."

She narrowed her eyes and gave him a side-ways glance. "All right. I'll hear you out. But don't expect an agreement to this condition should I find it unacceptable."

"Fair enough." He cleared his throat. "First of all, we need a little give and take here. If I concede this issue without further argument, then surely you can grant one small concession in return."

"I don't know if I can promise something I know nothing—"

"You can do this without undue hardship, I give you my word."

She hesitated as suspicion gnawed. "If you're going to ask me about my name again, then you—"

"This isn't about your name. Well, at least not in the way you mean."

She drew her brows together. "I don't understand what you—"

"Trust me, Essie."

Trust. Now why did he have to ask for that?

She let go of a sigh. "Fine, tell me what you want already."

Amusement filled his eyes long before it tugged on the corners of his mouth. He had her right where he wanted her and he knew it.

"You must promise to marry me, and I want you to marry me the minute we return to Llys y Gwalch, or at the very least, at the first feasible moment thereafter. For I love you Essie, far more than I ever thought possible and I simply cannot bear my life without you in it."

Chapter Twenty-Six

Garreth turned his gaze toward the woman he loved without exception and took pleasure in just looking at her. Though she paid strict attention to the movement of her horse and her surroundings, she still carried the same bemused expression that settled over her beautiful face the moment he asked her to marry him. Her wide-eyed gaze and sharp intake of breath told him she hadn't expected it. That suited him fine. Better to catch her unaware before she could devise a reason to refuse.

The passionate kisses they shared after she accepted his proposal, passion that stirred his very soul, both amazed and delighted him. Because, for the first time, she held nothing back. Yet, until that very moment he didn't know she had unknowingly safeguarded a small portion of her heart lest he should break it. He told her then that he wanted her beside him for all time, not just for an unnamed number of months or years ahead. Once she regained her ability to speak, she said yes. He didn't even need to lay out a single carefully constructed argument as to why she should condescend to marry a man such as himself, and he had several of them waiting in the wings. Good ones. No matter, he may need them later, should she have second thoughts.

"You seem more than a little pleased about

something, Lord Garreth," said Cledwyn with a knowing smirk curving his lips.

"Yes indeed, I've noticed that myself," Aneirin chimed in.

Cledwyn tilted his head to the side. "Of course, Essie seems to mirror that same expression. I wonder if there's a reason for that."

Ignoring their companions, Essie turned her golden brown eyes upon him and bestowed a dazzling smile. Garreth winked in response. "Perhaps it's because, finally, she *just* might be of a mind to reveal her name to me."

She shook her head and laughed. "I don't recall that ever being part of our bargain, m'lord Garreth."

"What?" He clutched a hand to his heart. "Oh come on! How can you keep that information away from your future husband?"

"Far easier than you think," she quipped.

He stared at her in disbelief. "Well—a wife shouldn't keep secrets from her husband, should she?"

She shrugged. "I see nothing wrong with a woman retaining a bit of her mystery."

"But then how will the clergyman marry us properly?" he countered.

"By saying 'husband and wife,' of course," she volleyed back. "I'm pretty sure he doesn't need to say anything more than that."

Both Cledwyn and Aneirin exchanged glances and then burst out laughing.

"You still don't know her given names, even after your betrothal?" asked Aneirin.

Garreth dropped his hand to his knee and exhaled the most pitiful sigh he could muster. "I'm afraid not and despite our newly acquired state, she still refuses to disclose it. But the thing is; I just can't imagine any name being all that hideous."

"Well, let's see if we can help you out with that." Cledwyn wiped at his nose and sniffed. "How about we try the universe again. Perhaps a planet and a moon this time, like Saturn Enceladus or even Saturn Europa."

Essie rolled her eyes and huffed out a derisive breath. "You're way off track, Cledwyn. Way off."

"I've toyed with the idea that perhaps her parents gave her the modern names of the countries they've visited," said Aneirin. "Countries that mayhap struck a chord or have profound meaning to them personally, countries like Somalia Estonia, Samoa Ethiopia, or even Slovenia Ecuador. What do you think?"

Garreth laughed out loud right over the incredulous expression on Essie's face and then joined in the fun. "Not quite right? Well then, how about we resume our list of mythological goddesses. I have several more to offer. Perhaps you are named for one of the Germanic deities like Sinthgunt Eir, or how about Sjöfn Eostre"

She flicked a length of hair behind her shoulder and lifted her nose a notch. "Do you want to know what I think? I think all of you have way too much time on your hands. That's what *I* think."

****

The guesses continued throughout the length of their tedious journey, but Essie truly didn't mind them. They helped pass the time and keep their minds off the task ahead. Besides, she didn't really need nor have any desire to pay attention to the ridiculous names they bandied about. Not when the man she pledged to marry could turn her whole world upside down with just a look, and the promise of forever took on new meaning. Now, instead of spending decades with the man she loved more than life itself, she would have centuries. Centuries. The very thought boggled the mind.

"Well, this place looks familiar," said Aneirin, cutting into her blissful thoughts.

He reined his mount to a halt close to the jagged rock protruding from the ground, just as they had once before. She shielded her eyes from the afternoon sun and contemplated the steep, rocky hill they needed to climb. The path looked just as daunting as it did the first time.

"We'll go ahead and leave the horses and supplies here," said Cledwyn. "There's plenty of water and grazing should our task take longer than we expect."

Garreth dismounted, made his way to her side, and assisted her to the ground. "Are you sure you're ready for this?"

She fixed her gaze to his as she dusted the back of her jeans. "Yes, quite ready."

A devilish grin emerged. "I don't suppose you'd be willing to wait here, watch over the horses, and guard the camp until we return?"

She dropped back on her heel and put a hand to her hip. "Guard the camp? Really, Garreth? Are you serious?"

A chuckle accompanied the slight shake of his head. "Well, I had to at least give it a try."

She breathed out a laugh, stood on tiptoes, and gave him a kiss. "I'll give you that—but I'm going with you, so you needn't waste your breath."

"Somehow I knew you'd say that."

Their Fair companions made quick work of setting

up camp and securing the horses. Then, after they retrieved their smaller packs, Garreth took hold of her hand and laced his fingers through hers. Together they trailed behind Cledwyn as he climbed the steep, winding path leading to the dragon's lair. They made their way through the forest of trees and dense foliage without undue hardship. Then, just as the sun dipped below the horizon, the petrified rock with its gnarly branch loomed before them. She gazed at the overhang of vegetation that marked the gateway to the dragon's cave. A shiver coursed through her body and along with it, a bit of unease settled into the pit of her stomach.

"All right," said Cledwyn as he waved a hand over his crystal torch and then held it aloft. "In we go—but please be ever mindful of the path."

"Point well taken," said Aneirin. "But with all due respect, if a misstep occurs, I should think you'd be the one to take it since you're the one leading. Therefore, should you fall on your face; the rest of us will surely avoid the pitfall."

He shook his head as he rolled his eyes heavenward. "Thanks, Aneirin."

They stepped through the tapered fissure and into the first chamber, one at a time. Cledwyn paused for a moment so their eyes could adjust to the dimmer light. Then, after marking a safe path through the stalactites, he led them to the passageway on the right. They traversed the musty corridor down the steep grade and into the second cavern. The smell of stagnant water permeated all around them and for whatever the reason, it seemed much worse this time. Because this time, not only could she smell the foul stench, she could taste it.

Garreth touched the tip of her wrinkled nose and

winked. "That bad, huh?"

A quiet laugh accompanied a nod. "Yep, I'm afraid so."

"Well, not much longer now," he said.

"That's right," said Aneirin. "We'll be in and out of here in no time at all."

No one bothered to say, "If all goes well," but surely each of them thought it.

Cledwyn leaned his torch toward the chasm where the treacherous stairs awaited them. "Let's proceed with caution. Remember these steps are quite fragile."

Garreth took hold of her hand as they made their way to the ledge. As a precautionary measure, Cledwyn stooped down and aimed his light down the stairway.

"I see no further signs of damage," he said as he rose to his feet and placed a foot on the first step leading downward. "So, let's get in there and get this done, shall we?"

"I'm all for that," Aneirin murmured. He looked at Garreth and with an exaggerated sweep of his hand, invited him to the stairs ahead of himself. "After you."

Garreth firmed his grasp and side by side they shadowed each cautious step Cledwyn took. They made it to the bottom step, traversed the narrow, sloping curve of the passageway, and entered the grotto.

Moonlight penetrated the shadows, sending beams of light through the open crevice on top of the mountain, and spilled onto the smooth, black surface of the stone platform. The beat of her heart accelerated as her gaze darted between the altar and Garreth. He gave her a reassuring nod and released her hand.

Aneirin stepped a bit closer. "Do you suppose you just climb up there and put the thing back?"

"I guess we'll find out here in a minute." From the side pocket of his backpack, Garreth retrieved the crystal, now void of light, and then dropped the bag onto the floor.

Each of them stepped over the dragon's skeletal form, and onto the platform, forming a semi-circle behind Garreth. He turned the hawk so the head faced upward and then placed it into the hollow cavity. Nothing out of the ordinary happened. No booby traps. No screaming phantoms. No fire wheels. Essie released the breath she unknowingly held. Garreth studied the seven symbols and then placed a finger in the indentation below the one for fire. He took hold of the wheel and yanked. The thing refused to budge.

"Something's wrong," said Aneirin, peering over Garreth's shoulder. "The wheel is supposed to turn isn't it?"

"According to the directions, yes." Garreth rubbed a hand against his chin as he studied the mechanism. "Perhaps we need to form a full circle around the thing."

"That might work," Cledwyn said. "Perhaps we ought to join hands as well."

Aneirin shook his head. "No, we can't do that. Garreth needs his hands to turn the wheel."

"Oh yes, that's right, and it would be impossible for the three of us to link hands around the entire platform. Still there must be something we're missing."

"Maybe I just need to place both hands on the rim," Garreth replied. This time he selected the symbols for both fire and water. The wheel still wouldn't give way.

"Now what?" Aneirin huffed out a breath. "Anyone have any bright ideas?"

Cledwyn grinned. "Yes, we should've insisted that Uvan come along with us, so he could tell us what we're doing wrong."

"The old man wouldn't have survived a second journey up a mountain, and you know that as well as I," Aneirin countered.

"Better hope he didn't hear you say that," Cledwyn replied.

"No one can hear us inside here, remember?" he countered.

Ignoring their banter, Garreth puzzled over the dilemma for several moments. "No, the scroll states the hawk will rise and that *his* hand will restore the fragile balance. Uvan said I would have to do this alone."

Her heart dropped. Essie shook her head in vehement disagreement. "I'm not leaving, Garreth."

"I don't think we have to leave the chamber completely, Essie," Cledwyn cut in. "I just think we need to get off the platform."

Garreth fastened his gaze to hers and gave her a wink. "I'll be all right, Essie, I promise."

She swallowed past the lump in her throat as everyone looked at her and waited. Finally, she nodded. "All right. But I refuse to leave this cavern without you."

Cledwyn offered her his hand. With a sigh of resignation, she accepted the inevitable. Once they all stood against the wall, Garreth retrieved the hawk. This time, the moment he had it in his hand, brilliant light pulsated from within the piece—just as it had inside the wizards cave. Their eyes met for a brief moment. He then turned his focus to the image of the black dragon. Once again, he placed the crystal inside the hollow. At once, a resonating hum filled the cavern and it sounded very much like the hum of the fire wheel. Just as she sucked in a breath, an umbrella of iridescent light descended over the center of the room in shimmering display, encasing Garreth inside its barriers. The hum increased in volume. She flung her hands over her mouth as the scene unfolded. Her heart doubled its pace.

Cledwyn dropped an arm around her shoulder. "Everything's going to be all right, Essie. You needn't worry. Garreth is doing what he's destined to do."

She didn't respond—she couldn't. Right now, she just couldn't tear her eyes, or her attention, away from Garreth. He chose the symbol for fire and turned the wheel three times. The sparkling white light transformed into one of brilliant yellow.

"He must be doing it correctly now," Aneirin murmured.

Cledwyn nodded his agreement, but said nothing in return.

Garreth changed the position of his hands and again turned the wheel three times. The brilliant yellow light turned cobalt blue. He chose another symbol, and then turned the disc counterclockwise, twice. The humming changed its pitch from low to high and then high to low before it leveled off. Garreth blew out a breath and then turned the wheel clockwise, four times. The blue light changed to one of vibrant red. In that same instant, the crystal hawk rose from its nest and while elevated, the canopy in a dazzling display of luminescent light, radiated all her colors. The lights crackled and then flung sparks in all directions. All the while, the hum grew ever louder. Cledwyn shouted out something, but she couldn't hear what he said. He nudged her shoulder and pointed below the dais. She dutifully dropped her gaze and looked.

The bones of the dragon moved—and they moved as if the creature still lived. The skeletal structure suddenly enshrouded itself with a thick, black, ethereal, mist and it scared the tar right out of her. The creature rose to its feet. Flames filled the sockets of his eyes. He twisted his head from side to side and then thrust his gaping jaws upward. A deep rumble emerged from the belly of the beast a scant second before the phantom belched flaming fire. In response, the crystal hawk slammed back into its nest while the entire stone altar exploded with shimmering light. Garreth took the brunt of the powerful seismic wave that followed the burst. She could see the pain he absorbed as he clenched his teeth and leaned forward with a hand clutching his chest. While, he struggled to retain his footing, the dragon foundered for several tense seconds and then collapsed into the same position from which he rose, taking Garreth down with him.

Essie didn't have time to gasp, scream, shout, or any number of things her frightened, chaotic mind demanded she do. For at that precise moment, the earth shook violently beneath her feet. The walls of the chamber cracked. Broken pieces of stone rained down upon the ground. All throughout the horrifying event, the canopy of light grew ever dimmer and then disappeared altogether. Instinct drove her feet toward Garreth for the overwhelming need to be at his side. Cledwyn and Aneirin remained but a step behind. As the earth quieted, she flung away the dirt and debris that littered Garreth's body. He lay so still. Too still. Blood oozed from the side of his head and trickled down the side of his face.

"Garreth," she cried. "Oh Garreth, can you hear me?" He didn't respond to her voice. Her panic intensified. She spared her Fair companions a glance. "We've got to get him out of here. Please help me—"

Cledwyn gave her shoulder a gentle squeeze and nodded. "Aneirin and I will assess the damage and find the best way out. I promise you, we'll hurry."

"Thank you." As she wiped at her tears she spied her backpack near the dais. She stretched her arm toward it and struggled to get hold of the straps using just the tips of her fingers. The effort took a couple of minutes but at last, she had the thing in her hands. She used it to cushion his head as she wiped away the blood.

Suddenly, his body stiffened and he struggled for breath. Dread washed over her. She gathered him into her arms in a bid to elevate his body even further, but it didn't serve any real purpose. He grimaced, agony marred his features as he lurched forward, coughed, and then fell limp.

A soft wail escaped her lips as tears fell down her cheeks. "No, Garreth, No! Please don't leave me. Not now. Please, you've got to stay with me!"

She brushed her fingers through his hair and as the tears streamed down her face, she willed him to awaken—willed him to live. A million times, she searched the corridor, hoping to see Cledwyn or Aneirin emerge. They remained elusive and while they searched for an exit, it seemed that Garreth slowly slipped out of her grasp. She placed a hand against his heart. Each beat of his heart seemed far slower than the one before it. No! She wouldn't allow him to leave her—she couldn't bear it if he did.

She mustered a firm tone. "Garreth, you need to open your eyes. You need to stay with me. You promised, remember? Now wake up!"

Finally then, with what appeared great effort, his eyelids fluttered. The effort cost him. He lifted a hand to her face and then dropped it onto his chest. At once she took hold of his hand.

"Essie..." he whispered so faintly, she could barely hear it. "I'm so glad...so glad that I finally found you...if even for the brief moment we shared. You own my heart, cariad...no matter what happens...you have my heart and my soul..."

"You're going to make it through this. You have to. So, just...just hang on Garreth. You're stronger than this. Now, Cledwyn and Aneirin will be here shortly. We're going to get you out of here. Do you hear me? I need you to stay with me because I love you more than you can possibly imagine. I can't live my life without you. I can't. Please, please don't ask me to do that."

"Essie—" Shallow, uneven breaths followed a sharp intake of breath. He struggled for air, and she just didn't know what to do or how to help.

"Essie, I need to know your name. I would like to have it tucked inside my heart...so that alongside...my memories... I can carry it with me...before I...before I..."

She wrapped him even tighter in her embrace. Fresh tears streamed down her cheeks. "No! Don't leave me Garreth, you can't."

He locked his gaze on hers while a weakened finger caressed the length of her cheek. "Please Essie, don't refuse me…"

She took in a deep breath and sniffed. Her eyes closed as she wiped a hand against her mouth and nose. She dropped her lips close to his ear so that only he would hear. Then, while running her fingers through his hair she swallowed past the lump in her throat.

"I love you Garreth ap Daffyd." She paused and it took everything inside her to give him what he asked, for she had not spoken the name aloud since early childhood. She gritted her teeth. "Strawberry Essence DeSpencer—loves you more than life itself."

A horrible wracking cough seized his body just as the words left her mouth. He labored for each breath he took. Fear gripped her heart. Her eyes flew open as she tugged him into her arms and clutched him to her heart. "Garreth?" she could hear the panic in her voice.

The terrible hacks slowly transformed into something entirely different then. It took her a moment to realize that he no longer coughed at all. He *laughed*. In fact, he laughed so hard tears ran down his cheeks.

Her mouth dropped as understanding flooded her mind. She pummeled his chest and then pushed him off her lap for his disgusting performance. He then sat up without any difficulty whatsoever. Heated indignation splashed onto her cheeks. "Ooh! Of all the conniving, deceitful, imposturous, underhanded, mean-hearted—"

He yanked her into his arms and though she fought hard for release, he refused to allow even so much as an inch of space to come between them. Then, he cupped her face with his hand and lowered his lips to hers. The ardent kisses that followed silenced her tongue as well as her anger.

Just as well.

She was running out of adjectives anyway, and the fact that he could give such powerful, passionate kisses told her that he would not leave her. Not now, not ever.

Finally, he broke free of her lips and grinned. "Strawberry Essence DeSpencer?" He shook his head. "As in a vessel that dispenses the aroma and essence of a sweet, ripened strawberry?"

"I don't think that's quite what my parents had in mind when they filled out my birth certificate." She paused and then released a deep breath of resignation. "As the story goes—on the night of my conception, my parents were celebrating an extraordinary triumph, months in the making. This being the case, my father wanted everything to be perfect. From their more remote location as well as the season in which the event took place, it took a great deal of effort on my father's part to gift my mother with all her favorite things. Amongst them, he presented her that evening with a delectable bowl of fresh strawberries and cream, strawberry scented bubble bath, and a bottle of strawberry wine. The memory is one they equally treasure and if you have even so much as a shred of affection for me at all, you will never utter my given names or the circumstances surrounding them again."

The humor never left his eyes. Nonetheless, he placed his hand over his heart. "On my solemn word of honor, no one else will ever hear your name from my lips."

The sound of hurried footsteps drew their attention to the passageway and ended their discussion. Aneirin emerged first with Cledwyn but a step behind. Their startled gazes darted between her and Garreth and then broad smiles appeared on their faces.

"Well, it's nice to see you've recovered somewhat from your ordeal," said Cledwyn. "Are you able to travel?"

Garreth gave her a wink as he stood and then assisted her to her feet. "That I am, and the sooner the better, for I've a wedding to attend before the bride thinks better of it and changes her mind."

Chapter Twenty-Seven

The recalled memory of those final, private moments they had shared inside the cave not only warmed her heart, but also prompted a quiet breath of laughter no one else would hear. Almost seven years had ticked off time's calendar since the Lord of Llys y Gwalch entered her life and claimed her heart, mind, body, and soul. During those years, Essie looked back on that day more times than she could count.

No, wait. That couldn't be right, could it? *Seven years?* The thought gave her pause.

Garreth said it would be so when one pondered the passing of time, but had it really been almost seven years? As she cast her gaze about the beauty of their glorious garden, she considered all the wondrous events that had taken place since her husband returned the crystal heart to the restless dragon.

True to his word and for his unbearable need to have her as his wife—or so he said—they were married within two weeks of their return to the castle. Only that because Lowri insisted it would take her that long to prepare a feast large enough to feed all the villagers and the invited guests from Llys y Helig. That suited her fine, for it seemed it took them every moment of those two weeks to provide those they loved with the details of their journey and allow them to fuss—and celebrate their success.

Their wedding rivaled any fairytale, myth, or fable known to man. From the exquisite dress provided by the Tylwyth Teg, the ceremony held in the glade outside the castle, to the reception that followed, the day could not have been any more perfect—or wondrous. Helyan not only gave her away, he also stood beside her as her 'Man of Honor.' Not a soul dared make light of—or question—his right to perform what he considered his greatest privilege to date. At the tail-end of the celebration, dear Aneirin and Cledwyn whisked them away from the realm of Llys y Gwalch with no one the wiser, and put them on a sleek ship bound for the Isle-of-Man.

They spent their honeymoon in a charming cottage on that island, veiled from mortal eyes by the magic of the Fair folk. This cozy little bungalow, nestled amongst the trees, sat very near the River Glass and during that time, no one on this earth—past or present—loved so deeply, completely, or passionately, as they did. Not that their passion for each other had waned—quite the contrary, it had only increased as they fell ever deeper in love with the passage of each day.

She rose from the bench and strolled along the cobblestone pathway as the cherished memories assailed her mind and splashed a rosy glow onto her cheeks. They stayed an entire month the first time they visited the cottage, and during that idyllic time, they discovered a stone hidden under the lush river foliage that contained an Ogham inscription. That inscription spoke of Manannan Mac Lir of the Tuatha De Danann, whom they had discussed years ago, and the dragon cave he discovered. That record sent them off on another wild adventure. Eventually, they found the cave, and the bones contained therein. She immediately sent the hidden location to a thrilled Ian Penrose. Other such exploits followed, for her noble hawk had an adventurous spirit that complemented her own. In that regard, they were too halves of a perfect, incredible, whole.

"There you are."

She whirled around and as Garreth made his way to her side, she fastened her gaze to his and gave him a smile. "I'm glad you're back. I missed you."

"As I missed you." He pulled her into his arms and as he caressed the length of her back, he dropped a sumptuous kiss on top of her lips.

Her hands traveled up his chest the moment he put a bit of space between them and gave her leave to speak. "Did you and Bran get everything done that you needed to do this morning?"

Humor filled his eyes as a grin emerged, exposing the beloved scar on the side of his face. "Yes, we did. Took a little longer than we expected though. Rhodri had to help us out a bit." He winked.

She laughed as she envisioned such a scene. "That little tot is just as rambunctious as his father, I'm afraid."

He nodded. "I'll have to agree with you there."

She nibbled at her bottom lip as she peeked up at him through her lashes. A host of brilliant fireflies swarmed inside her belly, creating delicious heat. Should she share her precious news now or wait until they retired for the evening? Absurd thought. She didn't want to wait another minute.

He tilted his head to the side as he regarded her

with a bit of suspicion. "Just what is it that you're all but bursting to tell me, hmm?"

A breath of quiet laughter accompanied the slight shake of her head. The man could read her like a book. Now, how did she want to phrase this? She only had this one chance to get it perfect. "Well, while taking in the beauty of our garden this morning, I waxed nostalgic and recalled the countless, treasured memories of our days together and all they entailed. The recollection made me wonder if our son or daughter would inherit the dynamic, incredible, magnificent, spirit of *his or her* father, for right now, that is my greatest wish for him or her."

The moment he understood what she meant, he sucked in a breath. His incredulous expression turned to one of immense joy. He tightened his hold as he lifted her off her feet and spun her around. They laughed together and they cried tears of joy together while the reality of the babe set in. Words escaped him for a time. Then finally, he regained a semblance of control over his tender emotions. She lagged a bit behind him, though.

"Well, this makes my gift all the more timely then," he said.

"Your gift?"

"Yes," he dipped a hand into his coat pocket and withdrew a square box, beautifully wrapped, which he promptly offered her. "I asked one of the Tylwyth Teg artisans to make this for me. I planned to give it to you on our anniversary, but when I saw it, I just couldn't wait, so I went looking for you. I had no idea you had a gift waiting for me as well, and one that would surpass my own."

She accepted the box from his hand, and together they made their way over to their bench. After they sat down, he dropped an arm around her shoulder and drew her snugly into his embrace. He gazed deeply into her eyes, needing to see her every expression. His anticipation grew as she removed the wrapping, taking great care as she did so. The moment she opened the lid, she gasped for the significant meaning of the gift. Delightful warmth filled her heart and traveled upward, causing her throat to swell.

Tears began anew as she lifted the green crystal goshawk music box from its nest. The sunlight revealed a rainbow of colors and to top it off, a delicate red strawberry, fashioned from a ruby, created its heart.

"Oh, Garreth," she murmured. "This is just so beautiful—especially for the meaning behind it." Her fingers traced over the details of the piece and then she turned the key. The music box played Elphame Lullaby, a personal favorite and the first song they danced to together. That momentous event took place on the day of their wedding, in front of all their guests, mortal and immortal alike. Tears formed in her eyes as she lifted her chin and gazed at her beloved husband.

"You own my heart, cariad," he whispered huskily. "You always will."

"As you own mine." An exquisite kiss followed the declaration and once the kiss finally ended, and she could speak, she put her thoughts into words. "I don't know how you do it, but you always manage to make me feel so loved and so cherished—"

For a moment he simply looked at her and then the smallest of smiles turned the corner of his mouth. "Do you remember the day we visited the tomb of the kings for the very first time?"

She dabbed at the corner of her eyes and nodded. "How could I ever forget?"

"As you might recall, Helyan spoke to me before we entered the crypt."

"Yes, I remember. The sound of his voice startled me out of my wits."

His finger traced along her jaw and then brushed through the length of her hair. He gave her the look then that always set her heart on fire. "Then you'll also remember that he noted your beauty. But then again, how could he not?"

Essie dropped her gaze for a brief moment. As always, she could feel the heat rise from the center of her belly and exit her cheeks as he bestowed the compliment he gave her so very often.

"But that's not all he said that day. Helyan also informed me that at long last, I had found my soul mate and that I could do naught but admit it. He laughed over the dumbfounded look on my face and then told me what a lucky, misbegotten cur I was, and—that he shared my joy."

Helyan's words, spoken in one of her worst moments of despair, tumbled into her mind.

A man can have many loves over the course of his lifetime. Don't let anyone tell you any different. However, he has but one soul mate. And when he finds her, it's like a raging bolt of lightning exploding inside his heart with tremendous force. The heat consumes him, and he is never the same again.

"He couldn't have been more right, Essie. I *had* found my soul mate and I knew then that no other woman would ever do, come even close, or take the place you have in my heart. So how can I not make you feel loved and cherished? For I *do* love and cherish you. I will continue to do so, all the days of my life and far beyond that."

"As I love and cherish you, forever and always," she whispered in return. "Forever and always, Garreth."

Another enchanting kiss followed her assertion—well, several kisses followed, actually. When at last he let her breathe, he dropped his gaze to her precious burden and then placed a gentle hand on top of him or her. "So does our son, or our daughter, feel up to a little adventure with his parents?"

She gave him a side-ways glance and smiled. "What do you have in mind?"

"I thought for our anniversary this year, we could take a couple of weeks, visit Tintagel, and see if we can find any *real* evidence as to the existence of Merlin's legendary cave. What do you think of that?"

"Sounds perfect, m' lord Garreth." The look in his eyes matched the devilish grin he tried so very hard to hide and all but turned her into a puddle of mush.

"Good, good. Now, if my beautiful wife will just accompany her completely besotted husband up the stairs to the privacy of their chamber, they can discuss the details of that trip, and uh—a few other urgent matters, just a little more in depth."

A word about the author...

Debbie has always had a soft spot for fairy tales, the joy of falling in love, and happily ever after endings. Stories of love and make-believe have filled her head for as long as she can remember.

When she is not busy conjuring her latest novel, Debbie spends time with the members of her very large family. She also pursues her interests in family history, mythology, and all things ancient and historic.

~*~

www.dk-peterson.com